THE HELL SCREEN

I. J. Parker, winner of a Shamus Award for "Akitada's First Case," a short story published in 1999,
lives in Virginia Beach, Virginia. This is the second
novel featuring Sugawara Akitada.

The
Hell
Screen

I. J. PARKER

PENGUIN BOOKS

PENGUIN BOOKS

Published by the Penguin Group

Penguin Group (USA) Inc., 375 Hudson Street, New York, New York 10014, U.S.A.

Penguin Group (Canada), 90 Eglinton Avenue East, Suite 700, Toronto,
Ontario, Canada M4P 2Y3 (a division of Pearson Penguin Canada Inc.)

Penguin Books Ltd, 80 Strand, London WC2R 0RL, England

Penguin Ireland, 25 St Stephen's Green, Dublin 2, Ireland (a division of Penguin Books Ltd)

Penguin Group (Australia), 250 Camberwell Road, Camberwell,
Victoria 3124, Australia (a division of Pearson Australia Group Pty Ltd)

Penguin Books India Pvt Ltd, 11 Community Centre,
Panchsheel Park, New Delhi – 110 017, India

Penguin Group (NZ), 67 Apollo Drive, Rosedale, North Shore 0632,
New Zealand (a division of Pearson New Zealand Ltd)

Penguin Books (South Africa) (Pty) Ltd, 24 Sturdee Avenue,
Rosebank, Johannesburg 2196, South Africa

Penguin Books Ltd, Registered Offices:
80 Strand, London WC2R 0RL, England

First published in the United States of America by St. Martin's Press 2003
Published in Penguin Books 2008

1   3   5   7   9   10   8   6   4   2

Maps courtesy of the author

THE LIBRARY OF CONGRESS HAS CATALOGED THE HARDCOVER EDITION AS FOLLOWS:
Parker, I. J. (Ingrid J.)
The hell screen / I. J. Parker.—1st ed.
p.   cm.
ISBN 0-312-28795-X (hc.)
ISBN 978-0-14-303562-6 (pbk.)
1. Japan—History—Heian period, 794–1185—Fiction.   2. Government investigators—
Fiction.   3. Kyoto (Japan)—Fiction.   4. Nobility—Fiction.   I. Title.
PS3616.A745H45   2003
813'.6—dc21   2003046550

Printed in the United States of America

To Cathleen Jordan,
editor of *Alfred Hitchcock's Mystery Magazine*—
in loving memory

She took a chance on a story by an unknown writer,
and the Akitada series came to life.
This novel will always be specially hers
because it began as a short story intended for her.
She was, is, and will be a part of all my work.

Acknowledgments

I owe a debt of gratitude to a group of faithful friends and fellow writers who read this novel in multiple drafts. They have spared neither criticism nor encouragement to keep me true to my purpose. They are Jacqueline Falkenhan, John Rosenman, Richard Rowand, and Bob Stein. Their friendship, patience, and loyal support have meant everything through the years.

My sincere thanks also go to my editors, Hope Dellon and Kris Kamikawa, for taking such care with my books and making me proud of them.

I do not know how I would have managed without Jean Naggar. She is the best agent in the world, but she is also a friend who has faith in me and makes me take heart when I get discouraged. Jennifer Weltz has earned my gratitude for her tireless and successful marketing of the novels in foreign countries. I have been blessed.

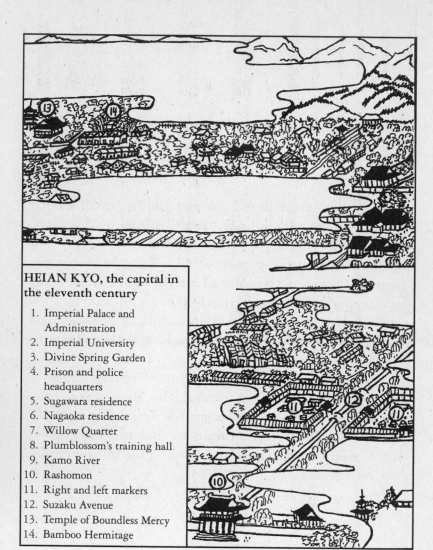

HEIAN KYO, the capital in the eleventh century

1. Imperial Palace and Administration
2. Imperial University
3. Divine Spring Garden
4. Prison and police headquarters
5. Sugawara residence
6. Nagaoka residence
7. Willow Quarter
8. Plumblossom's training hall
9. Kamo River
10. Rashomon
11. Right and left markers
12. Suzaku Avenue
13. Temple of Boundless Mercy
14. Bamboo Hermitage

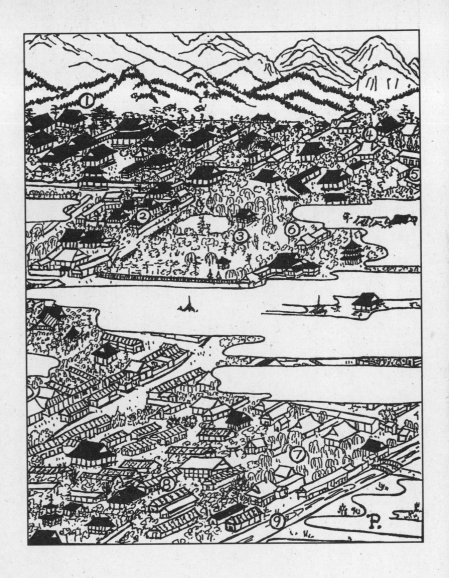

Characters

Kobe	Superintendent of metropolitan police
Dr. Masayoshi	Coroner
Abbot Genshin	Head of the Eastern Mountain Temple
Eikan and Ancho	Two monks
Noami	A painter
Yasaburo	Retired professor, father-in-law of Nagaoka
Harada	The drunken bookkeeper of Yasaburo
Danjuro	An actor with Uemon's troupe
Gold	An acrobat
Miss Plumblossom	Retired acrobat
Yukiyo	Her maid

The

Hell

Screen

Prologue

The snoring behind her changed to an unintelligible mumbling, and she turned her head sharply. But it was nothing, part of a drunken stupor. She returned her attention to the dark, wet courtyard outside. In a moment the snoring resumed. Men were such weak-minded animals!

Surely enough time had passed. It must be done by now. She shivered and pulled her silk gown more closely around her shoulders.

Earlier, when she had entered this room—a place of rest and prayer for generations of pilgrims—she had read with amusement some of the inscriptions they had left behind on its walls. One was accompanied by a drawing of a seated Buddha and the judge of the dead, King Emma. Smiling and praying figures surrounded the smiling Buddha, but in front of the glowering king, a fierce demon was spearing screaming people to put them in a vat boiling over a fire. The unknown artist had taken pains and achieved a certain gruesome realism. The inscription said, "Release me, Amida, from desire! Save me from eternal torment!"

She was intimately acquainted with desire, but fortunately she was not superstitious. No, she had no time for the foolishness of the religious.

Stiffening, she leaned forward intently. Had that been the sound of a door closing? This was the most dangerous time. A careless move by the one she was waiting for, some guest on his way to relieve himself, or a monk bent on predawn austerities, and all would be lost. But the courtyard lay silent again among the trees. Strangely, there were not even the cries of night birds or the stealthy rustlings of fox or badger. Perhaps the rain had spoiled their hunting.

There! This time she was certain. Another faint sound, closer this time, of gravel crunching underfoot. She closed the door a little farther, peering through a narrow crack.

The faint glow of the lantern at the end of the gallery was momentarily blotted out. Some large shape had moved across it. The loose board of the veranda steps creaked.

Her heart beating in her throat, she called out softly, "Is someone there?"

A grunt. "It's me. Open up! Quick!"

She jumped up and threw the door wide.

A man, dressed in a monk's robe, entered, bent under a large burden. She closed the door behind him and shot the latch. In the darkness, his rasping breath made a counterpoint to the snores of the sleeper. She groped for the candle and lit it.

The flickering light revealed the small, simple room, and the bowed figure of the visitor. He let his load roll off his shoulder onto the floor. It fell heavily, like all dead weights. The girl lay on her back, her eyes staring at nothing and her tongue protruding slightly between swollen lips. A hemp rope was still knotted about her throat.

The man sat down abruptly and buried his face in his hands.

"You took your time!" said the woman, giving him an irritated look. Then, turning her back to him, she started to undress. "Did you have any difficulties?" she asked.

He grunted something, staring at her, then nodded toward the sleeper. "What about him? What if he wakes up?"

"He won't! He's never had a head for strong drink and this time he won't wake until morning. And by then it will be much too late." She giggled, dropping her underrobe. He devoured her nakedness with hot eyes as she was bending over the dead girl.

"Here! Hold her up for me!" When he did not move immediately, she added impatiently, "Why are men so useless?"

He got to his feet meekly, averting his eyes from her breasts and groin. "I wish you'd put on some clothes!" he muttered.

"What?" She looked up, then smiled. "In a moment, my precious stallion."

His hands trembled as they worked, and when they were done, she came to him, passionately, pushing him back onto the floor, possessing his body with her own urgency, and bringing them both to gasping orgasm. When they had finished, she rose and dressed, grimacing with distaste, while he turned away abruptly and buried his head in his arms.

"Now what's the matter?" she asked. "Come! We're almost done. Don't get weak-kneed now! You know what must be done next." She went to a traveling box and picked up the sword which lay on its top.

"I can't," he muttered, watching her, his handsome face distorted with fear. "I can't look at her. You do it!"

"Don't be ridiculous! In her condition she won't feel a thing! You would think a man with your background wouldn't balk at using a sword!" She pulled it from its scabbard and extended it to him.

He shuddered. "We shouldn't have done it here! The spirits won't like it."

Coward, she thought, and cursed under her breath. She turned to draw the sharp blade across the dead girl's throat. It bit deeply, nearly severing the head from the body, but there was very little blood. Then she said softly to him, "Please get up!"

When he stood, she came to him, the bloodied sword in hand, and looked up into his eyes pleadingly. She knew he could not resist her. "Come, my love! I have made a start. You are strong, and must do the rest. Just do this one last thing, and we can put the past behind us and live like princes the rest of our lives."

His eyes wavered before hers. He nodded. She pressed the grip of the sword into his limp right hand and gave him a little push. He took the few steps to the corpse, raised the blade high, and brought it down. The bright steel flashed in the candlelight. Again and again he slashed, in a kind of frenzy, until the blade was black with blood and the girl's face was no more.

She stopped him then, and took the dripping sword over to the sleeping man, to wipe the blade on his clothes before placing it into his limp right hand. "There!" she said with a nod. "It looks well! Now quick, back to your quarters! I'll join you at dawn."

He gulped, his eyes on the horror he had made of the girl's head.

Opening the door cautiously, she listened, then waved to him.

When he had left, she glanced once more around the room, pushed the bloody head a little closer to the body with her foot, then extinguished the candle. Moving to the door, she raised the latch, listened, and slipped out.

The moist, chill night received her. Her nostrils flared with the excitement of this moment. It was done! She was free. Then she pulled the door shut behind her, tried it, and, when she found it still unlocked, slammed it more sharply. This time, the latch dropped into place with a click.

For a moment she stood undecided. The distant light caught her beautiful face, moist lips smiling, but the eyes hard and bright—the mountain lioness returning from a nocturnal hunt, her bloodlust slaked, but every sense alert to danger. Then she slipped away into the shadows quickly, gracefully.

Silence hung over the night-shrouded roofs until, faintly from a distant courtyard, the high, clear note of a temple bell called to morning prayer.

ONE

The Mountain Temple

The path was rocky and the horse's hooves slipped on the wet stones. Rain hung in the air like a thick mist. In a gully a miniature waterfall had formed, its muddy current splashing and gurgling downhill. Patches of wet fog hung between the sagging branches of tall cryptomerias like giant jeweled cobwebs.

The tall rider sat hunched forward in the steady downpour, his big sedge hat joining seamlessly with the straw rain cape covering his body. At a turn in the path he straightened and peered ahead. Ah, finally! The curving blue-tiled roof and the red-lacquered columns of the main gate to the temple lay just ahead. Beyond the plaster walls, dimly seen in the grayness of mist and rain, rose a graceful five-storied pagoda and the many roofs of temple halls and monastic outbuildings.

The tired horse smelled stables and shook his head, releasing a shower of water. Its rider was Sugawara Akitada, returning to the capital from one of the far northern provinces. Akitada was still young, in his mid-thirties, and physically strong, but days of forced riding had worn him out. The steady cold rain had made this particular day's journey across the mountains especially wearying, and now, in the fading light of early evening, he was forced to seek the temple's hospitality: a simple room, a hot bath, and a vegetarian supper.

Two other travelers had reached the gate ahead of him. The man had already dismounted and was solicitously helping a lady from her horse. They both wore rain gear similar to Akitada's, but the woman's broad-rimmed hat was also covered by a thick veil, sagging with moisture. She rearranged it impatiently and walked up the steps to the gateway, the lavishly embroidered hem of her gown sweeping through the mud behind her.

As Akitada stopped to dismount, her companion struck the bronze bell at the gate. Its high clear metallic sound broke the peaceful splash and drizzle of the rain. Almost immediately the gate opened and an elderly monk appeared, looking uncertainly from the couple to the tall rider waiting behind them.

The woman's companion, unaware of Akitada, explained, "We are traveling to Otsu and cannot go any farther today. Can you give us shelter?"

The monk hesitated. "Is the other gentleman with you?"

They both turned then to look in surprise at Akitada, who looked back calmly. Though he could not see the lady's face behind all that wet veiling, he knew she was young, for she moved quickly and with studied grace. The man was stocky, well-built, and in his late twenties. He wore traveling clothes of good quality and, like Akitada, had a sword stuck through his sash. A gentleman, perhaps. Certainly a member of the affluent class. His face was not handsome, but open and friendly, and he bowed politely to Akitada before telling the monk, "Oh, no. There are just the two of us. This gentleman is a stranger to my sister-in-law and myself."

The woman moved impatiently, extending a smooth white arm from under her rain cape to gesture to her companion to hurry. Multiple layers of fine silk, in shades from russet to lavender, peeked out from under the cream-colored satin sleeve of her robe. The embroidery on the sleeve and hem was of autumn leaves and chrysanthemums.

A very rich lady indeed, thought Akitada, who was tying his horse next to their mounts and noting the costly saddles. Bowing deeply to her, he hoped she would remove the veil so he could see her face. But he was disappointed, for she abruptly turned her back to him. He told the monk, "Please accommodate your guests first. I shall wait for your return."

The lady ignored Akitada's courtesy, but her companion bowed his acknowledgment.

"Are there many visitors here tonight?" the lady asked, slipping off her wet rain cape for the young man to pick up.

"Oh, yes, madam," the monk replied.

"And what sort of people might they be?"

"Oh, mostly ordinary," said the old man, turning to shuffle barefooted down the long covered corridor to the right. They followed him. Akitada stepped up under the gateway to watch them walk away.

"Ordinary?" she asked, her voice rising a little. "What do you mean?"

"Mostly pilgrims, madam. And a group of players who put on *bugaku* dances for the local people. But don't worry. They are in a different building."

She pursued the topic, but Akitada could no longer make out the words. He slipped out of his wet rain cape and took off the sedge hat, chuckling at the lady's fears that she might have to rub shoulders with the common people. He reflected ruefully that she had evidently not approved of him, either, when she saw him in his cheap rain gear and on a hired horse. Underneath the straw cape he wore a sober brown hunting robe over fawn-colored silk trousers which he had tucked into his leather riding boots. A long sword was pushed through his wide leather belt. His slender, deeply tanned face with the heavy eyebrows might have belonged to a scholar or a warrior, but was to his mind ordinary. And he thought his narrow straight back and waist and broad shoulders lacked both grace and muscular bulk.

He laid his wet straw cape and hat on the railing of the balustrade and looked out across the large courtyard toward the main temple hall. Memories stirred of visits to this place back in the days of his childhood. He had been accompanied by his imperious mother and two younger sisters, along with nurse-maids and servants. How would he find them now? Was his mother still alive? The message of her severe illness had reached them two weeks earlier, on their homeward journey, and Akitada had pushed ahead alone, leaving his wife and small son to follow more slowly with the luggage and servants.

Now he was only a short day's ride from the capital and worried about what he would find. Akiko, the elder of his two sisters, had married an official during his absence and moved away, but Yoshiko was still at home. He tried to imagine his mother ill, her fierce strength gone, and only the bitterness remaining. He sighed.

Steady streams of water descended along the chains suspended from the monstrous snouts of rain spouts above him and splashed with a great din into pebble troughs. Across the courtyard the tall pagoda rose into the mist, its top lost above the clouds. The scent of pines hung in the air and mingled with the sweetish odor of wet straw and sedge. But for this miserable rain he would have made better time and arrived home this very night. Instead, he and his horse were near physical collapse after hours of trudging through deep mud and roaring torrents.

The gatekeeper returned, his soles whispering softly on the smooth boards of the gallery. "Forgive the delay, sir," he said, glancing at Akitada's clothing and sword. "Has your honor come to worship or for lodging?"

"Lodging only, I'm afraid." Akitada produced a visiting card and handed it to the monk, who peered at it and bowed deeply.

"A great honor, my lord," he said. "May I conduct you to the abbot?"

Akitada suppressed a sigh. He was bone tired and in no mood for courtesies over fruit juice, but the visit was obligatory for men of his rank.

This time the monk turned to the left and led the way to the inner courts of the temple and its monastery. After an eternity of galleries and corridors, he paused before an unadorned door made of beautifully polished wood. It was opened by an acolyte, a boy of ten or eleven. In the room behind him sat a very old man on a small dais.

"His Reverence, Genshin," murmured the monk.

Genshin was frail, almost skeletal, and his skin stretched like yellowed paper across his shaven skull. He wore a dark silk robe and a very beautiful stole patched from many-colored pieces of brocade. A string of amber beads slid slowly through fingers thin as the claws of a bird. His eyes were closed, the lids almost transparent, and the thin, pursed lips moved silently.

"Reverence?" whispered the gatekeeper. "Lord Sugawara wishes to pay his respects."

A bead moved as they waited, and then another. Finally the thin lids lifted and faded eyes looked at Akitada. "Sugawara no Michizane?" Genshin's voice sounded like the rustling of dry leaves.

Michizane, long dead though never forgotten? "No, Your Reverence," said Akitada, stepping forward and bowing deeply. "I am afraid I have little in common with my illustrious ancestor. I am Akitada, most recently provisional governor of Echigo." He said it with an odd mixture of pride and humility. Echigo had been a punitive and punishing assignment, and only he knew how hard-won his achievements had been.

The abbot shook his head confusedly. "Governor? I thought . . ." His voice trailed off and the lids closed again.

Apparently the courtesy visit was going to be more difficult than Akitada had anticipated. He sought for words that might wake the old man to some semblance of conversation. "I have been recalled to the capital. A few years ago I held a minor position in the Ministry of Justice."

The lids lifted marginally. "Justice?" Genshin pursed his lips thoughtfully. "Yes. Justice. Why not? It's an appropriate choice.

Please be seated, Akitada. I am delighted that you have come to see me."

Akitada suppressed his puzzlement and sat, wondering how to explain to this senile cleric that only the accident of a rainstorm had driven him to this Buddhist temple. Aloud he said, "I am here for a brief rest only, Your Reverence, a chance to gather my thoughts and refresh my spirit." And that was not far from the truth.

"Ah!" Genshin nodded eagerly. "Of course. Then listen: He who seeks the Law will find it in the mountain groves. And remember, that which seems real in the world of men is but a dream and a deception. Though the reverse is also true. Now be at peace, my son!" He gave Akitada an encouraging nod and raised a frail hand in farewell, then closed his eyes again and resumed his prayers.

Disconcerted, Akitada looked at the gatekeeper. The man did not seem in the least troubled by his master's incomprehensible behavior.

"If you will follow me, my lord," the man whispered, "I will conduct you to your quarters."

Akitada got up, relieved that the visit was over, when the abbot said suddenly, "Show him the hell screen!"

The monk acknowledged the order, and Akitada followed him out, chafing under the need to view some painted screen before being allowed to retire.

The lateness of the hour and the overcast sky made the light poor. They passed through a labyrinth of dark, quiet corridors, emerging now and again into the gray light of covered galleries. Akitada caught glimpses of wet graveled courtyards and heard the sound of steady rain, before delving again into the silent obscurity of another hall or corridor.

Akitada lost all sense of direction and was following sleepily when they turned a corner and he came face-to-face with a monstrous creature. Light flashed from its bulbous eyes, and its slavering lips bared sharp fangs. Akitada saw a raised weapon and started back, his hand reaching for his sword. Then he took in the rest of the life-sized statue of a guardian spirit in ornate armor and the flaming sword raised threateningly above its head. The flickering of an oil lamp in the air current as they passed had caused the masterful carving to appear momentarily alive.

The room beyond the figure was filled with shelves of ritual objects used in Buddhist ceremonies: gilded bronze bells, thunderbolts, scepters, and wheels of the law jostled gongs and plaques of every size on stands and tables.

"It's getting dark," said his guide, and took up a pierced bronze lantern, lighting the candle in it from the oil lamp.

They went on. The flame of the lantern flickered as they walked, transferring gigantic swooping birds and moving branches from the decorative pattern of the lantern onto the walls and ceiling. Sharp looming shadows distorted pillars and doorways into swaying tree trunks and cavern openings until Akitada felt he had passed into another world. He stumbled with tiredness and disorientation. The long journey up the mountain and the strangeness of this temple had taken their toll. Shaking his head to rid himself of the sense of having wandered into some nightmare, he abruptly remembered his horse in the rain outside the temple gate.

His guide said, "Your horse has been stabled, my lord."

Akitada stared at the old monk's back. Had he spoken out loud, or was this monk a mind reader? And how much longer must he follow the shuffling footsteps?

"We are almost there," said his guide, and opened another door.

They entered a very large, empty hall. One whole wall was covered with dark curtains, and a strange smell, part mineral and part resin, hung in the air. The monk reached for a rope to pull up the draperies. Akitada's eye fell on one section where the fabric had parted first. He started back with a cry.

The lantern light shone on a gruesome image. A child, a

small boy no more than five or six, was sitting there. His rounded features were distorted in agony and he held up two bleeding stumps where his hands had been.

His guide said reassuringly, "It's very realistic, but it's only a painting, sir. That's the hell screen His Reverence wanted you to see. He is very proud of it. It isn't finished yet, but we think it will be quite wonderful. The artist is Noami, a man who is most devout and meticulous. He has been painting the screen for the past year."

Akitada nodded.

The monk held up his lantern to illuminate another section. "This is the hell of the slashing blades. It will be much clearer by daylight, of course, or when there are many candles burning in the hall."

Akitada sincerely hoped not. Even given the fact that the people in it were not really life-sized, the realism of the details was painful. The horrors of the scenes before his eyes were quite shocking enough by the faint light of a single lantern. Hell screens were, of course, not uncommon in Buddhist temples, being an aid to teach people the penalties of their sinful lives. But this . . . this was beyond anything he had ever seen before. He saw nude men and women who were writhing in the clutches of black demonic creatures, while streams of blood poured from terrible wounds made by swords, pikes, and halberds. The mutilated child was one of many victims. Near him his mother clutched a halberd which had entered her stomach and protruded from her back, while a huge black-winged demon slit her throat, releasing a fountain of gore. More demons were slashing the face of a beautiful lady with sharp knives, and her handsome young lord had lost both legs and was crawling away on the ground, leaving a broad trail of blood behind him.

The monk said proudly, "It looks very real, doesn't it? And look at the flames of the burning hell! It makes you feel hot just to look at it."

It did indeed. Red, orange, and yellow flames filled a large area of the screen, and in the flames humans could be seen, writhing, their skin scorched and blistered, their mouths and eyes wide with screams of agony. Here, too, demons, black-skinned and long-haired, drove reluctant naked creatures into the flames with burning torches or tossed them into a river of glowing lava.

Akitada shuddered. What kind of faith was this that celebrated human suffering, and what sort of mind could call up such scenes of horror and agony?

"Noami has been working here tirelessly day and night, except when he goes home to make more sketches for the next scenes," said Akitada's guide. "I have seen some of them. He will paint the judge of the dead next. Emma will be right here, in the center, and his attendants will stand around him, and the soul of someone just dead will be kneeling here, with demons waiting to take him to the hells of fire or of ice. The rest of the screen is also blank, but it will depict the freezing hell. Noami says he cannot start that yet until winter gets here."

Akitada blinked. "Until winter gets here?"

"Oh, yes. Noami always works from nature. I myself have seen him build a fire in the courtyard to paint the smoke you see there."

Akitada looked respectfully at the bluish black clouds which rose from the flames of the burning hell. They looked real enough to choke him. "Let us go!" he said. "I am tired."

The monk drew the curtain again. "It's not much farther," he said.

They left the hall of the hell screen and walked down another dim corridor. Turning the corner, the monk pushed open a sliding door. "Here we are. These rooms are reserved for official guests. It is much quieter here than in the visitors' courtyard. Especially today. We have a group of traveling actors staying with us. They have given a performance of *bugaku* and are to travel on tomorrow. I am afraid they may be very noisy tonight.

13

We do not allow wine in the temple grounds, but such people rarely abide by the rules." He went to light an oil lamp on a tall stand in the corner.

"I am too tired to care," said Akitada, hoping the chatty monk would get the message. The room was plain and perfectly empty except for a yellowed calligraphy scroll suspended on one wall.

"Someone will bring you food and bedding," said the monk. "The bathhouse is at the end of the gallery to the right. I hope you will rest comfortably. May Amida bless you!"

Akitada murmured his thanks, and the old man bowed and shuffled off.

The air was stuffy from disuse. Akitada walked across the bare floor and threw open the shutters. Outside was a tiny courtyard, no more than a few square yards enclosed by high plaster walls. It was getting dark, and the two small shrubs growing in one corner next to a stone lantern were indistinct in the gloom. They were surrounded by a patch of moss, black with moisture and outlined by swirling patterns of raked gravel. The gravel glistened wetly in the light from Akitada's room, but the rain had slowed to a drizzle and only trickles of water fell from the eaves above in a regular, soothing pattern of small sounds. Akitada breathed in the fresh, pine-scented mountain air gratefully. That hell screen had shaken him more than it should have. He had seen so much of violent death in his lifetime that a mere painting ought not to upset him to this degree. He shook his head. It must be his exhaustion. He decided to leave the shutters open to air out the room, and hoped the promised bedding would arrive soon. He needed sleep more than food.

His eye fell on the scroll. He carried the light closer to read the inscription: "Higher Truth and Common Truth are different and the two cannot be one, though they are known as the Twofold Truth." He frowned. It made no sense. The abstract philosophies of the Buddhists struck him as irrational, mere

14

conundrums to dazzle the ignorant. How much more humane and instructive were the teachings of Confucius, who had a useful lesson and practical virtue for every circumstance of life.

He replaced the lamp and decided to go in search of the bathhouse.

It was just where the old monk had said it would be. Mercifully, both the undressing room and the bath itself were empty except for the attendant, a young monk, naked apart from a loincloth and glistening with sweat and steam.

Relieved that the young man did not engage in chatter, Akitada stripped quickly, hanging his clothes on one of the hooks on the wall above the wooden benches, and walked naked into the bathing room. The attendant handed him a bucket filled with steaming water and a small cloth bag filled with rice bran. Akitada squatted near the drain and scrubbed himself down. The sudden warmth caused by the friction of the bran was pleasant. After sluicing off with the bucket of water, he climbed into the large wooden trough filled to the brim with almost unbearably hot water.

Gasping with the shock, he lowered himself gingerly to the submerged seat and let the water rise to his neck. Discomfort changed into a deep sense of well-being. With a sigh of relief, he relaxed, leaning his head back against the rim of the trough, and emptied his mind.

The attendant disappeared to the outside, and Akitada heard him stoking the firebox under the bath. He returned with considerately gentle movements and took his seat against the wall. The fire crackled softly, and the steam formed beads on Akitada's face. It was too much trouble to brush them away. He closed his eyes and dozed off.

Male voices and laughter penetrated his slumber gradually but persistently until he returned to awareness of his surroundings. On the other side of the wall someone was pounding out a rhythm on a wooden surface. A man was chanting. The words were inaudible, but the sounds were pleasing. Akitada sighed and closed his eyes again. He allowed his mind to drift with the melody and thought of his flute. He wished he had brought it, but the urgency of his mother's sickness had driven the matter from his mind. He wondered again how ill she was. His sister's letter had sounded frantic. Serious illness usually meant death, and as a rule it came quickly. Perhaps he would be too late even for the funeral. He sighed again, the weight of his fears back on his shoulders.

Next door the music ceased abruptly. A great stomping ensued, accompanied by hoarse cries and shouts. Akitada turned his head to stare at the wall. Whoever had disrupted his peace, it was neither monks nor pilgrims.

Just then a woman's shrill laughter made Akitada sit up in dismay. Females in the monks' bathhouse?

He cast a worried glance at the young attendant and saw that he was standing up, his eyes grown round with shock and his wet skin flushed all the way to his shaven head. What would he do if naked females invaded his celibate male space? Akitada was annoyed himself. All he needed after his miserable wet journey and the nerve-racking tour of the monastery was for some uncouth men and women to burst in on him in his bath.

The attendant gathered his courage and went into the changing room, closing the door behind him. The noise stopped instantly, there was a brief exchange, then the young monk returned, looking agitated. "My apologies, sir. It's the players. They must have taken a wrong turn somewhere. I told them that they were not permitted here, but they would not go away. I don't think they will come in, but I shall run and fetch help."

"Thank you." Akitada closed his eyes again, wondering how long the players would linger. There was the matter of walking back out to get his clothes.

A door slammed behind the attendant. Then there were voices again, some sort of argument. A man kept saying, "Why?" A woman was pleading. Other male voices joined in. Akitada caught a few words. Her name appeared to be Ohisa and she had been dismissed. Ohisa sobbed, and someone shouted, "He can't do that!" The voices grew louder and angrier. Akitada stood up and climbed out of the bath, his face thunderous.

Grabbing a towel from the rack, Akitada slung it around himself before flinging open the wooden door and glaring at the people in the undressing room.

He had a quick impression of startled eyes—four men and one woman, all fully dressed, the woman young and very pretty, the men of different ages—before they all gasped and rushed for the door in a panic, to disappear down the corridor. The scene was so funny that Akitada's ill humor fled and he began to chuckle. His amusement increased when he was joined by four or five elderly monks and the attendant. The old monks were voluble in their outrage at having their privacy invaded by a woman and cast dubious glances at him. He became aware of his wetness and undid the towel to dry himself. After scandalized glances, all but the attendant withdrew rapidly.

Akitada hung the wet towel on one of the drying racks and put his clothes back on, then made his way, still smiling, back to his room.

Someone had come in his absence to leave a tray table with food and drink and to unroll his bedding. The fare was vegetarian—rice cakes stewed with wild mushrooms, fried bean curd, pickled eggplant, cucumber, and green soybeans, along with a dish of toasted millet mixed with honey. Akitada sampled cautiously. It was delicious, and he reflected gratefully on generations of monks who had devoted their ingenuity to making palatable the grains and plants they were allowed to eat. He was sitting near the open door to the small garden, breathing in the moist mountain air and eating everything on his tray. When the bowls were empty, he drank thirstily the fruit drink in the small flask. It tasted peculiar but not unpleasant. Outside, the rain slowed until there was only a soothing, steady, soft drip-drip from the gutters.

His body pleasantly relaxed and sated, Akitada's eyes became heavy, and he crept into the quilts and went to sleep.

He slept very deeply, but soon he was troubled by a horrible dream. In it he was naked and pursued by blue demons who had flames spurting from their fangs and reached for him with curved claws. In his rush to escape them, he passed hundreds of other naked men and women, also running and screaming. He dashed toward a huge, steaming vat, thinking to hide behind it from his pursuers, but when he reached it, he found it filled with more screaming people. They were being boiled alive by two gigantic demons who were blowing their fiery breath against the sides of the vessel. The nearer demon scooped him up with a huge ladle, which he lifted over the bubbling cauldron. Akitada clutched the rim of the ladle, gauging his chances of jumping clear of the monstrous cauldron, and took a frantic leap into space. For a heart-stopping moment he hung suspended in the steam above the upturned faces of boiling souls; then he found himself landing on his feet in a courtroom.

The judge in gorgeous robes sat on a high throne. His large eyes flashed as he stroked his beard. Akitada fell to his knees and touched his head to the floor. But no one seemed to take notice of him. The guards, more blue demons, were dragging in an elderly woman, pale and aristocratic in her fine robes, her long white hair trailing behind her. To his horror, Akitada recognized his mother. Other demons stepped forward to lay charges against her, while she knelt in stoic silence. Akitada wanted to defend her, but his tongue was paralyzed. Slamming his baton on his knee with a loud *thwack*, the judge pronounced sentence, and the blue demons carried his mother away to hell. When Akitada raised his eyes to the judge to plead for mercy for her, he saw that he was looking at his own face.

He was the infernal judge, stroking his beard, hearing charges against poor sinners brought before him. Akitada heard himself pronouncing sentence after sentence: the burning hell for the coldhearted, the frozen hell for the lustful, the realm of the hungry ghosts for gluttons, and the torture of swords and knives for the violent. He gave sentence after sentence, thwacking his baton, watching the blue demons in their armor carrying the wailing souls out, his eyes following them to an execution ground, where the demons cut off limbs and heads with smooth strokes of their flaming swords, until the dismembered bodies piled up into mountains, and the blood flowed between them like a river. Then the mountains began to topple and the river of blood to rise, and Akitada was crushed by an avalanche of death and drowned in a torrent of blood.

Akitada came upright with a strangled shout. It was dark and he gasped for breath, flinging out his arms against the nightmare. Realization came slowly. He wiped the sweat from his face and pushed back his bedclothes. The cool night air felt good on his perspiration-drenched skin. He could not recall ever feeling a greater sense of horror and blamed the dream on his exhaustion and fear for his mother. The extraordinary sights he had seen the previous evening had then produced the particular phantasms which still haunted his mind, their very sounds lingering vividly in his memory. He listened.

But all was quiet and peaceful in his room. Outside, only an occasional drop of water broke the stillness.

Then, suddenly: a single high-pitched scream—stifled instantly.

TWO

Scattered Leaves

Akitada rushed into the corridor and from there to the nearest courtyard. It was empty. He had no idea where he was or where the scream had come from, but he listened for several minutes. The night remained dark and silent. All around him rose the temple halls, mysterious shapes looming against the night. Galleries led off to other courtyards and more halls. After walking briefly this way and that, Akitada gave up. He felt a little foolish now, no longer certain of what he had heard. Perhaps it had been an owl. Or a couple of lovers, the girl teasing an overeager admirer, and both long since gone, afraid of being caught.

With some difficulty he found his way to his own room and crept back into his bedding. After a long time he fell asleep again, dreamlessly this time, until faint bells calling to morning service woke him before dawn.

He dressed quickly and walked out into the courtyard. It was barely light. Heavy fog shrouded the temple buildings, muffling the tinkling of bells and somber chants. Akitada looked at the fog with dismay. It was common in the mountains, especially after a rain, and would stay until midmorning, slowing him down on the steep and hazardous mountain track.

After collecting his horse at the stables, he rode to the main gate. A different gatekeeper greeted him. They exchanged comments on the fog and the road down the mountain, and Akitada presented the monk with some silver, a donation to the temple in return for its hospitality. The gatekeeper hoped that the gentleman had had a restful night. Akitada said, "I was woken by some brief noise once. Did anyone else report a disturbance?"

"No, sir. Oh, I do hope it wasn't those noisy actors."

Akitada recalled the scene in the bathhouse the evening before, but shook his head. "No. But I thought I heard someone cry out in an adjoining courtyard." A thought occurred to him. The gatehouses of most major temples kept simple diagrams of the location of various buildings handy for visitors. He asked, "Do you have a plan of the temple here?"

The monk opened a cupboard and produced a wrinkled piece of paper. Together they bent over it and located Akitada's room.

"Whoever cried out must have been just there," Akitada said, pointing to an area between several long, narrow buildings.

The monk pondered. "It can't have been there. That's a storage yard," he said. "Only the monks assigned to kitchen or housekeeping use it, and never at night. Visitors' quarters are in this courtyard." He pointed to the opposite corner of the compound.

"Oh, well," said Akitada. "It probably was nothing. I'll be on my way."

The road was drier than the day before, but the downward slope made the journey difficult for horse and rider. Every rock and loose pebble seemed bent on starting a small avalanche. Fog shrouded all but the closest trees, and it was impossible to see the next turn ahead of time. They moved at a snail's pace.

In spite of his frustrations, Akitada thought the scenery quite beautiful. It was already the Frost Month and in the north winter would already have smothered the world in blankets of snow, but here autumn lingered. The unseen sun gradually illuminated wisps of mist until they looked like fairies dancing in silver and gold veils among the trees. The whole forest resembled something seen in a dream of the Western Paradise. Lit from within, its graceful branches released rainbow-sparkling jewels which fell soundlessly on cushions of green moss. Here and there the path was strewn with rich blankets of fallen leaves: orange, red, pale yellow, and deep russet. Above Akitada's head, a few crimson maple leaves mingled with the cobalt green of Sawara cypress and the deep emerald of cryptomerias.

The only sounds were made by the horse, hooves clinking against rocks, an occasional snort and puff of breath, the creaking of the saddle leather, and the soft slapping of the reins against his neck when he shook his head. But there were birds in the forest. Akitada saw them flitting across the path ahead of him, indistinct like silent moths. Once a rabbit appeared, sat up to eye them, and dove back into the undergrowth. Horse and man moved companionably through a misty cloud forest.

In time, imperceptibly almost, the fog lifted, the road leveled, sights and sounds became clearer, and Akitada caught glimpses of hazy mountaintops covered with a patchwork of fading autumn colors.

When he reached the place where the road to the temple branched off from the highway and an abandoned shack stood deserted near some pines, the world was as still and empty as the mountain had been.

But he turned his horse toward home, and soon the smell of wood fires announced small hamlets where cheerful men and women smiled at him and bowed.

He was making better time now and with the speed he felt a renewed sense of urgency. Every moment brought him closer to the real world of the living—or dying, as the case might be. For days now the specter of his mother's imminent death had driven him. Riding hard and long, changing horses at road stations when they went lame or flagged, he had been sore, hungry, and fearful of what he was rushing toward. Even now the enforced stay at the temple filled him with guilt. His nightmare of the hellish trial stayed with him, though common sense told him that it had been the result of an overactive and sickly imagination brought about by anxiety, exhaustion, and the sight of that extraordinary screen.

Then Akitada caught the first view of the capital. With the fog gone, the day turned out to be one of those perfect early winter days, with a limpid, cloudless sky and a brisk freshness in the air. In the clear morning light, Heian Kyo, the seat of government and residence of the emperor, lay spread across the wide plain, along the sparkling Kamo River. It welcomed him home after four long years of absence. Akitada stopped his horse and looked his fill, tears slowly running down his cheeks. How beautiful it was, his city, the heart of his country, the place he had dreamed of in the long winter months of the far north. Heian Kyo was the golden jewel in the palm of Buddha, the promised end of the dark journey, his home.

But he entered it almost shyly, by Rashomon, the two-storied red-pillared gateway with its curving blue tile roofs ending in gilded dolphin finials. As a provisional governor returning from official assignment, Akitada was entitled to travel with an impressive retinue of servants and bearers. Such an arrival attracted crowds and turned into something of a progress, even in a city like Heian Kyo, which saw such events on a regular basis. Not a man who had ever bothered much with consequence or protocol, Akitada had nevertheless pictured such a homecoming fondly. But his mother's illness had spoiled the thrill, and he crept in through Rashomon as unnoticed as any ordinary farmer or hunter.

Making his way quickly along Suzaku Avenue, the broad main street crossing the city from north to south, he saw that it was paved in molten gold with the scattered leaves of its willow trees. He paused at its end in front of the gate to the Imperial Palace. Normally he would enter to report his return before going on to his home. But today was different. He must see his mother first.

Their street was, like the rest, covered with decaying leaves. Mournful sights and sounds greeted him. The gate to the Sugawara mansion was closed, and solemn chanting could be heard all the way down the street.

Akitada pounded on the gate. It was opened slowly by a bent old man. Akitada recognized Saburo, his wife's old servant, whom he had left in charge all those years ago. The old man stood in the opening, peering up at him in surprise. Akitada rode past him into the courtyard and slid stiffly from the saddle. A group of saffron-robed monks sat on the veranda of the main building, chanting away, undisturbed by his arrival.

"Master!" cried Saburo, slamming the gate shut and hobbling his way. "You're back! Welcome home!"

Akitada stretched his sore limbs. "Thank you, Saburo. How is my mother?"

The old man's smile faded. He shook his head. "Not well, my lord. Not at all well, I'm afraid." He cast a glance over his shoulder toward the gate. "Her ladyship? She's not with you?"

"No. They are two weeks behind me." Seeing the old man's disappointment, Akitada added with a smile, "But she is very well, and so is our son. She has missed you."

Saburo laughed out loud, baring toothless gums. "Missed me, has she? Ho, ho. And she's bringing the young master. Ho, ho, ha! What a time we'll have!" He clapped his hands, a tear of joy spilling over, and said again, "What a time we'll have, yes. It's been sadly quiet here all these years."

Akitada patted his shoulder and went to the house. As Saburo helped him off with his boots, Akitada asked, "Are my sisters here?"

"Only Miss Yoshiko. Lady Toshikage resides in her husband's home."

The elder of Akitada's sisters had married in his absence, a match arranged by his mother. Toshikage was in his early fifties, and Akitada had wondered how the headstrong Akiko had fared.

He had hoped for a younger man for her, but she had been in her twenty-fifth year by then, well past her first youth or a time when she could expect many offers. And it had been his mother's wish. Toshikage was, by all accounts, a respectable civil servant, holding a senior secretaryship in the Bureau of Palace Storehouses. His first wife had died, and Akiko had taken her place, apparently content.

Yoshiko, two years younger than her sister and ten years Akitada's junior, had been left to take care of their bitter and sharp-tongued mother.

Akitada walked through dark hallways and rooms. All the shutters were closed because of his mother's illness. Yoshiko must have heard his step, for she suddenly appeared in the doorway to his mother's room, looking wan and worried. When she recognized Akitada, her face lit up with joy. She gave a little cry and ran to throw her arms around him.

"You came." She laughed and cried, hugging him. "And how well you look. But you must be tired. Have you eaten? Oh, Akitada, how I have wished for you!"

"I know," he said, holding her away a little. "You have had a hard time of it, Little Sister. Are you well?"

She brushed tears and a strand of hair away and nodded, smiling. "I am well. You know how healthy I am."

"And Mother?"

She shook her head. "She has been ill for three weeks now. It started with an ache in her belly. We have tried everything: gruels made from herbs, powdered thistle, parsley, red clover, and teas of barberry bark and catmint. The pharmacist walks in and out of our house as if it were his own."

Akitada glanced toward the closed shutters which could not shut out the chanting of the monks. "So you finally resorted to spiritual remedies?" he asked, raising his brows.

"Not for that reason," Yoshiko said, shaking her head impatiently. "I know how you feel about it, but how would it look if we did not? Besides, it was Mother herself who made the arrangements. I don't think she believes in the chanting, but she likes people to think that we do things properly. Oh, Akitada, she has changed so much, you will be shocked. She cannot keep her food down and is too weak to stand up. I do not know how she has lived this long, except to wait for you and her grandson to come home. You did bring Tamako and the boy?"

"When I got your letter, I rushed ahead. The others won't be here for a while. I did not want to risk their health."

Yoshiko's face fell. "She will be disappointed. But never mind. Come in!"

She led the way into the gloom of his mother's room. A large, rawboned maidservant quietly rose from her cushion beside the sick woman and moved aside. The elder Lady Sugawara lay on her bedding on the floor, her head propped on a porcelain head-rest, her pitifully thin body covered by a silk quilt. The room was dimly lit by a single candle on a stand, and the air was thick with incense, which did little to disguise the smells of sickness and decay.

Akitada almost did not recognize his mother. The long beautiful hair, her special pride, was gone, cut off short just below the ears. What was left was thin and snow-white. The strong handsome face had shrunk and her skin was bluish gray, the pale lips restlessly pursing and unpursing, the eyes closed, receding into dark sockets. Of the rest of her, only the hands could be seen, lying on top of the cover, gnarled, spotted, and feebly plucking at the fabric.

"Mother?" said Akitada softly, frightened by her appearance.

She opened her eyes. They were still black and as sharp as ever. "You took your time!" she said. Her voice was strong, and its tone the familiar reprimand. It was almost reassuring. Akitada knelt down next to her.

"I came as soon as I heard. Yesterday's rain slowed me down. I had to spend the night in the mountains."

"Where is my grandson?"

"He follows with Tamako and the servants. They will be here soon."

The eyes closed. "Not soon enough," she murmured.

"Only a week or so. You must get better quickly now so that you can hold your grandson and play with him. He is nearly three years old, active and big for his age."

"He is like his father, then," she sighed.

Akitada was deeply moved. He did not know what to say. Sudden tears rose to his eyes and he swallowed hard. "Oh, Mother!" he whispered, taking her hands in his.

His mother opened her eyes to glare at him and pulled her hands from his pettishly. "Well, what are you waiting for? I expected you to bring me my grandson. Go away now. I am tired."

Akitada left the room, followed out by Yoshiko, who closed the door and murmured, "You must not mind her. She is in pain all the time."

He leaned against the wall and sighed. "No. She was always the same. I should not have expected any softening. It grieves me that you have had to be at the mercy of her moods all these years."

Yoshiko hung her head. "She cannot help it. It is her nature. Besides, there is no one else."

"Akiko?"

"She has her own home and cannot come often. Never mind. It will be better now that you are here. But come, let's have some tea or wine!"

Akitada thought of the sickroom and shuddered. "Wine, I think. And something to eat. I left the monastery before the morning rice and have had nothing since last night."

Yoshiko cried out at that and made a fuss over him. She got him settled in his own room, which was spotlessly clean and adorned with a pot of fresh chrysanthemums. A maid brought warm wine and a plate of pickles. Soon after, bowls of rice, vegetables, and an excellent fish stew followed.

Akitada ate, while Yoshiko filled him in on recent events in the household.

"We have new servants," she said. "Saburo, of course, you remember. He has been most kind and helpful, but the work is getting too much for him, so I employed a boy to help him with the outside chores. Mother's old nurse died, as we wrote you, and her new maid has had to take much abuse. But she is a simple country girl, very strong and forgiving of Mother's ill temper. I apologized to her one day, when Mother called her an idiot fit only to clean out stables, and she said, 'Never mind, miss, she's hurting and it takes away a bit of the pain.' The cook is her cousin. I am afraid she knows nothing of elegant dishes, but we have had no occasion to entertain since you left. Is the food to your taste?"

"Delicious," Akitada said, and meant it. "If this is peasant fare, we must give it a fancy name and serve it to company." He lifted his bowl of fish stew and bamboo sprouts. "How does 'silver carp playing among the reeds and grasses' strike you?"

Yoshiko giggled. There was a little more color in her pale face now. Akitada put down the bowl and looked at her. Gone were the childlike innocence and gaiety, the soft prettiness of her face and body. She was paler, thinner, older, and much more fragile, but had gained an elegance which was quite attractive. In brighter clothes and with her hair loose she would be a different woman. Seeing her like this, in her dull cotton gown and with her hair pulled back and tied at her neck, he regretted bitterly that his younger sister's chances at happiness had been sacrificed to his mother. And to his own career, he thought sadly, for if he had remained at home, she, too, could have married.

"Have you not met any young men?" he asked bluntly. "Your sister seems to have managed very well."

Yoshiko flushed and turned her head away. "Someone had to stay with Mother," she said. "When Akiko's match was arranged, Mother said I was not to mind, that Akiko had a stronger character and was better able to put up with the sorrows of marriage. She implied I was lucky to be saved from all that."

Akitada was speechless. If this was indeed his mother's opinion, it provided a surprising glimpse of her own relationship with his father. For the first time he considered whether the bitter, autocratic woman who had made his life unpleasant all these years was in fact more to be pitied than blamed. Still, her treatment of Yoshiko showed selfishness rather than concern. He put softer emotions aside and said, "Well, I do not agree. You shall marry if you wish, and you shall have the same dower your sister had." He had provided the silver for the marriage settlement—and Toshikage had not come cheaply—as well as boxes of silk and brocade, household furnishings, and enough rice to feed five servants for a year. Akiko's good fortune had meant a year of deprivation for himself and his family in the far north. Now his finances were in better shape and he would gladly do the same for Yoshiko.

But his sister said bitterly, "It is too late. No one will want someone like me, no longer young and worn out from serving Mother as a maid."

He flared up, "It is not too late. You are young still, and pretty. What you need is a rest, some happy people around you, and pretty clothes. I shall see to it that you will have them. Is there any man you like?"

She looked at him then, and slowly her eyes filled with tears. "Oh, Akitada! You mustn't!" She sniffled. "Really. It is so kind, but . . . it's all over."

"What do you mean?" he asked, upset by her grief.

She shook her head wordlessly and buried her face in her sleeve.

"Yoshiko," he begged, "please tell me. I think it is my fault you are so unhappy. Perhaps there is something I can do to set it right."

"No," she cried, her voice muffled. "It has nothing to do with you, or with Mother. I was foolish. There was someone once. I thought that he liked me . . . and I hoped he would ask

Mother. But nothing came of it. He married someone else." She paused to heave a shuddering sigh. Then she squared her shoulders and lifted her face. "When Akiko married Toshikage, it did not really matter what Mother said. You see, after that I really did not want to marry anymore."

Akitada was taken aback. "This man," he growled, "did he visit you privately?"

Yoshiko waved this aside as immaterial.

"Did he?" persisted Akitada, his voice tense with anger.

She nodded with downcast eyes.

"How often?"

"Please, Akitada. It does not matter. It is all over. As I said, I was foolish. I thought of you and Tamako. But I see now that that was different."

"Do you mean that he came to you at night as a bridegroom and allowed you to think you had become his wife and then disappeared?"

"No," she cried, wringing her hands. "Oh, Akitada, stop! It is long past and forgotten."

Akitada bit his lips. Hardly forgotten! Something truly hurtful had happened to cause Yoshiko such unhappiness. He would get to the bottom of it but did not want to force the issue now. "I am sorry," he said. "I should not have questioned you about such a private matter. Forgive me."

She nodded, giving him a small, moist smile.

"You once spoke to me very bravely, when you were still a young girl and thought that I was making a mistake by staying away from Tamako. Do you remember?"

Her face brightened. She nodded. "And I was right, wasn't I?"

"Yes, you were, and we both owe you a great deal. I mention it because nothing would make me happier than to repay that debt someday. Will you allow me to do so?"

She said sadly, "I know you want to help, Brother, but it is too late."

"Very well," he said, yawning. "We will talk about it some other time. Now I shall get some rest, and early tomorrow I shall meet the servants and take a look at the house."

The next day, after Akitada had duly spoken to all his people, thanked them for their faithful service to his mother and sisters, and made a brief inspection of the property, he returned to the house. Yoshiko awaited him.

"Mother wants to see you again."

He followed her to his mother's room. If he had expected to find Lady Sugawara apologetic or in a more mellow mood, he was mistaken. She fixed her sunken eyes on him and asked in a peremptory tone, "Have you reported your return to the controller's office?"

"No, not yet. I came directly here."

"I thought so." She spoke with difficulty, forcing out brief phrases between gasps of pain. "You have not changed. Always irresponsible! Go immediately." She took a shuddering breath, and added, "You can ill afford to risk whatever little good will you may have gained with your last assignment."

Akitada protested, "But Mother, I thought you would want me to see you first. Besides, my official robes and all the documents are traveling with Seimei in the convoy. I assure you, the controllers do not expect me for weeks."

Rolling her head from side to side, she gasped, "Why are you arguing with me?" and pressed a hand to her chest, closing her eyes in pain. "Do you want me to die?"

Akitada bit his lips. "Of course not, Mother. I shall go immediately." He turned to leave.

His mother's voice pursued him to the door. "Hurry! How stupid of you not to think that the news of your arrival will be all over town by now!"

Akitada went to his room fighting depression. She had not changed at all. There was nothing he could do to please his mother. He flung open one of his old clothes chests. It contained robes which had been too worn to take along four years ago. He rummaged around and found an old suit of court robes. The gray silk robe was faded, mildew-stained, and threadbare, and the white trousers had yellowed and showed muddy splotches along the bottom. Both garments were badly wrinkled and smelled of mold. And the formal court cap, still trimmed with the colors of his former rank, had lost much of its lacquer and leaned limply toward one side. But he dressed in the costume that was compulsory for a visit to the palace, and left the house, walking the distance in the slanting rays of the winter sun.

The workday was nearing midday, and most officials, clerks, and scribes, hurrying to their homes for their noon rice, cast astonished glances at Akitada's disreputable appearance. Admitted to the controller's office only after long negotiations with a shocked clerk, he found one of the senior secretaries still in and explained his errand. The young nobleman, himself dressed impeccably in a freshly stiffened cap and gorgeous robe of figured silk over white silk trousers, wrinkled his nose, took in Akitada's costume, and raised his eyebrows in astonishment.

"*You* are Sugawara?" he said, staring at Akitada. "But you are not expected till the end of the month."

"I know. I received news of my mother's illness and rushed ahead by myself. I just arrived and thought it best to report to Their Excellencies as soon as possible."

"Hmm. Nobody's here now. I suppose you can leave a note." The young man rummaged among papers, found a sheet and writing utensils, and pushed them toward Akitada, who dashed off a few lines. When he raised his head, he saw that the young dignitary was still eyeing his clothes suspiciously. Taking the note, the young man read it with a frown, then asked, "Are you pressed for funds, by any chance?"

Interpreting the question correctly, Akitada said stiffly, "Not at all. If you are referring to my attire, I rode ahead of my entourage and did not bring any luggage. I had to make do with some old clothes put away years ago."

The young noble's face reddened, then relaxed into a smile of amusement. "Oh. I see. For a moment, I thought you might be someone masquerading as a ranking official. Well, you'd better go back home until you can equip yourself properly. Their Excellencies are very particular about dress. I'll see to it that they get your message. We'll send for you when you are needed."

"Thank you." Akitada did not return the young man's smile. The incident would, he was sure, make an amusing tale to pass around among the fellow's noble friends. Seething with anger, he gave the young man, who undoubtedly outranked him, a mere casual nod and turned on his heel.

He walked home quickly and without looking into people's faces. The sun shone, but there was a chill in the air. The blue of the sky and the drifts of fallen leaves under his feet had lost their brilliance and seemed merely a sickly pale and dull brown. Far from making a triumphant return after a dangerous and highly successful assignment, he felt he was taking up where he had left off. After all these years he still shrank in embarrassment from what people thought of him. It was as if his mother's reception had brought back a host of old miseries. In truth, he reminded himself, there was no reason for him to be ashamed. He was no longer poor and he had made a name for himself in the far north. He had handled difficult situations well and he would be of use to the emperor in the future. It was ridiculous that he still cringed before his dying mother and some noble youngster in an expensive robe.

When he got home, Akitada found that his sister Akiko had arrived. She greeted him with a big smile and immediately posed to show off an extremely handsome robe of embroidered silk.

"How do I look?" she cried.

"Wonderful," he said, and meant it. Akiko had filled out and looked rosy and contented. Her long hair almost reached the floor and shone with care and good health. He looked from her to Yoshiko. The contrast was painful. Yoshiko was the younger by two years, but her thinness and the plain robe, along with the unattractively tied-up hair, made her look like a middle-aged servant. His heart contracted with pity.

Akiko was still posing, sideways now, stroking her robe down over her belly and arching her back. "Do you really think so?" she asked, her eyes twinkling.

Yoshiko gasped. "Akiko! Are you sure?" she cried.

It took Akitada another moment. "You are expecting a child," he cried, and went to hug her. "How splendid to hear such happy news on the very day of my return."

Akiko sat down complacently. "I have known for a while now. Toshikage is beside himself with pride." She gave Akitada a look. "You knew that he has two grown sons?"

Akitada nodded. He had seen the documents when Akiko's marriage settlements were being arranged, a process which had frustrated everyone because of the long delays involved in carrying papers between Heian Kyo and the distant province of Echigo.

"Of course, my position was impossible until now. Unless I can produce a son, I have nothing to look forward to but widowhood living on your charity in this house." She made the fate sound like abject penury. "Toshikage is no longer young. He could die any day. And then everything will go to his sons, and nothing to me."

Akitada's jaw dropped at Akiko's cool analysis of her situation. It told him that her happy looks had nothing to do with marital bliss, a fact she confirmed almost immediately.

"It was not easy," she said, patting her belly with a sigh. "My husband is willing, but not always able. I am told men lose their desire with age. You cannot imagine what I've had to do to keep him coming to my bed."

Akitada said sharply, "I have no wish to hear such intimate

details. And if you felt that way about Toshikage, why did you consent to the marriage? You knew that I would take care of you."

Akiko laughed bitterly. "Oh, yes. But who wants to grow old serving Mother as a target for her ill temper, while going around looking like a common maid? Look at Yoshiko! Anything is better than that! I am Lady Toshikage now, with my own household. I have many beautiful gowns, my rooms are furnished luxuriously, and I have three maids. And now that I bear a child—a son, I think, and with luck the future heir—my position will be permanent."

Akitada looked at Yoshiko, saw the averted face, the clenched fingers in her lap, and felt anger at Akiko. "Your sister has too much work, with your mother so ill. Your place should have been here to help her," he said sharply.

Akiko's eyes grew wide. "With my own house to run? And in my condition?" she cried. "Toshikage would never permit it."

As if on cue, Akitada's brother-in-law arrived. He was a corpulent man in his fifties, and he approached smiling widely, until he saw Akitada's clothes. Then he stopped uncertainly.

Akiko followed his glance. "Heavens, Akitada," she said, "where did you find those old rags? You look absolutely ridiculous. Toshikage no doubt thinks you're some itinerant soothsayer."

"Not at all!" cried her husband. "I recognized the noble features of my brother-in-law. Pleasure, my dear fellow! Great to be related!" He approached and embraced Akitada, who had risen.

Akitada returned the pleasantries and invited him to sit down. When he congratulated Toshikage on his imminent fatherhood, his brother-in-law smiled even more widely and cast an adoring look at Akiko, who simpered in return.

"Lovely girl, your sister," he told Akitada, "and now she's made me doubly happy at my advanced age. I tell you, I feel quite young again." He laughed until his belly shook and clapped both hands on his pudgy thighs. "We are to have little children running around the house again! It will be wonderful."

Akitada began to like the man. As a proud father himself, he soon involved Toshikage in cheerful discussions of children's games and antics. Seeing the ice thus broken, the sisters withdrew, and Akitada sent for wine and pickles. In due course, he turned the conversation to news and gossip about the government. At first Akitada had only a vague sense that the subject depressed his brother-in-law. But Toshikage became increasingly ill at ease, fidgeting nervously, sighing, and making several false starts to convey some information.

"Is there anything the matter, Brother?" Akitada finally asked.

Toshikage gave him a frightened glance. "Er, y-yes," he stuttered, "as a matter of fact, well, there is something . . . that is, I could use some advice. . . ." He paused and fidgeted some more.

Akitada was becoming seriously alarmed. "Please speak what is on your mind, Elder Brother," he said, using the respectful form of address for an older blood relation, to encourage Toshikage.

Toshikage looked grateful. "Yes. Thank you, Akitada. I will. After all, this is a family affair, since it also affects Akiko and our unborn child. Er, well, there has been trouble in my department. Some false stories are being told about me." He gulped and gave Akitada a pleading look. "They are quite untrue, I assure you. But I am afraid——" He broke off and raised his hands, palms up, in a gesture of helplessness.

Akitada's heart fell. "What stories?" he asked bluntly.

His brother-in-law looked down at his clenched hands. "That I have . . . privately enriched myself with, er, objects belonging to the Imperial Treasury."

THREE

The Cares of This World

After a moment of shocked silence, Akitada asked, "Do you mean that someone suspects you of having stolen imperial treasures?"

Toshikage flushed and nodded. "It all started with a stupid misunderstanding. In an old inventory list I found that a lute called Nameless had been mislabeled 'Nonexistent.' Then some fool had drawn a line through the entry and made the notation that the instrument had been removed from the storehouse, but did not say by whom. When I started asking questions, nobody seemed to know what had happened to the lute, and there was no record that someone from the palace had sent for it. This started me checking all the lutes in the treasure-house. I could not find Nameless, but saw that another lute needed repair and restringing. Because it was the last day of the week, I took it home with me to have our usual craftsman work on it at my house. Foolishly I did not sign it out. It so happened that evening I was having a party for friends. Someone must have seen it lying there, for when I returned to work the next week, the palace sent for me and asked what an imperial lute was doing in my house. It was embarrassing, I tell you, especially since the person did not quite believe my explanation." Toshikage broke off and sighed deeply.

"Hmm," said Akitada. "I grant you that was a bit unpleasant, but I don't see that a single incident should cause you serious trouble. Surely you returned the lute?"

"Of course." Toshikage rubbed his brow with shaking fingers. "And I got strange looks from everybody when I did. You know how people are. They were whispering behind my back, snickering, exchanging glances. The worst was that they have been doing it every time I make some innocent remark, perhaps mentioning that I was thinking of buying a present for Akiko, or commenting on some misplaced object." He sighed again.

"Nasty." Akitada nodded. "Your colleagues must be rather unpleasant people."

Toshikage looked surprised. "I never thought about it, really. I suppose they are. What shall I do?"

"Who is behind it, do you think?"

"Behind it? What do you mean?"

"Well, if there is a plot to blacken your name, then there must be someone, or perhaps several people, who instigated it."

Toshikage's expression went blank. He asked in total astonishment, "Do you really think so?"

Akitada almost lost his patience. It was becoming clear to him that his new brother-in-law was naive and not given to pondering arcane matters. Instead of explaining, he said, "Of course. Who saw the lute in your house?"

"Oh, everybody, I suppose."

Akitada bit his lip. "Who was at your house?" To forestall another "everybody," he added quickly, "Their names, I mean."

"Oh." Toshikage wrinkled his brow. "Kose was there, of course, and Katsuragi and Mononobe. Then some people from the Bureau of Books and someone from the Bureau of Music, I don't recall their names, and some of my personal friends. Do you want their names also?"

"Perhaps later. Were the first three the only ones from your office?"

Toshikage nodded.

"Do you have any particular enemies among any of the men who attended your gathering and may have seen the lute?"

"Enemies?" Toshikage was shocked. "Of course not. They

may not all be close friends, but they certainly were not enemies. I am not in the habit of inviting enemies to my house."

Akitada sighed inwardly. "Could anyone other than the three from your office—what were the names—Katsuragi, Kose, and . . . ?"

"Mononobe."

"Yes, Mononobe. Could anyone else have recognized the lute as belonging to the Imperial Treasury?"

Toshikage shook his head. "I doubt even Mononobe would. He just started working in the bureau."

"Very well," said Akitada. "We are making progress. More than likely either Kose or Katsuragi, or both, recognized the lute. They may have pointed it out to Mononobe, and one or all of them later passed the story around your office. From that point on, someone, perhaps one of the three, perhaps someone else in the bureau, decided to make use of the incident to blacken your reputation. You will have to find out who that man is and put a stop to it."

"How can I do that?" cried Toshikage. "I cannot very well accuse them."

"Do you want me to pay your colleagues a visit and ask questions?"

Toshikage looked horrified. "Good heavens, no! I would really be in trouble."

Akitada looked grim. "Then I do not know how I can serve you in this matter."

"I thought you might find the missing items. Then we could return them quietly and the whole matter would die down."

Akitada stared at his brother-in-law. "What items? You said you returned the repaired lute. Do you mean that other instrument? What was it called? Nameless?"

"No. Everybody knows Nameless has been missing for a long time. The other things started disappearing later, after the gossip about my having taken the lute."

Akitada sat up straight. "What else is missing?" he asked, fearing the worst.

Toshikage closed his eyes and recited tonelessly, "A lacquer box with a design of wheels, given to the eighth emperor by a Korean ambassador; two amulet covers, gilded silver, once the property of Empress Jimmu; a painted jar, said to have contained the true toenail of the Buddha; a small carved statue of a fairy; a gilded censer; and the golden seal given by the Chinese emperor to one of our embassies to Changan."

Akitada breathed, "Good heavens!" Such a loss was a scandal of the first magnitude. "How many people know?"

Toshikage began to look frightened. "Only I know of all of them. I think Katsuragi has been checking the inventory, and he and Kose know about the jar and the box. Maybe the statue also."

"Have they reported the losses to you?"

"No."

"Didn't that puzzle you?"

"I supposed it was because they thought I had been taking the things."

Oh, Toshikage! "Have you mentioned the theft to anyone?"

"No, I was afraid to. I think we should try to find everything and put it back."

"Easier said than done. Shouldn't you have reported to your superior? Who is he, by the way?"

"The director is Otomo Yasutada. And no, I did not."

"I think you had better. It does not look good for you to keep this matter to yourself . . . unless there is something you are not telling me?"

Toshikage waved his hands. "No, no. I have no secrets from you, Akitada. Where do you think the items are?"

"That depends. If they were taken for resale, they could be in a shop or in someone's home." Toshikage looked shocked. "But if they were taken purely to get you in trouble, they may be hidden someplace."

"Oh. Well, you must find them." Toshikage bit his lip. "But why get me in trouble? I have not done anything to them."

"Since you cannot remember having made any enemies, there must be another reason. Who would get your position if you were dismissed?"

Akitada watched his brother-in-law digest this new thought. He was beginning to look distinctly uneasy and said, "Kose would be promoted in my place. But I cannot believe it of him. The thief must have sold the objects. Even that is terrible to consider. How can I clear myself?"

"It may be difficult. Well, I shall ask around in the shops. Cautiously, for it would not do for anyone to find out that we are looking for imperial treasures." Akitada found a sheet of paper and some writing utensils. "Here, make a list of the items for me."

Toshikage seized on this task eagerly. "Thank you, my dear Akitada," he muttered when he was done, passing him the list. "I shall, of course, pay you back if you have to buy the items." He paused, frowning. "I don't suppose it would be too expensive? They are all old things."

Oh, Toshikage, thought Akitada again. Aloud he said, "It all depends on the seller and the dealer. I have been away for a long time. Who might buy such things for resale?"

"If it's dealers in antiquities you mean, I only know Nichira. His store is near the eastern market. But since I am hardly in a position to squander my money on such baubles, I am not the best person to ask. As for private collectors, well, it could be anybody. All the Fujiwaras have the wealth, and several of them have famous pieces. Kanesuke, for example, and Michitaka, and the chancellor, of course. And then there is Prince Akimoto. But surely you cannot mean to visit any of them?"

Akitada shook his head. "Not the great men, certainly. I might look in on some of the dealers and antiquarians, though. That will do for a start. Meanwhile, I want you to make an initial report that you cannot locate certain items and wish to take an inventory."

Toshikage looked unhappy but promised.

Before Akitada could change the subject to something more pleasant, Akiko came back. "Mother wants to see you, Akitada."

His spirits sinking further, Akitada rose and went to his mother's room. Yoshiko was sitting next to the pile of bedding which covered the frail body. Lady Sugawara fixed her son with a glare from eyes sunken into the hollows of her thin face. Her pale skin flushed unnaturally. She snapped, "Surely you did not report to the controllers looking like that?"

Akitada glanced down at his disreputable gown in dismay. He should have remembered to change before coming to see her. He said apologetically, "I am afraid so. You see, I have not brought any suitable clothes, and you insisted I go immediately."

Lady Sugawara sucked in her breath sharply and turned her head away. "Oh! You are impossible!" she moaned. "You did this to spite me! No doubt you wish me dead and hope to speed me on my way by shaming me publicly. Go away! I cannot bear to look at you."

Outside in the corridor, Akitada stopped and took a deep breath to control the sudden sickness which rose in his belly like a live thing. She was an old woman and in pain, he reminded himself. He must not mind so much. Perhaps she did not mean it.

But the logic was in vain. He was both angry and sorry now that he had rushed home, hoping to make his peace with at least one parent before death parted them forever.

Instead of returning to Toshikage and his sister, Akitada went to his own room, where he sat until night fell, staring out at the dark garden until Yoshiko came.

"Toshikage and Akiko have left," she announced, adding, "You have no light." She went on silent feet to light a lamp, and brought it over to him. Sitting down near him, she waited. When

Akitada made no move to talk, she asked, "Will you eat something if I join you?"

He looked at her thin, drawn face and felt guilty. "Yes. Of course." He tried a smile. "Please do join me. I hate to eat alone."

They shared a simple meal, and when they were done, Yoshiko said hesitantly, "You may have to return to the palace soon. It occurs to me that we have a very nice piece of dark blue silk. Will you let me sew you another gown? I am very handy with my needle."

He was touched. "Thank you. It is a good idea, but one of the servants can do it."

"I am much better at it. I made Akiko's gown."

He recalled the elegant appearance of his other sister. "Did you? It was quite beautiful. I had no idea you have such talents." A thought occurred to him. "If I buy some silks tomorrow, will you sew two robes, one for you and one for me?"

She looked down at the plain cotton gown she wore. "I do not need anything. Fine silk is wasted on mere housework and nursing."

"It would give me pleasure to see you in it when we share our meals."

She smiled with sudden affection. "In that case, yes. Thank you, Elder Brother."

————◆————

Akitada went shopping the next morning. Leaving the house to the accompaniment of the monks' chants, he felt as if he were escaping from a prison. The weather was warm and sunny, and even the bare willows of Suzaku Avenue made a fine show against the limpid blue sky. The recent rain seemed to have washed the world clean, and the ordinary people in the streets looked remarkably tidy. The great thoroughfare bustled with foot traffic, ox carriages of noble gentlemen and ladies, and riders on urgent business.

He passed the red-lacquered gate of the Temple of the City God and turned right into the business quarters of the capital. Here well-dressed shoppers mingled with bare-chested porters carrying heavy bales and boxes on their backs. An occasional red-coated constable, bow and quiver slung across his shoulder, kept an eye out for pickpockets.

The increased traffic and noise told him that he was approaching the markets, and he turned into a street of large shops, looking for silk dealers and antiquarians.

He found Nichira's almost immediately. Whitewashed plaster walls and high screened windows covered with dark wooden fretwork faced the street. A sign announced proudly, "Nichira's Treasure House of Antiquities," but the shop door was plain. Akitada walked through and found himself in a stone-paved entryway just below a raised platform of polished wood. The wooden floor stretched all the way to the dim back of the building. As far as he could see, the walls were lined with floor-to-ceiling shelves, and rows of raised tables stood everywhere, forming passages crisscrossing the central space.

From nowhere, a thin young man appeared at Akitada's side and knelt to help him with his shoes. Stepping out of his own clogs, he led Akitada up onto the wooden floor, bowed, and asked what his honor would like to see.

"Hmm," said Akitada, glancing around him. Every surface of shelf space and every tabletop were covered with objects. There seemed to be hundreds of small boxes of every description, and thousands of small ceramic and porcelain vessels. The shelves held figurines and masks, rolled scrolls and yellowed books, lamps and candlesticks, carved writing utensils and jade seals, games and musical instruments, religious as well as secular items. "May I look around?"

The assistant bowed, and followed Akitada around the room. Closer inspection proved that none of the objects on display were of sufficient antiquity to qualify as imperial treasures.

Akitada gave up. Turning to the assistant, he asked, "Do you perhaps have a very old lute?"

The assistant bowed again and led him back to one of the shelves. It held some twenty different instruments, all of them nice, but none old enough to be "Nameless." Frowning, Akitada pursed his lips and said, "No, no. Nothing so ordinary will do. Don't you have something really special? Really old?"

The young man hesitated, then said, "Perhaps Mr. Nichira had better be called."

Mr. Nichira duly appeared. He was short, fat, and quite self-possessed. Casting an appraising eye over Akitada's brocade hunting robe, he bowed. "I am told the gentleman is looking for a very special old lute? Might I have some particulars about the instrument?"

Akitada bit his lip. They were getting on dangerous ground. How to ask for an object without describing it in recognizable detail? He pretended ignorance. "Yes. Well . . ." he said, glancing helplessly around the large room. "Not necessarily a lute, but something really special. . . . I suppose it need not be a lute as long as it is rare . . . it is a gift for someone highly placed, you see . . . very highly placed."

To his relief, Mr. Nichira smiled. "I quite understand. It is not always easy to find just the right thing for a connoisseur, is it?"

Akitada raised his shoulders helplessly. "No. I thought . . . But perhaps you might know better what . . ." He let his voice trail off.

"Quite. Might I ask your honored name?"

"Sugawara."

The name rang no bell for Nichira. Akitada was more relieved than hurt. The dealer said, "Ah, yes. If your honor is not particular about its being a lute, I may have some other very special objects to show you."

Akitada murmured something about putting himself entirely

into Mr. Nichira's hands, and was led into a private room behind the showroom. Here the dealer begged him to be seated on a fine silk cushion, poured a very strong, fruity wine from a translucent porcelain flagon into a jade green cup of Chinese origin, and then produced several silk-covered packages, which he began to unwrap. None of the lovely things were the missing treasures, but Akitada managed to chatter about antique seals, lacquer boxes of great antiquity, and statues of fairies—not because he expected Nichira to produce them, but in hopes that the dealer might have heard about such things from his colleagues or suppliers. No such luck. But the thought of suppliers prompted another question.

Picking a lovely old flute from among the items on the table, Akitada said, "How did you come by this? It is quite unusual."

"It is part of the estate of Lord Mibu Kanemori. The widow was in straitened circumstances and sent for me. She says it's been in the family for more than two hundred years."

Akitada turned the flute this way and that, studying the workmanship closely. "The arrangement of the finger holes is unique. Does it have a good sound?"

Nichira looked impressed. "Does your honor play?"

"A little," Akitada said modestly. He tried to place his fingers over the holes, itching to try out the sound produced by such an instrument. He once had a wonderful old flute himself, a present from a young noble friend, and he flattered himself on his skill playing it.

"Please allow me to hear you perform," begged Nichira. "I have no skill myself."

Polite fellow, thought Akitada, pleased, and put the mouthpiece to his lips. The sound which emerged when he blew was quite lovely, high and clear rather than mellow like his own flute. He attempted a more complicated piece of music, struggling a little with the unfamiliar finger holes.

Nichira listened with rapt enjoyment. Akitada was impressed

with the dealer's appreciation of music and said so when he finished. Nichira burst into highly flattering comments. After that they were entirely in charity with each other. Akitada bought the flute, trying not to wince at the price, and had no trouble getting Nichira to part with some useful information.

The other antiquarians likely to have very old and precious goods were called Heida, Kudara, and Nagaoka. Nichira helpfully supplied their addresses. Nagaoka was semiretired, handling a few transactions out of his family residence. All respectable dealers investigated the provenance of any articles brought to them.

"It is necessary to tell the buyer," explained Nichira. "You asked about the flute. Knowing the previous owners adds to the value of the item."

Akitada parted contentedly from Nichira, promising to return on another occasion.

He found a silk shop in the next street. This store was open to the street, its shutters raised to allow passersby a view of the large interior, where apprentices bustled about carrying rolls of silk to seated customers. Akitada entered, and a senior saleswoman introduced him to the treasures of the shop. Akitada, who was used to the meager offerings in the northern province, felt his head spin at the colors and patterns of silk and brocade which were offered for his inspection. His own needs were fairly easily met, but he lingered over the silks for Yoshiko.

The assistant was a graceful middle-aged woman of great patience. Akitada pleasurably pictured Yoshiko in a new wardrobe. A lovely deep rose silk which changed to paler pinks depending on how the light struck it seemed to him particularly elegant and youthful, but it was after all winter, and he eventually settled on a deep copper red. Then, on an impulse, he added the rose silk after all. Matching thinner silks for undergowns, five each, their colors complementary yet distinct, had to be selected next. The assistant brought the lengths of silk tirelessly, combining and recombining their shades in layers until he was happy with the results. The copper red fabric would cover layers of pale gold, lilac, sand, and moss green, while the rose silk would be lined in leaf green, deep red, light red, and white. Immensely pleased with his choices, Akitada paid another astronomical sum and had everything sent to his residence.

Poorer but happy, he stepped out into the street to the sound of bells. It was already time for the midday rice, and he decided to postpone visits to the other antiquarians, except for Nagaoka, whose house was on his way home.

The thought of home, reminding him of his mother, ruined his good mood. In addition it began to look more and more as though someone in Toshikage's office was hiding the treasures for his own purposes. The thought raised unpleasant possibilities. Was it merely an attempt to get Toshikage dismissed and so win a promotion? Or was the thief bent on vengeance and planning to have the treasures discovered on Toshikage's person or in his house? The offense of stealing from the emperor was serious enough to warrant public humiliation, confiscation of property, and banishment to a distant province. Toshikage's family would suffer the same fate as he. While Akitada, by virtue of bearing a different surname, would not be involved, his sister Akiko and their unborn child certainly would share her husband's fate.

Nagaoka lived in a quiet residential quarter, not quite for the "good people," nor for mere tradesmen, either. His house was a typical wealthy merchant's home on a double plot, hidden from the street by tall wood screening. A simple sign above the decorative doorway read, "Nagaoka, Antiquarian."

Akitada raised his fist to pound on the fretwork gate, when it was suddenly flung open and he found himself face-to-face with an old acquaintance.

The expression on the other man's face changed rapidly from surprised pleasure to acute suspicion.

"Kobe!" cried Akitada heartily. "What a coincidence! I intended to pay my respects eventually, but family matters have kept me occupied."

"What are you doing here?" growled the other man, as usual bypassing politeness to get to the heart of the matter.

Akitada raised his brows. "Now, that is hardly a friendly greeting after all these years," he said lightly. He realized belatedly that there was something quite different about the police captain: Kobe did not wear his customary uniform of red coat and white trousers. Instead he was attired rather formally in dark silk. "I was calling on the antiquarian for some information. But are you no longer with the police?"

Kobe's face relaxed momentarily and a smile twitched his lips. "Promoted," he said. "To superintendent."

"You don't say!" Akitada chuckled and bowed. "My sincerest congratulations. You deserved it."

"Thanks. You did not do so badly yourself. Provisional governor. And you crushed a rebellion or two, I hear. The New Year should bring a generous promotion."

"Not with my luck." Akitada paused and glanced at a servant who had cracked open the gate and was listening with an expression of avid curiosity. Kobe followed his glance and took Akitada's arm to pull him a few steps away. Behind them the gate clanked shut.

Akitada looked back and then in growing puzzlement at Kobe. "What brings you here? Is something wrong?"

"Murder," remarked Kobe placidly. "My men seem to be making a mess of the investigation, so I came to see what's what."

"The antiquarian has been killed?" If the trail of the imperial treasures ended here, Toshikage's predicament had just taken a new, more ominous turn.

But it appeared that Nagaoka was alive.

"His wife," said Kobe. "Apparently killed by his brother. A

love triangle. Pretty young wife agrees to meet elderly husband's younger brother in a romantic setting. Somehow they argue, and he kills her. Husband is understandably distraught. Mixed loyalties! Should he help the police and have his own brother sentenced for murder, or should he protect the man who killed his beloved wife? He has not been cooperative so far."

"I see." It was a tricky problem for a Confucian scholar. Was a man's first duty to his wife or to his blood brother? More to the point, Nagaoka would hardly be in a frame of mind to answer questions about antiques.

"What did you want from him?" Kobe's eyes studied Akitada's face with bright interest.

Akitada could hardly divulge Toshikage's problem to the police superintendent, yet Kobe must be told something. Akitada hesitated just a fraction too long, and Kobe's eyes suddenly became intent. "Aha! I was right. What do you know about the case?" he snapped, his good humor gone in a flash. "Come on! Your arrival is just a little too coincidental."

"I swear I know nothing about it," said Akitada, trying to think of some innocuous reason. Then he remembered his flute purchase. "I, er, have taken up flute playing, and am interested in antique instruments. Nagaoka's name came up as someone who might help me."

Kobe was unconvinced. "You are here to look at flutes?"

Akitada nodded. "I have had four long years in the northern wilderness to practice. You have no idea how soothing the sound of a flute is when you are snowed in and the cares of the world hang heavy on you."

Kobe looked at him askance. "Sounds depressing to me. I don't suppose you'd better bother Nagaoka at present. He has about as much of the cares of the world as any man can bear."

"I can see that. When did the murder happen?"

Kobe hesitated for a moment, then said, "Night before last. In a temple west of the capital. The brother was found with the wife's corpse in a locked room. It's a clear case and he confessed right away, but then Nagaoka talked to him in jail, trying to get him to withdraw the confession. I could see our case falling apart in court and came to warn Nagaoka off." Somewhere another bell rang the half hour. Kobe said, "I must get back. Are you walking my way?"

Akitada hesitated. He cast a glance back up the street at the closed gate of the Nagaoka residence, then said, "I am on my way home. My mother is very ill, and I had better not be too late. Can we meet tomorrow?"

"Of course. Stop by my new office in the palace. Sorry about your mother."

They exchanged bows and walked off in opposite directions. Akitada went around the next corner and stopped. A murder night before last? In a temple? Perhaps the Eastern Mountain Temple, where he had heard a woman scream in the middle of the night?

It was not really any affair of his, and Kobe would not take kindly to his meddling in police business again. But Akitada had never been able to resist a mystery.

Peering around the corner of Nagaoka's fence, Akitada made sure that Kobe was gone. Then he returned to the gate and knocked.

FOUR

Faceless Murder

After a moment, the fretted doorway opened a crack and the round, frowning face of the servant peered out.

"I am Sugawara," said Akitada in a businesslike manner. "I must speak to your master immediately."

This had the desired effect, for the gate opened wider and the servant let him enter. Akitada took in his surroundings. The unswept courtyard with its stone pathway was covered with fallen leaves, and the man had merely tossed a hempen shirt of mourning over his regular cotton clothes. He looked irritated, symbol of a household in disarray, but led Akitada politely enough into the house and helped him remove his shoes before bringing him to a small study in the rear of the building.

The room was bathed in diffuse light which came through the paper-covered openings of doors to the outside. Faded silk paintings and calligraphy scrolls hung against the dark wood of the walls, and carved stands displayed translucent jade bowls and vases. In the center of the room sat a thin, bent figure at a low black desk.

Nagaoka was a colorless man, gray from his hair to his dress. His clean-shaven face was ashen and deeply lined. He wore a robe of costly gray silk and was sitting hunched over, inert. When the door opened, he looked up without much interest. Even the sight of an unexpected guest caused no change in his expression. In a tired voice he said, "Not now, Sasho."

"The gentleman insisted, sir." The servant's tone was aggrieved.

Akitada stepped fully into the room. "I am Sugawara Akitada," he introduced himself formally, closing the door on the servant's curiosity.

After a moment's hesitation, Nagaoka took in his rank and came to his feet with a deep bow. He was almost as tall as Akitada, but narrow-shouldered and much thinner. "How may I serve you, my lord?"

"I came here for information about antiques," said Akitada, seating himself, "but find instead that I may be of some use to you in your present difficulty." At least he hoped he might. "Just now I met my old friend Superintendent Kobe outside your gate. He told me of the recent tragedy. You have my deepest sympathy on your loss."

Nagaoka still stood, looking down at him with a dazed expression. His face contracted suddenly. "My brother . . ." he said, his voice catching. "My younger brother has been arrested for murder. If you can help, I would be . . ." Tears suddenly spilled from his eyes. He broke off, put a shaking hand to his face, and collapsed on his cushion. "Oh, there is no help," he sobbed. "I don't know what to do."

The fact that Nagaoka seemed to grieve, not for his wife who had been the victim, but for the brother who had murdered her, struck Akitada as strange. When Nagaoka finally stopped weeping and dabbed his face with a piece of tissue, Akitada said, "May I ask where the murder took place?"

Nagaoka raised reddened eyes to his. "In the Eastern Mountain Temple. They were on a pilgrimage."

Akitada had expected it. The complexities of fate always had a way of catching him. The rains which had brought him to the Eastern Mountain Temple for the night of the murder, the old abbot's rambling talk, the hell screen, and his frightful dreams of screaming souls had all inescapably led him to this moment in Nagaoka's house. He felt a shiver of dread run down his spine.

He asked Nagaoka, "Why do you believe that your brother is innocent?"

Nagaoka cried, "Because I know him like myself. He is incapable of such a crime. Kojiro is the most gentle of men. Since he remembers nothing of the night and does not know how he got into my wife's room, he should not have confessed to something he did not do."

Akitada reflected that a loss of memory hardly constituted innocence, even if it was genuine, but he only said, "Perhaps you had better tell me his story."

But now Nagaoka balked. "Forgive me," he said, "but why is it that you are interested in my family troubles?"

"Not at all. I happened to spend the night at the temple and may have seen or heard something which could be of use to you and the authorities. Besides, I am fascinated by complicated legal problems and have had some luck in discovering the truth on past occasions. In fact, that is how Superintendent Kobe and I met several years ago. He was a captain then, and I served in the Ministry of Justice. I am sure he will vouch for me." Akitada had some doubts about this, but his curiosity about the Nagaoka murder was thoroughly aroused. "Suppose you start by telling me a little about your wife and your brother."

Nagaoka had listened with growing amazement. Now he nodded. "Yes, yes. Let me see. My brother is much younger than I, and more strongly built. He has an intelligent, cheerful look about him. Everyone takes to him right away."

Akitada nodded. "It sounds like a young man I saw when I first arrived at the temple gate. The lady with him was veiled."

"My wife was wearing a pale silk robe embroidered with flowers and grasses. She, too, is . . . was young."

"Quite right. They had arrived just before I did. I am afraid we did not exchange many words."

"What a coincidence!" Nagaoka said, shaking his head. "That gown . . . I had just given it to her. She died in it. When I saw her, her face was . . . disfigured, but she was very beautiful." He shuddered. "It is most kind of you to offer help. My brother and I . . ." His voice broke. "We are very close, and my being the elder . . . our father died young, and I have always felt like a father to Kojiro. This has all been most dreadful and I blame myself terribly."

"For what?" Akitada asked, surprised, then added, "I don't wish to pry into personal matters, but I would have expected you to be deeply grieved and shocked by the loss of your young wife. Instead you seem to be mostly troubled by your brother's arrest."

The antiquarian said bleakly, "Of course I am shocked by her death, but it is my brother who is alive, and he needs my help now. Besides . . ." He sighed deeply. "Our marriage had become a burden to both of us. Nobuko did not love me. I think she fell in love with my brother. It was to be expected. She was only twenty-five, and I am fifty. Look at me! I am an old man, a dull fellow who deals in old things. My brother is fifteen years my junior. He writes poetry and plucks the zither in the moonlight outside his room. What young woman could resist?"

Being happily married to Tamako, Akitada could not imagine what another husband might feel when his wife sought love from his own brother. It occurred to him that Nagaoka had a strong motive for murder himself. In spite of his explanations, the man's reactions were all wrong. A husband betrayed by both wife and brother should have been furiously, even murderously angry. But this man sounded apologetic about his wife's faithlessness and frantic over his brother's arrest.

Nagaoka took up his story again. "I should never have married again. At least not someone young enough to be my daughter." He moved his thin hands helplessly. "Nobuko was very lively when she lived in her father's home. She liked to dance and sing, and they always had young people around. I had hoped that children might fill her life, but we did not have any. I found out soon that she was unhappy with me, and so I started staying away. I claimed that my work kept me busy, but the truth is I could not bear to see her so unhappy. She only cheered up when my brother came, and I was glad." He broke off and stared miserably at one of the scrolls on the wall.

After a moment, Akitada said, "Forgive me, but are you suggesting that your wife took your brother as a lover because she was bored?"

Nagaoka looked shocked. "Of course not. They were not lovers, though I would not have objected. But Kojiro would never betray me . . . unless . . ." He flushed, then said firmly, "My brother would never knowingly do anything to hurt me, any more than I would hurt him."

"Knowingly? People don't commit adultery unknowingly."

Nagaoka looked away. "I do not believe it."

Akitada, having caught the small note of doubt, coaxed gently, "But there is something?"

Nagaoka cried, "I don't know the full truth. . . . Neither does he! Apparently Kojiro had been drinking heavily. When he drinks he often does not remember the next day where he has been or with whom. The constables from the pleasure quarter used to bring him home senseless. It was a great worry to me, because I was afraid that his drinking would ruin him." He sighed. "And now it has."

"Did your brother live here?"

"No, he stayed here only for his visits. He owns a place in the country. I helped him buy it with money from our father's estate. He has worked hard on that land and also managed Prince Atsuakira's estate nearby." Nagaoka clenched his hands. "Oh, what will the prince think! And why did this have to happen now?"

"What do you mean, 'now'?"

"Kojiro had stopped drinking. He had not touched wine in over a month." Nagaoka looked at Akitada beseechingly. "Please understand that Kojiro's behavior at the temple was a complete surprise. His previous drinking had been because of a romantic disappointment, and he'd got over that."

Akitada had his doubts. A man who had spent his leisure time drinking himself into a stupor in the pleasure quarter was not above drinking in a temple and assaulting his sister-in-law. But he said only, "How did he come to be at the temple with your wife?"

"It was Nobuko's idea to worship there. She wished to make a donation and say some special prayers because she had heard that women had conceived after reciting a particular passage from one of the sutras. I thought it was all nonsense, but she . . . Well, I could hardly stop her. But I did not want to go myself, and Kojiro offered to be her escort."

"I see. And how does your brother explain the condition he was found in?"

"He cannot. He swears he only drank some tea, but . . ."

"You suspect he is lying?"

Nagaoka fidgeted. "No, of course not, but I don't know how to explain it. He was found reeking of wine and there was a nearly empty pitcher of some cheap wine in the room."

Akitada nodded. "Go on. What else does he say?"

"Kojiro remembers feeling tired and sick and says he went to lie down in his room. That is the last he remembers, until the monks broke open the door of my wife's room and found him with her . . . dead."

"Then why has he confessed to the crime?"

Nagaoka clenched his hands in helpless frustration. "Because he cannot remember what happened all those other times, he thinks he must have killed her in some sort of fit. I tried to convince him to withdraw his confession. To let the police investigate further." He grimaced. "But the superintendent came today to tell me the case was closed and not to meddle anymore, that I'd just make things worse for Kojiro. He said the evidence is so solid against him that they must get a confession, and would use force to get it. Can they really do that?"

"Probably. Confessions are encouraged with bamboo whips."

Nagaoka cried, "But my brother is no common criminal. He is a respectable landowner. Can't you make them wait? There must be some explanation why Kojiro was in her room. Someone may have seen something that night."

They were interrupted by the servant. "Will you take your rice now," he asked, "or shall I let the fire go out in the kitchen?"

Nagaoka looked at him uncomprehendingly, then said, "Rice? Is it time to eat?"

"An hour past," said the servant, casting a resentful glance at Akitada.

"Oh, dear." Nagaoka looked helplessly at Akitada and suddenly remembered his manners. "Forgive me, my lord. I am afraid I lost all sense of time. Will you honor me with your company for the noon rice?"

Akitada had more questions, but they could wait. He must speak to Kobe as soon as possible. The longer he delayed, the angrier Kobe would be, and he would need the superintendent's help if he was to help Nagaoka. Rising, he thanked Nagaoka, assuring him that he would do his best on his brother's behalf.

Nagaoka also stood up. He looked relieved, but whether he was glad to be rid of Akitada or counted on his help was not clear. Bowing deeply, he said, "My brother and I are deeply obliged to you."

━━◆━━

Police headquarters occupied a city block on Konoe Avenue not far from the Imperial City. Akitada passed through the heavy, bronze-studded gate into the usual bustle in the broad courtyard. He walked to the main administration building and asked a young constable for Kobe. By great good luck, the superintendent was still there. Akitada found him in one of the eave chambers, deep in conversation with one of the jail guards. Kobe greeted Akitada with raised brows.

"Can I speak to you privately?" Akitada asked with a glance at the guard.

Kobe led him to another office, waving the occupant out. "Well?" he asked brusquely when they were alone.

"It is about the Nagaoka case."

Kobe began to glower.

"I had no intention of meddling—I swear it—but something you said made me wonder if I might not be involved anyway."

"How so?" snapped Kobe. He had raised his voice, causing Akitada to glance nervously at the door. "What do you mean, 'involved'? You just got back. How could you have anything to do with a local case? If this is another one of your tricks, you are wasting your time."

"Oh, come, now," said Akitada reasonably. "You were glad enough of my meddling the last time we worked together. I thought we had become friends."

Kobe relented a little and lowered his voice. "Well, it looks bad when you stick your nose into police business. For one thing, it makes us look incompetent. And now that you are a private person of some standing in the government, there might be talk about undue influence."

Akitada almost laughed. "I have standing? Heavens, Kobe, I am a nobody. I cannot even promote my own interests. And even if I had influence, you should know me better. I would never play political games."

Kobe sighed. "All right! Never mind! Explain how you are involved in something that happened three days ago in the Eastern Mountain Temple!"

"I spent the night there and heard someone scream."

Kobe's jaw dropped. "What?"

"The rain forced me to seek shelter in the temple. I arrived right after a young couple. During a restless night I woke up suddenly—why, I do not know. But once awake, I knew there was a woman screaming somewhere outside my room. I ran out, but being unfamiliar with the temple layout, I got lost. The next morning I left early. At the gate I mentioned the incident to the monk on duty, and he let me have a look at a plan of the monastery. He explained that there is only a service courtyard in the area where the woman must have been, and only monks use it during the day. Also, because of the rain, they had an unusual number of overnight guests, among them a troupe of actors who had given a performance the day before, and the actors were, as I had witnessed myself, an unruly bunch. They could well have wandered all over the place with their women. At any rate, I put the matter from my mind."

Kobe had listened carefully. "But you think it was something to do with the murder." Akitada nodded. "Well, I don't agree. You either dreamed the whole thing or, as you point out, it was probably some of those actors making a nuisance of themselves. But if it will make you feel better, I'll have my men go back and check it out. Were you staying in the visitors' quarters?"

"No. They keep apartments for special guests in one of the monastery wings. I stayed there. The visitors' quarters were quite a long way off."

Kobe said, "Well, there you are, then. Not anywhere near the murder site. In any case, there is no need for you to trouble with it further. You have reported it, and there the matter rests."

Akitada protested, "But what if it was the murdered woman I heard screaming? It is certainly a strange coincidence that an actress should have screeched outside my room the same night. Isn't it at least possible that she was not killed in her room or by her brother-in-law?"

Kobe glared. "That does not follow, and you know it." Narrowing his eyes, he asked suspiciously, "And how do you know where she was found?"

"Nagaoka told me."

Kobe flushed with anger. "So you went to speak to Nagaoka after all! No doubt he asked you to clear his brother."

"He did."

Kobe muttered under his breath and started pacing, casting angry glances at Akitada from time to time. After a few passes, he stopped in front of Akitada and asked through clenched teeth, "Did you inform him also about the scream and your theory that the murder must have happened elsewhere?"

"Of course not! I have no intention of undermining your work."

"Hah! You have done plenty of damage already. Now Nagaoka will persist in dragging out the case. I went to tell him that the evidence forces us to put his brother through interrogations until he signs a confession. If the man refuses, he will be dead in a week."

Akitada's stomach lurched. "You cannot do that! Your evidence is not complete. He was asleep or unconscious when they found him. He does not remember anything."

"That's what he says. He was drunk. It'll come back to him when he feels the bamboo whip."

Akitada searched for a convincing argument and failed. Biting his lip, he tried another tack. "What does your coroner say about the cause of death?" he asked.

To his surprise, Kobe became evasive. "Nothing special. Time of death sometime during the night. They never like to be precise. In his fit of anger, the killer cut her up pretty badly with his sword. Not a pretty sight. By the way," he added pointedly, "Nagaoka's brother still had the sword in his hand and was covered with her blood when we found them together."

Akitada felt his heart beating faster. "You still have the body?"

Kobe jerked his head. "In the morgue. It's messy. You don't want to look."

"I do want to look. Would you show me?"

Kobe turned away.

"Three days have passed," Akitada pleaded. "There is not much time before you will have to release her for cremation. How could my seeing her ruin your case?"

After a moment Kobe turned and nodded grudgingly. "Come on, then," he muttered, walking to the door. "I must be mad, but there is something that's been bothering me about that corpse. The coroner and I have an argument about the cause of death. I'd like to get your opinion. The doctor is still around somewhere, I think."

As they passed through the hall, smiling police constables and sergeants bowed snappily to Kobe. His new status had clearly won him their respect. He passed them with a joke here or a nod there, only pausing once to request that the coroner be sent to the morgue.

They left the administration hall by the back, crossed an open exercise yard, and headed toward a series of low buildings. The morgue was the farthest of these, a small building reminiscent of the earthen storehouses of most mansions and temples. A guard stood at the narrow door. When he saw Kobe approaching, he flung it open. Kobe led the way as they stepped over the wooden threshold onto a floor of stamped earth. The bare room held several human cocoons, bodies wrapped in woven grass mats, but only one corpse occupied its center. A faint smell of death hung in the cool air but was not yet offensive. Light fell through two high windows covered with wooden grates.

Kobe went to the body in the middle of the room and flung back the grass mat covering the naked corpse of a young woman. She was on her back. Next to her lay a carefully folded bundle of clothing. Akitada recognized the material, heavy cream-colored silk with an embroidery of chrysanthemums and grasses. He had last seen it on the veiled woman in the rain outside the temple gate. The lovely fabric was stained with blood and dirt, and Akitada, having priced expensive silks for his sister, guiltily wished it had not been wasted on a woman who had first dragged it through the mud and then allowed herself to be murdered in it.

"Well?" said Kobe, when Akitada's eyes had rested long enough on the clothing. "Look at *her!* What do you think?"

Akitada did as he was told. It was his second glance, and again he flinched inwardly. The first look had taken in the mutilated head and quickly escaped to the embroidered silk. The willful destruction of a part of the human anatomy which was the person's identity, the self which he or she saw every morning in the mirror, the means by which humans are recognized for who they are and by which they express their thoughts and emotions to others, shocked even him who had seen too much of violent death. He recalled wishing to see the face of the veiled lady who had moved with such lithe grace. Now he would never know if she had been beautiful. Gone was the mouth which once had smiled at husband or lover and had spoken words of love—or hatred! The eyes would never again see the beauty of the world and mirror thoughts of happiness or sadness. Instead of a human face he saw a bloodied mask of raw flesh, the nose and one eye gone, the other covered with gore, and the mouth gaping like some grotesque wound. The memory of the horrors of the hell screen flashed into his mind. He wondered if the painter had studied his craft in the police morgue.

It had been a vicious attack. The killer must have been either demented or so furiously angry with his victim that he was no longer rational. Akitada thought of Nagaoka, the husband.

Kobe, untroubled by either philosophy or psychology, urged impatiently, "Well, come on! Or are you waiting for the coroner to tell you what happened to her?"

"Talking about me behind my back again, Superintendent?" asked a high, brisk voice from the doorway. A small, dapper man in his fifties walked in with a bouncing step. He gave Akitada a glance, bowed slightly to both of them, but spoke to Kobe in a casual, almost jovial manner. "So? What gives us the honor of a second visit, Super?"

" 'Us'?" Kobe grinned, raising his brows. "Have you appropriated police headquarters, Masayoshi, or just the morgue? Or perhaps you have formed a closer relationship with the late Madame Nagaoka here?"

The dapper man cackled. "The latter, of course. It is a professional bond which always develops between the coroner and the latest victim of a crime. The intimacy of my investigation has much of love and passion in it." He winked at Akitada, who frowned back.

"I brought a friend," explained Kobe. "His name is Sugawara. He's the nosy fellow who likes to solve my cases. As he wanted a look, I thought you could use some help, being that you don't seem to be able to make up your feeble mind about the cause of death." Kobe turned to Akitada. "This is Dr. Masayoshi, our coroner."

Akitada gave the man a cool nod. He was scandalized by the coroner's flippant attitude toward the body of a respectable young married woman.

If Masayoshi noted his expression, he ignored it. "I've heard of you," he said. "There was a great deal of talk the time you pinned a strangulation of a girl from the pleasure quarter on one of the silk merchants."

Akitada stiffened. "Nobody pinned anything on the silk merchant. The man was guilty. It was a long time ago, and you cannot be expected to have all the facts. Also, it required no medical skills. I have since had opportunity to learn a few things from one of your colleagues, but could not, of course, match your expertise. Please give me the benefit of your opinion in this case."

"Ah!" said Masayoshi, his eyes twinkling. "I see how it is. The superintendent has brought an ally. It would hardly be fair if I spoke first. Tell us what you think happened to her."

Irritated by the man's manner, Akitada said, "Very well," and began an examination of the dead woman. Nagaoka's wife was of average height, as he knew from having seen her at the gate, and had a well-shaped and pale-skinned body. There were no visible wounds anywhere except, of course, for the mutilated face and shoulders. Nudity of men and women was too common a sight in bathhouses, or in ponds and rivers during the summer, to trouble him as he bent closer to scrutinize the well-shaped legs and arms, the small, firm breasts, flat belly, and rounded hips. "She was young and attractive, perhaps in her early twenties, and has led an active life," he said, and moved to study the soles of her feet and the palms and fingers of her hands. "Her skin is too smooth and white for a peasant," he noted, "and her hands and feet are well cared for, but . . ." He felt the upper arms and thighs, pursed his lips, and straightened up.

Kobe met his eyes impatiently. "Come on! What about the way she died?"

Akitada glanced at the terrible wounds made by the killer. Several of them could have been fatal. They had obliterated the face, nearly severed the neck, and left deep gashes in her shoulders. "The cuts were made with a sword, I believe. No knife could have left such deep, hacking gashes, but sword wounds look like that. I have seen many of them." Unwelcome memories rose; Akitada pushed them firmly aside and knelt again to look more closely at the wounds. "Strange," he muttered. "She must have been prone. Whoever wielded the sword stood over her, for the cuts are deeper at the top and quite shallow lower down. Also the swordsman, or perhaps it was a woman, must have cut the throat deliberately, for that required a change of direction."

Kobe said, "Hah!" and exchanged a triumphant glance with Masayoshi, who chuckled and asked, "Anything else?"

Akitada was still looking and probing with his long index finger. The wounds of the face gaped, puddles of dried blood mingling with cartilage here and there, and pieces of bone protruded whitely from the raw flesh. One eye was closed; the other had disappeared completely in a mass of bloody pulp. Where the lips had been, broken teeth glimmered against the coagulated blood which filled the mouth cavity. It was no longer a human face. Akitada controlled a shudder.

"There is not enough blood," he said after a moment, and looked up at Masayoshi, his face suddenly tense. "That means she was already dead when she was hacked to pieces, doesn't it?"

"Excellent!" cried Masayoshi, clapping his hands. His tone was that of a teacher praising a bright child. "But come, how then did she die?"

Irritated by the coroner's manner, Akitada looked at the corpse again. Except for the carnage about her head and shoulders, there were no wounds on the front of her body. He gently rolled her onto her stomach. The silken hair was tied in back with a bow, once white but now mostly dark with dried blood. The young woman's back was also without wounds. "Perhaps a head wound," he muttered, feeling the skull through the soft hair. Whatever blood the facial wounds had produced had run down her neck to gather between the shoulders. Her hair and bow had soaked up what little there had been. The skull itself proved to have neither cuts nor the soft depressions caused by bludgeoning. "No," he said, sitting back on his heels and looking at her thoughtfully. "If we eliminate poisoning, the cause of death must be hidden by her wounds. Her face and throat are slashed so badly that it is hard to tell how she died, but it could have been many things. An arrow or knife thrust through the eye or mouth, or through the throat, for example, in which case she would have bled to death elsewhere."

"I'm impressed." Masayoshi nodded, smiling broadly. "They do teach you young gentlemen something after all." His tone was openly offensive.

Akitada got to his feet slowly. From his full height he looked down at the short coroner and said coldly, "I gather from your remark that you know nothing about a gentleman's education. It would have been wiser to hold your tongue under the circumstances. Your specialized training is what put you in your present occupation. Confine yourself to that in the future."

Kobe gave a snort which could have been either surprise or satisfaction, but the coroner's face froze. He bowed stiffly, saying, "I beg your pardon, my lord. I forgot myself."

The man had a careless tongue, and Akitada did not like the manner of the apology, but he controlled his anger. He had no wish to humiliate people who performed useful tasks, but the coroner had taken intolerable liberties. A coroner was a mere functionary of the courts and he, Akitada, had held the rank of governor. He had been the one who administered justice and maintained good order among his people. He said brusquely, "Very well. Please explain your findings now."

Masayoshi bowed again and turned to the corpse. He pushed aside the woman's hair and pointed to the back of her neck. The blood had been washed off, and the skin gleamed softly white—except for a thin pink line, hardly noticeable, beneath one ear. "There it is," he said dryly.

"It is nothing," said Kobe quickly. "Anything could have done that. It certainly did not kill her."

Akitada bent to look. He slowly turned the woman's head, following the thin line until it disappeared in front under the torn flesh of the severed throat. Straightening up, he looked at the coroner. "I believe you are right. You think she was strangled with a rope or cord of some sort?"

Masayoshi nodded. "There are no other wounds on the body, and there is no evidence of poison, or of disease." He bent to lift the lid from the undamaged eye. The pupil was turned upward, but the white was suffused with broken blood vessels. "This is what happens when people cannot breathe," he said dryly.

"But," complained Kobe, "it makes no sense! Why would the man first strangle her and then hack her to pieces?"

"That, my dear Superintendent," said the coroner, rising, "is your job. May I be excused now?"

Kobe muttered, "Yes, yes. Sorry to have kept you, Masayoshi."

Akitada cleared his throat. The doctor's eyes flicked in his direction. "May I be of further service, my lord?" he asked tonelessly.

"I wondered if you had found any sign of sexual, er, activity."

"If you mean intercourse, the answer is no. Anything else?"

"No, thank you." Akitada felt that, quite unreasonably, he was being told that he had given offense and was being put in his place. When Masayoshi had left, he said to Kobe, "What a very unpleasant fellow! Where did you dig him up?"

Kobe frowned. "He's a good man. In his own way, he is as stubborn and opinionated as you are. But he is no respecter of the aristocracy, and your reprimand has made him angry. Now it will take me days to soothe him sufficiently to get any work out of him. You had no cause to humiliate him that way. Especially when you were wrong and he was right."

Akitada felt himself redden. "He was disrespectful. Remember, Kobe, I, too, am not the same man I was eight years ago. Up in the deep snow country I have learned some hard lessons about authority. The man was disrespectful of my position. Respect for distinctions of rank is necessary to maintain harmonious order. Common sense dictates that respect must be given and demanded or social chaos ensues. By mocking me, he mocked the order established by our emperor and the gods, and that cannot be not permitted."

Kobe burst into shouts of laughter.

Akitada froze, then turned to leave.

"Wait," cried Kobe. "Don't be ridiculous! I grant you the man lacks manners, but I have to take a more practical view. Masayoshi is a damned fine coroner, so I don't pay attention to his oddities. For instance, in this case, if he says she was strangled, then she was. Though it makes the case against Nagaoka's brother damned awkward."

Akitada snapped, "Well, it could not matter less, for the dead woman is not Nagaoka's wife."

Kobe turned to stare at him. "Not his wife? Have you lost your mind? The husband has identified her. There is no doubt about it. Besides, even Kojiro identified her as his sister-in-law."

"Nevertheless, they are mistaken." Akitada glared back with the certainty of conviction. "Perhaps they are lying for their own reasons. Without a face, the body could belong to a lot of young women. This particular one is well muscled, her palms are callused, and the soles of her feet are toughened from walking. She may not be a peasant woman, but neither is she a lady of leisure, as Nagaoka's wife surely was. I don't know how she came by the gown, but I think you should look for a missing servant girl. Apparently neither you nor your clever coroner have wondered why her face should have been destroyed."

Kobe started to laugh again. "This is your unlucky day! It so happens I asked about the muscles and calluses. Nagaoka says his wife was raised in the country and used to ride horses and climb mountains and everything. A regular tomboy, according to him." He stood, rocking back and forth on his heels, his eyes filled with glee.

Akitada gaped. "Are you sure? But why cut up her face like that, then? What was the purpose?"

Kobe took his arm to lead him out. "Never mind! You have done enough damage for one day. Why don't you go home now? You said earlier that your mother was very ill. Surely you are needed at home." His tone was paternal and thoroughly insulting.

Akitada shook off his arm. Through clenched teeth he said, "Could I have a few words with Nagaoka's brother first?"

"No." Kobe's tone was firm, and his eyes cold. "Not today or anytime. Put the matter from your mind! It is not your concern."

FIVE

The Shrine Gate

Perhaps four years earlier Akitada, less conscious of his consequence, might have persisted in his plea to see the accused, but
now, meeting Kobe's implacable eyes, he merely executed a stiff
little bow, turned on his heel, and left.

In his fury, he walked straight home without noticing the
change in the weather. The city shivered in a cold wind and
under a sky which was clouding up rapidly. People rushed along,
holding on to their hats and pulling their collars up against the
chill breeze. Leaves danced along the street, swirled up in little
eddies, and subsided in odd corners of buildings and along the
bottom of bamboo fences.

Saburo opened to his knocking, his wrinkled face breaking into a
welcoming smile. Akitada brushed past him. The chanting monks
had withdrawn from the windswept courtyard into the shelter of
the house. Their droning voices reverberated through the corridors.

Yoshiko heard his step and came running, her eyes shining.
"Oh, Akitada," she cried.

"How is she?" snapped Akitada, his face and voice stormy.

Yoshiko's happiness faded abruptly. "There is no change."
She faltered. "Is . . . is anything wrong?"

"No. Yes. Never mind! It has nothing to do with you. If
Mother has not sent for me, I'll go to my room."

"No, she has not. But . . . what has happened? Can you not
speak about it?"

She looked anxious, and Akitada felt guilty that he had inflicted his outrage with Kobe on her. "I am sorry," he muttered. "There is nothing for you to worry about. Just an injury to my own cursed pride and self-consequence. Come and I'll tell you about it, if you like."

She brightened at that and followed to his room.

"Did they deliver the silks?" he asked, glancing at her severe dark blue cotton dress.

"Oh, yes," she cried. "That is what I wanted to tell you. But Akitada, you should not have bought such very gorgeous fabrics for me. And why two sets, and with all the stuff for undergowns? I have never had anything half so expensive or lovely. It must have cost a fortune?"

He smiled at that. "Not quite a fortune. I am reasonably well-to-do these days, Little Sister, and it gives me great joy to imagine you in the finished gowns."

"I am so very grateful, my dear, but I may not get much use out of them, especially the rose-colored one."

"Why not?"

"Because of Mother."

For a moment his anger rose at the thought that the meanness of his mother might extend to forbidding her daughter a pretty gown. Then he understood. "Oh, dear," he said, ashamed of his thoughtlessness. "Yes, I suppose we must be prepared to go into mourning when the time comes. But it may not be for some time."

Yoshiko shook her head. "Certainly before spring. It will be soon, I am afraid. She has been spitting up some blood."

Misery settled on Akitada. "What does the physician say?"

Yoshiko looked down. "He says the end is not far away."

"And she has not asked for me?"

Yoshiko shook her head mutely. He sat, staring sightlessly at his clenched hands. How much she must hate me, he thought. And he knew that his mother was leaving him a legacy of self-doubt along with the memory of rejection. He sighed deeply.

"She is very ill," said Yoshiko gently, "not really herself, you know."

He said nothing.

"You look tired and . . . have you had your meals in the city?"

"What? No. There was so much to do I forgot."

She left and came back with a bowl of noodle soup and some rice cakes on a tray, and watched him as he ate. He had little appetite, but the food made him feel better. He put the half-empty bowl down and said gratefully, "It is so good to be back," then corrected himself quickly with a grimace: "I meant with you. This has never been a happy house for me."

Yoshiko looked stricken. "You mustn't feel that way! This is your home, not Mother's or mine," she cried. "Do not let her spoil it for you and Tamako and your son. It will be a happy home again. Our family has lived here for many generations and will continue to live here through you."

Akitada glanced around his room and out to the overgrown garden, now as covered with leaves at Nagaoka's courtyard had been. From the direction of his mother's room the voices of the monks penetrated even into his sanctuary. Like Nagaoka's, this, too, was a house in disarray, but Yoshiko's words touched something in his heart. She was right! It was up to him to give life back to the family home. Tamako would make short work of the weeds and choking vegetation outside and turn the garden into a flowering grove, while his son Yori, and in due time other children, would play outside, filling the place with their shrill shouts and laughter instead of the horrible drone of prayers for the dying. He smiled.

"There," said Yoshiko. "That looks much better. Now tell me what happened to upset you so."

He decided not to mention Toshikage's problem, but told her of his night at the temple, and how he had run into Kobe in the city and ended up becoming involved in the murder of Nagaoka's wife.

"It was foolish," he said, when he was done, "to become so angry with Kobe for refusing what I considered a courteous request, but I have become used to being obeyed. No one has spoken to me in that manner for a long time now." He added with a smile, "It will take some patience before I will become properly humble again."

Yoshiko did not smile. She was sitting very still. He was dismayed to see her so pale, her eyes large with shock. Cursing himself for frightening her with his gory tale of murder and nightmare, he apologized.

"No, no," she said, smiling a little tremulously. "It is nothing. But what will happen now? Who will help that poor man? Oh, Akitada, can you not do something? You could use your rank, perhaps. Or get some of your powerful friends to intercede."

He looked at her in astonishment. "Of course not. My arrogance is not quite that great. Besides, it is by no means clear that the man is innocent."

"Oh, but he is. He must be. You said yourself that you were not convinced of his guilt."

Akitada sighed. "Yes, my dear. But that is not the same as believing him innocent. I am not satisfied that he had a motive, and the fact that Nagaoka's wife was strangled before being hacked about suggests that she was not murdered by a drunken maniac. It is not logical. That is all."

"Anybody could have done it. What about the husband? He must have been angry with his brother, if he suspected him of being his wife's lover. Perhaps it was he who killed her and made it look as if his brother had done it. It would be the perfect revenge, wouldn't it?"

She had spoken fervently, leaning forward a little, her eyes pleading with him to agree, and he was amused. Of course, she was quite right about Nagaoka's motive, and he told her so. "But," he said, "my hands are tied. Kobe will not let me speak to his prisoner, and I must do so before I can get any idea of what

74

happened at the temple and of the relationship between the two brothers and Nagaoka's wife." He paused, and gave Yoshiko a glance of concern. "Are you quite well? You look a little feverish. Perhaps we had better not talk about the matter anymore. Do you think I should go to see Mother?"

His sister looked down at her hands and took a moment to calm herself. "Perhaps tomorrow. I am afraid that she may excite herself too much and bring up more blood."

Akitada nodded. No doubt Yoshiko thought the sight of him would be so abhorrent to his mother that it might hasten her death. "I think I shall read a little," he said, and watched his sister rise and leave without another word.

He spent the rest of the day depressed by his inability to cope with the assorted miseries he had found on his return. His mother's hatred for him, even in her present condition, was sufficiently demoralizing, but then there was the matter of Toshikage, potentially dangerous not only to Toshikage but also to Akiko and their unborn child. Yoshiko's unhappiness and his own pending report to the great men who held his future and that of his people in their hands also weighed heavily on his mind.

He missed his wife and son. Tamako and Yori, short for Yori-naga, had been his whole life until now. He hoped they were safe. Yori was only three, and by no means safe from the many illnesses which could strike young children so quickly and often fatally. And they might encounter highwaymen. He reminded himself that Tora and Genba rode with them and were both strong and experienced fighters. Besides, there were the bearers and some hired horsemen. Seimei, Akitada's secretary, was too old, of course, to be much use against robbers, but his wisdom would keep them well advised. Still . . .

Akitada eventually went to bed. He spent a restless night, tossing and turning as he revolved all his troubles in his mind. Outside, the monks' droning chants continued their unabated hum. He wondered at the cost and knew he would soon have to ask Yoshiko how large a gift the temple expected. Once during the night, he heard someone running, and the monks began a more frantic burst of chanting. Akitada rose and flung on some clothes, waiting for the summons which would call him to his mother's side.

But it did not come. The house fell quiet again, and Akitada returned to his bedding. Toward morning he finally dozed off.

He sought out his sister as soon as he was dressed the next morning. She met him, looking exhausted, at the door of her room.

"Is Mother all right?" Akitada asked. "I heard some excitement during the night."

"Another hemorrhage. A bit worse than last time. She finally fell asleep." Yoshiko passed a hand over her dark-ringed eyes. "At least I think so. It is hard to tell if she is asleep or simply too weak to bother."

"You are tired. Shall I go sit with her today?"

Yoshiko gave him a grateful look. "If you would. For just a few hours. I have not had any sleep. Don't wake her, though."

In the corridor outside his mother's room, some five or six monks sat in a line, their eyes closed and their lips moving continuously, while prayer beads passed between their fingers. Akitada stepped over them and opened the door. They neither looked up nor paused in their chant.

His mother's room was in semidarkness, the air overheated and thick with the smell of blood and urine. Braziers glowed here and there. The sturdy maid looked up at him with startled eyes, but Lady Sugawara lay still. She was on her back, hands folded across her stomach, sunken eyes closed, nose and chin jutting up sharply from a face which already looked more like a skull than a living human being.

Akitada gestured for silence and took a seat near the maid, whispering, "I shall stay for a while. Please do not let me trouble you. How has she been?"

" 'Twas bad in the night," the maid whispered back. "But she's been asleep the last hour or so."

"Good." Akitada prepared himself for a long vigil, but suddenly his mother's eyes opened and fixed on him. "Mother?" he asked tentatively. When she said nothing, he tried, "How are you feeling?"

"Where is my grandson?" Her voice was shockingly loud and harsh in that stillness. "Have you brought my grandson?"

"Not yet. They will be here shortly. In a . . ." He stopped, seeing her face contract into a mask of fury.

"Get out!" she gasped, choking. "Get out of my room! Leave me alone!" The gasping turned to convulsive coughing. "I can . . . not even die in . . . peace . . . without you rushing me along. . . . Curse you . . . for . . ." She raised up suddenly, pointing a clawlike hand at him accusingly, her eyes filled with implacable hatred. But whatever she had meant to shout at him was never said. A gush of dark blood spilled from her mouth and over the bedding, and she fell back choking.

Akitada jumped up in horror and stood helplessly by as the maid busied herself, mopping blood and holding the gasping, coughing figure of his mother.

"A doctor," said Akitada, "I'll get the doctor. Where does he live?"

The maid glanced up impatiently. "No, sir. He can't help. She'll calm down in a moment. But you'd best go away. It upsets her to see you."

Akitada almost ran from the room. In his haste he stumbled over one of the monks outside. The man grunted, and Akitada mumbled an apology as he fled.

In his room his breakfast waited. He stared at the bowl of rice gruel, then rushed out onto the veranda and vomited into the shrubbery.

Feeling slightly better, he returned to his room to put on his outdoor clothes. Then he left the house.

The weather was still overcast and chill. Now and then the frigid wind picked up and shifted some of the dead leaves. Most trees were bare already. A good time for death, Akitada thought morosely, hunching his shoulders against the cold.

He no longer hoped for a reconciliation with his mother. Her venomous hatred of himself had to be accepted. It seemed to him that it must always have existed, contained for all those years under a mantle of propriety. Now that she was dying and no longer cared what anyone, least of all himself, thought of her, she spat out the stored-up bitterness of a lifetime as if it had been her life's blood. At least it absolved him from further attendance on her.

But the thought gave him no peace. His mother's words had poisoned something in him, and for the first time in his life he wished her dead. In fact, he hoped fervently that she would die soon, before his family arrived, before she could poison also his beloved Tamako and the child she had given him! He hated the thought of those skeletal hands touching Yori, those wrinkled, hate-dripping lips kissing the soft, rosy cheek of his son. Bitter resentment twisted inside him like an awakening dragon. How dare his mother destroy the peace and happiness he had finally won after leaving his home? He clenched his fists in helpless misery and wished he had not returned. By heaven, now that he was here, he would not allow her to spoil his future and that of his family.

In his aimless walking, he had reached a quiet street in he knew not which quarter, but before him rose the tall gates to a shrine. It was one of the many Shinto shrines which occupied small tranquil spaces in the middle of the mercantile bustle around them. The *torii*, gateways of two tall upright wooden pillars topped with a gently up-curved top beam, marked the entrance to sacred space. A grove surrounded the modest thatched shrine building, but the trees were bare of leaves now, and the weather had driven worshipers away. The isolation of the place exerted a powerful pull on Akitada, and the shrine gate seemed to beckon. As if under a spell, he obeyed.

Once through the *torii*, he entered a world of silence. A thick carpet of leaves under his feet muffled his steps, and the human sounds of voices and wagon wheels dropped away behind. Somewhere a bird chirped. Turning a corner, Akitada found a stone basin. With a soft flutter of wings, a sparrow landed on its rim and drank. Akitada stood very still and waited until the bird had his fill and flew away. Then he approached and dipped some water with a bamboo ladle which lay on the basin. He rinsed his mouth with it, a familiar and comforting action, then spat the water on the ground. Next he rinsed his hands. The water tasted and felt cool and fresh, and it seemed to him that the symbolic cleansing had eased his mind and he approached the shrine with a calmer heart. Above the doorway, small paper twists tied to the sacred rice-straw ropes rustled softly in the wind, as if whispering the prayers inscribed on them by the troubled worshipers who had come here before him. He had brought no paper and, surprised at the impulse, regretted it.

At the door to the shrine he bowed. The sweet smell of fruit and rice wine, gifts presented to the god in small bowls on the plain wooden veranda, mixed pleasantly with a trace of incense. He looked into the dim interior, a space too sacred to enter. There were no images in this particular shrine, just a large carved box in the center of a table. It housed the spirit of the deity, an ancestral god associated with the neighborhood, perhaps. Akitada was about to turn away when his shoulder touched a thick straw rope suspended from the eaves of the roof. It was for ringing a bell which would announce a request. Akitada paused.

Then he turned back to the face the shrine, clapped his hands three times, concentrated his thoughts, and pulled the rope sharply. A muffled clanging sounded in the roof. He bowed again, stood a moment longer, and then left.

The ritual was as ancient as his people and familiar to him

from his earliest childhood. He felt strangely calm and at peace, as if performing the simple act of worship had exorcised his demons and had helped him see his way. He was grateful to the god of the shrine.

At home, in the house filled with his dying mother's curses, it had been impossible to think clearly, but now he knew that he must turn his back on a past which was dying with his mother and care for the future of the living. His sisters needed his help. His heart had gone out to Yoshiko, no longer the laughing young girl he remembered, but a sadly changed young woman who rarely smiled these days. He would find her a husband as soon as he had settled back into his work and met eligible men. Someone, he hoped, that she could laugh with.

But Akiko's problem was her husband. There was nothing Akitada could do about her marriage, of which, in any case, Akiko herself seemed to approve. He wondered if she would if she knew the trouble Toshikage was in.

And so, because of Toshikage, Akitada went to see Nagaoka again. He still had Toshikage's list of the treasures which had disappeared from the Imperial Treasury, but had never consulted the antiquarian about them.

When he knocked at Nagaoka's gate, the same servant opened. To Akitada's surprise, he was back in ordinary clothes, and the courtyard looked raked and tidy. Apparently Nagaoka had reestablished some order in his house and put aside mourning his wife.

Nagaoka was in his study, sitting behind his desk much as the day before, except that he was busy inspecting an object in a wooden box. When he saw Akitada, he rose and invited him to sit. There was something cool and formal about his manner which told Akitada that he was not really welcome.

"I apologize for another unannounced visit," said Akitada, taking the offered seat, "but there is something I forgot to ask you. I hope I do not intrude?"

Nagaoka sat also and pushed the open box aside. "Not at all, my lord," he murmured formally. "May I offer you some refreshments?"

Having left without his morning rice, Akitada became aware of feeling ravenously hungry, but in the present chill ambiance he decided against accepting hospitality. "Thank you, no."

A brief silence fell. Nagaoka apparently had no wish to discuss the murder. Akitada was puzzled and wondered what had brought about the change. He glanced at the box. "Have I interrupted your work?"

"I was merely looking at an antique I may sell. Are you interested in theatrical performances?" He tipped the box toward Akitada, who suppressed a gasp.

His first shocked impression was of a man's severed head. From the brocade folds surrounding it, a human face glared back at him. Disconcertingly, the disembodied head appeared alive. The forehead was wrinkled in a deep frown, bushy eyebrows nearly meeting above a large hooked nose, and the thick lips were compressed in a scowl. Fathomless black eyes stared angrily at Akitada. The head wore a folded cap resembling formal court hats, but the face was demonic rather than human.

Nagaoka's dry voice cut through the blur of Akitada's confusion. "A very fine specimen, don't you think?" His eyes lingered on the mask with an intent, almost passionate expression.

"Er, yes. Very lifelike. What precisely is it?"

"Oh, a *bugaku* mask. Quite old. Either Chinese or Korean in origin. It represents one of the Indian characters in a Buddhist play."

A mask for a dancer! Akitada reached across and lifted it from the box. He saw now that it was the hollow wood carving of the face and top of the head only. The ribbons with which the performer tied it on dangled from its edges. The mask's cap was really quite different in style from those worn at court, and the large hooked nose was definitely foreign. But the workmanship was masterful and it was painted in lifelike colors. The piercing eyes were holes through which the actor looked during a performance.

Bugaku dances were much admired at court and occasionally put on by great nobles to entertain the emperor and his family. A connection of this mask to the Imperial Treasury was quite possible. To be sure, no mask was mentioned on Toshikage's list, but perhaps this was a more recent theft.

"Is it valuable?" he asked Nagaoka.

Nagaoka pursed his lips. "It is almost certainly two hundred years old and in excellent condition. Yes. I would think for a collector or someone wishing to make a present to a great man or to a temple it might well be worth twenty rolls of brocade." He looked down at his hands, adding, "However, I do not expect an offer of that size."

"How do you come by rare objects like this?"

"Usually someone needs money and unearths something from the family treasure-house. Sometimes, more rarely, it is an import from Korea."

"And this?"

Nagaoka met his eyes with a hooded glance. "Part of my reputation, my lord, rests on the absolute confidentiality with which I transact business."

"Of course. But do you not wonder if such a precious object might really belong to the person selling it?"

Nagaoka smiled thinly. "I make certain. Besides, the buyer usually asks about the provenance. It adds to the value of the piece."

Akitada raised his brows. "What about the confidentiality, then?"

The smile widened a fraction. "It may be said to be confined to six ears only."

Akitada thought for a moment, then fished Toshikage's list from his sash. Handing it to Nagaoka, he said, "This does not involve a sale, so I hope the matter will be confined to only you and me. These items have been removed from a collection illegally and may have been offered for sale during the past month. Can you give me any information about such a transaction involving any or all of the items listed?"

Nagaoka stared at him a moment, then read the list. Frowning, he reread it, then looked at Akitada with a strange expression on his face. "You say these things were stolen?"

Akitada shook his head. "They were stolen only if they are being offered for sale. Otherwise they have merely been removed without permission."

"Ah." Nagaoka returned the list. His fingers shook slightly. "I am happy to say that I have no news to give you. Indeed, if they have been stolen, then someone has committed a sacrilege of the most serious nature. Such things would not be offered for sale to a reputable dealer like myself. Handling the transaction and being in possession of any one of the objects could mean death or deportation. I would most certainly report any rumors circulating among my colleagues, as I trust would they."

Akitada nodded. He was only mildly surprised that Nagaoka had recognized the origin of the objects. A man of his experience would certainly know what was contained in the Imperial Treasury. "Thank you. I thought so, but needed confirmation. What about taking the goods out of the capital and selling them in a distant province, or even in Korea?"

Nagaoka thought. "It is possible, but dangerous. You would have to assume in the first case that the thief has a buyer in mind who is already disloyal to His Majesty and is willing to pay a great deal to possess such goods. Such a man needs to be very secure in his position."

Akitada looked at Nagaoka with new respect. The man was extraordinarily shrewd. Perhaps his profession had taught him a great deal about the secret desires of the powerful. "And in the second instance?" he asked.

"The thief would have to approach one of the foreign traders either here or at the port city of Naniwa. We have not had any trade ships arrive from Korea in over a year and none are expected to leave for there, since there has been a cooling of relations between our countries. This has been very bad for men of my profession, but it almost certainly means that such objects would not be offered to Korean merchants. They could not leave the country and, as I said, possessing them is dangerous."

"Yes. I think you are quite right. Thank you. Do you yourself travel a great deal in your business?"

"Not often nowadays."

Silence fell. Akitada wondered how to introduce the subject of the brother, when Nagaoka cleared his throat and said, "It was very kind of you, my lord, to take an interest in my family affairs the other day, but I hope you will not trouble yourself further on my unfortunate brother's behalf."

"Oh? You have had reassuring news, then? The police have another suspect, perhaps?"

Nagaoka did not meet his eyes. "Not precisely. Forgive me. I am not at liberty to discuss the case with anyone, but I have hopes the matter will be resolved soon."

Now what had happened? Akitada hesitated, then asked the question which had troubled him all along. "I don't suppose there is any question in your mind about the victim's identity?"

Nagaoka stared at him dumfounded. "Of course not. I recognized my wife immediately."

So that eliminated Akitada's suspicion that the corpse was someone else!

Nagaoka looked miserable, but somehow Akitada did not think it was grief which had him so downcast today. Had Kobe threatened him? Or was there another, deeper reason? Had he decided it was too dangerous to have Akitada poke his nose into his family affairs? Either way the message was clear. Akitada was to stay out of the business.

Thanking Nagaoka again for his help with Toshikage's list, Akitada took his leave.

The servant, less sullen and in an unexpectedly chatty mood, was waiting at the door with his shoes. "Winter's here for sure," he said for an opening. "A bit chilly out today."

"So it is," agreed Akitada, sitting down. "I see you have had your hands full with all the leaves. It must be a big job to take care of everything by yourself."

"And little thanks I get from the master," grumbled the man, busying himself with Akitada's boots. "The funeral's coming up. That'll make more work, even if it is to be a small affair."

"Very sad, yes. Did you like your mistress?"

A strange, secretive look passed over the servant's face. "She was very beautiful." He paused, then added, "And much younger than the master."

"I suppose it must have been dull for a young lady here with your master gone so much from home?"

"Hmm," said the servant, rising to his feet.

Akitada reached into his sash and counted some copper coins into his hand. "Here," he said, "for your trouble."

The servant grinned and bowed. They walked companionably toward the gate.

"She was making eyes at the master's brother," the man volunteered suddenly. "Fair drove him away, she did. But the master was blind to her ways. Always among his old pots and things, or going out to buy more. The gods only know why people want such stuff."

"It is one of the mysteries of life. I suppose it was you who gave him the news about her death? That must have been difficult for you."

The servant nodded. "That it was. You could have knocked me down with a thin reed when the police came pounding at the gate that morning, asking questions as if I was a thief. I had to tell them he wasn't expected in till later and I had no idea where he'd gone. They kept at me like hungry gnats, but in the end they told me what'd happened and went about their business, leaving it to me to tell him. He got back soon after. I must say, he took it well enough. Turned right around and went to the jail to see his brother."

"Were you surprised that the brother was arrested for the murder?"

"A bit. But then I thought, who knows what goes on in the heads of people? He used to get drunk a lot, and a man is not accountable for what he does then."

It made for a simple and convenient explanation all right. But as Akitada walked homeward, he wondered where Nagaoka had spent the night of his wife's murder.

SIX

Painted Flowers

More than a week passed without news of any kind. Akitada's mother rallied a little over the next few days, but continued her steadfast refusal to see her son. Akitada was relieved. Since his visit to the shrine, he no longer actively hated his mother, but in his present detachment, he had no desire to face another scene. He occupied himself with drafting his report to the chancellor and reviewing his accounts. He visited the temple which supplied the monks whose chanting continued to fill the house, and presented several rolls of silk in payment for their services. He also negotiated the terms of the funeral rites, an action which met with disapproval from the *betto*, intendant of the temple, who murmured a gentle reprimand about having more faith in the prayers. He did, however, to Akitada's sarcastic amusement, enter into the financial arrangements with the utmost thoroughness.

Akitada's greatest concern was the lack of a letter from Tamako. He knew that they must be getting close to the capital by now, and it would have been easy to entrust a letter to one of the many government messengers who hourly galloped along the major highways leading to Heian Kyo. He fretted because he could do nothing about it.

Toshikage and Akiko had also not made an appearance for a number of days. Though no news was good news, Akitada could not help feeling uneasy about Toshikage's problem. This, at least, he could do something about, and so he sent a brief note announcing his visit. On a dry, cold morning with hoarfrost on the roofs and terraces, he set out to pay a visit to his brother-in-law.

Toshikage's house, though smaller than the Sugawara residence, was newer and altogether more impressive. It occupied four city lots in one of the best residential streets, and its gatehouse and main building were roofed with blue tiles and carved spouts like the imperial palaces, great temples, and houses of important nobles.

Akitada admired the complex from the street, reflecting that his own home, though in an old and prestigious quarter and certainly large enough by the standards which applied there, was sadly ramshackle and old-fashioned by comparison. His father and grandfather had been forced to sell off several parcels of the original grounds, so that the buildings now appeared cramped among the remaining huge trees and narrow gardens which surrounded them. To his own eyes and, no doubt, to his disapproving neighbors, they seemed sadly run-down. Worse, repairs had been done only as a last resort and the great roofs looked patched and ragged. The money had certainly never stretched to tile roofing, though it was far more durable than the thick, blackened thatch which covered the Sugawara halls, or the boards, held down by heavy rocks, which protected the outbuildings.

Akitada knew that his mother had been motivated by Toshikage's wealth when she had chosen him for Akiko's husband and he hoped wryly that all this would not be confiscated for theft.

He walked through the open gate into a wide courtyard. Servants were sweeping the gravel. One of them bowed deeply and ran ahead to announce him. Inside, a majordomo appeared, saw to his reception, and informed him with many bows that Lord Toshikage regretted that he was in conference. However, her ladyship would be delighted to receive her brother.

Akiko occupied a large, handsome room in the northern quarter assigned to the first lady of the house. Akitada found himself in a most luxurious and feminine setting. The entire wall facing him consisted of translucent oilpaper-covered sliding doors, closed now against the wintry weather, but promising a veranda and garden view outside. Shelves, filled with decorative objects, and cabinets took up the right wall, while a lovely painted screen and a series of lacquered clothes boxes occupied the left. The center of the polished black wood floor was covered with four thick grass mats which were surrounded by low curtain stands with richly tasseled brocade hangings.

Akitada's sister reclined languidly on the mat among her silken bedding as a young servant girl brushed her shimmering black hair.

"What, still abed?" he teased, walking to her.

"Don't be silly." She smiled up at him. "I am fully dressed. Though only just. Toshikage insists that I take it easy." She patted her stomach, a tightly rounded shape covered by a saffron yellow silk gown under an embroidered Chinese jacket in chestnut brown.

"You look very fetching," acknowledged Akitada, seating himself on a cushion. "That is a lovely jacket. And I had no idea that your hair had grown so long."

Akiko was pleased. "Yes. It is nice, isn't it? I have it brushed for an hour every morning." She sat up abruptly and turned to the maidservant. "That is enough. You see I have a visitor. Go and fetch some wine."

"Too early for wine," protested Akitada. "I don't suppose you serve tea?"

"Naturally. Toshikage gets me anything I like. Very well, Sachi. Make some tea instead, and bring some of the sweet rice cakes."

When they were alone, Akiko rose. "How do you like my room?"

Akitada glanced around the large, elegant space. Filtered light came through the paper-covered doors. The room was comfortably warm, for large braziers filled with glowing charcoal stood about everywhere.

Akiko walked to the doors and opened one a little. "My private garden," she said proudly.

Akitada joined her and looked. Beyond the open veranda with a red-lacquered railing lay a landscape in miniature. A tiny stream meandered among mosses. Spanned by a curved red-lacquered bridge, it flowed through a small pond and out under the tall plaster walls which enclosed the area. Hillocks rose and undulated around the waterway, cleverly planted with shrubs and dwarfed trees to resemble a wooded scene. A small wooden pagoda, precise in every detail, to the gilded bells at its eaves and the golden spire on its top, stood among some rocks, and a carved stone lantern beckoned from beyond the bridge as if the tiny path continued past a dense shrubbery into another scene.

"That one there is supposed to be Mount Fuji." Akiko pointed to the largest hillock. "Does it look like it?"

Akitada had seen the sacred mountain. "An exact replica," he lied. He glanced at Akiko fondly. "I am glad to see you so happy and that Toshikage is such a good husband to you."

She laughed lightly. One of the nicest things about Akiko was her tinkling laughter. It lacked the infectious spontaneity of Yoshiko's, but fell very pleasantly on the ear. For a moment, Akitada felt a strong sense of affection for both his sisters.

Akiko shivered and pushed the door shut. "It is so cold today," she said. "How is Mother? No doubt she ordered more braziers for her room until you cannot breathe at all. I do not see how Yoshiko stands it day after day."

Akitada's warmth toward Akiko faded a little. His eyes fell on the large screen. It was painted with baskets and vases of flowers. The colors and shapes were lovely and natural, and the realistic detail with which the artist had rendered wisteria, bluebells, kerria, camellias, maiden grass, and many other plants astonished Akitada. Tamako would know them all by name, along with their medicinal properties. The painted flowers had been gathered in a number of charming painted baskets, porcelain bowls, and bamboo birdcages.

It occurred to Akitada that Tamako would find only bare rooms, stripped of their ancient and broken furnishings. Toshikage's generosity made him painfully conscious of his own neglect. With her love for gardens, Tamako would enjoy such a screen above all the other luxuries he owed her.

"This is a lovely screen," he told his sister. "Who is the artist? I would like Tamako to have one."

"I have no idea," Akiko said. "Toshikage ordered it for me. You must ask him. The colors are very bright, aren't they? I expect it was expensive. Everything Toshikage buys is expensive. Just look at all the things in this room!"

Inwardly amused by his sister's warning that the screen might be too costly for him, Akitada wandered about the room looking at hanging scrolls and carved vases, lacquered boxes, painted clothes trunks, silk-covered curtain stands with heavy silk tassels, and writing sets, games, makeup stands, and mirrors in gay profusion.

One item gave him sudden pause. It was a small ceramic figurine of a floating fairy, dainty, detailed, and painted in faded but exquisite colors, down to the gilding of her headdress and drooping jewelry. "Did he give you this also?" he asked, his heart beginning to pound in sudden panic.

Akiko glanced at it without much interest. "I don't remember that!" she said, vaguely astonished. "He must have sneaked it in to surprise me." She looked at the figurine more closely. "Pretty, but a bit old, isn't it? It looks foreign. Like some of the Chinese statues of Kwannon in the temple."

"Yes." She had a surprisingly good, if untutored, eye. The figurine was certainly old and dressed in Chinese costume like the representations of the Goddess of Mercy. However, unless he was mistaken, the little lady was one of the missing imperial treasures. Surely there could not be two of these around. He looked at Akiko and wondered if her husband was a thief after all.

"What is the matter?" she asked.

Seeing her standing there, a worried look in her eyes, her hand pressed against the swelling abdomen, he decided he could not burden her with his suspicions. He walked back to his cushion and sat down. Warming his hands over one of the braziers, he said lightly, "I was thinking that I have not treated Tamako very well. It is high time that I showed some appreciation for my wife."

Akiko trilled one of her laughs and came to sit with him. "And so you should!" she said, shaking her finger at him. "Men are always wrapped up in business, taking us for granted when night comes. Thank heaven Toshikage is still attentive. It is no wonder so many highborn ladies take lovers on the side."

The maid came in with the tea. She filled their cups from the bronze pot, placing it on one of the braziers afterward to keep warm. Before she left, she bowed and told Akitada, "The master's guest has gone. The master says he will see you when you have finished your visit with her ladyship."

Akitada thanked her, but Akiko pouted.

"You just got here," she complained. "I thought you wished advice on what to buy for Tamako. I know all the best shops for silks and gewgaws."

Akitada sipped his tea and smiled. "I shall come back often now that I know the way. And the other day I went to a silk merchant near the market to shop for some fabric for a court robe for myself and some silks for Yoshiko. They seemed to have an immense selection." He mentioned the name of the establishment.

Akiko nodded. "Yes. That one is good. But why in heaven's

name are you buying stuff for Yoshiko? She never wears any-thing but old cotton rags."

Akitada rose. "That is precisely why I did it. Unfortunately, the lovely colors were a little too lively. She reminded me that Mother might put us all into mourning shortly."

"Oh!" Akiko struggled up. "What a horrid thought! It is bad enough that we will be in seclusion for weeks, with taboo tablets hanging at the gate and around our necks! I do wish that they would shorten the mourning period for a parent. It seems so pointless."

And so it was, thought Akitada on his way to Toshikage's study, though Akiko's pronouncement lacked proper sentiment. But he of all people could hardly fault her, for he felt neither love nor grief for his dying mother.

Toshikage was looking unexpectedly glum and was not alone. A young man in the dark robe of a government clerk rose when Akitada entered. Akitada recognized him in an instant as one of Toshikage's sons. He had his father's round face, though he had not yet run to fat.

"Welcome, dear brother," cried Toshikage, coming to embrace him. "Please forgive the delay. I had a rather unpleasant visit from my superior. This is my son Takenori. He is my confiden-tial secretary and knows all about the, er, problem."

Akitada bowed to the young man, who returned the bow politely, his face expressionless.

"Come, let us sit down. Some wine for your illustrious new relation, Takenori!"

Akitada took his seat on one of the silk cushions in the cen-ter of the room. Like Akiko's quarters, Toshikage's study was the epitome of comfort and luxury. Here, too, large braziers spread their pleasant warmth. Here, too, mats covered the floor and papered doors filtered light from outside. Toshikage's doors had carved grilles and, instead of painted screens, scrolls covered his walls, and the doors of the built-in cabinets were painted with landscapes. Shelves above the cabinets held his books and document boxes, and his writing utensils and paper were laid out on a low window seat under a round, screened window. A bell with a wooden hammer hung there also, suspended from a silk rope, in case he wished to summon a servant.

The son poured, and Akitada accepted the cup, saying pleasantly, "You must be a great help to your father, Takenori. I had no idea that you were already old enough to hold a position of such responsibility. Did you attend university?"

"Yes, sir. Thank you, sir."

Akitada wondered if the young man was shy. He certainly did not engage in conversation.

To ease the awkward moment, Toshikage filled in. "Takenori is twenty-eight years old. My other son, Tadamine, is twenty-seven. He serves at the northern front and was recently promoted to captain." Fatherly pride and something else—a sadness?—sounded in Toshikage's voice.

"You are to be congratulated on your children. Are there daughters also?"

Toshikage brightened a little and chuckled. "No such luck, or I could make some shrewd connections with the ruling Fujiwaras. Are you by any chance asking because you wish to take another wife?"

Akitada was taken aback by the suggestion. He would never take another woman into his household while Tamako occupied it. Renewed worries about his family's welfare surfaced and were banished. "Not at all," he said firmly. "I am well content with my present arrangements."

"And so am I," cried Toshikage. "Your sister is all an old man like myself could wish for. She has such elegance and beauty it takes my breath away."

Akitada smiled warmly at his brother-in-law. When he glanced at Takenori, however, he noticed the young man's clenched hands. So there might be some ill feeling here! Not a pleasant situation for Akiko, who had probably been a bit naive to congratulate herself on being the mother of the next heir. She had planned without considering Toshikage's grown sons.

Toshikage, unaware of the effect of his speech on his son, continued happily, "And now she is to be a mother soon. She tells me it is to be a boy. Women know about such things, don't you think? What about your wife? You have a son, I hear. Did she carry him high in her belly? For that is what Akiko does. A lively child! He kicks already to open the door to life!" Toshikage laughed and his own belly trembled with merriment. His son got up abruptly and busied himself with some papers at the desk.

"Well," said Akitada blandly, "if it is not a son, you will have a daughter to play marriage politics with. And, in any case, you have sons already."

Toshikage's face fell. "My sons are well enough," he said, "but Takenori here is promised to the church. He has postponed taking the tonsure to see me through the present problems at work but will enter the Temple of Atonement in Shinano province in the coming year. And Tadamine insisted on joining the army last year. There has been a great deal of fighting up north." He sighed deeply.

Akitada looked at Takenori with surprise. The young man returned his glance stolidly. Akitada told him, "You are to be admired for such a serious spiritual choice at your age. Few young men are so devout, though it is said the Buddha himself followed the calling before he had reached the prime of life. But will you not miss your family and the life of the capital?"

Takenori said, "I see my path clear. There is nothing for me in this world."

Toshikage shifted uncomfortably. Akitada wondered whether Takenori had rejected the temptations of a worldly career or felt abandoned by his father. He glanced uncertainly at Toshikage and thought he saw tears in his brother-in-law's eyes. So it had been the young man's own choice, just as apparently it had been

95

the other son's wish to become a soldier. To have both sons turn their backs on a career in the capital where they could support their father and eventually carry on the family name was a tragic blow. But eventually, of course, it would benefit Akiko, particularly if she did bear Toshikage more sons, and if Tadamine lost his life on the battlefield. No doubt his sister had taken these things into account. Thus were grief and happiness forever intertwined in the rope of fate.

"Takenori," said Toshikage with a sigh, "stop your fidgeting and sit down. We must tell Akitada about our visitor."

It developed that the director of the Bureau of Palace Store-houses himself had called on his assistant to express his dissatisfaction with certain rumors he had heard.

Toshikage was distressed. "Apparently the story of my having the lute got out past our department," he said. "The director does not show his face very often in the office. His is one of those appointments which merely produces a good income. He was angry because someone made insinuations about lax administration at a party he was attending."

Akitada watched his brother-in-law as he reported on the director's visit. Toshikage appeared more frustrated than conscious of guilt. His son looked angry. When he met Akitada's eyes, he cried, "It was an intolerable insult to my father and may cost him his position."

Akitada said soothingly, "Well, nobody takes gossip very seriously. Next week they will have something else to talk about. I meant to tell you that my questioning the local antiquarians has at least given us the encouraging news that the thief, if there was one, has not offered any of the objects for sale." He gave Toshikage a hard look. "I don't suppose they could simply have been misplaced. Perhaps, like the lute, they were removed temporarily only and will be returned?"

"Impossible," cried Takenori. "Father and I checked carefully. They have been missing for months."

Toshikage nodded with a sigh. "Yes, I am afraid Takenori is right. We have made a most careful search since I last spoke to you. We did so after hours so as not to attract the notice of my colleagues."

Fleetingly Akitada wondered if Takenori was taking refuge in Buddhist vows because he foresaw his father's downfall and exile. They would certainly protect him from prosecution. But what about the figurine in Akiko's apartment? "Are you quite certain, Brother, that you have not forgotten bringing home some of the things? They could easily have become mixed up with your own treasures."

Toshikage stiffened. "Of course not. I am not yet in my dotage even if I am quite a bit older than you."

"Sorry. I did not mean to imply anything." Seeing the anger in Toshikage's face, Akitada broke off awkwardly. How was he to pursue the matter? Any suggestion of his suspicion might offend Toshikage so seriously as to lead to a break between the families, or worse.

Toshikage had fallen into a hurt silence, but Takenori looked flushed with anger. When he saw Akitada's eyes on himself, he protested, "My father is most meticulous in his duties. It is so unfair! I think that we should propose that this house be searched. It will establish his innocence once and for all."

Toshikage cried, "Heavens, no! I forbid it. What are you thinking of? It would upset Akiko, and in her delicate condition that could endanger the child."

Akitada, more than ever at sea about Toshikage's culpability, sought desperately for something else to say and remembered the screen.

"Forgive me, Brother, for speaking so carelessly. I really was thinking of the many wonderful things I saw in Akiko's quarters."

Toshikage looked slightly mollified. "It gives me pleasure to surround beauty with more beauty," he said sentimentally.

"She is a lucky woman. And you are a remarkable collector with a fine eye for art. I particularly admired the screen with the flowers."

"Oh, that! Yes. Does it look well there? It cost a pretty penny. The fellow is getting a name at court."

There was something not quite right about Toshikage's response. Had the man not seen it for himself? Akitada said, "It looks very well indeed. Was it you who chose to place it just to the side of the sliding doors to the courtyard? In the summertime it must look as if the garden had moved into the house."

Toshikage beamed. "Hah! Very good. No, Akiko must have put it there. Clever girl!"

So Toshikage did not venture to his wife's room regularly. Apparently, like the emperor's consorts, Akiko proceeded to her husband's quarters for their intimacies. More importantly, it was possible that Toshikage had nothing to do with the suspect figurine. It made the problem more complex, for someone else in the household could have placed it there. If, indeed, it was part of the imperial treasure and not some similar piece.

Akitada turned to Takenori. "By the way, your father has given me a description of the missing items. It occurs to me that you, too, may be familiar with them. Could you give me your recollection of what they looked like, please? It will help confirm your father's memory."

Takenori turned out to be less than helpful. He stumbled through some vague descriptions, getting the colors of the figurine wrong and being corrected by his father, and finally gave up with the comment that he did not take much interest in such things. The outcome was largely inconclusive, except to confirm that Akiko's figurine was at least a close replica of the emperor's and that Toshikage was not aware of its presence in his house.

Well, he could do no more at the moment without alerting father and son to his suspicions. With an inward sigh, Akitada gave up, and then remembered the screen. He said to Toshikage,

"I am really impressed with the flower screen. Akiko could not tell me the name of the artist and referred me to you. I thought I might commission something similar for Tamako. She is very fond of gardening."

Toshikage clapped his hands. "That is an excellent idea. Takenori took care of the commission for me. Please look up the address and tell Akitada how to get there, Takenori!"

His son obediently rose and went to the shelves, where he opened one of the document boxes and searched through the contents. He returned with a sheet of paper, which he handed to Akitada. "This contains the information, sir," he said politely.

It was a copy of a bill of sale for "one screen, four panels, decorated with flowers of the season in exotic containers" to be delivered by the end of the Leaf-Turning Month to His Excellency, the assistant director of the Bureau of Palace Storehouses, in return for ten bars of silver. The bill was signed, "Noami, of the Bamboo Hermitage, by the Temple of Boundless Mercy."

Ten bars of silver! It was an enormous price to pay a mere artisan. Artists usually scraped together a living hawking their wares at markets and during temple fairs. Akitada said, "At these prices the man must live in a palace. Where is this Bamboo Hermitage?"

Toshikage laughed. "I told you the fellow is becoming the fashion. Did you notice the detail? He is said to study a flower from the time the bud opens through all the stages of bloom until the petals fall. Such patience costs money. But I have an idea. I have wondered how to express my gratitude to you, dear Brother, and to welcome you home properly at the same time. Allow me the pleasure of making you a gift of such a screen. Takenori shall go with you, and you shall tell the man what you want. When it is done, I shall have the screen delivered to your lovely wife."

Akitada was embarrassed. Under no circumstances did he wish to obligate himself to Toshikage, at least not until he knew exactly where his brother-in-law stood in the case of the missing treasures. "Thank you, Brother! You are most generous, but this particular gift to Tamako must be my own. You understand, I am sure?"

Toshikage raised an eyebrow and grinned knowingly. "Say no more, dear Brother! I understand completely. The lady must be reassured of your affection. I know the feeling." He chuckled.

Akitada turned to the son. "There is no need for you to come, but perhaps you can give me directions to the artist's house?"

It appeared that the painter lived in the western part of the city. Takenori hinted that it was in a rough neighborhood.

"What's this?" cried Toshikage. "You said nothing to me about the place being dangerous."

Takenori lowered his eyes humbly. "Forgive me, Father. I did not know until I was accosted by a pair of aggressive beggars. I got away from them easily enough, but Lord Sugawara may not be so lucky."

Toshikage tsk-tsked. "The western city is getting so bad you cannot walk the streets any longer without being in fear for your life. Takenori is right. You had better take an armed servant with you. I cannot imagine why a successful painter would live among such riffraff."

"Oh," said Takenori, "his house is quite substantial, if a bit overgrown. I suppose it is his family home, but he lives there alone."

"Well, it is time I were on my way." Akitada got up, still frustrated by his suspicions about the figurine in Akiko's room. After a moment's hesitation, he said to Toshikage, "I think my sister might benefit from your explanations about the origin and meaning of some of the charming objects which decorate her room. I am sure knowing their history will increase her enjoyment greatly."

Toshikage looked pleased. "Certainly, certainly. What a very good idea! It will give me great pleasure to do so. Please convey my regards and hopes for improvement to your lady mother."

An empty wish, that, and they both knew it. Akitada bowed and took his leave.

After the pleasant warmth of Toshikage's rooms, the cold air outside took his breath away, and he strode out briskly to let the physical exertion warm his blood. He intended to take care of the matter of Tamako's screen as soon as possible. Takenori's warning he ignored. The suggestion that he could not handle himself at least as well as that young man had been offensive and he ascribed the slight to the fact that young Takenori not only resented his father's young wife, but by extension her brother also. He might have realized that Akitada had dealt single-handedly with far greater dangers than a couple of hungry beggars.

More irritating than the imputation of faintheartedness or a walk through a bad neighborhood were the painter's prices. But this time he would not let money stand in his way. Tamako should have her screen, come what may.

Little did he know the price he would ultimately have to pay.

SEVEN

The Bamboo Hermitage

Two days later Akitada went to see the painter. He had not set foot in the western city since his return. It was here that almost five years ago he had suffered soul-wrenching grief when his wife's family home had been burned down with her father inside it. Since then, he had avoided this part of the capital.

It was another bitterly cold day. Winter here arrived not with the heavy snowfalls of the north country, but with an icy wind which bit more keenly, and the prevailing gray and brown hues of bare trees and dried grasses looked dirty and dismal in contrast to the sparkling snow cover in Echigo.

There were fewer people in this part of the capital and they seemed to hurry along with their chins tucked into the collars of their padded robes. A few women, with thick scarves draped around their heads and shoulders, walked clutching their baskets or small children with one hand, while the other held the scarf in place.

When he passed Konoe Avenue, he glanced down it toward the imperial flags flying over the prison. The capital had two of these, just as it had two city administrations and two markets. The division of the capital into an eastern or left half and a western or right half, with Suzaku Avenue the central dividing line, had created two worlds, for the two halves could not be more different. The eastern city was crowded, bustling, affluent, and mostly law-abiding; the western half had sunk into a rapid decline and now was inhabited mostly by the poor and desperate. The prison on this side of town was always crowded and the court docket full.

Nagaoka's brother was in the other prison, but was suffering, no doubt, the same daily beatings until he signed his confession. Akitada's stomach twisted at the thought of it and he drew up his shoulders with a shiver.

The artist's studio lay in the westernmost quarter of the city. He walked quickly to keep warm in the cold air, tucking his chin into the collar of his quilted robe. But there was little he could do to keep his ears warm, and they began to hurt unpleasantly.

Once there had been fine private homes in large gardens here, but they had fallen into ruin or burned to the ground. The "good people" had moved away to the other side of town, leaving behind a tangled wilderness. Squatters occupied the empty spaces now, and here and there thin spirals of smoke rose from huts and abandoned pavilions.

Poorly dressed people gave him a wide berth after a brief glance at his silk robe and black hat. He was one of the "good people," an oddity like a piece of brocade among hemp, or—as he soon realized when he could not get close enough to anyone to ask for directions—a fish out of water.

He began to regret his good clothing even more when he attracted a following of about six or seven ragged young men who seemed to wait for him to turn down one of the narrow side streets where there would be no witnesses to a quick robbery.

He got directions eventually from a laborer carrying a load of roof tiles on his back, no doubt salvage from another abandoned villa. He gave them grudgingly enough, along with an astonished glance at Akitada's formal silk robe. The farther Akitada walked, the more uneasy he became. His clothes shamed him among the poor and ragged creatures who inhabited the makeshift shacks by the side of the weed-grown and rutted roads. When his surroundings became more densely populated, the character of the quarter became even worse. Workers' tenements crowded together, interspersed with poor shops and leaning stalls. Now and then he passed a shrine or small temple, and once a somewhat more substantial house which bore the insignia of the local warden, but in most blocks cheap wine shops alternated with eateries stinking of rancid fish oil and rotted vegetables.

The Temple of Boundless Mercy was a surprise when he finally reached it. It occupied a large area and was dominated by a towering main hall and a three-story pagoda. These and other, smaller buildings stood inside a vast courtyard surrounded by the remnants of tall plaster walls which had lost most of their plaster and had collapsed altogether in some sections. The temple grounds lay in a haze of thin gray smoke and, from what he could see through the gaping holes in the wall, appeared to be a sort of local market.

He stopped to look at the temple, wondering how to find the painter's house, when he felt a violent push to his back and stumbled forward. Hands pulled at his sash and felt his sleeves. Reacting by instinct, he whirled, his fists clenched and lashing out at his attackers. His right made sharp contact with a body. There was a yelp, and a slight figure scurried away. But he had no time to waste on that one, for he had grabbed hold of a second attacker with his left and flung him face down on the ground. Falling on his prostrate opponent with his knees, he knocked the breath out of him and caught the flailing hands by the wrists, pinning them into the dirt. His prisoner screamed in a high, thin voice, and Akitada realized that he had caught a youngster, about fourteen or fifteen years old. Pickpockets, he thought disgustedly, and shifted his knees from the boy's back, wondering what to do with his captive.

The answer became quickly obvious. A small hostile crowd gathered around him. Kneeling on the street, Akitada saw their feet and legs first, mostly naked or in ragged straw sandals, except for one pair of massive leather boots right before his eyes. Large as the boots were, the wearer had had to cut them open to make room for some enormous dirty toes. Akitada's eyes traveled upward and found that their owner matched them in size and uncleanliness. A bearded giant glared down at him. Worse, on either side of him stood no fewer than ten or fifteen burly, hostile males. Akitada swallowed. The bearded giant alone easily outweighed him by a third.

"Let him go!" the giant growled down to him.

Akitada rose to his feet but jerked the youngster up with him, his fist firmly grasping the boy's flimsy shirt by the neck. The young thief had stopped wailing and struggling and was awaiting the outcome of the confrontation with renewed confidence.

At eye level, or near eye level, for the big man was almost a head taller than Akitada, the bearded giant did not improve. The part of his face which was not covered by the unkempt bristly beard was badly pockmarked, and a fleshy nose and thick lips did nothing for his appearance. They eyed each other in mutual disgust for a moment; then Akitada said matter-of-factly, "This boy and his companion tried to steal from me. I'd like a word with his father if you can tell me where he lives."

The big man's jaw dropped a little, but he recovered quickly. "I said to let him go. It's none of your business. We don't need your kind here, giving our kids a bad name, calling them thieves." The others muttered their agreement and shuffled up a little more closely.

Akitada pushed the boy forward without loosening his grip. "You claim to care about your children. Open your eyes!" he challenged the big man. "Look at him! Today he tried to grab a few coppers from my sash, but in another year or two he'll be pulling knives on helpless old men and women. Do you want him to turn to murder or be killed himself? How many of your boys are running wild now? How many of your sons end up dead or in chains?"

The other men's muttering turned angry, but the big man stared at the youngster, and Akitada could see his conviction waver. "Kinjiro's a good kid, one of eight," the man said defensively. "I know his folks. They're poor like the rest of us. His father's been sick and his mother's just had another kid. Maybe he just bumped into you. Hey, Kinjiro? Did you try to take the gentleman's money?"

The boy burst into tears and sobbed explanations in a dialect which Akitada could not make out. But as the big man listened, his face lengthened. When the boy stopped with a sniffle and a swipe at his running nose, he put a big paw on the thin shoulder for a moment. "All right," he said. "Don't worry! I'll take care of it. You go home now." He looked at Akitada. "You can let him go. I'm Hayata, the warden of this quarter, and I'll go talk to them. The new babe died this morning and they have no money for a funeral."

"Oh." Akitada released the boy instantly. "I am sorry," he said, helpless in the face of such sadness and so extreme a want. His hand went to his sash for money, but he changed his mind. He had no proof if what he had been told was true or merely a trick to get his money.

The bearded giant nodded to the youngster. "Off you go! And don't ever let me catch you and Yoshi again." Then he waved away the other men, who dispersed quickly. When they were alone, he gestured to Akitada's clothes and remarked, "It is easy to see that this is not your kind of place, sir. Best go home now." Having said this, he turned and walked quickly after the boy.

The message was clear: he was not welcome. Angered by this reception into stubborn persistence, Akitada brushed off his robe and crossed the street to the temple.

He entered through the sagging gateway and wandered about the vast courtyard filled with people gathered around open fires or haggling with vendors. Children tumbled about among the adults, shouting and chasing each other. Near one of the fires, ragged men sat on the ground gambling with dice. On the temple steps, a storyteller held a group of gaping adults and children spellbound. And everywhere men and women were selling things: cheap wine, soup, amulets, vegetables, old clothes, chipped utensils, and medicinal drafts, potions, and balms for every imaginable ailment. And ailments there appeared to be many. One man was missing an eye, another hobbled on a crutch, one foot hanging mangled and deformed, while near the storyteller an old crone sat coughing weakly into a bloodstained rag.

In spite of these surroundings, Akitada became aware of a ravenous hunger. Following an appetizing smell, he made his way through a group of poor people, who fell back from him in silent awe, and found a young woman, cleaner than the rest, stirring a large pot of soup over a small fire. He held out some coppers, and she ladled a generous helping into an earthenware bowl.

Warming his cold hands on the bowl, Akitada wished he could do the same for his ears. The soup appeared to consist mostly of assorted vegetables and beans. He took a cautious swallow. It was as good as it smelled. He thought he could make out turnip and cabbage, but there was another leafy vegetable, deep green, which had a slightly bitter but pleasant flavor. He emptied the bowl quickly and asked for another. The woman smiled at him this time and watched him eat. He asked her what the green vegetable was. Dock, she said. It was plentiful hereabouts, especially in the old monks' burial grounds behind the temple.

Akitada choked down the last bite and looked where she pointed. In a nearby open area some six or seven small boys were gathered near leaning wooden tablets where one of them was spinning a top. Akitada had played with tops himself as a youngster, and smiled. The boy with the top looked to be about five or six and was most adept. His top spun and danced, flew through the air, and returned. He made it dart in and out between his friends and kept it moving precisely where he wanted it.

Akitada chuckled. "He's good, that little one," he said.

The woman said proudly, "He's my son. He loves his top. There's not much else he can be good at, poor boy."

Akitada handed back his empty bowl and said, "What do you mean? He looks like a fine boy."

She cast a glance toward the children, and he saw that tears welled up in her eyes. "A fine cripple," she said bitterly.

Stunned by her words, Akitada looked again and saw now that the small boy was not merely holding his right arm close to his body but seemed to lack his forearm altogether. The right arm ended just below the elbow. Among his people, who relied on the skill and strength of their hands to make a living, he would be unable to support himself by any useful trade and become dependent on alms tossed him by the more fortunate. This part of the city was full of crippled beggars sitting at street corners and on the steps of temples with their begging bowls. Any number of accidents could cut short a productive life and reduce a man to this sort of misery. But this was only a child.

Suddenly an unpleasant thought arose in his mind. Saburo had warned him that this temple had an unsavory reputation based on some gruesome local superstitions. It was said to be inhabited by flesh-eating demons who roamed its grounds after dark to attack unwary sinners on their way home from a debauch. The occasional discovery of a dismembered body testified to the truth of such stories, which were additionally embroidered by the warning that the unhappy souls of the dead had turned into hungry ghosts, forced to live near the temple, feeding on excrement and garbage while wailing for food. Akitada glanced around him with a shudder. Some of these poor living creatures looked hungry enough to be ghosts themselves.

To still such imaginary horrors, he asked the mother what had happened to the child.

"An accident, foolish boy. He won't tell. A kind man brought him home. He said he found him by the road, bleeding, his severed arm gone, and a gold coin clutched in his other hand. Lucky this man found him and stopped the bleeding. He thinks my son saw the piece of gold in the road and was snatching it up just when a cartwheel caught his arm. Foolish child!" She sniffled and wiped her eyes.

"A terrible accident," Akitada said sympathetically. "What will you do about his future?"

She cheered up a little. "Oh, he'll be a monk. This same good person who found him got him a place at one of the big temples outside the city. May the Buddha bless him forever! It was a great relief to me."

Akitada looked at the boy again, the young face rosy-cheeked in the cold air, teeth glistening as he burst into triumphant laughter at performing a skillful trick. So kindness was not dead in this slum. Perhaps it was even more alive here than among the wealthy—an irony when the need here was so much greater and the resources so pitifully slender. And Akitada admitted grudgingly to himself that for once the monks were performing a useful and generous act in taking in this poor child.

"I am glad," he said. "He will do well. Look at how many friends he has made already."

She smiled. "At first the boys wouldn't come near him. They thought the demons had caught him and eaten his arm and were going to come back and eat the rest of him. But in time they took to him because he's so clever with his top. He's a good boy."

The incident depressed Akitada further and he left the temple compound, glancing up with a shudder at the great hall which loomed dark and forbidding above the scrambling humanity. The temple of the flesh-eating demons!

At the gate, Akitada asked directions to the Bamboo Hermitage from an old man selling incense sticks. He pointed down a narrow side street across from the temple.

"Is it far?" Akitada asked, eyeing the unpainted row houses with small shuttered windows dubiously. He got no answer. The old man was making rasping noises in his throat and pointed to his mouth. He was dumb, another cripple. Akitada put some coins in his bowl and walked away.

The narrow street resembled more an alley than an ordinary thoroughfare. It looked empty except for some debris and garbage, but Akitada kept his eyes open and soon noticed some furtive movement up ahead where a tangle of trees and the corner of a shed obscured the view. He felt sure that someone was hiding there and slowed his steps, cursing himself for setting out alone after having been warned. Suddenly there were quick steps behind him. They were accompanied by a familiar flapping sound, and Akitada whirled around. The bearded giant with the pockmarked face was blocking the lane behind him. Trapped! So much for the local warden, thought Akitada, and backed against a house wall.

"Looking for someone?" the giant asked, smirking a little.

Akitada looked him over. He appeared even bulkier than before, and infinitely more threatening in these surroundings. Looking to the right and left, Akitada searched for a weapon. There was nothing but a loose piece of lath a few steps away. It was shorter than a man, part of a broken fence, a puny weapon, but Akitada had some skill at stick fighting. He inched toward it, asking, "What do you want?"

The giant followed his eyes and made a strange rumbling deep in his chest. It sounded exactly like a dog's growl, and Akitada moved a little faster toward the thin length of wood. The pockmarked face split into a broad, gap-toothed grin and the growl became a chuckle. "I mean you no harm," the giant said, raising both hands to show he carried no weapon. "Just making sure you're all right. This place is a bit rough and we don't get rich gentlemen very often. If you'll tell me where you're going, I'll walk with you."

It was an impasse. The man could, of course, be lying. But there was something about him worth taking a chance on, and after a moment, Akitada detached himself from the wall. "Thank you. I thought I saw someone hiding up ahead. I am on my way to a place called Bamboo Hermitage."

The warden raised bushy brows. "So! Old Noami's got another customer. Well, come along, then. We think a lot of Noami around here. He's got an open hand when it comes to the poor."

Akitada felt himself flush. He reached into his sash and produced a string of coppers. "I have been thinking about that youngster's family," he said. "Perhaps you might give them this to help bury the little one."

The big man looked astonished, but he took the money, saying, "Thank you, sir. May the gods reward you for your kindness. It was the only time that boy's ever been in trouble and he'll never do it again. Well, let's be on our way, then."

He strode off, his torn boot soles slapping the frozen ground. Akitada followed.

When they got to the shed, two rough characters jumped out into the street, barring their way. The moment they saw his companion, their ferocious scowls turned to horror and they bolted.

"Hah!" shouted the warden after them. "Come back here! I've seen you bastards! Don't think that you'll get your ration this week, you dirty scoundrels!" They paid no heed, and he muttered angrily, shaking his fist.

"Do you know them?" Akitada asked, astonished.

"Do I!" he grumbled. "They'll be sorry! Well, there you are! That's Noami's place over there! Excuse me, but I've got to go catch those two. Don't hang about till dark, and take the other way out. There's a busy street that way." He gestured ahead, the way the two would-be robbers had gone, and strode off after them, boots flip-flapping in a purposeful manner.

The Bamboo Hermitage had been named for the dense

growth of bamboo around the thatched buildings. A tall fence woven from bamboo canes surrounded the property. Next to the gate a small sign, beautifully lettered in Chinese, proclaimed its name and identified it as an "artist's studio." Both gate and fence were in excellent repair and reinforced with beams and sharpened bamboo spikes along the top. No wonder Noami took precautions against thieves in this neighborhood, thought Akitada. Considering the fortifications, he was mildly surprised when the gate swung open at his touch.

He entered, calling out, but got no answer. It was very silent here. Only the dry bamboo leaves rustled in the cold air. Bamboo grew so thickly and so tall that the tops screened out the sky, and Akitada walked in their shade between the dense, thick canes to the front door. When he reached it, a raucous cry overhead made him jump. A chain rattled above him, and then another cry sounded. Akitada peered up cautiously and saw a huge black crow on a projecting roof beam, eyeing him with its beady eyes and fluffing up its feathers. The chain around one claw was fastened to the beam and clinked again.

Apparently the bird was a primitive yet effective system for announcing visitors. Akitada waited for the artist to appear, but nothing happened. He could see through the open door into a large dim hall. Scrolls hung suspended from rafters, and long tables held pots of paints and stacks of papers. A half-painted screen stood near a set of sliding doors at the back.

Akitada called out again, the crow joining in his effort. When this noise produced no better results, he took off his boots and stepped onto the wooden floor of the hall to look around. Almost instantly an irrational feeling of danger seized him, and the hairs on the back of his head rose.

Too much talk of demons, he thought, and forced himself to look around. The wooden floor of the hall was dull with dirt and splotches of paint and ink. New rolls of paper and silk lay stacked in a big pile in one corner. From the low, smoke-darkened beam in the center of the room hung a heavy bronze lantern, suspended by a chain from a massive hook. The studio had the appearance of belonging to someone who cared nothing for comfort or cleanliness, and everything for his work.

Akitada strolled over to the half-finished screen and saw an autumn scene in the forest. In the foreground some large rocks had been sketched in with elegant strokes of black ink, and the background was a misty wash of blue and gray, subtly hinting at wooded mountainsides. But a leaning maple tree in the center was already outlined and painted in all its crimson glory, every leaf daintily detailed, so real that one could almost see it trembling in the breeze. A similarly realistic large black crow, a double of the one outside, perched on one of the rocks, and a few sparrows were pecking at seeds in the foreground.

Small dishes of paint and containers of water stood about in front of the screen, along with bowls containing remnants of dried food and half-eaten pickles. Brushes of all sizes lay everywhere. Akitada bent to touch one dish filled with crimson paint. It was still moist. So the painter had been at work here not too long ago. Where could he be?

Akitada slid open one of the back doors. They led to a garden behind the house. A vast wilderness of vegetation had closed in on the building here also. He thought he could hear faint sounds from the far corner of the property. "Hoh! Is anyone home?" bellowed Akitada. "Master Noami?" He thought he heard a shout, but nobody came and Akitada turned back to his exploration of the studio.

Idly, he wandered around, picking up loose sketches of flowers and birds, marveling at the painstaking skill of execution. Toshikage had not exaggerated. This man was a consummate, even obsessive artist.

He was just bending over the large stack of sketches which had been piled higgledy-piggledy into a dark corner when there was the sudden sound at the back door. Almost simultaneously he heard a string of curses and rapid slapping footsteps across the floor.

Akitada turned quickly. A short, wiry individual in a dirty, paint-smeared monk's robe glared at him from a head shaped like a kickball, his skull shaven but covered with a thin stubble, the eyes like dark berries on either side of a flat nose, and the mouth a mere slash above the thin strands of a chin beard. He was neither young nor old, indisputably ugly, and indefinably menacing.

"Get away from there, you whoreson piece of excrement!" the odd creature screeched at Akitada, waving his arms in the air as if he were shooing away dogs. "Away, I say! Don't touch anything!"

The unexpected crudity, exceeding as it did even the most extreme example of disrespect, shocked Akitada. Looking at this astonishing being, he had the disconcerting feeling of having walked into some demonic tale, so unreal seemed the encounter and so grotesque the person's appearance and manner. Perhaps the man was mad.

He stepped quickly away from the sketches and raised his hands into the air. "I beg your pardon," he said. "No one answered my calls when I arrived."

The wiry man said nothing, just stood scowling and studied him with his beadlike eyes as if he were memorizing every line of his face, every hair or fold of his robe. He was barefoot, his feet liberally caked with mud, his hands covered with earth. Akitada decided that this must be the painter's assistant, evidently a half-wit. "Where is your master?" he demanded.

The man said in his strange high voice, "I'm Noami. Who wants to know?"

Akitada suppressed his surprise and introduced himself, explaining his errand.

"A screen?" asked the painter, relaxing visibly. "Like that one?" He jerked a thumb toward the autumn scene.

"Yes. Very much like it," said Akitada. He walked back to the screen and looked at it again. "You are to be commended for your skill with the brush." Surely, he thought, he could transact his business quickly and leave this unpleasant place, hopefully never to return. "I expect my wife to join me soon," he continued, "and would like to surprise her with something to remind her of her garden. She loves flowers. When I saw the screen you painted for my brother-in-law, Toshikage, I thought of it. Only, could you have the flowers growing in a garden? Perhaps different ones for every season on each panel. And some birds or small creatures that live in a garden? I like the crow and sparrows in this one."

The artist had come to join him. "Maybe."

Akitada looked at him with raised brows. "How do you mean?"

"To paint all the seasons will take a full year, for I must study plants and animals in their proper time. It will therefore be expensive. Ten bars of silver for each panel." His earlier vulgarity notwithstanding, Noami spoke like an educated man.

"Ten bars of silver?" Forty bars altogether! That was four times what Toshikage had paid for Akiko's screen. Akitada said so, and Noami explained coolly that Toshikage's screen had been assembled from existing sketches. He seemed disinclined to accommodate a new customer.

Seeing his long miserable errand wasted, Akitada said, "I had hoped to surprise my wife now. Do you have something ready which might please her? Then we could perhaps negotiate about the screen later?"

Noami pursed his thin lips. "I have no flowers. Only a scroll with dogs."

They walked across the room. The painting was of a small boy playing with three black-and-white spotted puppies. The child, a little older than Yori, looked vaguely familiar and the entire scene was charming. Having agreed on a fairly reasonable price, Akitada paid.

As Noami took down the scroll and rolled it up, Akitada asked, "How do you manage to find your subjects and have them hold still for sketching? That little boy with the dogs, for example?"

The artist froze for a moment and stared at him blankly. Then he bent to tie the scroll, saying in a flat voice, "People are very poor around here. Most are outcasts. The children are willing to model all day for a copper and some food. The dogs are free for the taking." He paused and his thin lips twisted. "It's the getting rid of them that becomes a problem."

Akitada nodded. The artist's willingness to employ the unemployable would bring with it the frustration of their importunities. The children, no doubt, interfered with his work as well as his paints. Akitada suddenly realized that this might be the man who had been a benefactor to the crippled boy in the temple courtyard. The big warden had spoken highly of him. Noami, a successful artist living in the midst of this slum, was in a rare position to do good to his poorer neighbors. Ashamed of his earlier dislike for the man, Akitada said more warmly, "I can see that the offer of payment and food is enough to fill your house with all sorts of needy creatures and provide you with useful models at the same time."

Noami stared at him again and then cast a glance around the room. "Why do you say that?" he asked sharply. "There is no one here but myself."

Again Akitada felt an irrational hostility in the man. He said soothingly, "I merely meant that your neighbors surely appreciate your generosity to their children."

"My neighbors?" Noami's voice rose shrilly. "They are all liars and thieves!"

"Never mind." Akitada extended his hand for the scroll, adding coldly, "My name is Sugawara Akitada. If you decide to accept a commission for a screen, you may come to see me. Lord Toshikage can tell you how to find my house. But I should like to see some sketches before I approve a commission of that size."

Noami bowed, and Akitada escaped the studio to the raucous cries of the crow.

On the whole it had been one of the most unpleasant afternoons Akitada had spent in a long time. By comparison even home with his dying mother seemed preferable. Tired and footsore from walking, chilled to the bone, and irritated by his encounter with the eccentric artist, he took a shortcut through the Imperial City. The tall halls and groves of pines were some protection from the icy wind which whistled down the thoroughfares of the capital, and he was safe enough from acquaintances. At this time of day the bureaucrats were busily planning and wielding their brushes inside their offices.

When he entered his half of the city, he found himself on Konoe again, but this time near the eastern prison. It was as good a way as any to take home and, miserably aware that his feet were so cold that they had lost all feeling and that his legs hurt abominably, he reflected that he was no longer used to walking such distances.

There were more people about here. The prison gate, its flags snapping in the wind, was guarded by red-coated constables who jogged steadily back and forth to keep warm. Other constables, city clerks, and ordinary men passed in and out. The problem of Nagaoka's brother nagged at him again and he promised himself to look into it as soon as his family was safely home. Perhaps some news from them was waiting for him even now. He sped up a little. Ahead a woman walked in the same direction, her head wrapped in a large kerchief against the cold, and a basket over her arm. He wondered idly if she had come from the prison, perhaps a constable's wife who had taken her husband his dinner. For a moment there was something oddly familiar about the way she moved and held her head, then she disappeared around a corner.

He thought of Tamako and Yori in this cold weather, wishing that he might find them waiting for him at home, hoping that there would be at least some message by now, and limped homeward at a steady pace.

Saburo let him in, crushing his hopes quickly. They had not come and there was no news. Sick with worry, Akitada cursed under his breath and staggered to the house. Saburo watched his master's stumbling progress across the courtyard with open-mouthed concern.

"I'm home," Akitada called out, sitting down in the entry to ease his swollen feet from the boots.

Yoshiko appeared behind him. She was in her outdoor clothes and folded a scarf into a basket. "Welcome, Brother," she said. "Are you hungry?"

Akitada looked up at her and smiled in spite of his disappointment. Her cheeks and nose were pink from the cold air and she looked like the little sister of the past. "A bit, but mostly cold and footsore," he said. "I have been all the way to the other end of the city to buy Tamako a painting." He held up the scroll, then glanced at her basket. "Have you been out, too?"

"Yes. Just to the market for some things for supper. Let me check on Mother first and then we can have some tea in your room and you can show me the picture." She padded off softly on stockinged feet.

Akitada stood up himself, groaned, rubbed his icy ears, and hobbled toward his room, wondering why his sister had claimed to have come from the market when her basket was empty.

EIGHT

Temple Bells

In his room, neatly folded on his cushion, Akitada found an elegant court robe. He unfolded it reverently, marveling at the tiny stitches with which his sister had sewn together the panels of rich silk. Now he was ready for the summons from the palace, whenever it would arrive, and would not have to be ashamed before arrogant youngsters like the secretary in the controller's office. He took off his quilted outdoor robe and slipped into the new garment. It fit comfortably, and he was looking for a sash to wind around his waist when Yoshiko came in.

"Well?" she asked. "Do you like it? You look absolutely wonderful! Not even the chancellor will make a greater figure than you. I cannot wait to see you walking in the official procession to present New Year's wishes to His Majesty."

His pleasure and her words momentarily wiped all doubts from his mind. "Thank you, my dear," he said, choking a little with emotion. "It is beautifully sewn and must have taken you many long, weary hours. I am afraid it was too much for you, when you already have Mother to take care of."

She came closer, smiling, and gave his robe a little tuck here and there. "A sash," she muttered, "it needs a sash, and I think I know just the fabric. The train of Father's court robe is just the right shade of silver gray. It will look well with this dark blue."

"No," he said quickly. "Nothing of my father's." Seeing her

startled eyes, he added lamely, "You can hardly mutilate his best robe. What would Mother say?"

"Nonsense! It is already damaged by mildew. You cannot waste things for sentimental reasons. And Mother won't know. I have made up my mind that we must decide our future from now on. You and I have endured far too long the will of parents who cared nothing for our happiness."

"Yoshiko!" Akitada stared down at his sister slack-jawed and shocked to the core. She, a woman and the youngest member of the family, had just rebelled against centuries of Confucian laws fixing immutably the duties of children toward their parents, and, for the first time in his hearing, voiced an outright criticism of their parents. Suddenly she seemed a stranger to him. What had happened to change her so?

"Well?" she demanded, her chin pushed out stubbornly. "Am I wrong? Has either of them ever demonstrated any love or care for either of us? Our father threw you out of the house, and Mother forbade me to get married because she wished to keep me around as a cheap bond maid. It is a credit to you that you have succeeded anyway. As for me"—she turned away abruptly and her voice broke—"any hope of happiness has come too late."

His heart contracted at her despair. He put both hands on her shoulders to turn her toward him. "It is not too late. You shall have a fine dower and I will do my utmost to find a good husband for you. You will see, in another year you, too, may look forward to your first child."

"You are very kind, Akitada." It was no more than a breath; then she moved away from him, saying brightly, "Now tell me about your day and show me Tamako's picture!"

He went to unroll the painting.

Yoshiko clapped her hands. "Oh, Akitada! It is charming. The little boy is adorable! Just so must Yori look, I think. We must get your son a puppy."

"Yori is a little younger, but he is big for his age." Akitada narrowed his eyes and made mental comparisons. "He has finer features, I think, and larger eyes. And his hair is quite thick so that the braids over his ears stick out more. But he has the same sturdy arms and legs——" He broke off. She looked at him, questioning, and he told her, "I am so worried that there has been no news from them that I can hardly think of anything else. Tomorrow I ride back to see what has become of them."

"Oh, but Akitada," cried his sister. "What if . . . ?" She paused, her eyes large with concern.

He misunderstood and said impatiently, "Mother has repeatedly refused to see me. She can hardly expect me to sit around at her door like those cursed monks. And if she should take it into her head to die while I am gone, it cannot be helped."

"Yes, of course. I was thinking of the palace. What if they send for you?"

Her worried face made him smile. "I shall only be gone a day or so. Make my apologies and claim an urgent message has called me away."

<hr />

The next day was cold and overcast, but the post horse was fresh and Akitada, warmly dressed in a thickly padded hunting robe and lined boots, set out at a smart pace.

In the three weeks since he had passed this way, the colors of the mountains ahead had shifted from the golden bronze of late autumn foliage to a dull grayish brown of winter. Only the pines and cedars had kept their green, muted to a duller shade now under the cloudy sky. Nights of freezing cold had turned the roadside grasses sere, and the fallow rice fields looked nearly black.

He soon reached the foothills and began the steady climb. Once he encountered a small caravan of travelers and stopped to ask about his family, but they had come from the south and had no news. He wondered how far he should go. All the way to Lake Biwa? He could not stay away too long without incurring imperial displeasure if he were called to report. If only his mother had not insisted that he go and announce his return!

Eventually he came to the place where the road to the temple joined the highway. A wooden shack, boarded up and seemingly abandoned on his last visit, was now open, serving refreshments to travelers and pilgrims. With its shutters raised, Akitada saw a small wooden platform inside, with a woman in a blue and white scarf and gray apron sitting next to a tiny stove, an earthenware pitcher, and several bamboo baskets.

He dismounted and tied his horse to a tree. The woman, young and deeply tanned, shot up and skipped down from the platform. "Welcome! Welcome!" she cried, running and bobbing bows every few steps. "Welcome to the Abode of Celestial Mountain Breezes, your honor! First-class accommodations! Refined wines and delicacies from the capital! Served hot to warm you on a chilly ride. Please enter and allow me to wait upon your honor."

With the end of her speech she came to a halt before him, bowing so deeply that he was looking down at her back and the nape of her neck, and so she remained in apparently rapt contemplation of his boots.

"Thank you," he said dryly. "I shall have a cup of wine before I go on."

She bobbed up, revealing briefly a round, smiling face with eyes so narrow that they were mere slits, before rushing back to her shack, where she busied herself with a cup and ladle, with which she dipped wine from a small container on the stove.

Akitada followed more slowly and sat on the edge of the platform. The wine was cheap and rough, as he had expected, but it warmed his stomach in the chill mountain air. He peered into one of the baskets and decided to buy a dumpling. It was hardly capital fare, being a cold rice dumpling stuffed with chopped vegetables, but none the worse for that. He ate hungrily, complimented her, and asked for another.

She had a pretty way of blushing and confided that she had started preparations the night before and risen well before sunrise to boil her dumplings before walking to this little shack with her food and wine supplies.

He smiled at her. "You are strong as well as a good cook. I missed you when I passed this way a few weeks ago. But it was raining very hard."

"I remember the day," she cried. "Did you go to see the temple dancers?"

Akitada shook his head.

"Oh, you missed a treat. I closed early that day and walked up to the temple with my husband. It was a fine show. The celestial fairies were so beautiful I thought I was in the Western Paradise." She looked rapt, then added confidingly, "My husband says if business is good we'll go to the plays in the capital. Have you ever seen those?"

"No, but since you recommend them, I shall perhaps go this year. Did you hear about the murder at the temple?"

"Yes. The next day. Horrible, wasn't it? We missed all the excitement, my husband and I. We walked home in the rain right after the plays. Wet as drowned rats." She laughed, then offered Akitada more wine.

"Perhaps one more cup," he said. "Do you happen to recall the name of the performers?"

"They called themselves the Pure Land Dancers, but that name is just for temples. When they're playing in the capital for ordinary people, they do more exciting stories about heroes and monsters, and there are acrobatics, and some things that'll make you laugh. They call themselves Uemon's Players then. That's because the old man who runs the group is called Uemon, you see."

"Yes. I see." Akitada nodded with a smile at her enthusiasm. He glanced up the narrow, stony road which led to the temple. Perhaps he could make a brief detour and still reach Lake Biwa before dark. Farther than the lake he dared not travel. He hoped to meet his family on the way, or at least pick up some news of them from passing travelers. "Will you be here for a few more hours?" he asked the woman.

"Till dark," she said with a sigh, glancing at her baskets. "Business picks up toward evening because travelers are trying to get to the capital before dark."

Akitada took a silver coin from his sash and extended it to her. "For the food and a favor," he said. "Would you keep an eye out for my family? My name is Sugawara and I expect my wife and three-year-old son, along with an elderly man and two strong young warriors on horseback and in wagons, with bearers and some mounted guards. If you see them, will you ask them to wait here for my return?"

She promised eagerly, tucking the coin inside her robe.

This time Akitada reached the temple quickly. It was nearly midday and cold, but the road was dry. The great roof of the gate where he had last seen Nagaoka's wife and her brother-in-law still had silvery hoarfrost on its tiles. The colors of the vermilion columns and blue-tiled roofs were sharp and the gilded spire of the pagoda disappeared into the clouds above.

The sound of his horse's hooves brought the gatekeeper running out to greet him. By good fortune it was the same man who had offered Akitada a glance at the plan of the temple that other morning. They recognized each other instantly and with mutual pleasure.

"Welcome, welcome, my lord!" cried the monk, taking the bridle of Akitada's horse. "Have you heard the news? There really was a murder the night you visited."

Akitada dismounted. "Yes. That is why I am here. The police in the capital have the suspect in custody, but there are some aspects of the story that trouble me and I thought I would come and take another look."

"Then I have won my wager!" cried the monk happily, tying Akitada's horse to a post.

"Wager?"

"I bet my friend that you would return. Oh, my lord, I hope you will forgive the impertinence, but after I spoke to you, I looked up your name in the visitors' book. Then it came to me that you must be the same Sugawara who solved all those murders not many years ago."

Akitada was astonished. "But how could you know about that? I have been in the far north for many years."

"I have a cousin, my lord, who is a schoolteacher. He was one of your students when you taught at the university and told me all about those university murders. His name is Ushimatsu."

Ushimatsu. Akitada instantly recalled the backward, shy, middle-aged student, the butt of his classmates' jokes, who had humbly and cheerfully persisted in his studies. He smiled at the memory. "How is Mr. Ushimatsu?"

"Oh, very well. He teaches at a country school and has a wife and two little sons by now. He says he owes it all to you."

Akitada was embarrassed. "Not at all. He was a very hardworking student who would have succeeded in any case. I am very glad to hear he is doing so well. Please give him my regards next time you see him."

"Thank you, my lord, I will." The gatekeeper rubbed his hands. "Now, what may I show you?"

"The service courtyard and the visitors' quarters, I think. But are you at liberty to do so?"

They had climbed the steps to the gate. Inside the gatekeeper's office, Akitada could see a young novice sweeping the floor with a straw broom. Somewhere a bell was ringing, its sound clear and high in the still cold air.

The gatekeeper rubbed his hands eagerly, "I am completely at your service, my lord. It's too early for visitors. Just a moment." He put his head in the door of his office and gave the novice instructions, then returned to Akitada's side. "Ready, my lord! By the way, my name is Eikan."

Akitada thanked him, relieved that he did not have to visit the abbot again to explain his purpose for the present visit. It had been bad enough last time, when he had used the temple to get out of the rain as if it were a roadside hostel. This time his reason for coming was even more dubious. He could claim neither official standing nor that he was acting on Nagaoka's behalf.

Fortunately, his companion seemed to find nothing wrong in his curiosity. As they crossed the graveled courtyards of the public section of the temple, he told Akitada, "After the murder was discovered, I went back myself to look at the service yard where you thought you heard the woman screaming, but there was nothing to see. Still, you will have a better-trained eye for such things. I suppose not even the smallest drop of blood on a pebble would escape your attention?"

"I doubt we shall find any blood. It rained hard that day, and by nighttime the ground was still soaked with water." Akitada did not mention that the murdered woman had been strangled before her face was mutilated. Strangulation rarely left traces apart from signs of struggle, and those would long since have been obliterated by the passage of monks and the incessant raking of gravel.

They passed through the covered galleries and reached a plain wooden door. Eikan opened it, and they stepped down into a courtyard, surrounded on three sides by low, plaster-walled buildings with thatched roofs and on the fourth by the gallery they had just left. A grayish column of smoke rose from a chimney of the central building. Long rows of firewood were stacked against its wall, and wooden kegs against the building on the right. In the middle of the courtyard stood a well, surrounded

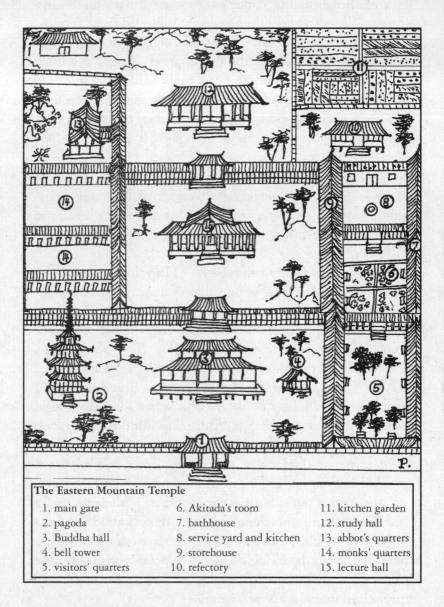

The Eastern Mountain Temple

1. main gate	6. Akitada's toom	11. kitchen garden
2. pagoda	7. bathhouse	12. study hall
3. Buddha hall	8. service yard and kitchen	13. abbot's quarters
4. bell tower	9. storehouse	14. monks' quarters
5. visitors' quarters	10. refectory	15. lecture hall

by a waist-high wall of darkened wood on a platform of large stones. A wooden bucket hung over it suspended from a winch.

"The kitchen yard," said Eikan. "The building across from us is the monastery kitchen. To the right are the pantry and bathhouse, and to the left a storehouse for religious objects and statues. You may have passed through it on your way to your room."

"Yes"—Akitada nodded—"yes, of course. I remember now. I was very tired, but you are quite right. My room must have been back that way. We passed through such a building. I recall being startled by a life-sized statue of a demon king." He turned to gauge distance and direction. "Now that I see it in the daylight, I am more than ever convinced that it was near here, or in this service area, that a woman screamed in the middle of the night."

Eikan shook his head dubiously. "There is no one here at night. The last hot meal is prepared at midday. We have midnight prayers and have to be up before sunrise for meditation. The bells remind us of our duties. Perhaps the scream came from the other side, the visitors' quarters? If, as you say, you were very tired, you might have been drowsy and confused."

"No. I am quite certain the sound came from here. And a murderer would hardly be deterred by a 'no admittance' sign. Neither, for that matter, would drunken youngsters bent on mischief."

"Ah, you are thinking of the actors." Eikan nodded. "It is possible. Do you suspect one of them of having killed the lady?"

"No. At this time I am merely wondering if someone might have seen or heard something unusual." Akitada wondered again if Nagaoka could be the murderer, either by committing the crime himself or by hiring a killer. The police had checked the names of all the visitors that night, but Nagaoka would hardly have signed in under his own name.

The door to the storehouse suddenly opened and a figure in monkish garb hurried out with a pail. He was walking to the well. There was something familiar and unpleasant about him. After a moment Akitada recognized the eccentric painter Noami. He had fortunately not seen them and began to lower the creaking bucket into the well.

Akitada said urgently, "Come! I have seen enough here. Let us go to the visitors' quarters now."

But the creaking had attracted his companion's attention. He cried, "Oh, what luck! Noami is here today. You must meet the famous painter who is working on our hell screen." Paying no attention to Akitada's gestures, he shouted across the courtyard, "Master Noami? A moment of your time. Here's someone you must meet."

The painter turned slowly to peer at them, then approached. He scowled when he recognized Akitada.

"Lord Sugawara," said Eikan, looking from one to the other, "this is Noami. Noami, this is the famous lord who solves all the crimes in the capital. Imagine, he has come here to investigate."

Noami's small, sharp eyes flicked from the monk to Akitada and back. "I have had the honor already," he said in his strange, high voice, shrinking into his patched and stained robe.

"Really?" cried Eikan. "Oh, that's right. You did spend the same night here, Noami. I had forgotten. Your comings and goings are so irregular."

"What do you mean, 'irregular'?" snapped the painter. "I am not a member of this monastery and consequently free to go as I please. Now, if you will excuse me, my lord, I have work to do." He turned and went back to fill his pail from the well bucket. Picking it up, he trotted to the storehouse without another word or glance, went in, and slammed the door behind him.

"Oh, dear," said Eikan apologetically. "So rude! He is peculiar, but the most gifted artist of this century."

Akitada looked after the man thoughtfully and said, "The

century is not over yet, and I cannot admire the gory scenes he seems to excel in."

"Oh, you have seen the hell screen. Yes, it makes me shudder, too, but that is after all the purpose. It is said that if we can just save one soul from sinful living by impressing him or her with the sufferings of their afterlife, it has served its purpose."

"I expect so," said Akitada, and turned to leave, but at the gallery he paused and looked back. "You said Noami spent the night of the murder here. Where does he sleep?"

"Sometimes in the room where he works, sometimes in one of the empty monks' cells. He used to be a monk, you know."

"Used to be? Did he renounce his vows, or was he dismissed for improprieties?"

Eikan spread his hands. "Nobody seems to know, my lord." He grinned suddenly. "And believe me, we have tried to find out. Though I shouldn't say it, life has a certain sameness to it day after day in a monastery. You have no idea how interested everybody is in the murder. The abbot has already assigned three penitential meditations to stop such worldly concerns. For those we stay up all night, kneeling on the hard floor, our backs straight as pine trees. If we drowse off or slouch, we are struck with a bamboo cane by the hall steward. But even that has not stopped the young monks from whispering about it."

"Under those circumstances I feel guilty asking your help."

They looked at each other. Then Eikan said, "Not at all, my lord. It is my duty to aid in the investigation." They smiled at each other in complete understanding.

The accommodations for lay visitors to the temple were in the southeastern corner of the temple grounds. Akitada's own room, thanks to his rank and the abbot's hospitality, had been in the monastery proper.

They entered the visitors' courtyard through a small gate. The buildings of the quadrangle resembled monks' cells. A rectangular courtyard with a few pine trees was enclosed by one-storied buildings, two long wings to either side and a shorter one closing off the end. Many doors led to rooms accessible from a veranda which passed around the quadrangle. Every six doors or so, steps led down to the courtyard, where two young monks were busy with chores.

Eikan turned to the right and they walked along the veranda until he stopped before one of the doors.

"This is the room which was given to Mrs. Nagaoka's brother-in-law," he told Akitada.

The door was not latched, and he merely pushed it open on an empty room. It literally held nothing, not so much as a clothes chest. The bare space was only ten feet deep and wide, perhaps to fit the monastic ideal of the ten-foot-square hermit's hut, and had a floor of plain boards. The rough wooden walls, decorated with the scribbles or drawings of generations of pilgrims, had only two openings, the door and one small window in the back wall. As accommodation it was hardly luxurious.

"Have they removed the furnishings?" asked Akitada, astonished.

"No. All the rooms are like this. Bedding and a lamp are provided if there are guests. On cold nights also a brazier of coals. And, of course, water and a simple vegetarian meal. All of those things, except for the brazier, were left for the gentleman." Eikan paused, clearing his throat meaningfully. "He did not make any use of them."

"Oh?" Akitada noted a coy expression on Eikan's face.

"It is one of those facts, my lord, which has filled the younger monks' minds with conjectures of a worldly nature and imposed the penitential meditations on them." Eikan winked with a straight face.

Akitada almost laughed aloud. He was beginning to like his companion. "You are suggesting that the lady's brother-in-law joined her in her quarters soon after their arrival. What about his luggage?"

"Oh, he left that behind, money and all."

Akitada's brows shot up. "All but his sword," he murmured thoughtfully.

"Ah," cried Eikan, rubbing his hands. "I follow your thinking, my lord. You believe that he had already made up his mind to murder the poor lady and proceeded immediately to her room, taking his sword along?"

"That is one explanation."

"But that means that he was not bent on seducing his brother's wife, as most of us have assumed. He did not kill her because she spurned his advances?"

"It would seem unlikely that he would take his sword on an errand of love."

"A brilliant deduction, my lord." Eikan eyed Akitada with admiration. "I am willing to wager that the police have not thought of that. They kept asking if anyone had noticed improper behavior between the two."

Not being in Kobe's confidence, Akitada could not pursue the subject. He asked instead, "Who discovered the crime?"

"One of the novices. His name is Ancho. The novices are assigned to cleaning duties in the guest quarters. Ancho and Sosei had the duty that week. I made a note of it and questioned Ancho after I discovered your identity, my lord, just in case you should return and ask me this question."

Akitada thanked him gravely.

"It is a pleasure to be of service. In any case, Ancho and Sosei started their duties after the morning lecture. That is well after the hour of the dragon, when most guests have risen and are at their devotions or have departed. Ancho knocked at the lady's door, and when there was no answer, he assumed the room was empty and used his special key. He was horrified to find the bloody corpse of a woman and the lifeless body of a man. Being young, he went screaming for help. Sosei came from another room and looked. He, too, ran, but he had the sense to get a senior monk from the monastery. Ancho, confused, stayed in the courtyard within sight of the room. He saw a few guests gathering to peer into the room until some of the senior monks arrived. It was only then that someone noticed the man was alive and merely in a drunken stupor. They tied him up, and the prior sent for the capital police."

"Did the man sleep through all this commotion?"

"It took the police several hours to get here. He woke up in the meantime and had to be restrained. The monks got more ropes and sat on him when he got violent. The police felt it proved his guilt."

Akitada had no trouble picturing the scene. Nagaoka's brother, Kojiro, woken up by a rude shaking, and, while still dazed with the aftereffects of drink, tied up by a group of monks, would have panicked. He nodded and said, "I think I should like to see that room next."

They walked along the veranda to the short wing of cells.

"This is where the women stay," Eikan said. "The male actors occupied rooms across from this wing. It seemed better to separate them. The mind is supposed to be pure when preparing for worship."

Akitada grunted somewhat disrespectfully. Eikan ignored it and threw open another door on a room identical to the last one. Akitada stepped in and looked around. The floorboards had been scrubbed, of course, and there would not have been much blood in any case. Finding nothing out of the ordinary, he turned his attention to the door. There was a latch on the inside which could be lifted from the outside only by a special key inserted through a small hole. Akitada asked, "Who has keys for this lock?"

"There are only two. They are kept in the guest prefect's office. Only the novices assigned to cleaning duties carry them. They are issued keys on the morning of their duties by the work supervisor, and they return them to him when they are done. Empty rooms generally are not locked."

"I see. Do you suppose I could have a word with this Ancho?"

"Nothing easier. He's outside."

They stepped out onto the veranda, and looked toward a young monk who was raking the gravel at the end of the courtyard.

Eikan put his hands to his mouth and shouted, "Ancho." The young monk dropped his bamboo rake and came running.

"Ancho," said Eikan, "this is the great lord I mentioned to you. He has come to investigate the murder and has a few questions for you."

Ancho's rosy cheeks, flushed by the cold air or his labors, paled a little and he cast a fearful look toward the open door. "I don't know," he said nervously. "Master Genno has forbidden us to think about such things. It is very difficult, but I have endeavored to obey."

"Never mind," said Eikan. "This is a special situation. You know His Reverence has told us to cooperate fully with the authorities."

Seeing the young man's uneasiness, Akitada said soothingly, "I will be as quick as I can. I am sure you must find all this upsetting."

Ancho nodded gratefully. He looked like a bright youngster, not much more than eighteen, Akitada guessed.

"Well, then, Ancho, are you certain that the door to this room was locked when you came to clean the room?"

"Yes. When there was no answer to my knocking, I pushed against it. Usually the guests leave the door unlatched when they leave. I knocked again, and when there was again no answer, I inserted my key and tripped the latch."

"May I see the key, please?"

Ancho exchanged a glance with Eikan—who nodded firmly—and handed over a thin metal gadget he carried tied to the rope around his waist.

The key was peculiarly shaped, and Akitada saw immediately

that it was made especially for this kind of latch. He inserted it into the hole and heard the small click as the latch moved. A slight twist released it again. Satisfied that only an expert thief, and one who had come prepared, would be able to unlock the door without this special key, Akitada returned it to the young monk.

"Now I must ask about some things which you may find upsetting," he said. "Please forgive me and do the best you can. First, tell me exactly what you saw when the door opened."

The young monk closed his eyes. He grew a bit paler, but spoke readily enough. "I saw the lady on the floor. Her feet were toward the door. I recognized the robe right away. Very pretty it was, with chrysanthemums and golden grasses embroidered on it. I thought she was asleep, but she was not on her bedding. She was on the bare floor and lying strangely. Then I thought she had become ill and fainted. I went in to help her." He shuddered and swallowed hard. "There was blood and her face . . . there was no face . . . it was all cut up. I knew she was dead then and I ran." He opened his eyes and looked at Akitada miserably.

"You are doing very well," said Akitada reassuringly. "Were you at all aware that there was someone else in the room?"

Ancho shook his head. "There wasn't much light, only what came from the open door, and I only looked at the lady, never thinking that a man might have joined her." He flushed painfully and averted his eyes.

"You said you recognized her robe. Had you seen her the night before?"

"Yes, my lord. When I brought her bedding and some food and water."

Eikan cried, "You had served her? You never told me."

Ancho said simply, "You never asked me."

For a moment Eikan looked irritated, then he brightened. "How about that? Only someone like you, my lord, would discover such a very important fact from a casual word. I have much to learn, it seems."

Akitada's mouth twitched. "Do you expect to need such skills in your way of life?"

"Certainly, my lord. You'd be surprised at the sorts of tricks our youngsters get up to, though not murder, of course. Also, with so many visitors, and low types like those actors ... though I believe the abbot plans to review the policy of permitting acting groups and women to stay here. It is written: 'All degeneration of the Law begins with women.'"

"I confess I was startled that the temple admits lay women free access to the monastery. I found some of the actors, men and a woman, in the bathhouse that night."

Eikan looked profoundly shocked. "A woman? Are you certain, my lord? That area is strictly forbidden to lay persons of either gender. What about the bath attendant?"

"He went to speak to them, but with little effect. I thought perhaps the rules had been lifted for the occasion of the festival."

"Not at all, my lord. The actors were supposed to remain in their rooms here." He shook his head. "No wonder the abbot is upset."

Akitada turned back to Ancho.

"Tell me about the evening before, when you saw the two people alive."

"They sent me to serve new guests, a gentleman and a lady. I stopped first in the kitchen. It was closed already, but I put cold rice cakes and two pitchers of water into a basket. These I took to the veranda before the lady's room. Then I fetched a roll of bedding from the storeroom and knocked. The lady opened the door. I tried not to look at her, but noticed the pretty gown. I took in the bedding first and put it under the window." He flushed. "We are not supposed to spread it out. As soon as I had done that, I went back for some of the rice cakes and a pitcher of water. I put those just inside the door and went to do the same for the gentleman."

"I see. You did not speak with either of the guests?"

"No, my lord. It is discouraged. The gentleman thanked me."

"Did you notice any luggage?"

"Yes, my lord. The gentleman had a saddlebag and his sword, and the lady had just a saddlebag."

"How did they seem? Cheerful, nervous, bored, or irritated?"

"It is hard to say. The gentleman gave me a smile and a nod. He looked tired, I think. The lady was walking about. Perhaps she was nervous. I don't know. She did not smile, and did not so much as look at me. I'm afraid that is all I can tell."

Somewhere a bell began to ring again, high and strident. Ancho glanced over his shoulder and began to inch away.

"The bell for our noon meal, my lord," said Eikan.

"Just a moment more," said Akitada. "As you were on duty that evening, did you have occasion to serve another visitor who would have arrived later? He would have been in his fifties, gray-haired and thin."

"Oh, no, sir. There were no other visitors later that night. And I don't recall seeing anyone like the man you describe."

So Nagaoka apparently had not followed his wife and brother. "One more thing: did any of the other guests express an interest in the lady who died?"

Ancho shook his head. "Not to my knowledge, sir."

"Thank you. That is all. It was very good of you to think back to something which must have troubled you a great deal."

Ancho bowed briefly and then ran. Eikan lingered behind, watching as Akitada pulled the door to the murder room shut behind him and found that it would not latch. "There is no need to lock it, my lord," he said.

Akitada stared at the door fixedly. Then he pulled it to again, harder this time. The latch jumped into place with a loud click and the door was locked.

"It locks from the outside," Akitada said with pleased surprise. "And that explains why Ancho and his fellow attendant have keys and why he opened the locked door with the key after knocking. He assumed it was empty and had slammed shut."

"Of course. People sometimes slam the doors so hard that they lock by themselves."

"But that makes all the difference," said Akitada. "While no one could enter a locked room without a key, it was quite simple to leave a room locked. Thanks to your help, we now know that someone other than Kojiro could have killed Mrs. Nagaoka."

Eikan looked blank. After a moment he said, "I am not sure I understand. May I ask if my lord suspects one of us?"

"Not necessarily. Someone who was in the temple or monastery the night of the murder. There were, by all accounts, many outsiders here that night. But you will miss your meal and I must continue my journey. I shall not forget your generous and invaluable assistance."

Eikan brightened slightly. "I have time. Someone brings my food to the gate. Will you come back, my lord?"

"Perhaps. But whatever happens, I shall let you know the outcome."

They parted company pleased with each other, and Akitada mounted his horse again and hurried back down the mountain road, anxious to make up for lost time.

Not completely lost, perhaps, for he had at least enough information now to speak again to Kobe. But there were so many uncertainties, not the least of which was the troubling person of Noami. The man seemed to be everywhere, a perpetual, ominous presence in the background.

He fell imperceptibly into glum discouragement again as he reviewed the past weeks. He was no closer to the solution of the murder of Nagaoka's wife, at home his unforgiving mother lay dying, one of his sisters was desperately unhappy and the other had married a man under suspicion of theft from the Imperial Treasury, he himself had yet to make his report to the palace, and he had so far failed to solve even one problem.

The mood persisted until he passed through a clearing and caught a glimpse of the valley and the highway below him. At the little shack where he had stopped earlier he saw a great bustle of carts, horses, and people. A group of travelers had paused on their journey to the capital.

His eyes sharpened, and he counted. Yes, two carts with oxen and a number of horses, at least fifteen. And there, just inside the shack, he saw the blue robe of a woman, and then a man stepped out, carrying a small child on his back. They had finally come!

Giving a shout of joy, Akitada slapped his horse into a neck-breaking gallop down the road to greet his family.

NINE

Family Matters

Their reception at the house was less than climactic. To be sure, Saburo grinned hugely when he saw his mistress again, and Yoshiko came running, brushing at her cotton gown and smoothing her hair back, but the other servants were strangers and merely peered curiously into the courtyard filled with horses, wagons, and strange men. But with the elder Lady Sugawara at death's door, and the chanting of the monks casting a pall over the return, there was no sense of celebration.

Tamako and Yori looked well after their long journey, healthy and tanned by the sun. Yoshiko's sickly pallor was all the more apparent by contrast.

Tamako knew about his mother's condition from Akitada, but now asked Yoshiko for the particulars. The two women, Yoshiko with Yori in her arms, walked toward the elder Lady Sugawara's room, while Akitada followed glumly behind. He had felt a strong urge to prevent this meeting, to protect them from the poison of his mother's disturbed mind, but Tamako had quickly informed him that it was her duty as daughter-in-law to pay her respects and present her son. So he hung back, stopping outside the door among the chanting monks, while the women disappeared inside.

He had a long wait, which he passed in morose thought, staring down at six shaven heads and thinking of the mountain temple; the murder; the painter Noami, once a monk himself; the hell screen; and finally of his gift for Tamako. The last thought cheered him, for presenting the scroll of boy and puppies reminded him that he would soon be alone with his wife. They would have a chance to talk, make plans for the future, touch hands, and then perhaps make love.

When Tamako emerged from his mother's room, her face drawn with distress, she was surprised to find her husband smiling at her happily, his hands extended eagerly.

"Finally," he cried. "Come, let us go to my room. I have missed you dreadfully."

One of the monks choked over a line, causing the chant to disintegrate and falter into silence. Six pairs of reproachful eyes were raised to Akitada. Then the oldest monk nearest the door cleared his throat and raised a hand. At his signal, they all picked up the chant again and continued.

Tamako took Akitada's extended hand and drew him away quickly. "She is dying," she murmured, partly in reproach and partly to express her own sadness. When they had put some distance between themselves and the monks, she added, "It cannot be long now. But she knew me, and she raised a hand to caress Yori. Only she was too weak even for that. Oh, Akitada! We returned barely in time."

Akitada looked into his wife's tear-filled eyes and marveled at her grief for a woman she had barely known. He knew his mother to be undeserving of such kindness. "I returned too soon," he said harshly. "If I had taken my time, it would have saved me the knowledge that my own mother hated me enough to drive me from her presence with curses."

"Oh, Akitada!" Tamako looked deeply distressed. "You did not tell me."

He turned away and started walking toward his room. "I did not mean to poison your mind, too," he said. "I stay away from her, waiting for the end, hoping it will come soon and release all of us so we can begin to live our lives like everyone else."

He opened the door to his room. It was cold. No one had thought to bring a brazier or hot water for tea. Akiko's luxurious quarters came to his mind, with their many glowing braziers, the silken bedding, and the cushions spread on thick straw mats and protected from drafts by screens and curtain stands.

"Forgive me," he said, turning toward his wife. "Nothing is ready. My mind has been on other things. This is a dreadful homecoming for you."

For all that, they rested well that night. The following morning, the bustle of settling in began. Akitada went early to inspect the stables and greet his horses. The weather was cold, windy, and overcast, causing him anxiety. A large portion of the stables was roofless, and cold currents of air stirred up the straw spread for the animals. He gave instructions to Genba and Tora about temporary weatherproofing and blamed himself for not having taken care of this before.

When he returned to his room, he found Tamako shivering under a winter robe. "I am sorry, my dear," he said. "My mother's illness keeps the servants busy. And here you are in a cold room with not so much as a hot cup of tea." He suddenly missed his son. "Where is Yori?" he asked, glancing anxiously back toward the door.

Tamako smiled a little. "Don't fret. Yoshiko has taken him to your mother again. She seems better when she looks at him, and he does not mind being around her. And do not worry about me. Now that I am here, I shall be able to give a hand to Yoshiko, who must have had a dreadful struggle taking care of your mother and you, too. She has only one housemaid to help her, she says."

Akitada flushed guiltily, thinking of the robe his sister had sewn for him.

"I am worried about Yoshiko," Tamako said, unpacking clothing and draping it over clothes racks to air out.

He grimaced. "I know. Too much work, my mother's sharp tongue, her illness, loneliness! It has been no life for a young woman of her class. I promised to find a husband for her. With a home of her own, she will soon be her own self again."

Tamako laughed. "Oh, Akitada! It is not that simple!" Turning serious, she said, "No. There is something else. Apparently she is keeping it to herself, and that means trouble of some sort."

Akitada cocked his head and smiled at his wife. "You are just looking for someone to dose with one of your magic potions," he said fondly. His wife's skill with herbal remedies had been a great boon to his family and household during the long years in the north. Even Seimei, his old friend and a family retainer, had turned over his box of salves and teas to her and concentrated instead on his new role as Akitada's personal secretary. "It is enough that we have my mother's illness to deal with," he said firmly. "Yoshiko is quite well, just tired and housebound."

Tamako went to open the shuttered doors to the overgrown garden. Cold air blew into the already chilly room. "Your mother is beyond my help." She sighed, looking at the sad tangle of shrubs and trees.

Akitada had followed her to the door. "I have not had time to get things tidied up," he said apologetically. The evergreen shrubs had grown to tree height, and frost-blackened weeds and choking piles of dead leaves and fallen branches covered everything else.

But Tamako smiled. "Never mind! I have always liked this room best. It gets sunlight most of the day and yet the garden is like a private world. It will be good to garden again. No more long winters and crushing snows. We shall sit on this veranda and sip tea, admiring the azaleas and camellias, peonies, and autumn chrysanthemums." She turned to him impulsively, her eyes shining. "Oh, Akitada! It is good to be home."

Akitada was so deeply touched by his wife's words that he did not realize for a moment that he was about to lose the room he had always occupied, the place where he had slept and worked and found refuge from the disdainful eyes and words of his parents. Well, he would find another room if Tamako wanted this one. "You know," he said, pulling her against him, "I was never happy in this house until now."

Instead of answering, Tamako buried her face against his shoulder with a happy sigh. Outside, a breeze picked up a handful of brown leaves and whirled them into the air. He shivered and wrapped his arms more tightly around her. "It has turned winter early," he said. "And there is no heat in this room. You must be cold. I wonder what happened to the servants. I have not had time to see about hiring more staff, either. Let me go get your maid and see about some tea and braziers."

She chuckled and released him reluctantly. "It does not matter, though a cup of hot tea would be nice."

He closed the veranda doors and went in search of the maid. Except for the distant chanting of the monks, the house seemed deserted, it was so quiet. When he went outside, he saw that the carts still stood in the courtyard only half unloaded.

In the low kitchen building he found the cook and his mother's tall rawboned maid in eager conversation with Tamako's dainty maidservant, satisfying their curiosity about the new mistress and Akitada's people. Apart from a bit of a small fire under the rice steamer and a small pile of chopped vegetables on a board, there was no sign of food preparation.

Feeling more than ever that this negligence was his fault, he snapped, "Why are there no braziers in my room? And where is the hot water for tea?"

The cook and the big housemaid rushed toward the stove and the empty braziers.

Akitada glared at Tamako's pert little maid and growled, "You are a terrible gossip, Oyuki. Go to your mistress immediately to make her comfortable!" The girl rose, grinning impudently, and disappeared.

The cook was pouring boiling water into a teapot, and the housemaid transferred glowing charcoal from the hearth to one of the braziers.

"When you have taken that brazier," Akitada ordered, "come back for another. The room is very cold."

The maid goggled at him. "I can't. The old mistress won't allow more than one brazier, sir," she protested.

"I am the master here now," Akitada corrected her with a flash of anger, "and from now on you do what I say, or what my wife tells you to do. Do you understand?" He directed a quelling glance at the gaping cook and added, "Both of you." Then he extended his hand for the teapot. "Get busy with the morning rice," he told the cook. "There are many mouths to feed."

The cook wailed, "There's not enough food for the rest of the day."

He almost cursed. But it was not, after all, the woman's fault. "Get more and do the best you can!"

Carrying the pot of hot water, he preceded the big maid with her brazier to his room, where he found Tamako admiring Noami's scroll painting and her maidservant unpacking a clothes box someone had brought in. Piles of gowns lay strewn about the room, and mirrors and cosmetics cases covered his desk. He sighed inwardly, but said only, "The scroll is a present for you. Do you like it?"

"It's beautiful," she said. "I don't think I have ever seen anything so lifelike. You can see every whisker on the puppies and every hair in their tails, and the little boy is charming. Wherever did you find this?"

The maid had placed the brazier next to his desk and left. Akitada poured hot water and brought Tamako her cup of tea. "Akiko's husband Toshikage found the artist. He commissioned a screen for her room. When I saw the screen, I knew I wanted you to have one, too, but the painter is a very strange creature, not at all pleasant even if he is very skilled. He insisted that he would have to observe the flowers for a whole year to paint a screen of plants for all seasons."

"How odd! I would like to meet the man sometime. How *is* Akiko? Yoshiko told me she is expecting a child."

"Yes. She seems in excellent health and very happy." He decided not to mention Toshikage's troubles and said only, "I like her husband, and he seems to dote on her."

Tamako studied his face. "Good! I shall look forward to meeting him."

The door opened, admitting Tora and Genba with more boxes. When they had gone, the second brazier appeared.

Akitada put down his empty cup. "There is much to do. I forgot to let Akiko know about your arrival. And I suppose I had better speak to Seimei about finding me other accommodations. And then I will lend a hand to the stable repairs. The place is not in good condition, I am afraid."

Tamako smiled at him. "Never mind! It will all come right now."

Akitada encountered Seimei in the hallway leading to his father's room. The elderly man was lugging a heavy box of documents.

"Wait," cried Akitada, rushing up to relieve him of the load. "You should not be doing this," he scolded. "It is much too heavy. Tora or Genba can carry the boxes and trunks. Where are you going with it?" He recognized his own writing set and personal seals among the items in the box.

"To your father's room," said Seimei. "It is fitting that you should be there now."

Akitada stopped abruptly. "No! Not there!"

Seimei looked up at him, his eyes sympathetic in the heavily lined face. "Ah! Old wounds are painful."

146

"You should know better than anyone," Akitada said harshly, "why I cannot work in a room filled with such memories."

The old man sighed. "You are the master now. And your father's room is the largest and best room in the house. It is expected that you should occupy it."

The thought crossed Akitada's mind that Tamako had assumed the same thing, but he simply could not face the prospect. "Some other room will do for the time being. Until we get my father's things cleaned out," he promised lamely.

"They have been put away already," Seimei informed him, and headed down the corridor. "There will be talk if you do not assume your father's position in this house. A man does not forget what is owed to either his home, his family, or himself."

His master followed dazedly with the box. When Seimei flung back the lacquered doors to his father's study, Akitada made one last desperate appeal. "My father did his best to prevent my taking his place. No doubt he will haunt this room if I use it."

At this Seimei chuckled. "Now you sound like Tora. I do not believe you. In any case, remember that patience is bitter, but its fruit is sweet. I have dreamed for many years of this day, hoping to live long enough to see you installed in your father's place."

Akitada looked at Seimei in astonishment. The old man had been with him all his life, doing his best to protect the child and youngster against his father's anger and his mother's resentment, but he had done so without ever committing the offense of criticizing, either. His loyalty to the Sugawara family had been exceeded only by his love for young Akitada. Akitada was more deeply touched than he cared to admit and gave up his resistance.

"Oh, very well," he said, and lugged the box into the room. Then he looked around. The light was dim, with the doors to the garden closed against the weather. The air smelled stale and musty.

There were the familiar shelves against one wall, but his

father's books and document boxes were gone. Gone also were the calligraphy scrolls with the Chinese cautionary precepts and the terrifying painting of Emma, the king of the underworld, judging the souls of the dead. This picture in particular had always instilled a special terror in young Akitada when he had crept into his father's room, expecting punishment. The resemblance between his father and the scowling judge had been striking, and Akitada had always suspected that that was the reason the painting held such a prominent place in the room.

The broad black-lacquered desk was also bare of his father's writing utensils and his special brazier and lamp. Only the atmosphere of stern and unforgiving judgment lingered. Akitada shuddered at the thought of receiving his own son in this room.

Seimei opened the doors to the veranda. Fresh, cold air came in. There was a private garden outside, with a narrow path leading to a fishpond, now covered with floating leaves. As a boy, Akitada had never been allowed to play here. Seimei tut-tutted at the state of the shrubbery, but Akitada stepped outside, glad to escape the room, and went to peer into the black water of the pond. Down in the depths he could make out some large glistening shapes, moving sullenly in the cold water. He picked up a small stick and tossed it in, and one by one the koi rose to the surface looking for food. They were red, gold, and silver, spotted and plain, and they looked up at their visitor curiously. Yori would like this place.

"Perhaps," said Akitada, "with some changes, the room might do."

Seimei, who had waited on the veranda, watching his master anxiously, gave a sigh of relief. "Her ladyship has directed which screens, cushions, and hangings are to be brought here. And, of course, there will be your own brushes and your books, your mementos from the north country, your tea things, your mirror and clothes rack, and your sword."

"Hmm. Yes. Well, make sure your own desk is placed near

mine," said Akitada, giving the old man a fond smile, "for I refuse to work here without you."

Seimei bowed. "It shall be so." There was a suspicion of moisture in his eyes as he turned to go back into the room.

Akitada followed, saying with a pretense of briskness, "I must go see about the horses and will send Tora to you. But could you dispatch a message to my brother-in-law Toshikage's, letting them know that the family has arrived?"

"I took the liberty to do this earlier, sir."

"I should have known." Akitada touched the old man's shoulder with affection, painfully aware how frail it had become. "I shall always think of you as my real father, Seimei," he said, tears rising to his own eyes.

Seimei looked up at him. His lips moved, but no words came. Instead he touched Akitada's hand on his shoulder with his own.

—◆—

It was not until the afternoon that Akitada was free to help with the stables. A good part of the building had been torn down years ago, when he was a child. The Sugawara finances had made the keeping of horses and oxen impractical when there were neither grooms for their care nor money for their fodder. Since then a part of the remaining section had lost its roof, and piles of wet leaves covered the rotten boards where once horses had stood.

He found Tora and Genba busy erecting a rough wall between the roofed area and the stalls that were open to the elements. In this freezing weather, you could not leave animals unprotected. Akitada's four horses and the pair of oxen which had drawn the carts were crammed together in the most sheltered part, where they had dry flooring covered with fresh straw.

The big gray stallion, a gift from a grateful lord, turned its handsome head to look at Akitada and whinnied. He went to the animal, running his hands over its body and down the slender, muscular legs, then did the same with the other three, a bay and two dark brown geldings. They had made the long journey in good condition. The bay was smaller than the others, but finely made and belonged to Tamako. They would be able to take rides into the countryside together. And soon, he thought contentedly, he would have to buy a horse for his son.

Protecting his horses was more important to Akitada than arranging his books. He worked companionably with his two retainers. Genba, a very big man, broad-shouldered and heavily muscled, had once been a wrestler. It was a sport he still engaged in at odd times, but he had, with great difficulty, lost much of the weight he used to carry and was perpetually hungry or fantasizing about foods.

Tora was willing enough to put his hand to a bit of rough carpentry when there were no pretty young women around to distract him. He had joined the household during Akitada's first assignment, when his master had taken a chance on the ex-soldier and saved him from a murder charge.

It got much colder when darkness fell, but the efforts of lugging about boards and climbing up and down ladders kept them warm enough, and the exchange of news passed the time.

Genba and Tora listened spellbound to his account of the events at the mountain temple. But when Akitada spoke of the hell screen and the painter's studio near the Temple of Boundless Mercy, Tora stopped hammering nails and stared at him.

"That place is haunted!" he announced. "Hungry ghosts are thick as flies there and every morning the outcaste sweepers find parts of human bodies."

Working side by side in the flickering light of torches while the animals quietly munched their hay and moved about in the straw went a long way toward laying the ghosts haunting Akitada's mind. Tora's imaginings were so far-fetched that both Akitada and Genba laughed at some of the details.

"Not a bad job," remarked Genba when they were done, and

had looked over the makeshift wall. "I think I've earned an extra helping of the evening rice. I meant to ask you, sir, how's the cook? Not too stingy with fish in her soups and stews, is she?"

"She is from the country and cooks hearty meals, but you were not expected. There may not be enough food in the house."

Comically, Genba's face first fell, then brightened again. "I could run out and get some of those vegetable-stuffed dumplings, and maybe some soba noodles. Yori likes those."

Akitada was putting on his robe. "Very well," he said with a smile. "But don't buy more than we can eat."

Tora hooted. "That's like telling the cat not to eat the fish." As Genba headed out the door grinning, Tora turned to Akitada. "I'm ready to get started on that temple murder tomorrow."

Akitada had planned to speak to Kobe as soon as possible, but now there were other things to be done. It would have to wait. He told Tora, "First we must get the family settled."

Tora waved a dismissive hand as they headed out of the stable. "Done in no time!"

It was nearly dark outside. Akitada glanced across the dim courtyard at the looming shapes of the residence and felt another pang of regret that in his absence little had been done to take care of it. "There are also the repairs to the house and gardens."

Tora's eyes opened wide. "But winter is coming, sir. It'll be best to wait until spring."

They walked to the well to wash their hands. The water in the bucket was icy, and the night air bit their wet skin painfully.

"Well," said Akitada, grimacing as he hurriedly dried his hands on the fabric of his trousers, "if you do have some spare time, you might ask around about those actors. They seem to have roamed all over the monastery that night. One of them may have seen something. And try to find out if any of their women were outside around the hour of the rat. They call themselves the Dragon Dancers and work for an old man by the name of Uemon."

"The easiest thing in the world," cried Tora, rubbing his hands. "A man like myself knows all the wine shops along the river where the actors usually spend their money—" He broke off as Seimei joined them.

"Beware of letting the tiger loose in the market," Seimei said to Akitada, with a meaningful nod toward the grinning Tora. Tora meant "tiger" and he had lived up nobly to the name since he adopted it. But he fancied himself as an assistant investigator of crimes, and he had had some success, though his methods involved copious drinking bouts and bedding material witnesses, much to the disapproval of Seimei.

"Thank you, Seimei. The advice is well taken." Akitada chuckled. "But you did not come for that, I am sure."

"Oh, no. Lord Toshikage and his lady have arrived. They are in her ladyship's room."

Akitada hesitated. He had no wish to see his mother. But Seimei corrected himself. "I meant *your* lady's room, sir." After another moment's confusion, Akitada realized that Seimei referred to his own room, or rather his former room.

Shaking his head at the changes wrought in a few hours, he headed that way. Yori's giggles and women's laughter came from behind the door, and he braced himself for a scene of chaos, with the women excitedly digging through Tamako's wardrobe, which would be flowing from innumerable trunks and covering every available surface, while his son romped about freely amid the general upheaval. He opened the door, hoping to extricate his brother-in-law from the chatter of women and children, but found to his surprise a tidy room with a happy family seated decorously on cushions around his desk.

All the trunks were closed and placed neatly against the walls, and a small painted screen and several handsome curtain stands stood around the gathering to protect them from the cold air coming from the doors. The faces turned toward him shone with laughter and good cheer in the light of candles. Tamako sat near the teapot; Yoshiko was holding Yori on her lap; Akiko, all smiles, had placed a hand protectively on her stomach; and Toshikage, next to his wife, rose to greet him. It suddenly struck Akitada that an extraordinary change had come over this house which, until most recently, had been filled with nothing but the mournful chants of the monks and nervous whispers of servants in the corridors.

The most profound change had nothing to do with his mother's illness. He could not recall ever hearing laughter in this house, or the shouts of children, or indeed seeing a happy gathering of family all under one roof. Feeling a surge of gladness, he greeted Toshikage with a hearty embrace.

The women were drinking tea, but Toshikage had a flask of warm wine, and Akitada accepted a cup of that, warming his frozen fingers on the bowl before letting the warm liquid spread a glow through his stomach. The two braziers, together with the screens, kept the chill at bay, and he relaxed into blissful leisure. Tamako informed him that she had entertained everyone with stories of the far north, and that now it was his turn. He obliged, and as they listened, asked questions, and chattered, they passed a giggling Yori from hand to hand. It was a more pleasurable time than Akitada could have imagined.

It was Akiko who broke the happy mood. "By the way, Mother looks dreadful," she suddenly informed him in a tone which was almost accusatory, though whether she held him accountable for his mother's decline or blamed him for her unpleasant experience was not immediately clear to him. "She cannot last the night. You had better think of the arrangements, Brother."

He sighed. "Don't worry. The arrangements have been made. How are you feeling, Akiko?"

This distracted her. She gave Toshikage a coy smile and patted her stomach. "We are very well, my son and I," she said proudly. "And Toshikage is quite charmed with your Yori, so he will take enormous care of us. Won't you, Honorable Husband and Father of our Son?"

Toshikage smiled broadly and bowed to her. "The most tender care, my Beloved Wife and Mother of our Child." He turned to Akitada and said, "You are blessed with a delightful family, my Brother, and I count myself the luckiest man alive to be a part of it."

Akitada was touched and made a suitable and affectionate reply, but thought privately of that unhappy young man who was Toshikage's oldest son. These thoughts led inescapably to the problem of the thefts from the Imperial Treasury, and he would have taken Toshikage aside to discuss the matter if the door had not opened to admit Tamako's maid with the evening rice.

Genba had outdone himself. There were platters of pickles, bowls of fragrant fish soup, mountains of soba noodles, and piles of stuffed dumplings. These delicacies were accompanied by rice and steamed vegetables from the cook's own kitchen. Dinner was another pleasant interlude, but finally Yori became tired and fretful. The women rose together to put him to bed.

On her way out Akiko had to pass Akitada and paused briefly. "By the way, Brother, it is the strangest thing, but that little figurine of the floating fairy you were so interested in? It has floated away again, and Toshikage swears he knows nothing about it. Have him tell you about it."

Akitada's eyes flew to Toshikage and he saw the other man flush to the roots of his hair. He waited till the door had closed behind the women before he asked, "So you recognized the figurine?"

Toshikage raised his hands. "I never saw it. I remembered what you said about instructing Akiko about the history of the little treasures and went to visit her room the very next day. She told me about the figurine, but when we looked for it, it was gone." He gulped down a cup of wine and sighed.

"And?"

Toshikage said miserably, "Akiko described it. Your sister has an excellent memory. It sounds like the floating fairy from the treasury. I don't think there could be two of them. I swear to you, Akitada, I did not put it there!"

"I believe you, but someone in your household must have done so."

"Impossible. Who would do such a thing? For what purpose?"

"I wonder why it was left in Akiko's room, and where it is now."

"Why leave it at all?"

"Perhaps as a warning to you?"

Toshikage looked absolutely confused. "A warning? About what? I don't understand."

Akitada sighed and thought.

After a moment Toshikage said, "It's a miracle the director did not see it. Remember the unpleasant visit I had from my superior?"

Akitada nodded.

"I had meant to show him the screen in Akiko's room and would have done so if you had not called to see your sister. Can you imagine what would have happened if the director had seen the thing?"

"Yes. But I thought you said the director was there to reprimand you. Why would you show him around under the circumstances?"

"Oh, it was not like that. I had mentioned the screen to him a few days earlier at the office and invited him over. In fact, at first I thought that was why he had come." Toshikage subsided into a misery of sighs and head shakings. "What can it all mean?" he muttered.

Akitada was beginning to have an idea. But it was hardly one he could share with Toshikage. If he was right, the truth would be a far bigger blow to his brother-in-law than a mere dismissal from office, no matter how embarrassing the circumstances.

TEN

The Dark Path

Lady Sugawara died the next morning.

It was Tamako who brought the news to Akitada. He was in his father's room, remote from the women's quarters, and thus unaware of the event. Rising early, he had slipped from under the covers gently so as not to disturb his sleeping wife and had walked softly to the kitchen to fetch a brazier and some hot water for tea, and then to his new study.

The room still depressed him. He lit as many candles and oil lamps as he could find against the darkness of closed shutters, but still a clammy, unpleasant aura remained. For a while he walked around rearranging his things where once his father's had stood. In the process he found the old flute he had bought from the curio dealer and decided to cheer himself up with some music.

He was badly out of practice but found some old scores and soon became immersed in the intricacies of fingering and timing the notes.

He was not aware of his wife until she walked up quickly and took the flute from his lips.

"What is the matter?" he asked blankly. "It was not all that bad, was it?"

Tamako looked down at him sadly. "No, Akitada. But you must not play anymore just now. It is your mother."

He rose abruptly. "Heavens! Am I not even permitted such a

small pleasure in my own house? That is intolerable, and I shall not allow her to dictate my life any longer."

Tamako looked at him with tragic eyes and sighed. "Yes, I know. Your mother is dead."

He gaped at her. Dead? His first reaction was relief that it was finally over, the long dying, the dreadful pall which had lain over this house so long. The relief immediately made way for shame, and then depression. Perversely, the event, so long expected, now seemed sudden, badly timed, too soon. "When?" he asked, and felt his heart contracting.

Tamako put a hand on his arm. He had not realized that his fists were clenched at his sides. His right hand hurt and when he raised it, he saw that it still held the antique flute, broken now; a splinter of bamboo had cut one of his fingers. Tamako gave a soft cry and took the pieces, laying them on his desk. Pulling the splinter from his hand, she said, "A short while ago. Another hemorrhage. Your sister was feeding her the morning gruel. I found Yoshiko covered with blood and incoherent with shock and took her away. The doctor has already seen your mother, and the maid and I have tended to her." She hesitated. "Do you want to go to her now?"

So Tamako had spared him the sight of his mother's blood-covered corpse. With a shudder he recalled the terrible scene when his mother had cursed him, the gaunt, distorted face, the sunken eyes blazing with hate, heard again the hoarse voice spitting out her vilifications until the words had drowned in a flood of gore.

Tamako gently stroked his arm. "Don't look so. You knew it was going to happen. It was time."

Akitada turned away from her sympathy. How could she understand that he felt mostly hatred for his own mother? Anger, regret, hopelessness, pain, but above all hatred. "Yes. I knew," he said harshly. "I even wished it. And, oh, yes, it was time! She poisoned everything she touched. My life, Yoshiko's,

Akiko's also! She would have poisoned yours, too, and our son's! I am glad it is over!" He laughed. "Finally it is over!" Looking around at his father's room, he shouted, "They are both gone! Gone! The house is ours! Our lives are our own! We can finally find peace and happiness. . . ." He collapsed on his cushion and covered his face with his hands.

"Shh! Akitada!" Tamako came to kneel beside him and touched his arm. "Don't! The servants will hear you! Please, you must not!" She saw that his face was wet with tears and, with a small moan of pity, took him into her arms.

"My own mother hated me so much," he sobbed into her hair, allowing her to hold him, rocking back and forth with the pain, "that she died without taking back her curses. What have I done to deserve that? Tell me, what have I done?"

"Shh!" Tamako crooned, patting him as if he were little Yori, "Shh, she could not help it. Death came too quickly."

Eventually he calmed himself and straightened up. "I suppose," he said, drying his face with his sleeve, "I had better go pay my respects."

Akitada had seen death often. It had never been a casual encounter, even when the dead person had been a stranger. But he had never hesitated or flinched as he did now at the door to his mother's room. He had stood here many times in his life, never eagerly, always wishing himself elsewhere. But always he had faced up to the encounter, because it was expected of him. With a sigh, he opened the door.

His mother's room was brighter than it had been in her lifetime. Many candles shone on the thin figure of the old woman as she lay, surrounded by the figures of the chanting monks. She was wrapped in the voluminous folds of a heavy white silk gown. Someone (Tamako?) had cut her hair like a nun's, suggesting a deathbed devotion which Lady Sugawara had never felt in life. It made her look younger, and her features seemed peaceful.

Akitada forced himself to study the face which, when alive, had regarded him with irritation, dislike, cold fury, and indifference, but never with love. He thought it ironic that those who had led blameless lives and whom he had loved had often died with contorted features. There was great perversity in death.

For the benefit of the chanting monks he knelt and bowed, staying in this reverent pose for an adequate time before rising and withdrawing. It was done!

The next days were taken up with funeral preparations. He concentrated on his duties, putting aside his bitterness for a calmer time. Both the house and its inhabitants wore willow-wood tablets with the "taboo" character inscribed on them, to warn outsiders of the ritual contamination of death. The taboo did not, of course, discourage the Buddhist monks, who seemed to take over the house and the lives of its inhabitants and would until after the funeral. But theirs was a different faith from the old religion, which abhorred the very thought of death.

No business of any type could be transacted during this period, and no visitors appeared, though Akitada received many messages of condolence from friends and from his mother's and father's acquaintances. It was all very proper and expected, except for one incident.

The day after his mother's death, Yoshiko came to see him. She was still very pale and looked frail in her rough white hemp gown. Kneeling in front of his desk, she looked with a sigh down at her folded hands. "There is something I have to tell you," she said. "I have thought about it a long time, for it may be painful for you." She looked up at him then, her eyes large and serious. "You know, I would not hurt you for the whole world, Akitada."

Akitada's heart fell. He had been worried for a while now that she was in some sort of trouble, and Tamako had suspected the same. Hiding his fear behind a smile, he said warmly, "I know. And there is nothing you could tell me that would make any difference in the way I feel about you, Little Sister. Please speak!"

She did not return his smile, saying bluntly, "I am afraid I caused Mother's death."

Her tone was so flat that Akitada stared at her. This lack of emotion was quite unlike Yoshiko, who had always had a soft heart. For a moment he wondered whether her presence during the final paroxysms had perhaps deranged her mind. To reassure her, he said briskly, "Nonsense! She was dying. What could you have done that would have made any difference in that certainty?"

Yoshiko shook her head stubbornly.

He searched his memory for Tamako's report, regretting for the first time that he had not seen his mother's body immediately. A hemorrhage, Tamako had said. Probably just like the one he had witnessed himself. But Yoshiko had not been with him then. He tried again, "Mother died of a hemorrhage. How could that be your doing?"

"Oh, Akitada. Can't you guess what happened? I quarreled with her. I knew how she felt about you, knew that one more provocation could bring on a final attack, but I could not keep still any longer."

Half-afraid of the answer, he asked, "What did you say?"

"I asked her why she would not see you, why she treated you so badly when you had rushed all that way to be at her side. She got very angry and said it was none of my business, but I would not leave it alone. I argued with her and accused her of lacking a mother's feeling for her son. That was when she started screaming at me."

Akitada winced. So it had been his mother's hatred for him that had finally killed her after all. Looking at Yoshiko's white, strained face, he said, "Don't blame yourself! It was kind of you to speak for me, but pointless. I have known for a long time that she did not love me. It is clear that I was foolish to think she would change on her deathbed. As for motherly feelings, I suppose she simply never cared for me. I have tried to account for it by the fact that she was as disappointed in me as was my father. I am so sorry that I should have been the cause for your distress."

Yoshiko cried, "Oh, no! That wasn't it at all. Oh, Akitada, I didn't come here because I needed you to console me. It is true, I blame myself for provoking her, but I know Mother was dying, and perhaps it was good that she spoke to me before she did." She paused and looked at Akitada anxiously. "You see, I don't think she was your mother at all."

After a moment's stunned silence, Akitada said, "You must have misheard something. My father never had any secondary wives."

"He did! We just did not know. I think your mother died when you were born, and you were raised by our mother. And I think she never forgave you for being another woman's son."

Akitada blinked. He felt as if he had walked into a dense fog. He wondered again if Yoshiko had gone mad under the recent strain. But she looked calm enough except for the nervous twisting of her hands. "What makes you think so?" he asked.

She leaned forward a little, her face tense, her voice high with emotion as the words tumbled out. "Mother said so in so many words. Actually, she screamed it at me! It was horrible, but if you think about it, it explains so much! I have thought about it ever since. Imagine all that resentment, years and years of it, holding it in for fear of Father. And when Father was gone, she still would not speak because you were the heir and could have ordered her out of the house if you had known. Oh, she probably knew you would not abandon her totally, but she was afraid that you would find her another place to live, and she could not have borne that. Only now she was dying, and you had brought your wife and heir home, and she knew there was no point in keeping quiet any longer. All the hatred and jealousy of nearly forty years, of knowing that Father preferred your mother to her, that your mother gave him a son, when she had no children at all, until Akiko and I were born, all of it poured out. She ranted on until she choked on her own misery, and then the blood came up and she died. It was dreadful!" The stream of words halted abruptly on a little gasp, and Yoshiko looked at him tearfully.

Akitada's mind reeled. "What exactly did she say?" he demanded. "What were her words?"

Closing her eyes, Yoshiko thought back. "She said, 'He's no son of mine!' and then, 'She was a person of no importance! What did he see in her?' and then she said, 'He insulted me and my family by bringing her child into my house, to raise him as his heir for all to see and pity me!' " She opened her eyes. "There were many hateful words about this other woman."

Akitada was silent, caught in the monstrous shock of the thing. He stood up and walked to the veranda door, opened it, and stepped outside. Standing on the edge of the veranda, he stared down at the fishpond, where a few dead leaves mimicked the golden and scarlet fish beneath the dark waters. Just so his father must have stood many times. What thoughts had been on his mind? The bond between himself and his father suddenly seemed strong and unbroken. It was as if he had always known deep inside of himself the truth he had just been told. *The truth within!* Somewhere he had read those words, but could not now recall where.

His sister sat wringing her hands in her lap. After a long time of watching him anxiously, she whispered timidly, "I am so sorry, Akitada. I did not mean to hurt you."

Akitada had been thinking of his father loving another woman, who was his mother, and was startled. "You have not hurt me," he said in a tone of wonder. "On the contrary, it is a great relief to me. Only, now my father's dislike for me seems even more strange."

His sister said quickly, "I thought about that, too. I think he must have pretended to dislike you because of Mother."

Akitada turned to look at her uncertainly. That idea would take some getting used to. How do you divest yourself of almost forty years of resentment toward your father in one moment? There were too many bad memories to be explained away, one by one. It was not going to be easy. He sighed and said, "At least it should not be difficult to find out the truth."

"You are not angry with me, then?"

"Of course not. And stop worrying about having caused . . . your mother's death. The slightest aggravation would have done the same." As he watched Yoshiko rise, her slender figure obscured by the stiff folds of the hemp gown, he forced a smile. "I suppose I shall have to wait until the forty-nine days are up before I see you in one of your pretty new gowns."

"Forty-nine days? We mourn a parent for a full year."

"No, Yoshiko. As head of this family, I decree that after the funeral we shall wear dark colors until after the ceremony of the forty-ninth day. Then all mourning will be put aside. So get busy with your needle."

She opened her mouth to protest, then smiled. "Yes, Elder Brother. As you say."

After she left, Akitada examined his feelings. On the whole he felt enormous relief that he was the child of another woman, as yet a mythical figure. It was one thing to be hated by one's own mother, but quite another if a stepmother had done so. A woman's jealousy of a rival could well cause her to reject that woman's child.

He felt a mild curiosity about that long-dead young woman, so hated by her rival, and so beloved by his father. For if he had not loved her, surely the woman whom Akitada had thought of as his mother would not have hated her son so bitterly and long. He recalled, too, moments when his stepmother's guard had slipped and she had revealed her bitterness toward her late husband, her many complaints about his political and financial failure, her bitter reminders that she had married someone unworthy of her own family. And gradually the stern, unforgiving image of his father softened in his memory until it became almost human.

He was still pondering these relationships when the door opened softly and Seimei entered with another message of condolence.

Seimei! Akitada looked at the old man with new eyes. He put the message aside unread and said brusquely, "Please take a seat!"

Seimei was surprised but obeyed.

"I have just had some extraordinary news, and it occurs to me that you must have known about it for many years."

The old man looked blank. "What is that, sir?"

"It seems the woman who claimed to be my mother all these years unburdened herself on her deathbed and told my sister that I am another woman's son."

Seimei paled slightly, but his eyes did not flinch. "It is true, sir," he said. "Lady Sugawara was not your mother. I regret that you had to find out before I could speak."

Akitada stared at him. How could the old man be so calm? A bitter resentment rose in his stomach. "Why did you not tell me?"

"I was bound by a promise to your honored father, but I was about to do so now, since Lady Sugawara has passed out of this sad world."

Akitada felt stark disbelief. This Seimei was a stranger to him, not the friend he had trusted from childhood, to whom he had confided every hurt and all his uncertainty about his parents, and whom he had loved like the father he had wished for. This man had kept a secret from him through all those years, a secret which would have saved him so much heartache! How could he have done it?

Seimei was still looking fully at him, but there were tears in his eyes now. "I gave my word, sir," he repeated.

His word! Was keeping one's word more important than a child's misery? Was it more important than seeing the adult struggle with self-recrimination? As recently as yesterday Akitada had still agonized over the relationship between himself and his supposed mother.

Seimei said softly, "I promised your father, because we feared for your life."

"What are you talking about?"

Seimei flinched at the harshness of Akitada's voice. "Lady Sugawara believed she would have a son of her own. There came a time when she was certain she was with child and she made arrangements for an accident to happen to you. Your father discovered it in time and sent you away."

All these years Akitada had believed that his father had driven him out of the house because he disliked him so intensely that he could not bear his sight any longer. He was moved profoundly by the thought that his father had cared for him after all. He stared at Seimei, but the tears welling up in his eyes blurred the old man's image until he could barely see him, and he turned away to regain his composure. The news raised more questions. After a moment he asked, "If he discovered his wife in such a plot, why did he not divorce her?"

"He, too, believed her with child. By the time it became apparent that she was not, you were quite happy in the Hirata family and refused to come home."

Yes, that was true. His professor at the university had taken him in. Hirata and his daughter Tamako, now Akitada's wife, had both welcomed the deeply distressed Akitada with such unaccustomed kindness and warmth that he had rejected out of hand his father's rapprochement.

"But why did you not speak after my father's death?" Akitada asked. "And why did my father not leave a letter for me?"

"Your father asked for my silence again on his deathbed. I do not know if he feared for your safety or wished to protect Lady Sugawara and your sisters. I could only give my word that I would do as he asked." Seimei quoted softly, " 'First and foremost be faithful to your lord and keep your promise to him.' "

Akitada closed his eyes. Confound Confucius! He had much to answer for in this case, he thought bitterly.

"You would not wish me to break my word to you, sir, would you?"

Akitada looked at the old man and saw tears sliding down the wrinkled cheeks into his straggly beard. He sighed. "No, I suppose not. Tell me about my mother!"

"Her name was Sadako. She was the only child of Tamba Tosuke, one of your father's clerks. Her family was provincial, very poor but respectable. When his wife died, Tamba Tosuke suddenly took Buddhist vows without a thought to his daughter's welfare. People took it for a sign of his extreme devotion, but your father was angry and he paid for the young lady's support. In time he fell in love with her and married her, though arrangements had been made for another marriage to the late Lady Sugawara. Your mother died when you were born, sir, and then your father brought you to this house to be raised by Lady Sugawara, hoping she would be a mother to you." Seimei paused, then added diffidently, "Her ladyship came from very different circumstances than your poor mother."

Akitada knew it well enough. Of course she despised the child of a woman of the lower classes, one who had been her predecessor and her rival. She had never allowed anyone to forget her own pedigree.

A sudden thought struck him. What if she had passed some of her qualities on to Akiko? Had not Akiko also wished to be rid of the sons of her husband's earlier marriage? He was immediately appalled at his lack of faith in his sister. Akiko was merely spoiled, not evil. She could be selfish and thoughtless, but she was not cruel. Still, she might already have caused trouble in Toshikage's house. He had to make an effort to undo it! That, too, was one of the legacies his stepmother had burdened him with. He considered bitterly that he was about to become the late Lady Sugawara's chief mourner in an elaborate funeral ceremony. It was ironic. In a way he was bound as irrevocably as Seimei to carrying out the wishes of the dead.

—◦—

The funeral took place after dark. They set out for the cremation site in procession. Torchbearers and monks chanting Buddhist mantras walked ahead. Lady Sugawara's corpse, washed again and wrapped in white cotton sheets perfumed with incense, lay in an ox-drawn carriage behind drawn curtains made of her embroidered court robes. Ahead walked Seimei, carrying the sacred lamp, and Saburo followed behind with a censer from which clouds of incense perfumed the night air. The mourners walked behind, Akitada first, followed by Yori in the arms of Tora, and Toshikage. The three women followed in hired litters. After them walked the Sugawara servants and friends. The long line moved slowly, silent except for the chanting of the monks, through the deserted streets of the capital.

The cremation ground was outside the city. A site had been prepared for them, with white sand strewn about the funeral pyre, and temporary shelters had been erected for the mourners.

Akitada took his seat among the men and prepared for the long night's watch. There was a clear sky with many stars, and it was bitterly cold. He had made arrangements for open braziers to be placed in all the shelters, but they made only a slight difference. He glanced worriedly at his son, who sat next to him. Yori was bundled into so many quilted robes that his round, rosy face looked absurdly small among all the silken coverings. Akitada had insisted that hemp was to be worn over ordinary clothing and only by his sisters and the servants. He, Tamako, and Yori wore dark silk robes instead. He had chosen that single subtle gesture because he was no blood relation to the dead woman. Since both dark silks and hemp were customary in mourning, outsiders would hardly realize the significance. If anything, they would ascribe the silk to his position as head of the family.

It was a very small act of defiance, for otherwise Akitada mourned Lady Sugawara publicly with all the expense and proper behavior of an only son.

Akitada saw that Yori's eyes were large with excitement as he watched the flames of the funerary pyre being lit by one of the monks. When the moment came, Akitada rose and ceremoni-ously placed Lady Sugawara's favorite possessions, her elegant toiletry boxes, carved rosary, zither, and writing utensils, along with the token coins to pay her way in the other world, into the flames.

The monks began their chanting again, and the flames rose higher, crackling softly, sending a long column of darker black smoke into the night sky, slowly obscuring the stars. The fire consumed symbols of emptiness, for life was no more than a wisp of dark smoke fading into night.

Yori fell asleep after a while, and his father pulled him close into his protective arm. Across the way, in the women's shelter, someone sobbed loudly. Akiko, no doubt, Akitada thought wryly. She always knew what was expected of her in public. Toshikage half turned to cast anxious looks that way, and Aki-tada thought, not for the first time, that Akiko had been very lucky to have found such a husband.

Of course, Toshikage's problem also affected her, and if Aki-tada was right in his suspicions, Akiko was the cause of it. Either way, he had a duty to help Toshikage. But this death had made things very awkward. None of them could go about naturally for the next seven days. They were, for all intents and purposes, housebound. And even after that Akitada and his sisters would have to observe restrictions of normal activities for another six weeks, until the ceremonies of the forty-ninth day had been completed and the soul of the deceased had departed the world.

On the positive side he need not worry about being called to court for the coming weeks. But meanwhile Toshikage's situation was pressing. For all they knew, the director of the Bureau of Palace Storehouses was already planning an investigation into Toshikage's stewardship. It was dangerous to let another day pass without taking action, and Akitada pondered this problem as the hours passed slowly.

The fire began to burn out after a while, and more wood was added to the pyre. The air became saturated with the smell of wood smoke and incense and, very faintly, of burnt flesh.

Tora came quietly to take the sleeping child to his mother. When he left, Toshikage whispered, "Do you think the ladies are warm enough?"

Akitada nodded and glanced at the sky. "It will be dawn soon," he murmured. "Come to my house to warm up before returning home."

Toshikage nodded gratefully.

Akitada thought how easily the words "my house" had come to his lips. It was truly his home now, no longer poisoned by memories of his parents' supposed rejection of him. He recalled his father's stern mien, so harsh and frightening in his childhood memories, and tried to see it as a mask put on to reassure a jealous wife that he felt no love for this son and merely tolerated him. And he thought much of the young woman who had been his mother. How short her life had been! Had she loved his father? If she had lived, would his life have been different? He felt in his heart that his mother would have loved him.

With the first light of the dawn, the monks stopped chanting. They went to pour water on the smoking remnants of the fire, then sprinkled the ashes with rice wine. Later they would collect the bones and inter them near his father. Akitada wondered where his mother's remains lay. The mourners straggled to their feet stiffly, and attendants went to get the litters ready for the women. Yori, still asleep, would ride with Tamako, but Akitada and Toshikage walked back side by side.

On the way from the cremation grounds, they stopped to perform the ritual purification at one of the canals which crisscrossed the city. The water was icy, and they hurried their ablutions.

"A fine funeral," remarked Toshikage, wrapping his wet hands into the full sleeves of his gown.

"Yes. It went very well," replied Akitada. One said such things, when there was nothing else to say. Certainly Toshikage knew better than to assume that Lady Sugawara was sincerely mourned by anyone, including his wife Akiko.

But this did not stop Akiko later from reciting lines of poetry about the melancholy event when they gathered for some hot rice gruel and warm wine. She dwelt with many sighs on the emptiness of life, and spoke of that sad period spent in "a night of endless dreams" before entering "the dark path" into death, meanwhile eating and drinking heartily between moments of inspiration.

Toshikage watched her complacently, remarking that the enforced period of mourning would give him a chance to see more of his wife. "I shall not be expected at the office," he said, adding with a distinct note of fatherly pride, "Takenori is quite capable of carrying out my duties for the next week. The boy is really a great help to me these days."

⊷

Akitada went to visit Takenori later that day. It was early afternoon, and he had had only a few hours of sleep. The weather was still wintry, but the sun shone brightly and warmed the air. He had dressed in a plain gray robe and formal black cap which could pass for either mourning or ordinary wear, but wore the wooden taboo pendant attached to the cap. It would stop casual acquaintances and strangers from engaging him in conversation on his way across the palace grounds.

He left the house quiet and shuttered, the large taboo sign at the gate warning visitors away from the contamination that a recent death placed on a household. The morbid presence of these reminders of death cast a dark mood over his errand. Much—no, everything—depended on Toshikage's son, and their previous meeting had not been encouraging.

When he reached the Greater Palace, the streets and buildings of the large enclosure hummed with activity: officials and clerks bustled about and messengers ran to and fro, carrying documents and records; the Imperial Guard made a splendid show at the gates, and performed a snappy drill in front of their headquarters. Akitada had his private doubts about the guard's effectiveness in case of an armed attack on the emperor. It had become a much-sought-after profession for the sons of minor nobles and provincial lords who wished to give their offspring exposure at court. But the guardsmen were young and looked sharp enough in their stiff black robes and feathered hats as they rode their horses in tight circles and twanged their bows.

The Bureau of Palace Storehouses was in a large building immediately to the north of the imperial residence. It contained not only offices but storage for the treasures belonging to the sovereign and other members of the emperor's family. The entrance was guarded by two young guardsmen who cast sharp glances at Akitada, noting his cap rank as well as the taboo marker, and let him pass.

Akitada was not prepared to answer searching questions about his identity and business there, so he was pleased to find Toshikage's name on a door almost immediately. He knocked, heard a firm young voice inviting him in, and entered, closing the door behind him.

Takenori was seated at his father's desk, bent over a ledger into which he was making entries. When he saw who had walked in, he froze, brush in hand, and stared openmouthed.

"Good afternoon, Takenori," said Akitada pleasantly, seating himself across from the young man.

Takenori dropped his brush into the water container and scrambled to his feet to bow. "Good afternoon, my lord," he gasped. When he straightened up, he still looked utterly confused. "Er, allow me to express my condolences, my lord," he stammered, then ruined the conventional courtesy by blurting out, "But your honored mother's funeral was only last night. My father is at home because of it. How is it that *you* are here?" He stopped and, with sudden panic showing in his face and voice, cried, "Something has happened! Is it my father? Is he ill?"

Akitada noted this reaction with approval and relief. So the young man did care about his father! That made things easier. He said, "No. Nothing of the sort. Please be seated. I had hoped to have a chat with you while your father is elsewhere, that is all."

Slowly Takenori sat down. His brows contracted, and some of his former antipathy returned. No doubt he wondered what could be of such importance that Akitada would break the social and moral rules of mourning so flagrantly to consult him personally.

Akitada smiled at him. "Though I have not known your father very long, you should know that already I feel a great affection for him."

Takenori barely suppressed a look of distaste. He clearly did not believe Akitada, but said politely enough, "Thank you. You do us a great honor, my lord."

"And that is why I am very concerned about the missing items. I think you must be aware of the seriousness of your father's situation. Should he be found guilty of this theft, he along with his whole family would be exiled to some very unpleasant, faraway province."

Takenori flushed. "My father is innocent and will prove it."

"Furthermore," continued Akitada as if Takenori had not spoken, "his property, large though it is, would be confiscated and all of you, you and your brother included, would be penniless."

Takenori became quite still. He looked at Akitada for a long time, clenching and unclenching his hands. Then he asked harshly, "Did you come here to tell me that you wish my father's wife, your sister, to return to her family because you fear for her future?"

Akitada raised his brows. "That was not only rude, but silly," he said. "I would not discuss such a matter with you, but with your father."

But Takenori had worked himself into a seething temper. "Well, if it was not your intention to dissolve the marriage," he said, "you must forgive me, for I cannot imagine that anything but an urgent crisis affecting your own family could bring you out during the ritual seclusion. And what else could you have to discuss with me?"

Akitada cocked his head. "Come, now, Takenori, we both know who took the missing objects, don't we?"

Takenori stared back at him. He slowly turned pale. "Wh-what do you mean?"

"Where are they? In your room in your father's house? Or somewhere in this building?"

"Why would you accuse *me*? Anyone could have stolen those things."

Akitada noted that so far the young man had avoided an outright denial. He pressed his advantage. "No. Not anyone. Only you or your father could have removed anything from this place and brought it to your house, and I saw the figurine in Akiko's room myself. No one else in that house had access to the treasures, and no one here had access to her room. As I said before, I have come to like your father a great deal. He is as incapable of theft as of lying about it afterward. You, on the other hand, are a stranger to me."

Takenori stared back at him. The color came and went in his pale face.

"I have wondered a great deal lately what sort of person you are," continued Akitada thoughtfully, folding his arms across his chest and studying the young man. "Are you, for example, greedy for wealth and power? Or do you feel such resentment toward your father that you are willing to sacrifice your whole family and yourself to punish him for putting you and your brother aside for the child my sister bears? Or perhaps you are merely playing some sort of childish game by which you hope to break up your father's marriage to my sister?"

Takenori flushed scarlet and bit his lip.

"Ah, so that was it. I thought so. Well, it won't work, young man. You are playing with fire. The other day you hoped to provoke a scene between your father and his superior by placing the emperor's figurine in my sister's room, thinking that your father would take the director there to show him the new screen. If I had not happened to visit that day, disaster would have struck. Your father would have been arrested. How did you hope to extricate him from the trap you had built?"

Takenori cried, "They would not have dared arrest him. He does not need to steal. He is rich. It would simply have been ascribed to thoughtlessness as before. But *you* would have heard about it and thought he was guilty. And *she* would have left my father."

"I see. Tell me, why do you resent my sister so much?"

Takenori looked away. "I have served as my father's secretary for several years now and I saw the marriage settlements. My brother and I plied the matchmaker with wine, and he told us all about it. Your sister married my father only for his money. Your

174

mother and your sister apparently were quite frank about it during the negotiations." He gave Akitada a sudden, bitterly resentful look. "Cruelly frank, I might add."

Akitada grimaced. That had the ring of truth about it. "Does your father know about this?"

Takenori flashed, "Of course not. We would never tell him what was said. My brother and I tried to talk Father out of this marriage, tried to make him renege on the contract, but he refused. When my brother became too insistent, my father got angry and sent him away." He clenched his fists and added bitterly, "He sent his own son away to die. I know your sister suggested it to him, because we stand in the way of her unborn son. When I saw what had happened to my brother, I decided to become a monk. At least a monastery is safer than a war." He buried his head in his hands.

Akitada knew only too well the pain of feeling rejected by a parent. "You do not really desire the monastic life, I gather?" he asked gently.

There was no answer.

Akitada sighed. "My sister has her faults," he said after a moment, "but she had nothing to do with your brother's decision. Neither did your father. He told me that he tried to talk Tadamine out of it. It appears that your brother is just such a hothead as you, but unlike you he is enamored of soldiering. Unfortunately, since you both made such drastic changes in your lives, Akiko has come to look at the unborn child as the natural successor to your father. It may, of course, be a girl, but there will be other children. Still, if my sister's children succeed to the entire estate, it will be no one's fault but yours and your brother's. I suggest you reconsider your own plans and urge your brother to return. He can always carry out his martial activities here as a member of the Imperial Guard."

Takenori raised his face from his hands to stare at Akitada. "B-but I thought," he stammered, "that you and she wanted it this way. I . . . I assure you, the marriage contracts are very specific about her rights."

"I know all about the contracts. I signed them and provided my sister's dower. However, I had nothing to do with the terms. My late . . . mother was a shrewd businesswoman when it came to providing for her daughter. I may not approve of all that passed in my absence, but it is right that Akiko and her unborn child should be secure if something were to happen to your father. However, that does not mean that anyone wished you and your brother to be disinherited."

"Oh." Takenori looked suddenly lost, uncertain about what had just taken place, and not yet believing in his good fortune.

Akitada rose. "I cannot stay. Someone might come in, and I have no desire to be caught in explanations. Your plan was quite irresponsible and extremely dangerous. I trust that you would not have let it come to the point of your father's arrest?"

Takenori started. "Oh, no! I would have confessed immediately."

"Well, whatever you may have thought, your father loves both his sons and is very proud of you and Tadamine. It would hurt him badly to know what you did. That is why I had to come to speak to you without his knowledge. You will keep the matter to yourself, and I rely on you to return the missing items immediately to their proper places. Find a plausible explanation for how they came to be misplaced."

Takenori scrambled to his feet. "Yes. Right away. I . . . am so sorry about all this. You were very good to . . ."

But Akitada had already slipped out of the door.

Outside, the same winter sun shone brightly. Akitada blinked his eyes against the brightness. The day no longer seemed sad to him. If life was a path through darkness into death, then at least it was good to extend a helping hand to another traveler. Besides, the past had taught him lessons which would light the way in the future.

ELEVEN

Miss Plumblossom

As it turned out, it was a whole week later before Tora and Genba were free to visit the city. They were by now well into the last month of the year, and appropriately the weather was bitter cold. There had been too many chores to do in the sadly under-staffed household. But after some of the most urgent—and quiet—repairs had been made, even Akitada could see that hammering and sawing were not appropriate in a house of mourning, at least not until the taboo tablets had been taken down from the gates.

The pair were on their way toward the riverfront in the south-ern part of the capital. It was late afternoon, and already the light was fading. The weather was not only frigid, but a heavy gray cloud cover threatened snow. They wore their quilted robes and lined boots and stepped out briskly, eager to sample the night life.

Their way took them through residential streets, quiet and sedate, lined with tall plaster walls which hid low-roofed pavil-ions in large tree-shaded gardens. Here servants swept the street in front of important double gates, and litters picked up the inhabitants for their errands.

The farther south they walked, the more the character of the streets changed. The houses moved closer together and added second stories whose roofs almost touched, and the gardens shrank to a few trees which grasped for the leaden sky with skeletal branches through narrow openings between roofs. Here the merchants lived, doing business in the house which they occupied with several generations of their families. Their wives or kitchen maids swept the street here, and customers and apprentices hurried in and out of many narrow doors.

Genba attracted the usual admiring stares. His size made him noticeable, for he was half a head taller than Tora, who was no midget himself, and much heavier. In fact, Genba was so big and broad that his wide shoulders and barrel-like torso resembled more a moving tree trunk than a man. His gait, developed after years of lifting weights and wrestling, had something to do with this also. He moved from the hips with a wide-legged stride, placing each foot firmly and deliberately before shifting the rest of his body, causing him to sway ponderously from side to side. The wrestler's walk is easily recognized, and wrestlers were universally idolized. No wonder, then, that people stopped and stared after them.

He looked about him happily, like a child on an excursion. Smiling broadly at people, he remarked to Tora, "It's getting close to the hour of the evening rice, isn't it?"

"Too early." Tora was nearly as cheerful as his companion. "Let's go through the pleasure quarter. Maybe some of the girls are out."

"Not in this weather," said Genba firmly. "People stay in and put some nourishing hot food inside themselves." He gave Tora a measuring glance and added, "How about some nice restaurant? The girls will be there on a day like this."

"Hmm," said Tora.

They reached the Willow Quarter, but as Genba had predicted there were only a few customers hurrying to assignations, and no women at all. Tora walked along the street, peering into each grated window, disappointed to find it closed by paper screens or curtains.

He proposed stopping in the quarter for a cup of wine, but

Genba had more substantial things in mind. "The master wants to know about the actors. Let's go where the actors eat!" he said.

They had to leave the protective streets and alleys of the city to reach the windy riverfront. A cold blast of air from the mountains in the north blew up the skirts of their robes and sent icy needles of air through their leggings and down their collars. Heavy black clouds were gathering above Mount Hiei, and the Kamo River moved choppily.

"Whew! Bad weather coming!" Tora peered down the street which followed the river. Fishermen's huts and warehouses gave way to long rows of eateries overlooking the broad gray waters of the river. Like the icy wind, the river came from the mountains in the north and flowed in a southerly direction past the capital, forming its eastern boundary. It was here, along the riverfront, that Tora and Genba hoped to find news about Uemon's Players.

Tora was for putting his head into every wineshop and eatery they passed to ask for them, but Genba made for a large building with a nondescript exterior about halfway along the block. Over its low door hung a badly written sign which read "Abode of the River Fairies," and it seemed to be doing an excellent business. A low hum of voices emanated from the door and the screened windows. A rich smell of cooking fish emanated also and started Genba's nostrils quivering and his lips smacking in anticipation.

Their arrival in the dim, lamp-lit room went unnoticed. Most of the space was taken up by rough tables and wooden benches, the kind one usually finds outside for the convenience of travelers or people in a hurry. Their practicality here was due to the fact that the establishment had a dirt floor. The tables and benches were arranged around a cooking pit in the middle of the room. Several huge black iron cauldrons simmered over a charcoal fire, watched over by a bare-chested, muscular fellow with a bandanna tied around his hair and sweat glistening on his face and chest. From time to time he paused his stirring to use a huge ladle to fill a bowl held out by one of the waiters. A lively exchange of jokes passed back and forth between this cook and some of the guests.

Tora paused to study the women, but Genba had no eyes for them. Smiling happily, he seized Tora's elbow and made for a table close to the steaming cauldrons, where he slid onto a bench already occupied by an elderly man who was staring morosely into his wine cup.

"May two thirsty fellows join you, brother?" Genba asked, using the local dialect. The man was in his fifties and wore a stained brown cotton robe. His thinning gray hair was stringy and unkempt, and a heavy stubble on his chin showed that he had not bothered to shave for several days. Tora took him for the neighborhood drunk.

The man looked up at them with bleary, bloodshot eyes. "Why not?" he asked, his voice cracked and the sounds slurring. "Drinking alone causes depression, and depression is unhealthy, as the ancients tell us."

Tora and Genba looked at each other. The man's speech was educated, incongruous in these surroundings and in someone of his appearance. The drunk seemed to read their thoughts, because he suddenly gave them a crooked grin and lifted his cup. Emptying it, he waved it toward the muscular cook and cried, "More of your elixir of happiness, Yashi! I feel the blue demons coming on again."

Blue demons? It crossed Tora's mind that the man might be one of those soothsayers who sell their spells in the marketplace. Some of them claimed to be wizards who could call up demons whenever it pleased them. He eyed the drunk warily.

The cook glanced over, took in the two newcomers, and shouted back, "You've had enough! I'm not putting you up again. And your master'll have your hide if you spend another night in the gutter and get killed."

This ridiculous threat reassured Tora. The man was only a servant after all.

The elderly man, however, glared at the cook and rose, swaying a little. "My good man," he said with enormous dignity, "I resent your inference as much as your tone. I'll have you know I am no servant. Indeed, my education makes me the equal of the gentleman lucky enough to enjoy my services at the moment." He then spoiled the gesture by belching and tipping backward so suddenly that Genba had to jump up to catch him.

"Thank you, my humble friend," the man muttered, feeling about in his sleeves. "A touch of dizziness. It is a warning I recognize."

"A warning of what?" asked Tora.

"Ah," said the man, glancing across at him from watery eyes, while still feeling about in his robe. "You and your friend here are both too young to understand the sorrows of an academician come down in the world. You have not lived long and painfully in a country inimical to intellectual pursuits. What I meant was this: I always get dizzy when the blue demons are imminent. And now I seem to have misplaced my money, too."

Tora cast a glance around the room for the blue demons, but saw only ordinary people who were more interested in their food than the odd man at their table. "Where are these devils? I don't see them."

Genba chuckled. "He means his sad thoughts for which he drinks. Perhaps you would care to join us, sir," he said to the elderly man, pulling out a string of coppers. The elderly man bowed his acceptance and Genba waved down a waiter. "Here, bring enough wine and food for the three of us!"

"Most kind of you to help a stranger in distress, sir," said the man. "Allow me to introduce myself. My name is Harada, doctor of mathematics, but at present estate manager for my colleague, Professor Yasaburo, in Kohata. May I know your honorable name and dwelling so that I may repay the debt?"

"I'm Genba and my friend is Tora. But what are a few coppers between fellow visitors to the capital? We hate to eat and drink alone."

Harada bowed, expressed himself charmed to make their acquaintance, and offered himself as a guide to the local attractions, which he had just begun to describe when the waiter returned with a jug of wine, two more cups, and a large platter of pickled radish. Mr. Harada poured, spilling only a little, and Genba sampled the radish.

"So you're really just an overseer of a farm?" Tora asked, still thinking about the blue devils. "I mean, you don't tell fortunes and call up spirits on the side?"

The cook shouted across, "The only spirits he calls up are in his cup. He's a hard drinker."

Harada, far from taking offense, said, "On the contrary, my friend of the steaming pots. Drinking is the easiest thing I do. The world rests heavily on my shoulders and the worries of my days fray at my nerves."

"And the wine makes the world go round till you're too dizzy to see straight," grunted the cook, ladling out a large platterful of steamed chunks of fish and vegetables. "See," he said to Tora and Genba, passing the bowl to the waiter with a jerk of the head toward their table, "it's like this: When he's out of sorts, he drinks. After the first cup he feels more like himself. So he has another and now feels like a new man. But the new man wants to drink, too, and so he goes on drinking till, pretty soon, he feels like a babe ... bawling and crawling all the way home!"

Laughter greeted these witticisms. When Harada protested, "I drink only to calm myself," one of the guests shouted, "Yeah! Last night he got so calm he couldn't move! Ho ho ho!"

"Fools!" muttered Harada. He pushed away disdainfully the bowl of fish and rice the waiter placed before him and instead refilled his cup from the pitcher. "The Chinese poets understood about wine!" he said, holding up the cup and squinting at it. "It frees a man's genius from the shackles of physical existence." He emptied the cup. " 'I will fill my cup and never let it go dry,' said Po Chü-i. And Li Po said, 'I can love wine without shame before the gods.' Li Po knew there's no point in explaining this to a sober man. Poets must nourish their souls, not their bellies." He glanced around the table and saw that both Tora and Genba had their noses deep in their bowls of fish stew. His nose twitched, and he eyed his own bowl thoughtfully for a moment, then reached for it.

Genba was emptying and refilling his own bowl with such speed and complete enjoyment that his lip-smacking and belching attracted the pleased attention of the cook, who promptly sent along a heaping platter of steamed eel, compliments of the house.

"So you're a poet?" Tora asked their companion. "I thought you just said that you manage a farm."

"Not a farm. An estate." Harada looked at him blearily. "You may not be aware of it, young man," he said with a fruity belch, "but poets have never enjoyed a regular income without a generous p-patron. P-professor Yasaburo, my old friend and classmate, is the closest I could find to a p-p... magnanimous p-erson, and he makes use of my many other skills as he has need of them." Taking another gulp from his cup, he belched again, and added, "At the present time, you behold in me an ambassador of good will, a bearer of happy tidings, a p-purveyor of the substance which makes even the dull p-pragmatists happy. In short, I have completed an errand of mercy." With a great sigh, he folded his arms on the table, laid his head on them, and went to sleep.

Tora, who had listened with only half an ear, now turned to Genba. To his surprise, Genba had stopped eating. He sat, slack-jawed, staring past Tora's shoulder, an expression of stunned amazement on his face. The platter of eels in front of him was barely touched, and he still held his chopsticks with a juicy morsel suspended halfway to his open mouth.

Tora looked to see what had shocked Genba into immobility. The restaurant was full of people. Behind them six men, of the ordinary riverfront variety, were exchanging stories over their wine. Near a pillar, several women were eating fish stew and chattering among themselves. Against the back wall, an old man presided over a table filled with members of his family. And near them a husband and wife were engaged in an argument. Tora could not see anything likely to cause that look in Genba's eyes. He reached across to take the chopsticks from Genba's rigid fingers. "What are you staring at?"

Genba jerked. "Huh? Oh!" He blushed scarlet. "See the young lady over there? She's the most stunning creature I've ever seen."

Tora scanned the women. Pretty girls, he thought, surprised and pleased that Genba finally seemed to take an interest in the opposite sex. He must mean the pert one with the look of a playful kitten. But the others weren't bad, either. An older woman presided over them, their chaperone or perhaps an auntie. Tora took in her size and blinked. She was enormous, towering over the girls and taking up the space of two men. Big shoulders, a huge jutting bosom, and bulging arms, all covered in shiny black silk, and a round, red-cheeked face topped with coils of hair which were decorated with red silk ribbons dangling coyly down on either side. Tora almost laughed out loud at the sight of her. No wonder she was fat; she was eating with a speed which astonished even him, and he was familiar with Genba's appetite. Her large fat hand holding the chopsticks darted quickly among the many bowls in front of her, picking up a tidbit here and a pickle there, the small finger extended daintily, the red lips closing with little smacking sounds around each morsel or dipping quickly toward the rim of a soup bowl to suck up broth and fish alike. He turned to Genba. "Pretty girls, but look at that madam! I've never seen a woman eat like that. No wonder she's as fat as Hotei!"

184

Genba stared at him. "What do you mean?" he asked, frowning. "She's the most handsome female I ever laid eyes on. Look at that rosy skin, the pretty mouth, and that fine body! And she eats most elegantly. Daintily, like a lady! Which is more than you can say about her companions. I never could understand what you see in those bony little bits you seem to prefer."

Tora gaped. "Have you lost your mind?" he asked. "That's some whore grown too fat to get customers, so now she runs the house, taking out her girls for their evening rice. Leave her alone! She'd make short work of an innocent like you and take you for every copper, having a good laugh with her girls afterward."

Genba got up, his face like thunder. "Good night!" he growled.

"Where are you going?" Tora cried, pointing to the uneaten food. "We aren't finished, and we haven't even started asking questions."

"You can do your own investigating," Genba said over his shoulder, and headed for the table of the women. Tora looked after him in stunned surprise. This was not like Genba, who was normally shy around women. But there he was, bowing to the fat woman, and then to the girls around the table. The girls wore the heavy white makeup of street women and clearly were not averse to male company, for Genba took a seat next to a slender girl whose eyebrows had been plucked and painted high on her forehead, in the manner of certain court ladies or actors playing women's roles. Tora shook his head. Genba would be sorry. He made a move to follow, feeling it his duty to protect his companion from the wiles of the professional women of the quarter. But when he took a step toward them, Genba looked up and scowled so ferociously that Tora quickly sat back down. Very well! Let him learn his lesson, then, he thought, and turned his attention to the food.

Harada was snoring softly. Tora caught the cook's eye. "What will you do about him?" he asked.

The cook gave the drunken man a glance. "Him? Nothing. He can stay. He's not a bad sort, comes to town on business for his master, takes care of whatever it is, then comes here to drink away whatever money he brought with him. As he spends it here, I feel obliged to look out for him. In the morning I'll put him on the road home."

Tora took a sip of his wine. "I'm told you see quite a few actors here when they're in town," he said to the cook.

"Sure. Some are back already. Getting ready to put on shows for the winter festivals and the driving out of the evil spirits at the end of the year."

"Ever hear of a troupe called Uemon's Players?"

"Uemon? Sure. Everybody knows of him. Mind you, he's getting old, but his people are good. They even get asked to perform for the good people." He scanned the room. "Danjuro, his lead actor, is really good. He used to come, but I haven't laid eyes on him since they got back from their tour. I guess him and his girl Ohisa got married at last and set up house."

"Would you know where I might find this Uemon?"

The cook hesitated, looking Tora over. "Why are you looking for him?"

Tora said, "Personal interest, you might say." He stroked his mustache and winked. "There's a very pretty girl in that troupe."

The cook suddenly became distant. "If you're after one of Uemon's girls, you can forget it. He's a respectable man and his people are strictly class. Better go talk to one of the aunties in the quarter."

Tora smirked. "Come, now! Maybe he doesn't know everything the youngsters get up to. I happen to know better. You ever meet any of them?"

The cook grinned. "Sure. They come in pretty regular for a meal or some wine. In fact, since you've met them before, you must've seen the girls with Miss Plumblossom. They were here when you came in."

Tora cursed himself for having missed his chance. Now he would have to follow them. "Well, where do they live when they're in town?"

"You're pretty persistent, aren't you?" said the cook, narrowing his eyes. "I don't know what you're up to, but you're lying. Maybe you're a rapist or the slasher. Maybe you're a constable. Come to think, there's something official-looking about you. Anyway, I can't help you."

Won't is more likely, Tora thought. He wanted to deny being either a rapist or a constable, but knew it was too late to come up with another convincing tale. Places like the Abode of the River Fairies, though not precisely hangouts for criminals, were sensitive about protecting their clientele. He sighed and looked around for Genba, but the table where he had sat was now empty. Genba had left him stuck with the bill for their meal and Harada's.

Outside, night had fallen with the abruptness of the season. Tora pulled up his collar and looked up and down the street. There was no sign of Genba. The wind still blew from the dark mountains and whistled through the alleys which led away from the river. The lanterns in front of the businesses swayed and bobbed with every gust. Their feeble lights were reflected in the dark, slow-moving waters of the Kamo and resembled madly dancing fireflies. A few customers hurried past, their collars raised around their ears and their arms buried in their deep sleeves.

Tora shrugged resignedly. He had little choice but to try his luck in some of the other eateries and wineshops.

An hour later, half-frozen and discouraged, he entered a ramshackle dive near the end of the quarter, and here his luck changed. The host of this dubious establishment was Tora's age, but unlike Tora incredibly ill-kempt. His long hair and beard were matted with dirt, and he wore nothing but a pair of stained cotton pants, held precariously in place by a knotted rope tied below his hairy paunch, and a dingy cotton shirt which was too small for him and hung open in front. He looked more like a street ruffian than a legitimate innkeeper. And apparently he was not only careless about his appearance, but also foulmouthed.

When Tora heard the first string of colorful curses, his face lit up. He joined the three barefooted laborers who were leaning on the counter and cried, "By the bare ass of a monkey! A man from Tsukuba!"

His host eyed Tora's neat blue robe. "Yeah?" he said. "And who are you, then?"

"Why, you filthy piece of ox dung, you pail of cat's piss, you dog's turd, you stinking pile of bear's vomit! Are you too stupid to recognize your neighbors?"

The host's dirty face relaxed. "Well, fry my balls!" he grunted. "You do sound like it. What village?"

"Ohori."

"No!" the host cried with delighted surprise. "I was raised across the river from Ohori. My old man and me fished the river and sold the catch in your village. You bastards used to throw rocks at us from the shore. Me and my buddy came across one night and let the water out of all your cisterns."

Tora guffawed. "You missed us. Half the village had to squeeze into our bath the next day. Say, what brought you here?"

"The cursed army. I was a kid when they grabbed me, the filthy bastards. I ended up here. How about you?"

Tora's smile faded. He did not like to remember the day when the soldiers had come to their farm. He had never seen his parents again. "Me, too," he said casually.

His host gave a knowing nod. "Hard times, but you look prosperous enough now. Lucky devil! The gods've been good to you. Me, I'm slowly starving." He slapped his bare belly and chuckled.

Tora laughed. "I've had some fighting, a little trouble, and a lot of luck. The name's Tora, by the way."

"Hah! The tiger, eh?" The fat man nodded sagely. Everyone knew the value of a pseudonym when you had to leave the military service abruptly. "Me, I'm not so fierce. They call me Ushi because I look like a big old clumsy bull." He reached under the counter and brought up a pitcher, poured two cups of wine, and pushed one toward Tora. The three laborers looked sadly into their empty cups and swallowed. "All right! All right!" the Bull said, and refilled their cups from an open barrel. "There. It's on the house! To celebrate this auspicious meeting with my countryman."

The three grinned, bowed, and tossed back the raw liquor.

Tora tasted. Ushi's private brew was strong but excellent; the fire it lit in his belly was welcome after the cold night outside. He raised the cup again and emptied it in one slow smooth gulp. "You live better than you think, Bull," he said with a grin, and belched.

Ushi's laugh rumbled and shook his belly like jellied bean curd. "So what sort of work do you do? You got your own business?"

"No. I'm in service, but my master appreciates my talents and treats me well."

"Ah! Lucky dog! A roof over your head, fancy clothes, three squares guaranteed, and money to spend." Ushi shook his head in envy, and returned to the past. "Say, speaking of strong wine, you ever get a taste of that stuff the monks used to brew in the temple on the Tone River? They called it mountain berry juice or some such and sold it in all the villages up and down the river. Strongest berries I ever tasted!"

Tora remembered it, and much more besides. After an exchange of reminiscences, he managed to ask about Uemon.

"Uemon? Too proud to set foot in my place," said the host, making a face. "I hear they go to Miss Plumblossom to practice. You after some girl? Better watch your step with the lady, my friend, and keep your hands to yourself. Miss Plumblossom don't tolerate low manners. She's a famous acrobat and served at court."

Tora did not believe that for a moment. Females in the theatrical profession had a very poor reputation. Many made their living with prostitution between engagements. He could well imagine what passed in Miss Plumblossom's establishment.

The Bull reached for the pitcher again.

"No, thanks," said Tora. "I've got to go. It's getting late, and I've got my bowl of rice to earn like the rest of you. Just tell me how to find this Plumblossom's place, and I'll be off."

The Bull frowned. "Say, you're not on the lookout for a bed partner for your master, by any chance? You'd better try the Willow Quarter. Or does he prefer men?"

Tora's arm shot out, grabbed the rope holding up Ushi's pants, and jerked forward hard. The fat belly hit the counter, and Ushi gasped and cursed. Still holding the man by his belt, Tora put his face next to Ushi's and snarled, "You filthy-minded piece of offal! What do you think I am, a pimp for a pervert?"

"Sorry, brother," whined the fat man. "I didn't mean it. Let go!"

Tora slowly released his hold. "Well, you've got your nerve," he grumbled, "assuming such a thing of a fellow countryman. I'd rather bite my tongue than ask you how you got out of the army."

The host blanched a little and said nervously, "No need to explain, brother. Whatever it is you're doing, I wish you luck! We all have our secrets. Just remember not to offend Miss Plumblossom. She's been keeping her eyes open since the trouble and will have your balls if you so much as smile at her girls. Her place is behind the Temple of the War God, two streets back from the river. You can't miss it."

"What trouble?" Tora asked.

"You haven't heard? Some bastard's been cutting up whores. Miss Plumblossom took one of 'em in. They say she looks worse than a monkey, now her nose is gone and her mouth's been rearranged. What a woman that Miss Plumblossom is! What a soft heart!" The Bull cast up his eyes and sighed in admiration. Tora thought it more likely that the lady needed a cheap maid.

One of the laborers suddenly found his tongue and cried, "A devil did that! The devils are loose at night. One of 'em tried to do the same thing to me. I only got away because I have an amulet and called on the Buddha." He reached into his ragged jacket and pulled out a filthy, odorous bag which was tied around his neck.

Tora suppressed a shudder. "Thanks for the wine, Bull, but I'd better go. Looks like the streets aren't too safe after dark."

Outside, the wind caught at his robe, and something moist and soft touched his face. He blinked against the light of a swinging lantern. In its golden aura danced the first snowflakes of the year.

He found Miss Plumblossom's establishment easily enough, though it did not look much like a brothel. The building was a long, low structure like a warehouse. It had solid plaster walls and a wooden roof held in place with large rocks. He stood for a few minutes deciphering the sign above the door. Even his untutored eye saw that the lettering was elegant. "Training Hall of Celestial Grace. Miss Plumblossom, Proprietess." What a joke! It certainly sounded like no brothel he had ever visited. Light came from behind the bars of two small windows high up, and he could hear muffled thumps, shouts, and grunts. Perhaps the place offered some novel sexual pleasures, and he was definitely not averse to learning new things.

Tora grinned and applied the wooden clapper vigorously to the brass gong which swung from a hook next to the door. It emitted a pleasant clear sound, and the door was flung open from inside.

He stepped into a dim entry. Through a half-open inner door, he could see a segment of a brightly lit room which had a wooden floor with some thick grass mats on it. Suddenly some female flitted past the opening. She seemed to be naked. Then another girl passed and the first one returned with a bounce. Tora swallowed hard. He was by no means easily impressed by the sexual pleasures normally available in the capital, but now he wondered what services these two might be expected to render and felt warm under the collar.

A cracked voice broke into his erotic imaginings. "How may we serve the gentleman?"

Tora took his eye off the cracked door and looked down. An ancient man was closing the outer door against the snow and peered up at him.

"I was told," Tora croaked, "that Miss Plumblossom ... er ... entertains ... that is, actors come here from time to time?"

"So they do. And other gentlemen, too. Miss Plumblossom's name is well-known in the profession. And what might the gentleman's preference be? Something acrobatic? Perhaps the gentleman prefers to engage in the masculine sport of swordplay? Or halberds?"

Tora glanced toward the lit room. He could imagine the acrobatics of lovemaking, but swords and halberds? Perhaps this research would necessitate certain expenditures. "Would it be all right to have a look before I decide?" he asked the old man.

"Certainly. Please enter!" The old man flung the inner door wide and preceded him. He hobbled to a bench against the wall next to the entrance and sat down, inviting Tora to join him. "I shall be happy to answer the gentleman's questions," he offered.

Tora stopped just inside the room, his jaw sagging with surprise. He had expected to walk into a small reception area where the girls displayed themselves to the customers. In fact he was in a huge training hall. And he saw now that the tumbling young women wore loincloths and that they practiced with young men in similar undress. The agile youngsters were working out on the mats, bouncing, rolling, jumping over and under each other, the men tossing the women into the air and catching them. Their movements were so skillful and continuous that there seemed to be nothing but bobbing breasts and twisting buttocks in sight. Tora slowly backed toward the bench and sank down, his fascinated gaze on the acrobats. After a while, he managed to separate the flying bodies into three young men and two young women and realized his mistake. This was no brothel, but a training hall for acrobats and entertainers.

There were others in the room, more conservatively dressed. In one corner, an old man sat cross-legged on the floor, beating a small drum, while two very pretty young women in silk dresses swayed in elegant dance steps. In another corner, two men were engaged in a mock sword fight, accompanying their lunges and feints with hideous shouts. Tora shook his head at such unmilitary behavior, and then looked toward the back of the room. A wrestling bout seemed in progress, though his view of the contestants was blocked by some onlookers. Then he got his next surprise. A large chair, like an abbot's, had been placed on a raised dais and on it sat the fat woman from the restaurant, all glossy black silk and red ribbons.

Tora gasped, "Who the devil's that?"

"Miss Plumblossom. Giving some pointers to the wrestlers. Very fond of wrestling, is our Miss Plumblossom. Never misses a contest, though she's an acrobat herself, of course."

Tora was trying to digest that piece of information when Miss Plumblossom suddenly leaned forward and cried, "Open your hands, Master Denchichi! No punching! Ah! Very good, Master Genba! Haven't seen that particular hold for years."

At first Tora thought he had misheard, but just then the onlookers started applauding and he could see the wrestlers. And there stood Genba, stripped to his loincloth and grinning inanely at Miss Plumblossom, while his opponent picked himself up off the floor.

TWELVE

The Prisoner

Tamako rarely entered her husband's room while he was at work, and Akitada glanced up in surprise from the family accounts when he heard her voice. She hovered at the door, after saying softly, "Forgive me for interrupting you, but there is a small matter on which I would like your advice."

Seimei rose from his papers, bowed to both of them, and left the room. Akitada looked after him unhappily. Their relationship had been strained since he had discovered that Seimei had concealed his parentage from him all these years. Seimei was aware of his coolness and bore it with a sad resignation, but Akitada chafed under the bitter resentment bottled up inside himself. He wished he could talk about it with Tamako, but with her fondness for Seimei she would urge him to put the matter from his mind. Easier said than done!

He watched her sit down across from him. She looked very elegant in the dark blue silk robe which showed only the narrowest band of her white silk undergown at the wrists and neck. When she had adjusted her trailing skirts and raised her eyes to his, he gave her a smile of affection. "The gown suits you," he said softly. "Even better than the one I took off you last night." He watched the rosy blush rise from her neck to her face, wondering why she did not smile. He caressed her face with his eyes, urging it into joy. Her eyes were clear and steady, like shining jewels set into the translucent skin, but the soft, pink lower lip trembled. He cocked his head. "I think," he murmured, "you must be growing more beautiful with every year."

That finally produced a fleeting smile. "What nonsense you talk," she said, but reached across his desk to touch his hand affectionately. "This is not about us. It concerns your sister."

"Ah." Which one, Akiko or Yoshiko? Akiko had been on his mind almost constantly since he had spoken with her stepson. But he knew that Tamako meant Yoshiko. "Is something wrong?"

Tamako nodded, looking at her hands, which lay neatly folded in her lap. "I am afraid it will sound as though I am spying on your sister, which I am not," she said with a sigh. "Even though I am worried about her, I do not keep a watch over her. Still, living in the same house, we can hardly avoid meeting. I noticed that your sister left the house every day at the same time, always between the hours of the monkey and the rooster. She left before sunset and returned after dark, just before the evening rice. And she carried a basket each time."

Akitada sat up. The day he had returned from the painter Noami, Yoshiko had come home just before he did, and she had held a basket. An empty basket, though she had claimed to have been to the market. "Have you asked her about it?"

"How could I? She never volunteered an explanation and it is none of my business. She is a grown woman, and this is her home. But today, just a little while ago, the same thing happened again. Only this time, she rushed past me without a greeting and ran to her room. I wondered if she was ill and followed. I stood outside her door and heard her weeping. Oh, Akitada, she was weeping dreadfully hard. I was afraid to intrude, but what if she needs help? What should I do?"

Akitada got to his feet and started toward the door.

"Wait, Akitada," cried Tamako, getting up also. "Don't rush in! You may make things worse. This is clearly a private matter. Perhaps, if anyone is going to burst in on her grief, it had better be me."

She was right, he thought, suddenly fearful. Something had happened, wherever she had been. Or it might be some female ailment. Or—heaven forbid—rape. The thought of some man doing violence to Yoshiko made him clench his hands. "I suppose you are right," he said. "Go to her, then. Only come back and let me know."

Tamako nodded and left.

Akitada sat back down and stared sightlessly at his accounts. His troubles seemed to be multiplying when they should have been at an end. He was finally free of a lifetime of blaming himself for the dislike shown to him by the woman he had believed to be his mother. His father no longer was the unfeeling authoritarian of his memory. He had come back to his home, truly his now, and was taking care of his own family as his father had done, at the desk his father had used. His career for once seemed secure. Yet peace and contentment escaped him. Happiness was slippery as an eel. Just when you thought you had a solid grip on it, it twisted this way and that, and was gone again. Oh, Yoshiko!

Seimei, his other point of discontent, came back in. "A visitor, sir," he announced with a bow. Seimei had become very formal lately.

The visitor turned out to be Kobe, and his arrival at this moment was anything but welcome. The superintendent strode in stiffly, nodding instead of bowing, and announced abruptly, "I must speak with you privately."

Akitada glanced at Seimei, who asked, "Shall I bring wine or tea before the gentlemen begin?"

"Nothing for me." Kobe stood waiting impatiently for Seimei to leave the room. When the door had closed behind Akitada's secretary, he waited, then walked quietly to the door and jerked it open. The corridor was empty. He grunted and slammed the door shut again with such force that the panels shuddered. Akitada watched with rising anger as Kobe returned and sat down stiffly across from him.

"My secretary," Akitada said coldly, "is not the kind of person who listens at doors. I gather from your manner you bring bad news of some sort."

Kobe stared at him for a moment. "Unpleasant for you, at any rate. I have discovered your little plot. How dare you compromise my investigation by slipping your minions into the prison? You will immediately produce your accomplice. She is under arrest. It is regrettable that I cannot do the same with you because of your position. However, I shall make an official report of the affair and protest in the strongest terms against your abuse of power." Fists clenched on either knee, he leaned forward and glared at Akitada. "I once thought better of you, by heaven, than that you would resort to sending a woman where you are forbidden to go. This time you have gone too far, Sugawara. This time I shall do my damnedest to put a permanent stop to your meddling."

Akitada wondered what new trouble was brewing. Kobe appeared furiously angry about some incident at the jail. It was all a mistake, of course, regrettable because he had hoped for a congenial discussion of his discoveries at the temple. Kobe looked angry enough to mean his threats. He said, "I haven't the faintest idea what you are talking about."

Kobe's face darkened and he struck the desk. Boxes, water containers, and ink stones jumped and rattled. "Don't lie to me!" he shouted. "You know precisely what this is about. Today we followed her, and she walked into this house not an hour ago."

Yoshiko! The answer came to Akitada unbidden, unwanted, and dreaded. His certainty was linked to a memory of a woman with a basket, familiar to him even at a distance, walking away from the prison where Nagaoka's brother was being held. What had Yoshiko done?

Kobe snarled, "I see you know what I am talking about. Call her! I want to speak to her. I don't care who she is to you—your wife, for all I care. After she tells me everything that's been going on, she will be under arrest."

Akitada felt himself go cold with fear. He knew very well that Kobe could carry out his threat, and he also knew the man well enough to fear his temper. He must try to find the right approach to defuse the other man's rage.

"You are mistaken, Superintendent," he said as haughtily as he could manage. "I am still completely in the dark about what you accuse me of, except that it must have something to do with Nagaoka's brother. Considering your threats against me and mine, I must remind you that it is customary to make certain of one's facts before laying accusations against persons of rank. I have only recently returned from—"

Kobe interrupted, "No, my lord, not even your fine record in the north is going to protect you from these charges. Flagrant abuse of power and perversion of the due process of justice will disqualify you from all future administrative positions."

For all his bluster, Kobe seemed a bit less certain of himself. Akitada considered his position. In spite of a fine record up north, Kobe could make trouble for him here. Akitada still had some enemies at court, and while he had been very successful, he had not always followed the rules. A charge of high-handedness in the capital so soon after his return could be used against him.

But at the moment Akitada was less concerned about his career. He was innocent. No, it was the danger to Yoshiko which worried him. In her present state, she could not handle what Kobe had in mind for her. He tried another tactic.

"I must remind you that my family is mourning the recent death of my mother," he said, keeping his voice low and firm. "My wife and son only arrived a few days ago, hours before my mother died. The funeral is barely over. The only women in this house besides my wife are my sister and a cook and two maids. I hardly think that any of them is likely to be involved in a murder case."

Kobe stared at him. It was impossible to guess what was going through his mind. Akitada knew better than to think he would now apologize and depart. What he wished to avoid at all costs was that Yoshiko would be dragged off and subjected to interrogation. Even women were stripped by constables and beaten with bamboo whips if the investigating judge or officer was not satisfied with their account. He must hope that Kobe would hesitate to inflict this indignity on a member of his family.

The superintendent finally relaxed his angry posture. "I forgot," he said, looking away. "I did hear that Lady Sugawara had died. Your mother, you say?"

Akitada nodded, keeping his face bleak and expressionless.

"Yes. Hmm. Sorry to hear it. Come to think of it, there was a taboo tablet at the gate. Hmm."

Akitada waited.

Kobe sat undecided for a moment, his hands now relaxed, the fingers drumming on his knees. Then he grumbled, "Er, the situation is awkward, and I regret my poor timing, but you must see that I had to investigate this matter immediately. Repeated visits of an outsider to a prisoner about to come to trial very likely will compromise the case. I must be in a position to give a full explanation to the judge or I, along with the people who were responsible for the prisoner, may be dismissed from office. I won't allow that to happen just to observe the proprieties."

Akitada nodded again. "That is understandable. Your mind is on your duties, as mine is on family matters. We must find a compromise. Perhaps you had better tell me what happened and what precisely you suspect us of. How many visits were there?"

Kobe's high color faded. He answered in a normal tone. "The female has come every single day since the time you and I met outside Nagaoka's house. Always in the evening."

Akitada thought back. Had he mentioned the Nagaoka case to Yoshiko? Yes, he recalled sharing some of its frustrations with her over dinner that day. And she had taken the brother's side. A bit too vehemently, perhaps? Did Yoshiko know the suspect—what was his name?—Kojiro? He asked Kobe, "How did she get in?"

"She claimed to be his wife, bringing him his dinner. It was not until yesterday that I heard of it and told the fool of a guard that Kojiro's not married. Idiot!" Kobe angrily blew through his nostrils.

That explained the empty basket! No doubt it was exactly what she had done, taken the prisoner food. He was not about to have Kobe probe into this mystery before he himself knew what was going on, and said, "Look, Superintendent, I cannot at the moment explain why this mysterious woman should have come to my house, and I shall certainly try to find out what is going on. But under the present circumstances, I must ask you not to trouble my family. If you agree, I shall come to you as soon as I have information. Tomorrow morning, early. For the present, I can only repeat that I knew nothing of this."

Kobe frowned and was about to make some comment. Akitada added quickly, "I do, however, have some information I discovered on another visit to the Eastern Mountain Temple. Only my family's arrival and my mother's death have intervened."

Kobe looked interested. "Oh? Well, what is it?"

Akitada outlined his visit to the temple and his conversations with the gatekeeper Eikan and the novice Ancho. He explained the mechanism of the lock and his theory that the murder could have been committed by someone other than the prisoner.

Kobe sat frowning as he digested the information. When Akitada finished, he pointed out that this discovery did not clear Kojiro. Still Akitada's reasonable and cooperative manner had not only calmed the stormy waters, but given Kobe something to think about. He even looked slightly ashamed of himself when he said, "It is unfortunate that the death of your mother has intervened. I am pressed for time, or I would not insist on your looking into the other matter right away. Shall I expect you tomorrow morning, then, at the hour of the snake? I'll be at the eastern prison." Kobe rose.

Akitada stood also. They bowed formally to each other, and the superintendent left, closing the door almost gently after himself.

Now that his fear for Yoshiko's safety had been allayed, Akitada could not remember when he had last felt so angry with anyone. How could she have done this to him? He tried to control his fury before going to his sister's room, but the memory of Kobe's charges and the thought of what lay ahead the next day upset him anew. He would have it out with her now.

He entered Yoshiko's room without knocking. The two women sat huddled together, Yoshiko weeping softly and Tamako with her arm around his sister's shoulders. They both looked up at him, Tamako clearly put out by his sudden unannounced arrival.

Akitada ignored the unspoken reproach and said to Yoshiko, "I just had a most unpleasant visit from the superintendent of police."

Yoshiko gasped and turned white.

"It appears," Akitada continued, "that you have been paying regular visits to a prisoner who is about to come to trial. Superintendent Kobe assumes that I arranged these visits in order to communicate with the man after being warned away from him. He intends to file an official complaint."

The two women cried out together, protesting vehemently. Akitada raised his hand and snapped, "One at a time." He glared at Tamako. "And I believe I was speaking to Yoshiko."

Tamako flushed and bowed stiffly. Yoshiko rose and came forward, kneeling before him, her head bowed.

"I beg your pardon for having offended you, Elder Brother," she said, her voice catching. "I acted most selfishly and foolishly and I have brought shame and embarrassment upon my elder brother and this family. Whatever amends I can make, I shall gladly perform. My rash behavior has already brought grievous pain to Kojiro—" She broke off and fought for composure. After a moment, during which Akitada ignored a pleading gesture from Tamako, she continued, "When you told me that Kojiro had been arrested for murder, I had to go to him. Kojiro and I . . . we were once very close . . . many years ago." She hesitated to glance quickly up at Akitada's face. "He is the man who wished to marry me. I know I should have asked your permission before going, but I was afraid you would not give it. And I could not ask Mother." She dabbed at her tear-stained face.

It was worse than he had feared. "You are quite right," he snapped. "I would certainly not have allowed a sister of mine to masquerade as a common slattern carrying food to her criminal husband. I assume, of course, that no marriage has taken place between you and this man, formal or otherwise?"

"Of course not." Yoshiko flushed and raised her head proudly. "Both Kojiro and I have behaved with the utmost propriety. He wished to marry me. I accepted, and he immediately spoke to Mother, who refused his offer with many cruel remarks. We never saw each other again until now."

Akitada found her calm admission infuriating. "Your behavior, then as now, was reprehensible," he said coldly. "He is the brother of a local merchant, a mere farmer himself, and certainly not a suitable acquaintance, let alone husband, for a daughter of the Sugawaras. You had no right to accept an offer of marriage, or to encourage it."

Yoshiko was looking down at her hands. She was quite calm and firm. "You were away at the time and you never met Kojiro. It is not well to judge a man one does not know. Master Confucius teaches us to be kind to everyone and to seek out the good in men. Kojiro is a good man."

At first Akitada thought he had misheard. Yoshiko had never spoken this way to him, or anyone, before. Had she really dared reprimand him? After her behavior? After all the trouble she had caused? He felt his anger begin to boil over and clenched his hands together behind his back to keep from striking her. Through his teeth, he said, "I have no wish to discuss your shameful past with this man any further. I barely prevented your arrest tonight. Unless I can convince Kobe of your innocence tomorrow morning, you will find yourself in a cell—in the same jail as your lover. And you, too, will be stripped of your clothes, in front of male prison guards, and beaten with bamboo rods until your back is lacerated from shoulders to buttocks or until you confess to having plotted with me to get Kojiro's charges dismissed. You will be asked about the lies I told you to suggest to Kojiro, and after a while you will tell them what they want to hear."

Both Tamako and Yoshiko stared at him in horror.

"No," cried Yoshiko. "I would never say what isn't true. I would die first."

Tamako said, "They would not dare lay a hand on your sister."

"Don't be a fool!" Akitada stormed at her. Then he looked from one to the other. They were well-brought-up young women, belonging to the "good people," their skin white and soft because they did not have to work for their food, their hair long and glossy because they had leisure to brush it. What did either of them know of the extremities of existence? He said harshly, "You know nothing of such things, but I do. As part of my duties I have had to witness such interrogations, and once or twice in my life I myself have come to know what it is like to go beyond caring about anything but the unbearable agony."

Tamako paled and bowed her head. "Forgive me, Akitada," she murmured.

But Yoshiko's stubborn chin was raised. "I am as certain as I can be that you did not dishonor your name on those occasions," she said, her eyes flashing. "But I, too, am Sugawara and, I tell you, I should rather die than submit."

"Keep in mind that your lover will undergo the same treatment as you. Will he also be willing to die to protect your family?"

"Yes. Kojiro has already suffered through one interrogation without telling them about me," Yoshiko said proudly. "It was because of me that he was beaten today. His guard told me when I got to the prison."

"That was the reason Yoshiko was so distraught when she came home," said Tamako.

"You were followed," Akitada informed his sister.

Yoshiko nodded. "Yes. I am very sorry to have caused you trouble, Akitada," she said. "And I am even more sorry for Kojiro. He has suffered for my sake. But I am not sorry that I love him. Once he is cleared of the murder charge, we shall be married."

"What?" Akitada ran his hands through his hair in frustration. Was there no way he could assert his authority in his own family? First the trouble with Akiko, and now Yoshiko, too! It must be their mother's blood which made them so unmanageable, so bent on causing mischief. He shouted, "You will do nothing of the sort. I forbid it! He is not a suitable husband for a sister of mine."

Yoshiko was quite pale now, but her chin was still up and she looked him straight in the eyes. "I am only your half sister. You owe me nothing. Having brought disgrace upon you, it will be best if I leave this house. I shall go to my sister. Toshikage will speak to Superintendent Kobe to explain to him that you knew nothing about my relationship with Kojiro. Then, if the superintendent wishes to arrest me, at least he will not need to come to your house to do so."

Their eyes locked. The pain of her rejection twisted like a knife deep in his stomach. Belatedly appalled at his treatment of her, he stammered, "You cannot do that . . . why Akiko? . . . or Toshikage? What can they do for you that I cannot do? Have I not always stood by you? By both of you? Why are you doing this to me, Yoshiko?"

Yoshiko's eyes faltered. She murmured, "I am sorry, Akitada, but I have given my word to Kojiro and I cannot break it."

Seimei's phrase! Everyone in his family seemed eager to pledge allegiance to others! Who would desert him next? Staring bleakly down at his sister, Akitada shook his head, turned on his heel, and left the room.

He did not share his wife's bed that night but spent restless, guilt-ridden hours in his father's room, trying to find answers to his family troubles. Tamako came once, perhaps in an effort to make peace, but he said, "Not now. I must think what to do." She inclined her head and left silently, returning much later with his bedding, which she spread for him without a word. He felt intensely lonely after she had left again.

Sometime during the night it began to snow. When the shadows of the room began to close in on him, Akitada threw back the shutters onto a pitch-black night. It was cold, but there was little wind now. The light from his lamp caught the large flakes as they fell slowly, drifting a little on unseen air currents, spinning in circles before floating gently to the ground. Shimmering like moving stars, they seemed to arrive from a void beyond, materializing only within the reach of his study light. The nearer shrubs and trees showed dimly with faint white highlights, but the gravel and the veranda boards were solid sparkling silver. Only the surface of the fishpond lay like a black mirror reflecting a black universe beyond.

Akitada stood for a long time, watching the mysterious arrival of the snow, before he closed the shutters and returned to his bed.

When he woke the next morning, the blackness outside had

changed to a uniform gray. The snow had stopped, but heavy low clouds seemed to brush the stark treetops, and the light was so faint that the snow on the ground and on the roof of his house looked dull like unbleached silk.

Akitada dressed quickly in a dark robe, his court hat with the taboo pendant, leggings, and boots. Seimei knocked and entered with a bow and murmured a greeting, bringing a dish of rice gruel and a pot of hot water for tea. He asked for instructions for the day.

Akitada sipped his tea. "Do what you like! Carry on with the accounts," he said. "I have to go out this morning."

Seimei hesitated, looking unhappy, then bowed and left.

In spite of the early hour, Kobe was waiting at the prison when Akitada was shown to the office set aside for his use. Kobe's mood was almost conciliatory. He offered Akitada warm wine.

"No, thank you." Akitada found it impossible to produce a polite smile. Seating himself across from Kobe, he plunged into his speech. "Last night I was shocked and angered by your accusations. Today I find that I must apologize for the foolish and dangerous actions of a member of my family. As head of the family, I take full responsibility for what happened, even though I had no knowledge of it."

Kobe nodded. He looked politely attentive. "Please continue!"

"I am afraid that the woman your men followed from the prison to my house is my younger sister Yoshiko."

At that Kobe's eyes widened. "Your sister?"

"Yes. It appears that she formed an attachment to the prisoner many years ago. I am to blame for her visits, because I carelessly discussed the Nagaoka murder with her. At the time, I had no idea that she knew anyone in that family, and she did not tell me."

Kobe seemed too astonished to doubt Akitada's words. "I see," he murmured. "How very unpleasant for you! It would hardly have occurred to you that your sister would form such a very unsuitable . . . relationship with a person of that type. You have my sympathy."

For a moment, Akitada thought he was being mocked. But Kobe's face expressed only shock and concern. Perversely, this easy acceptance of his explanation, entailing as it did revelations of a personally embarrassing nature, angered Akitada. Surely the man Yoshiko had become involved with was not so completely contemptible. Nagaoka was a merchant, but a highly respected one and a man of considerable culture. And the man Akitada remembered meeting in the rain at the temple gate had appeared gentlemanly. Then he realized that, to Kobe, Kojiro was a criminal, and that his sister's reputation depended on clearing her lover of the murder charge.

He pulled himself together and said, "I am much obliged to you for believing me, Superintendent. Since my sister is now deeply implicated in the case, I wonder if you might reconsider your position and allow me to assist you." He steeled himself for another refusal.

To his surprise, Kobe pursed his lips and studied the ceiling thoughtfully. He said, "Hmm," and after a moment, again, "Hmm."

Encouraged by this, his heart beating faster, Akitada promised rashly, "I would, of course, do nothing but what you had approved beforehand, work under your supervision, so to speak."

Kobe brought his eyes back from the ceiling and looked at him. He seemed amused; the corner of his mouth twitched. "I did not think the famous Sugawara would ever say such words to me. Will you go another step, my lord, and promise to be bound by my decision?"

Akitada flushed with shame, but said steadily enough, "Yes."

Kobe rose. "Come along, then. You shall speak to the prisoner. In my presence."

Akitada hardly knew what to make of Kobe's sudden compliance and assumed it had been bought with his own humiliation. So be it! As they walked through the outer offices and past scores of police officers and constables toward the wing of the building where the cells were, it occurred to him that he had no idea how to proceed. The man's relationship with Yoshiko made any thorough questioning awkward. And Kobe's presence at this first meeting between them was more than just embarrassing.

The figure who rose with a rattle of chains and stood, supporting himself against the wall, bore little resemblance to the sturdy young man at the mountain temple. Both his hair and beard had grown untended, he wore a ragged, stained shirt and loose cotton pants, and stood barefoot on the cold dirt floor of the cell. There was a smear of blood on his shoulder where the shirt had slipped, and more traces of bleeding on his chin from biting his lower lip.

Akitada had seen men look like this before—too many times—and he met the eyes of the prisoner. The eyes usually told the story. If they had that dull, hopeless look, a sign of having stopped fighting against a stronger force, one knew that the prisoner had told all he knew. He had come to wish for it as much as it sickened him, for it meant there would be no more beatings.

Kojiro did not have that look yet. He seemed both defiant and indifferent as he glanced from Kobe to Akitada. He frowned, then returned his attention to the superintendent. Apparently he did not remember their meeting. He neither bowed nor spoke, but an expectant silence hung heavy between them.

Akitada wondered what Yoshiko could have seen in this man. True, he was not at his best at the moment, but even cleaned up, he would only be an ordinary man of middling height, certainly shorter than either Akitada or Kobe, squarely built, with a face which was neither distinguished nor handsome. The cheekbones were broad, the nose flat, and the lips too wide and thick. He looked like what he was, a peasant. To be sure, he was not as blackened by the sun, nor as stringy and bent from labor in the rice paddies, but he certainly lacked every vestige of male grace as it was defined by people of Akitada's rank. Akitada was not vain and thought poorly of his own appearance, but he had formed certain ideas about the sort of men women admired. Kojiro did not fit them.

It was Kobe who broke the silence first. "Well, Kojiro. I understand you continued your stubbornness during questioning yesterday."

The prisoner did not answer, but he moved his shoulders slightly, as if he wanted to remind himself of the occasion. Akitada had seen the backs of "stubborn" prisoners and knew the man was in pain.

Kobe continued, "It was a waste of time, you know. We found out who the young lady was."

Something flickered in Kojiro's eyes, but he said nothing. He fears a trap, thought Akitada, mildly surprised that the peasant had attempted to protect Yoshiko's honor with his own skin.

The prisoner finally opened his lips and croaked, "What do you want, Superintendent?"

Kobe grinned unpleasantly. "I? Nothing. I am here because this gentleman has some questions to put to you."

The man turned to look at Akitada warily.

Akitada did not like the cat-and-mouse game. He said brusquely, "My name is Sugawara. Yoshiko has told me of her visits here."

That brought a reaction. The prisoner jerked and his eyes grew large with shock. A slow flush rose from his neck into his face. He said hoarsely, "It was nothing. The young lady took pity and brought food a few times. A charitable act to please Buddha. If some people have chosen to put a dishonorable interpretation on her generous gesture, it only shames them. The guard can testify that nothing passed between us but a few rice cakes."

"I am not here to discuss my sister's visits, but to see if you can be helped in some way."

A sudden wild and joyous hope flashed in the man's eyes. "You mean to help us?"

Akitada snapped, "You make a mistake. If I have anything to say in the matter, you will never see my sister again. A union between your family and mine is, as you have been told before, out of the question." He saw the light die in Kojiro's eyes without regret. It was best to be brutally frank in such matters.

The prisoner said tonelessly, "I see. Or rather, I don't see. Why bother to come, in that case?"

Akitada cleared his throat. "My interest in your case predates the recent revelations about your . . . acquaintance with my sister, as Superintendent Kobe will verify. In fact, we met once briefly at the temple gate. It was raining, and you were with your sister-in-law."

Kojiro nodded. "Yes. I do remember now. However, that still does not explain your interest in me, my lord. It is, of course, very good of you, but I must beg you to leave the matter alone. Under the circumstances, you will find it only distasteful, and I have nothing to lose." He turned away from them to face the wall. They could see the large dried bloodstains on the back of his shirt now.

Akitada bit his lip. If his sister had not meddled, this man might not have been tortured. He said, "My distaste extends only to injustice," with a glance at Kobe, who pursed his lips and studied the ceiling of the cell. "I have been told that you confessed to the murder of your sister-in-law, but later withdrew that confession. Are you innocent?"

Without turning around, the prisoner said, "Guilt or innocence, my lord, are relative terms. Of all the people I know, only one is truly innocent, your sister. The rest of us manage to gather enough sins of the flesh or against our fellow creatures to make suitable game for the demons of hell."

Akitada stared at the bloodied, chained, sagging figure of the man. Where had a man of his class learned such language? And why was he so uncooperative when his life was at stake? Instead of eagerly accepting the proffered help, he had made Akitada uncomfortably aware of his own shortcomings, and—in view of recent events—of those of his parents. He thought fleetingly about their sins and their likely fate at the hands of the mighty judge of the dead. Noami's hell screen depicted vividly the punishments in the netherworld, and he recalled his nightmare in the temple. The chained and bloodstained Kojiro looked little better than Noami's persecuted souls in the hell of the sharp knives. The human world also had its demons.

Struggling for control, and for patience with this obstinate man, he said, "I was there that night, though I did not stay in the visitors' quarters. I heard a woman scream. I am not convinced that you killed Mrs. Nagaoka. If you will allow me, I shall do my best to find out what really happened. I am afraid the evidence against you is too strong to clear you of the crime, but perhaps we may find the real killer."

Kojiro turned around. He looked at Akitada and then at Kobe. To Kobe he said, "Have you changed your mind also, Superintendent?"

Kobe shook his head. "Not at all. But I am a fair man."

Kojiro turned back to Akitada. "I cannot fathom your motives for wishing to clear me, but I am prepared to do what I can. Mind you, I still do not care what happens to me, but she would wish me to. She hoped once that you would take my case. For her sake, I shall tell you what I remember and answer all your questions, but do not expect much. There was a time when I thought I was guilty."

Akitada was irritated by the renewed reference to Yoshiko but decided to overlook it. "Begin by telling me about your relationship with your sister-in-law."

"My brother met his wife on one of his periodic buying trips in the country. Nobuko was the daughter of a retired academician with a small country estate. She was younger than my brother, but eager to find a husband of suitable background and income." Kojiro grimaced slightly. "Some young women," he said, "seem to wish for a life of luxury, and the trade may, after all, be a fair one. My brother was middle-aged and, no doubt, rather dull company for a pretty and lively young woman. But he had two advantages. He had money and he resided in the capital. Her father's motive was more complicated, I think. Professor Yasaburo is an educated man who struggled to make ends meet and could not afford to pay for a dower for his daughter. No doubt he wished to provide for his only child. In any case, she came to my brother's house and I acquired a sister-in-law. I liked Nobuko very much at first. She was close to my age and talented in music. On my visits, we used to play the lute and sing songs together while my brother watched and listened." A sadness passed over Kojiro's face. "My brother was deeply attached to Nobuko. He could not take his eyes off her, and I was glad. But this soon changed." The prisoner moved uncomfortably and sighed.

They were all uncomfortable standing there on that filthy, cold floor, thought Akitada, but Kojiro, chained and in pain, was much the worse off. Still, there was nothing to be done about it. To hurry the tale along, Akitada urged, "What changed?"

Kojiro said bleakly, "One day my sister-in-law asked me to make love to her. She claimed that my brother could no longer . . . satisfy her and that she could not sleep for love of me. I was appalled and immediately left my brother's house. From then on I stayed away as much as I could, but my brother would send for me. I could not tell him what had happened."

"You never acceded to her wishes?"

"Never. I detested that woman from the moment she offered to betray my brother." Kojiro's hard stare dared Akitada to doubt it. "I avoided her like the smallpox."

"Hah!" Kobe interrupted suddenly. "That is part of the

string of lies you told us. If you had been avoiding her so much, why did you go off with her on trips around the countryside, eh? And without a maid or chaperone? I tell you what you really did: You seduced your brother's wife and when diddling her got a bit difficult in his house, you took her on little excursions. You intended to take your sexual pleasures at the temple. The night of her death, you both got drunk, and you killed her. Maybe it was an accident, or maybe she refused you. When you saw what you had done, you panicked and slashed her face, so she would-n't be recognized and you could get away. But you didn't make it. The wine proved stronger."

Kojiro gave Kobe a contemptuous glance. "No," he said. "I have done nothing but think about that night. I do not know how I got into her room, but I did not drink anything but tea at the temple, and I certainly had no desire to make love to my brother's wife. I went on the trip because my brother asked me to accompany her, and I could not refuse without telling him why. Her maid did not come with us because she was violently ill the day we left. Nobuko insisted on going, and my brother supported her. He will confirm this."

Kobe said, "Oh, he did. But then, he has done his best to cover for his little brother all along."

Kojiro glared at Kobe, and Akitada said quickly, "I have been told by your brother that you used to drink too much. In fact, he said you had prior episodes of forgetting where you had been and what you had done. Is it not likely that this happened again?"

"I don't deny that I used to drink. Wine has always affected me worse than other men, and there was a time in my life when I welcomed oblivion for a few hours. However, by the time my brother married, I had stopped." He paused. "I repeat, I did not drink at the temple. At least, I did not do so knowingly. It would have been difficult in any case, because I did not bring wine with me, and the monks, of course, do not serve wine."

"Yes. I had thought of that." Akitada nodded, exchanging a

look with Kobe, who merely raised an eyebrow quizzically, as if to say, *Believe what you like!* "Did you spend any time with Mrs. Nagaoka after you had been shown to your rooms?"

"No!" The denial was emphatic and bitter. "I stayed in my own room, except for a brief visit to the bath. When I returned, I had a cup of tea and immediately went to bed. I was very tired. And that is the last thing I remember."

"Tea?" asked Akitada surprised. "I thought the monks served only water."

"There was tea in a pot on a small brazier when I returned from my bath. I do not like tea, and this tasted very bitter, but I was thirsty and the water had been removed."

Akitada exchanged another glance with Kobe, who frowned.

"You said that you remember nothing after you went to sleep in your own room. Did you have any dreams?"

Kojiro looked startled. "No," he said, "but when I woke up I felt exactly the way I did after a night of drinking. My head was pounding, I was nauseated, and my sight was blurred. And I could hardly speak. It was as if my tongue had turned into a heavy rock, and my mouth was full of sand. They told you, no doubt, that I reeked of wine and that an empty wine pitcher was next to me. I can only theorize that I was knocked out and the wine poured over me."

Kobe snorted. "We checked your head. Nobody knocked you out."

"Hmm!" Akitada stared at the prisoner thoughtfully. "Do you have any ideas who could have killed your sister-in-law and set you up as the killer?"

Kojiro's face lengthened. He shook his head. "No, my lord, I do not. No one knew us there. Only the gatekeeper saw us arrive together. And he was an old man and a monk. You saw him yourself." He sagged against the wall, his face suddenly drawn and very white. "I warned you," he said tiredly. "I know of nothing that might help my case."

"You do not suspect your brother of the murder?"

The prisoner came upright with a jerk and a rattle of chains. "What do you mean?" he cried, his eyes suddenly blazing. "My brother was not there. And he loved her to the point of madness. He would never have laid a hand on her . . . or implicated me! If you plan to shift the blame to my brother, I want none of your help. I will confess to the crime myself before I'll allow that to happen."

Kobe suddenly looked like the cat who caught the fish. "Well, Sugawara?" he asked. "Are you finished?"

Akitada nodded. To Kojiro he said, "I shall try to find out the truth. If it falls on your brother, so be it. You have spent all your time here thinking about what happened that night at the temple. I now want you to think about your sister-in-law. Anything you recall about her life before and after her marriage may be important. All her interests, her relationship with your brother and with anyone else in his house."

Kojiro opened his mouth, but Akitada raised his hand. "No. Not now. Rest and take your time! I shall return . . . if the superintendent permits it."

Kobe unlocked the cell door. "We shall see!" he said noncommittally.

Akitada nodded to the prisoner and turned to leave. Behind his back the chains rattled, then the hoarse voice said, "Thank you, my lord."

Once they were away from the cells, Akitada confronted Kobe. "You heard him. He was drugged, of course. With that tea. I spoke to the monks who serve the visitors. They never provide anything but water."

Kobe only grunted.

"Have you turned up anyone else who might have had a reason to kill Mrs. Nagaoka?"

"No one but her husband. By all accounts, she was a woman of few morals."

"Yes. But I met Nagaoka. He was strangely unemotional about her death. His whole concern seemed to be for his brother. Perhaps he suspected an affair between them."

Kobe cocked his head. "I've had the same thought just now. He was supposed to be besotted with her. But why defend his brother? Maybe he's a good actor. Why don't you look into it?"

Akitada thought of Nagaoka handling the mask the day he had visited. Could he have known the actors at the temple? Could he have paid some starving entertainer to murder his wife and make it look as though his brother had done it?

They parted at the gate. The weather was still depressing. Dense, low clouds and a leaden atmosphere hung over the city. Now and then a snowflake drifted down, settled on the mud of the roadway, and melted.

Akitada remembered miserably what awaited him at home.

THIRTEEN

Actors and Acrobats

"Genba!"

Tora walked purposefully toward the small group at the end of the training hall. Genba swung around to stare at him. "How'd *you* get here?" he demanded in an unfriendly tone.

Tora ignored the question and bowed to the enthroned Miss Plumblossom. "I beg your pardon for interrupting, madam," he said with an ingratiating grin, "My name is Tora. I see my friend got here before me."

The fat woman moved her fan slowly back and forth in front of her large chest and eyed Tora's fine figure and good looks with approval. "Not at all. You are welcome, Tora. What brought you here?"

"Your fame, madam. I heard about you in one of the wine houses on the river, from a big fellow who goes by the name of Bull and happens to be a fellow countryman of mine. He couldn't say enough about you and this establishment, so I made my way here in spite of the late hour and the snowstorm." Tora gave her his widest smile and added, "And now that I'm here, believe me, it was worth it to behold your charming face!"

Genba snorted with disgust, but Miss Plumblossom tittered and toyed with one of the red ribbons in her hair. "What a prettily spoken fellow your friend is, Genba." Her voice was girlishly high and she lisped a little, but Tora got a closer look at her face and doubted that she would see forty again. She wore paint on her face and rouge on her cheeks, and her eyes were outlined with lampblack, which had seeped into tiny wrinkles and laugh lines. Only the makeup and the giggle suggested her past as a famed acrobat.

Genba growled, "Don't waste your time with him, Miss Plumblossom. He's the biggest liar in town."

Miss Plumblossom frowned. "Oh? So you disagree with him? Well, that was certainly not prettily said!" she remarked tartly, and sniffed.

Genba colored and shot Tora an angry look. "No, no! You—you misunderstood," he stammered, "That's not what he—" He broke off helplessly. Miss Plumblossom had already turned her back to him.

"Well," she said to Tora, peering flirtatiously over the top of her fan, "and what precisely did you come for, Tora?"

Tora glanced at Genba, wondering how much he had given away about them while in the throes of his infatuation with this female. Genba compressed his lips and glared back.

"Apart from your charms, you mean?" Tora asked the lady.

"Silly man!" She fluttered her fan at him and then hid her face coyly behind it.

Tora almost burst into laughter. "Well, as I said, I was just chatting with Bull and happened to mention how rusty I was getting"—Tora glanced about the room for inspiration and saw the bamboo fighting sticks in their racks—"at stick fighting. That's when he mentioned you. I was a bit surprised that a lady should be in this sort of business, but he said yours is one of the best training halls in the city. I had to come see for myself. One rarely encounters both business sense and talent in a beautiful woman, madam." Tora made her another bow.

"You may address me as 'miss,' " remarked Miss Plumblossom, patting the coils of her hair. "I'm a single girl." She shot him a glance to see his reaction.

He grinned. "Really? What blind fools some men are! Or maybe your superior talent frightened them away?"

She giggled. "Flatterer! Though you're not wrong. When I was still a working girl, my career took up all my time. Love interferes with training. Acrobats need the self-control of champion wrestlers or archers. So I abstained. It was hard. Very hard, in fact, because mine is a hot-blooded nature." She sighed. "In the end it ruined my career. One day, when I performed at court, there was this particular gentleman, a gentleman of such august station and such romantic looks ... No, I won't say more, except he was most persistent!" She smiled and raised her fan to hide her blushes.

"Ah." Tora nodded. "A humble person like myself may only admire from a distance what the august personage desired." And that would be easy, thought Tora, casting appraising glances at the young women cavorting about the room. There was hardly a plain one in sight.

"Naturally," said Miss Plumblossom, lowering her fan, "I am a woman of high principles, and this is a respectable business. I have to set a good example for the profession." She waved a pudgy hand in the direction of the lithe acrobats and dancers. "If you'd like to come for a workout, you're welcome, but I won't have anything improper going on. Understood?"

Tora humbly promised to behave himself. Her face softened. She smiled, patted her coils some more, and added, "Trouble is, none of the yokels I employ is much good at stick fighting. I suppose I'll have to do it myself. I don't suppose you're an actor?"

Tora had been listening with only half an ear, wondering how to introduce the subject of the actors. "Oh, no," he said quickly. "Ex-military man. At the moment I hire myself out to gentlemen who want protection, so I have to stay in shape."

Miss Plumblossom nodded and pursed her lips. "A good business, that," she said. "The streets are not safe anymore for men or women. It's scandalous that the authorities allow depraved creatures to roam about freely. Well, Tora, I'll try to accommodate you, though stick fighting is not my specialty. Say, once a week, an hour each time, for a hundred coppers each?"

Tora was momentarily speechless. Had this obese lump of female flesh offered to instruct *him* in the art of stick fighting? And at such a price? The idea that he might have to face this huge woman in front of people appalled him. He would be laughed out of town.

She misunderstood his dismay. "Oh, very well," she said. "I suppose you're broke like all the rest. Pay me fifty coppers whenever you have some money." She stood up. "How about a small sample right now?"

Tora backed away. "No, no," he said desperately. "You are too kind, but I couldn't possibly impose on you tonight. You're all dressed up in that pretty robe and ribbons. Some other time I'd be deeply honored."

"Nonsense," she snapped, and untied the sash about her wide middle, dropping it on the floor. A quick shrug disposed of the black silk robe, which puddled about her ankles. Like the girl acrobats, she wore only a loincloth underneath. Tora looked away quickly and saw a young woman in a blue cotton robe with a white fan pattern bending to gather up the clothes, fold them, and place them on the chair. Her face was averted, but Tora noted that she had a supple narrow waist and rounded hips under the simple cotton robe, and her hair, tied with a white bow, was long and glossy as silk. The maid was a great deal more promising than the mistress, he thought, and turned his startled eyes back to Miss Plumblossom.

The loincloth was covered with a little red tasseled silk apron in front. It did nothing to hide the large breasts and a belly of magnificent proportions. As he stared, she raised her arms to her hair and, lifting the beribboned coils from a shaven head, handed the stiffly lacquered wig to the maid. Then she stepped off the dais, and walked past him with all the nonchalance of a male wrestler. Her legs were short, but the thighs rose massively to huge, dimpled buttocks, which in turn joined a broad back and thick arms. In spite of her gender, she was built like a male wrestler. Tora glanced at Genba, hoping that the sight had cured him of his infatuation, but found instead that his friend was watching her with a besotted expression.

Miss Plumblossom paid no attention to either of them, but selected two bamboo poles from a rack. The lighter one she tossed to Tora before taking her position across from him. "Your move!" she ordered.

"Madam—"

"Miss! What are you waiting for?" she snapped. "In a real confrontation, you'd be dead already." Before she had quite finished her words, she let her pole flash out and around while turning on the ball of one foot as the weapon transcribed a hissing circle aimed at Tora's head.

His eyes incredulously fixed on massive mounds of flesh bobbing and heaving before him, Tora parried belatedly and awkwardly.

"Slow," she commented, and aimed a stab between his legs.

Tora jumped and this time managed to flip up her pole. He followed through with a lightning-swift attack to her feet, intending to make her lose her stance. To his surprise, she dropped her pole, became airborne, flipping away, heels over head in a smooth backward somersault, and landed with a thud which made the heavy boards under his feet reverberate. Little clouds of dust rose from the cracks.

He still stood, his mouth open in shock, when she swept up her pole, whirled toward him, and, this time, succeeded in tripping him up. He landed painfully on his backside. All around him applause broke out. Genba shouted, "Well done! A beautiful move!" and Miss Plumblossom bowed all around.

Tora was still struggling to his feet when she charged again.

Cursing inwardly, he put his mind on business and parried smoothly. What followed was several minutes of challenge because Tora could hardly attack a half-naked woman and had to confine himself to adroit defensive moves and an occasional attempt to disarm her. Finally, she came at him so abruptly and quickly that he was faced with either meeting the charge and allowing her to impale herself on his bamboo pole, or throwing up the contest.

He did the latter.

She stopped neatly in front of him, puffing a little, red face breaking into a wide grin. "Hah! Had enough, I see."

"Er, yes," said Tora. "I didn't expect . . . that is, that backward somersault was an interesting move, but I've never really seen that used before in stick fighting."

She took the bamboo staff from his hand and replaced it, along with her own, in the rack. "That little jump of mine?" she asked over her shoulder. "Just something from my former career. I used to do a hundred of those all around a temple courtyard, up and down stairs, over all sorts of obstacles people would put in my way. Of course, I was a bit smaller and younger then and used to wear a shirt and pants like a boy."

"You must've been something to see," said Tora, wondering how this large woman could ever have resembled a boy. "But don't you think it might be dangerous during a real fight? I mean, you lost your weapon when you did the somersault."

She was putting on her gown again, tying the sash firmly around her enormous middle. "Seems to me you do whatever works at the moment," she said practically. "Surprise always does the trick. Half the time you stood there looking like a gasping fish, so I had time to grab the staff and attack. Still, even if you had followed through, I would have rolled myself into a ball and come up at you from underneath to toss you on your face."

"Without the staff?" Tora widened his eyes. "But that's not stick fighting. Only wrestlers do that."

She clapped the wig back on her head and got into her chair. "Didn't you mention that you're training to fight criminals? If you need practice for sporting contests, I'm not your woman."

Tora said quickly, "Oh, you are! You are! I think you're fantastic."

She nodded and pointed to the dais next to her. "Come and sit, then. My advice to you is to learn a few unorthodox tricks. Your regular technique is probably better than mine anyway."

Impressed against his will, Tora went to sit at her feet. He felt out of his depth with this strange female. The small crowd that had gathered to watch the bout dispersed again, laughing and chattering, and returned to various athletic exercises. Only Genba remained. After a moment, he came and took his seat on the other side of Miss Plumblossom.

They sat together companionably, watching the activity in the room. The sword fight had resumed, the dancers moved in carefully measured figures, and the tumbling youngsters began a new routine of jumping and flipping. Tora saw in amazement that the diminutive girls took their turns catching the two men. They looked alike to him. Both were small-waisted, full-breasted, and graceful. He could not make up his mind which would be the more delicious bed partner. It had been a long time since he had had a good bout of lovemaking. A well-rounded man had to stay in practice in more ways than one.

"Those four youngsters tumbling about must be acrobats?" he said to Miss Plumblossom.

She took her eyes from the men with the swords. "Not really. They are all working for Uemon. This is their night to practice."

Tora's interest perked up, and an idea began to form in his mind. "I didn't know they used acrobats in plays."

"They don't. These four have worked up an act to make some extra money. The girls are twins. They call themselves Gold and Silver. Gold, the one whose hair is coming loose, has some talent. But the others . . ." She waved her hands dismissively. "They should stick to acting. Trouble is, young people have no discipline or patience. They want to be rich now, and with the winter fairs coming up there's always a demand for acrobats and jugglers to entertain the crowds. The money's good, so when they're not onstage, they do their stunts."

"I suppose they travel about a bit. From temple fair to temple fair?"

Miss Plumblossom nodded. "Uemon's come back from putting on some religious show outside the capital."

Tora shook his head, looking at the girls' nearly naked bodies. "How come Uemon allows them to cavort about like that? I mean, they're women."

She snapped, "And what's wrong with women performing in public if they're talented? You're just like the rest of the men! Uemon included. Him! Never mind what he thinks about women. The hoity-toity old stick says acrobatics aren't respectable, but for all that he's put some funny scenes into his plays so the youngsters can do a bit of their stuff. The crowds love it." She sniffed. "Pah! Not respectable! I say let *him* give command performances before imperial princes!"

"And all the others here also work for Uemon?"

Miss Plumblossom nodded. "The women mostly sing and dance. But the handsome fellow with the sword is Danjuro. He's Uemon's top man."

Happy that he had come to the right place, Tora looked at the two sword fighters. No wonder they did all that stupid jumping and shouting while laying about them with their wooden swords. It was all make-believe. Clearly Danjuro was meant to be the hero, while his opponent, a broad-faced, bearded fellow, was cast as the villain. It was well done, really, especially the moment where the villain used a dirty trick to disarm the handsome youth and then leapt at Danjuro with his naked sword raised high. Danjuro sidestepped at the last moment, caught the villain in midair, and tossed him aside like a bag of rice. Then, wrestling the villain's sword from his hand, he plunged it into the man's belly.

Tora half rose in shock, but both actors laughed, picked up their swords, and strolled off.

"That was good," Tora said admiringly. "That Danjuro doesn't look big, but he must be very strong to catch and throw a man his size."

Miss Plumblossom pursed her lips. "He is. And he's a good actor. Uemon's people get asked to private houses to perform."

It was said grudgingly, and Tora asked, "Something wrong with him?"

She sniffed. "Too good-looking for his own good! Women throw themselves at him, stupid creatures."

Tora eyed the actor again. So he had a reputation of breaking hearts. Perhaps Miss Plumblossom's with the rest. As a ladies' man Danjuro did not impress him. The fellow was slender and well muscled, and he seemed agile enough, but that smooth face with the round eyes was positively girlish, and as for his handling of the sword . . . ! "He may be a good actor, but he couldn't fight a bout with a real swordsman!" Tora said disdainfully.

Miss Plumblossom chuckled. "That's the way they do it onstage. Anyway, sword fighting's not the sort of exercise a girl's looking for, eh?" She leaned forward to poke Tora's shoulder. "Bet you're quite the gallant yourself in the clinch. Got a wife or girlfriend?"

Tora's eyes went across to Genba, who had paled at the exchange. "Can't afford either," he said lightly, trying to think of a way to detach himself from Miss Plumblossom. He felt the strongest aversion to this female, who seemed to have designs on him. Besides, he was eager to talk to some of the actors. Or actresses, as the case might be.

Miss Plumblossom chortled and gave him another poke. "Nobody's getting any younger. Best get on with it."

"This Danjuro? I suppose he carries on with the women in

the troupe, too?" Tora cast an expert eye over the female members of Uemon's Players. There was a very good-looking girl among the dancers, the tall one who was whispering with Miss Plumblossom's maid. The maid still averted her face, but she was every bit as shapely as the dancer. And the twin acrobats were charming. The twin whose hair was coming loose in wisps caught his admiring glance and gave him a wide smile. He smiled back and remembered that her name was Gold.

Miss Plumblossom said, "Not anymore. Old Uemon put a stop to it. Told him to settle down or get out. So he got married and hasn't so much as looked at another woman since."

Tora exchanged another warm glance with the little acrobat and rose. "I think I'll introduce myself to the others," he told Miss Plumblossom. "If I'm going to be back for lessons, I might as well get to know them."

The acrobats had started another routine, so Tora strolled to the end of the hall to get a closer look at the dancer and the maid. The maid scurried away, but the dancer was a real beauty. He bowed to her, but her glance flicked disdainfully away. Piqued, he next tried some suggestive compliments about her figure. Suddenly there was a painful grip on his shoulder and he was jerked around.

"Make yourself scarce!" the actor Danjuro snarled.

Tora shook off the hand and glared. "What business is it of yours?"

Danjuro was almost as tall as he and possibly stronger. On close inspection Tora did not like him any better. His posture was a strange mix of male arrogance and feminine pettiness. The eyes were hostile but a bit too soft, the lips too full and red, and the skin too white and smooth for a man.

"You are annoying the lady."

And he talked like some schoolteacher. For an actor, Danjuro was certainly giving himself airs. Dancers and actors belonged to the lowest class and often had bad reputations. Tora sneered.

"What lady? I was complimenting one of the dancers. As a rule they enjoy a bit of action on the side."

Immediately the beauty whirled on him and spat in his face. "Dog!" she hissed. "How dare you insult me?"

Danjuro said sharply, "Don't bother with him. He's just some ignorant idler."

She turned on Danjuro. "And what are *you*, to let this lout get away with insulting me?"

What a snooty bitch this one was! Tora's interest changed to virulent dislike, and he hoped that Danjuro would put the woman over his knee later. He wiped his face on his sleeve and cast a baleful eye on the actor. "I guess," he drawled, "he thinks he's the grand chancellor himself and you the Kamo Virgin!"

The other man eyed him haughtily. "I am Danjuro," he said, as if that explained everything, "and you have insulted my wife. Your ignorance about the status of actors excuses your behavior somewhat, but I suggest that you stop interfering where you don't belong. Buy a ticket to the show if you can afford it." He turned his back on Tora and started to lead his wife away.

Stung to the quick, Tora cried after him, "I'll have you know that in my profession I deal with all sorts of people. When you're working with the criminal element, you learn to spot a sham."

They both turned to stare at him. Then the actor snapped, "Well, whatever you do, leave us alone!"

Satisfied that he had scored the final hit, Tora made his way across the room to the acrobats. They were taking a break. Hoping for a better reception, he approached the young woman who had smiled at him.

"Is it permitted to speak to you, little sister?" he asked cautiously.

She was sitting down cross-legged and had her arms raised to rearrange her hair. Tora admired a pair of taut breasts with an appreciative smile. Unabashed, she grinned up at him and said,

"Sure, handsome. I saw your bout with Miss Plumblossom. You're good."

Tora sat down next to her. "So are you. I've been watching you, too. Could hardly keep my eyes off you, in fact. I'm Tora."

She made a growling noise in the back of her throat. "A tiger, eh? I like it. They call me Gold."

"It suits you. You are rare and precious, truly a fortune any man might desire." He moved a little closer.

She had, no doubt, heard it before, but she giggled and batted her lashes at him. "What brings you here, Tiger?"

"Oh, I was looking for a place to practice."

"What sort of work do you do?"

"I hire myself out to rich cowards. For protection."

Her eyes widened. "Isn't that dangerous?"

He laughed. "Not if you know what you're doing. The stuff you do looks more dangerous to me."

"Only if you make a mistake, or your partner does, and then you break a bone. It hurts for a while and you can't work, but that's all. The money's good as long as you're working."

"But you're really an actress, right?"

She nodded unenthusiastically. "I used to like acting, but things have changed. Master Uemon was all right, but he's getting old and now he's turned over the running of the shows to that bastard Danjuro." She glared across the room and Tora followed her eyes. The actor stood talking to his wife and looking at them. "He thinks he's the gods' gift to acting," Gold said bitterly. "And his wife's a bitch. I saw her spit at you. What'd you say to her?"

Tora considered his answer carefully. "I asked her how long she'd been dancing, because she seemed sort of clumsy."

Gold burst into a trill of laughter, but immediately stifled it, hiding her grin behind her hand. Danjuro and his beautiful wife were still watching them with scowls on their faces.

"You got that right," said Gold. "She's new and still learning, but she thinks she can order us around because she's beautiful and Danjuro's wife. It's been worse since she got her inheritance. Now she's ordering Danjuro around and talking about buying out Uemon. Can't imagine why Danjuro picked that one when he could've had a sweet, pretty girl who would've waited on him hand and foot."

Tora frowned. "You?"

"Don't be an idiot," she snapped. Then her eyes widened. "Wow! Here he comes, looking like the thunder god himself. I bet she sicced him on you. You'd better go. I can't afford another black mark."

Danjuro was indeed heading their way with a purposeful stride. Tora rose immediately. "I've got to see you again," he begged urgently.

She looked panicky. "In the back alley. As soon as I can slip away," she whispered.

Tora made her a bow, saying in a loud voice, "A pleasure to meet you, Miss Gold. I look forward to seeing your performance," and strolled away.

Behind his back, he heard Danjuro asking angrily, "What did he want?" Gold's reply was inaudible, but Danjuro came back with, "Keep your mouth shut about our business or I'll see to it that you never work again."

Tora wandered around thinking about the incident. He tried to approach some of the other members of Uemon's troupe, but Danjuro's warning to Gold had been overheard. They turned their backs on him or left with a brief apology. Something was not quite right with these people. He finally made his way back to Genba and Miss Plumblossom.

"It's getting late, and I've got to get back," he told the lady. "Thank you for the bout and for letting me look around."

She winked. "Come back soon, my handsome fellow!"

Tora shuddered inwardly, but managed to agree enthusiastically before turning to Genba. "Ready to go?"

Genba scowled. "No."

Tora nodded. Genba was acting like an idiot, but that was his affair, and Tora still had some business of his own.

Outside, the snow still fell, but more thinly and in large wet flakes. Tora looked at them morosely. The wind had died down a little, but it was no night for romantic cuddles in dark alleys. He found his way with some difficulty. The alley was a narrow thoroughfare between the blind walls of buildings. Unidentifiable debris cluttered his path and lay in piles against the walls. The thin cover of snow shed a faint, eerie light reflected by dirty plaster, and he saw a few narrow doorways like black slashes in the gray walls. Up ahead something moved. A darker shape detached itself from one of the black rectangles.

"Hsst! Tora." Gold huddled against the cold in a thick wrap of some heavy dark material. "I haven't got much time," she whispered. "Danjuro's having a fit. He thinks you're a constable."

"I'm not. And why do you let him order you about?" Tora growled, putting protective arms around the shivering girl.

She cuddled against him. "It's not so easy to find another job. Uemon's troupe's got the best reputation."

Tora managed to insert a groping hand under her wrap and found bare flesh. "Where do you live?" he muttered hoarsely into her ear. "It's too cold out here."

"Let go!" She slapped his hand away and straightened her wrap, giving him a stern glance. "That wasn't very nice," she scolded. "I'm not a common whore."

Tora hung his head. "I'm sorry," he said. "It's just . . . well, you're really something, and I couldn't help myself. I keep thinking about your body twisting through the air and bouncing about." He swallowed and gave her a pleading look. "I meant no disrespect. It's just . . . every part of me wants to hold you and touch you and—" He broke off and extended a hand to brush a loose curl from her face. She did not pull away, and he traced the lines of her face gently with his forefinger. "You're the sweetest girl I ever met."

She grew still, her eyes luminous in the light of the snow. Her lips quivered a little. "Oh, Tora," she murmured. Then she flung herself suddenly back into his arms and whispered, "I want you, too."

After a moment's passionate embrace, Tora said urgently, "Where can we go?"

She wailed, "I don't know. I have to go back to our inn with the others, or I'll be in trouble."

"What inn?"

"The Golden Phoenix. It's near Rashomon. But you can't go there. They keep an eye on us."

Well, it would have to wait. Tora cursed inwardly and removed his hand from her breast, trying to control his baser urges. "Can you meet me tomorrow?" he asked.

"Maybe. Where?"

"I have a woman friend in the Willow Quarter." He felt her stiffen in his arms. "It's not like that," he said quickly. "I once did a favor for her and she'll let us use a room in her place. I know you'd rather not go there, but it's the best I can do at the moment. I'm broke."

"All right, Tora," she whispered, burying her face against his neck and kissing it softly.

He groaned and let his hand reach for her naked breast again when there was a loud squeal of rusty hinges. She gasped and tore herself free.

Ahead a dark head poked out from the door of the training school, and a soft voice called, "Gold? Is that you? Danjuro and the others are ready to leave!"

The girl in Tora's arms cried, "Coming!" then whispered to Tora, "It's Miss Plumblossom's maid. I've got to go. Tomorrow at this time? Where's the place?"

Tora shrank behind a pile of lumber, pulling Gold with him

and into his arms for another quick passionate embrace. Then he whispered instructions in her ear and let her go.

She disappeared into the building, but the door remained open. Tora waited in the shadow of the woodpile, but nothing happened. He peered cautiously toward the door. Through a crack between the wall and the edge of the door, he could see a bit of blue cotton with white fans on it. Miss Plumblossom's pretty maid still stood there. Waiting to catch him? Why? Tora had a profound conviction that women liked him and that everything that happened, happened specifically to keep his life interesting. He moved from the shadow on soft feet and rushed the door. Pulling it wide, he seized the girl, and drew her out, placing his hand over her mouth. She struggled wildly in his arms.

"Shhh," he whispered in her ear. "Don't shout. It's me. I'm not going to hurt you, my pretty. I just want to talk to you. A lovely thing like you has no need to spy on other girls." She stopped struggling.

He was about to remove his hand from her mouth when she bit him hard. With a curse he released her. She jumped back inside, but for just a second before she slammed the door he saw her face and recoiled in horror.

FOURTEEN

A Taste of Ashes

When Akitada entered his study, the short, rotund figure of his brother-in-law was sitting on a cushion by his desk cheerfully sipping wine. As soon as Toshikage saw Akitada, he arranged his face into suitable gravity.

"Good afternoon, Brother!" he said with a bow. "I hope you don't mind my waiting in your room. Seimei brought me some warm wine. Please have some. It takes the chill off the weather. You look frozen."

"Good afternoon, Toshikage." Akitada touched his face and ears. They were icy. Preoccupied with his family troubles, he had forgotten to turn up his collar against the wind. He untied his hat and went to warm his hands over the glowing brazier, then held them over his ears. The cold had given him a headache. "You are always welcome here, Brother," he said to Toshikage, who filled a second cup with wine.

Akitada had become fond of his brother-in-law, but his presence here today struck him as ominous, because of Yoshiko's threat of leaving. Apparently she had been serious. The situation left him utterly helpless. His solemn resolve to take care of his family had already ended in the first failure.

Toshikage extended the wine cup. Akitada attempted a smile and drank. Toshikage was right. The wine, sweet and mellow to the tongue, lit a fire in his belly. He felt marginally better. All day he had been as tightly strung as a bow, afraid that his self-control would shatter. He rubbed his temples, waiting for the headache to recede.

Toshikage, searching Akitada's face, said, "We both came the moment we received Tamako's message. What does the superintendent say?"

"Oh! You brought Akiko?" Then the full implications of Toshikage's words struck Akitada momentarily speechless. *Tamako* had sent for them! She had taken Yoshiko's side and sent for Toshikage and Akiko the moment his back had been turned. No doubt the three women were together even now, packing Yoshiko's clothes and making plans for her life in Toshikage's household. He felt slightly sick. Between them the women had cast him in the role of the ogre.

Toshikage's face wrinkled with new concern when he saw Akitada's expression. "What is it? Bad news? Will she be arrested after all? It is outrageous! We must stop him. I tell you what: I'll go to Kudara. He's a major counselor, a member of the Great Council of State. Kudara's the sort of man who insists on class privilege. He'll tell this Kobe fellow a few things and we'll have Yoshiko back home in no time."

Toshikage's offer was kind, but Akitada's way, no matter how mortifying, was preferable. He had no desire to put himself into debt to one of the great men. Such favors came with a price, and the price was too often one's integrity. He hurriedly reassured Toshikage, "No, no. The case is not as desperate as all that. I have managed to stave off the worst by throwing myself on Kobe's mercy." The memory of that difficult step was still painful, and he grimaced. Toshikage raised his brows questioningly, and Akitada confessed, "I doubt he was motivated by mercy. The situation was fairly humiliating."

Toshikage bristled. "That man gives himself too many airs!"

"We don't get along too well because he thinks I meddle in his affairs. On this occasion he thought I had finally overstepped the bounds of legality by smuggling messages and instructions to a prisoner about to come to trial. Has Tamako told you Yoshiko's story?"

Toshikage looked uncomfortable. "Yes, er, that is, I under-stand that this Kojiro is a former suitor and she went to visit him in prison."

"Yes. Repeatedly. And it is worse than that, I'm afraid. She appears to be besotted with the man. He is totally unsuitable, but she insists on marrying him as soon as he is cleared of the murder charge. I have forbidden it, of course."

"Ah, hmm." Toshikage nodded, avoiding Akitada's eyes and fidgeting.

Akitada was not encouraged by Toshikage's manner to hope that he was on his side, but he decided to get it over with. "She has defied me and informed me that she will leave this house. I assume you are here to take her back with you?"

Startled, his brother-in-law looked up. "Heavens, no. I came to offer my support against those high-handed police authori-ties. I had no idea things were as bad as that. She is leaving? Oh, dear, I have no wish to come between you two." He paused to digest this new information. "By the Blessed Buddha," he said, shaking his head, "if it's not one thing, then it's another. I've only just settled my own problems, when here is this new thing cropping up. But my dear Akitada, you are the head of her fam-ily. She must obey you. What do you want me to do? I am com-pletely at your service."

"Thank you." Akitada did feel profoundly grateful. It meant a great deal that Toshikage at least recognized his authority and would support him against the women. "I want Yoshiko to stay here," he said, "but I will not force her beyond reasoning with her. If worse comes to worst, I would be very grateful if you offered her the shelter of your home."

"But of course. She is Akiko's sister and I am very fond of her."

"How is Akiko?"

Toshikage beamed. "Blooming! In view of your trouble, I am

almost ashamed to admit that my own home has never been happier. And just think, that little problem of the missing treasures has been straightened out. Stupid of me to trouble you. All the lost items have turned up. It was just a silly mistake. I am so glad that you did not have to become involved."

So Toshikage's son had managed to return everything without arousing his father's suspicion. Akitada feigned ignorance. "Really? Where did you find them?"

"Oh, that careless son of mine forgot that we had sent a large number of things to be cleaned and repacked in new boxes along with other items. Takenori should have checked them off the master list. The fellow who does that sort of thing for us delivered most of the things last month, but he brought these back only yesterday. Everything is there, thank the heavens. Of course, in theory I am responsible for knowing where things are, but Takenori went before the director, threw himself full-length on the floor, and confessed his oversight. The director was very understanding. Silly boy! Of course, he should have been more careful, but I was quite impressed with his behavior. And let's face it, I have been laying too many of my own duties on his shoulders lately." Toshikage's face brightened. "And there is even better news. I have thought of a plan to bring his brother Tadamine home for good. There will be several openings in the Imperial Guard come New Year's Day. If he wants to play soldier, let him do it here in safety. What do you think of the idea?"

Biting his lip to keep from smiling, Akitada said he thought it the perfect solution. Privately he suspected that young Takenori had considerable hidden talents for a political career. Apparently he had had no trouble convincing Toshikage that the cleaning of the treasures and the reassignment of his brother had been his father's idea all along.

Toshikage rubbed his hands gleefully. "Yes, isn't it wonderful? I shall soon have both my boys back with me, and another one on the way." He positively glowed with happiness.

Suppressing a sigh, Akitada congratulated him on his good fortune and poured more wine to toast the happy news.

Toshikage recalled the reason for his visit. His face fell. "Forgive me, Brother. I should not have forgotten Yoshiko's problem so quickly. What did Kobe say?"

Akitada grimaced. "He commiserated with me on having a sister who could shame her family to the degree of claiming to be the wife of a peasant jailed for raping and murdering his own sister-in-law."

Toshikage sucked in his breath. "Surely she did not do that!"

"She did. It was the only way she could gain access to him. They allow wives to bring food to the prisoners."

"Oh, dear! Oh, dear! How angry you must have been! Did you beat her?"

Akitada was taken aback. The thought of striking his sister, or any woman, had never entered his mind and he felt slightly sick at the notion. "Of course not," he said. "Besides, she is a grown woman."

Toshikage shook his head and waved a monitory finger. "All women are children. And the provocation, my dear Akitada. I admire your restraint. I would have beaten my son if he had embarrassed me half as much."

"But not a daughter or sister." Or your wife, Akitada hoped, thinking of the troublesome Akiko.

Toshikage, guessing his thoughts, grinned. "Well, perhaps not quite so hard. Women cannot be held to the same standards as men." He sighed. "It's a fine mess. What will you do?"

"Of course Yoshiko will not be permitted any further contact with the prisoner. But Kobe has agreed to let me investigate the case with certain conditions. I am to work under his command."

"Oh, dear! Oh, dear!" Toshikage muttered again, shaking his head. "With your rank! How very embarrassing for you."

Akitada felt himself flush. "I had no choice. Kobe and that man have my sister's reputation in their hands. One word from either of them, and she is ruined. In fact, unless I can clear Kojiro of the murder charge, she may never be able to hold up her head in polite society again."

"Amida!" said Toshikage, and fell silent, momentarily bereft of words. They sat and considered the situation. Gossip ran like a firestorm among the "good people," and a scandal involving his wife's sister would touch Toshikage's family also. To Akitada's surprise, Toshikage was not thinking of himself. "Poor girl!" he muttered. "We must do our best to protect her. What sort of man is this Kojiro? Does he strike you as capable of the crime? Is he likely to use Yoshiko to protect himself?"

"I am positive that he is not capable of either." Toshikage had put his finger on something which had been troubling Akitada ever since his meeting with the prisoner. "I don't know why I am so certain. The man puzzles me. He appears surprisingly well educated. Quite gentlemanly, as a matter of fact. And he behaved well about Yoshiko. He tried to cover for her. Of course, Kobe did not believe him. In fact, I was very favorably impressed until he thought I had come to help him because Yoshiko asked me to. At that point, I am afraid, I got very angry at his brazen assumption that I might countenance such a relationship. Since Kobe stood there watching to see how I would take it, I disabused them both quickly of such an idea. Kojiro became quite stiff after that."

"But you will attempt to clear him?"

Akitada nodded. "He denies having had an affair with his sister-in-law, and I believe him. I also think he is sincere about his feelings for Yoshiko. His brother told me that Kojiro started drinking because of an unhappy love affair. I think the occasion was the rejection of his suit for Yoshiko."

Toshikage's eyes grew a little misty. "Heavens! Knowing your honorable mother's firmness of purpose, that must have been painful in the extreme. A truly romantic tale. Too bad you don't like the fellow."

Akitada raised his brows. "My dear Toshikage," he said brusquely, "it has nothing whatsoever to do with my liking or disliking the man. He is a commoner."

"Ah. Yes. That is very true. I forgot."

Akitada gave his brother-in-law an irritated look. "To get back to the murder: Kojiro's story suggests that he may have been drugged. On my visit to the temple, I observed that the young monks bring only water to the guests, but Kojiro says he was given tea. Being thirsty, he drank it and immediately fell asleep. When he was woken by the monks, he was in his sister-in-law's room. To this day he has no idea how he got there. He says his head felt fuzzy and someone had poured a pitcher of wine over him so that everybody assumed he was drunk. He thought so, too, at first, remembering the blackouts he used to suffer when he was still drinking. Wine affects him worse than most men. But he swears he stopped drinking, and I tend to believe him. Anyway, it explains why he confessed to the crime in the beginning but later changed his mind. I think there was something in the tea. The bitter taste would hide whatever sleeping powder someone gave him."

"Of course! How clever of you to figure that out." Toshikage paused. "But wasn't the door locked from the inside?"

"Slamming those doors will make them lock of their own accord. Guests are asked to leave the doors open when they depart, but the monks have a key in case someone forgets."

"The monks have a key? But that means one of the monks could be the murderer."

"Yes." Akitada was surprised at his brother-in-law's sharpness. He had not expected it from Toshikage, who had been totally helpless about his own problems. "Quite right. A monk, or someone else who knew where the key was kept. I cannot help thinking that there is more involved here than mere lust. Someone wanted her dead."

"Her husband?"

"Perhaps." Akitada decided to share his thoughts more often with his brother-in-law. It was helpful to have someone to listen to and comment on his theories. "Nagaoka was away from home the night of the murder. And Kobe is receptive of the idea."

His brother-in-law smiled. "There you are, then."

"Yoshiko won't be much better off having her name linked with a killer's brother. Kojiro, by the way, threatened to confess again, if we accuse Nagaoka. His affection for his brother is quite strong." Akitada grimaced. "I have some difficulty accepting that Nagaoka could treat his own brother so cruelly."

"My dear Akitada, our history is full of instances of fratricide."

Seimei came in with another flask of hot wine. Clearing his throat apologetically, he said, "The ladies have asked me to tell you that they are anxious to hear what happened at the prison."

Akitada rose. "Yes, of course. I forgot. I suppose we had better go now." He sighed. His head still ached and he dreaded the coming interview.

Seimei followed them, carrying the wine and their cups.

At first glance the gathering of the three young women looked charming and normal. Dressed in pretty silk robes, dark because of the mourning period, but most becoming, their long, lustrous hair spread out behind them, they sat or reclined on cushions placed around a large brazier.

But the faces they turned to the men were not cheerful. Akiko looked angry, and Yoshiko was sickly pale, with bluish circles under her red-rimmed eyes and a general air of frailty.

Akitada's eyes passed quickly from them to Tamako. His wife was sitting stiffly upright, her normally placid face tense and stern. His heart misgave him. Feeling guilty that he had delayed so long with Toshikage, he stumbled into apology. "Forgive me, but we were discussing the case against Nagaoka's brother." As soon as he had spoken, he felt that this excuse simply made the matter worse. Lately he always seemed to be saying the wrong thing to Tamako. Their easy, companionable relationship had changed to one of disapproval and hurt feelings. He went on hurriedly, "The news is good for Yoshiko at least. Kobe has agreed to leave her in peace for the time being."

Tamako said quietly, "Thank heavens for that!"

Akiko was less pleased. She cried angrily, "I should hope so! Who does the man think he is?"

Only Yoshiko did not speak. She looked down at her hands, plucking at the fabric of her robe.

Akitada was aware of new irritation with his youngest sister. She clearly had no idea what danger she had been in and what it had cost him to protect her. What had she expected? That he would get her lover released and bring him home to meet the family? He suppressed an urge to shout at her and instead seated himself next to Tamako. His wife immediately rose, offering her cushion to Toshikage, who accepted.

Seimei filled their cups with wine. When he was done, he hesitated and looked at Akitada. But his master's eyes were following Tamako, troubled that she had withdrawn from him, trying to catch her eye. Being ignored, the old man withdrew on soft feet.

"Well?" Akiko demanded impatiently. "What happened? Don't keep us in suspense, Akitada!"

"What? Oh. I told Kobe your sister's story. Under the circumstances, only the truth would do. He expressed shock and sympathy. Since he did not question it, the rest was easy enough. I asked to be allowed to investigate the crime in order to clear Kojiro. He agreed, provided I work under him." No point in going into the unpleasant details of the interview.

Tamako looked at him now and he knew that she understood his humiliation. He tried a reassuring smile, but she only bit her lip, glancing away again. His sisters received the information differently. Yoshiko's face lit up with hope, and Akiko clapped her hands. "Wonderful!" she cried. "That should take care of the problem neatly. You will prove the fellow innocent, and everyone will forget Yoshiko was ever involved in the matter."

"Thank you for your faith in me," Akitada said dryly. "At the moment I am not nearly as sanguine as you are." He glanced at Yoshiko. She had paled again, and her fingers resumed plucking and pleating her gown. "Well, Yoshiko?" he asked, hoping his voice was not as harsh as it seemed to him. "What have you decided to do?"

Without looking up, she said softly, "I shall wait."

"For what?" Akiko demanded. "Put the fellow from your mind and go on with your life. If it were not for this stupid mourning period, Toshikage and I would soon have you in the right company to meet *gentlemen*."

Though Akiko expressed Akitada's views precisely, her tactlessness irritated him. He asked again, "Yoshiko?"

She raised tear-dulled eyes to his.

"Will you remain here, in your home, for the time being?"

"Of course she will," Akiko cut in. "All this nonsense about leaving because she brought dishonor to you! How would it look, for heaven's sake?"

Akitada and Yoshiko were still looking at each other. He saw the helpless tears gathering in her eyes and opened his mouth to reassure her, but it was too late. The tears spilled over. "I shall stay—as I stayed with Mother," she said in a tone of utter hopelessness, half choking on the words, then jumped up and ran from the room. Tamako, with an inscrutable look at her husband, rose to follow.

"Now what?" said Akiko in an annoyed tone, staring after them. She started to get up also, clumsily, because of her pregnancy, and muttered, "Heavens! The stubbornness of that girl! She must be made to see reason!"

"No." Akitada was up. "Don't strain yourself. Stay here with your husband. You have done enough." He headed out the door, pleased for a moment with the ambiguity of his words, but tension, and with it the throbbing behind his eyes, returned. He was not sure whether he was more frustrated by Yoshiko or her insensitive sister. At the moment he felt like blaming both for the strain between himself and his wife.

He heard Yoshiko before he reached her room. Her voice was desperate, high with passion, and carried quite clearly. "No! You are wrong!" she cried. "My brother has made up his mind against it. He's the kind of person who despises men who are not as nobly born as he and thinks them no better than animals."

Akitada stopped abruptly. His mind rebelled at her opinion of his character. He fought his anger. It was not true, of course. She did not know him, could not know how fond he was of Tora and Genba, neither of whom would dream of aspiring to marry his sister.

There was a pause, presumably for Tamako to respond, but she spoke so softly he could not hear her. Yoshiko cut back in with, "Honor? It is he who is dishonored by forcing me to break my word to Kojiro."

Akitada bit his lip, then knocked.

Tamako opened, her eyes widening at the anger in his face. Akitada said stiffly, "Leave us alone." Tamako flinched, then her eyes narrowed. She compressed her lips and left.

Yoshiko stood in the middle of her room, a very pleasant one as her brother saw, his glance sweeping over screens and painted clothes boxes, lacquered sewing kits and writing utensils, a bamboo shelf with narrative scrolls and collections of poems, and paper-covered doors to the outside. That she should be so unappreciative of the comforts provided for her angered him more. He glared at her flushed, tear-stained face and said coldly, "I shall not force you to remain under my roof against your will. However, in this matter both Toshikage and Akiko support me. I cannot imagine that your stay with them would be much more pleasant than putting up with me."

Yoshiko stared at him. Slowly the tears started again. Her voice was unsteady. "I know. Thank you, Akitada."

He looked away and glanced around the room again, searching for words. He finally said stiffly, "It appears that I cannot make you see that I have only your best interests at heart, and this naturally pains me. But if you decide to remain, there will be a condition. I will not tolerate your putting your affairs between myself and Tamako. Do you understand!"

She gasped and made an imploring gesture with her hands. "I . . . I didn't intend . . . I am sorry." Then she began to sob in earnest. Her words were so muffled that he could barely hear her. "I am sorry and shall obey you in the future." She bowed, weeping silently. He could imagine what such a promise had cost her, and felt a little ashamed, sickened at having reduced his sister to this pitiful weeping thing—no matter that he had done so with words instead of blows; it had been just as effective.

He returned to his guests in a bitter mood. Toshikage was standing before the scroll of the boy and the puppies. He glanced at Akitada, but with great tact he did not ask about Yoshiko. Instead he said, "This is by Noami, Akiko says. What did you think of him?"

Covering his distress, Akitada became almost voluble. "A remarkable artist, but I did not like him. For one thing, he is insufferably rude. For another, there is something unpleasant about him. Did I tell you that he is painting a gruesome hell screen for the temple where Nagaoka's wife was killed?"

"You don't say! What a coincidence! Well, he is becoming very popular. I suppose his patrons think it's artistic eccentricity. Will he paint a screen for you?"

Akitada wanted Tamako to have the finest screen in the capital, even if it meant paying an exorbitant amount to a man he instinctively detested, but he hesitated. "I don't know. The thought of visiting his studio again appalls me. I am not superstitious, but I had the strangest sense of evil while I was there."

Toshikage chuckled. "I have met him. He would make a fine demon, I think."

Akiko yawned noisily and shivered. "How you men chatter! It is cold in here."

Toshikage rushed to help his wife into her quilted jacket. "It is getting late and Akiko is worn out," he said apologetically. "If things are settled, we will go home."

Akiko was either too tired or had the good sense to say no more on the subject of Yoshiko's lover. Leaning heavily on her husband's arm, she waved a languid good-bye to her brother.

Akitada saw them off and then returned to his own room. The charcoal in the brazier had turned to ashes, and it was chilly. His head still ached, and he wondered if he was getting sick. He did not have the energy to call Seimei. Besides, the old man had been doing enough. Throwing an extra robe around his shoulders, he sat down behind his desk and tried to think. The meeting with his wife and sister had gone about as badly as he had feared. Although he considered his anger justified after Tamako had taken Yoshiko's side against him, he dreaded facing her.

A scratching at the door interrupted his morose imaginings of what his wife would do or say to him after he had ordered her from his sister's room.

"Come in," he called, wishing whoever it was to the devil.

It was Yoshiko. She bowed very humbly. "Please forgive the interruption," she said, creeping in on tentative feet, her voice toneless, her eyes lowered. Taking a deep, shuddering breath, she raised her eyes to Akitada and burst into speech. "I regret deeply having caused trouble for you and Tamako. Thinking of you as only my elder brother, I am afraid I forgot my duty to you as the head of my family. Akiko and Tamako have both reminded me that since I am unmarried, my first allegiance must always be to my family. I promise to accept your decisions for my future and to remain here as long as it pleases you." She took another deep breath and reached into her sleeve. With trembling fingers she extended a letter to him. "If you please, this is for Kojiro. You can read it. It explains why I cannot marry him. Will you give it to him?"

Akitada stared at the oblong of elegant paper as if it were red-hot. He had triumphed over her willfulness, had forced her to break her word to Kojiro, but victory tasted as bitter as the ashes in the cold brazier. Yet he could not reverse his judgment. The man in prison was simply not an acceptable husband for his sister. He hesitated so long that Yoshiko's extended hand began to shake and the letter slipped from her fingers. He caught it before it fell and put it in his sleeve.

"Yes. Of course," he said thickly. "I . . . I am very sorry, Yoshiko. He knows already, for I told him. I wish things were different. You must see—"

She bowed without a word and left his room.

Akitada took the letter from his sleeve. It was not sealed. The thin mulberry paper showed the brush strokes on the inside. Yoshiko's brush strokes were elegant and fluid, the hand of a woman of grace and culture. How little he really knew about his sister! A memory came into his head, of how he had offered to help her marry the man her mother had rejected! A foolish promise made out of love for the little sister who had years earlier brought him and Tamako together. Sickened, he laid the letter on his desk and rose to pace the floor.

Suddenly the room felt too close. It seemed to be pressing in on him, worsening his headache. He opened the shutters and walked down into the garden. The snow had melted, and he could see the shapes of the fish moving sluggishly beneath the surface of the small pond. As he leaned down to scoop a handful of dead leaves from the surface, the carp rose to his hand. Sorry that he had no food for them, he let them probe his fingers with gentle inquisitive mouths. Their touch resembled caresses. Had his father ever stood like this, alone and alienated from those around him?

When he returned to his study, his head still aching, he found Tora and Genba waiting. Caught up in his private thoughts, he did not notice right away that they sat as far away from each other as possible.

"We came to report, sir," announced Tora stiffly.

"Oh, yes, the actors. Did you find them?"

"Yes, sir," they answered in unison. Genba added, "They use a riverside training hall to practice. I was lucky enough to meet the lady proprietor in one of the restaurants."

Tora made an impolite noise. "Never mind that obnoxious moon cake of a female! She knows nothing, but one of Uemon's girls has promised to meet me tonight." Tora smiled, stroking his mustache. "I'll try to get the goods on their lead actor Danjuro. He's a very suspicious character."

Akitada's eyes had moved from one to the other, trying to make sense of their words. Slowly he realized that something was wrong. They pointedly avoided looking at each other. Tora and Genba had always been on the easiest, friendliest terms with each other. What could have happened? He saw Tora looking at him expectantly and tried to recall his words. "Er, what do you mean, 'suspicious'?"

Tora gave a succinct account of events as they led up to and followed his clash with Danjuro, skipping only over his stick-fighting ordeal and the cuddle in the alley. "So you see," he summed up, "they all turned into clams when I tried to ask questions. And all because he thought I was a constable. Which naturally made *me* think he's got something to hide."

Akitada stared at him. "He thought you were a constable? Whatever gave him that idea?"

Tora reddened. "Can't imagine. Must've been something I said."

"What?" Akitada persisted.

"Well, he *was* giving himself airs about being the great Danjuro and told me that I was some lowlife who had insulted his lady wife."

Genba muttered, "Which naturally he had."

"Shut up, you," snarled Tora. "You weren't there. You were too busy ogling that fat cow to keep your mind on work."

Genba glared. "I found the place first. And I get results without getting into fights and quarrels and abusing every poor girl in sight."

Akitada had enough. "Stop this ridiculous bickering this instant! You can settle your differences later. What facts have either of you found out that links these people to the murder of Mrs. Nagaoka?"

They shook their heads.

"Nothing at all?"

"Well," said Tora, "they were at the temple, and Danjuro is afraid of the police. Surely that—"

Akitada snapped, "You wasted my time for that? Actors do not have to be involved in a murder to fear the police."

"Hah," cried Tora triumphantly. "That's exactly what I told the fellow! With my experience as an investigator, I told him, I know better than to believe actors and acrobats are law-abiding citizens. Nine out of ten times they're nothing but thieves and harlots."

Genba growled, "That's a lie! And you're a fool to give yourself away like that! Of course they wouldn't talk to you after that. I've lived longer than you and met more entertainers. They don't like the police because they're harassed by them. Most of them are as decent as you and me. No, more decent than you, for most of them would never look down on a man just because he's only a peasant or a sandal maker. Miss Plumblossom didn't look down on you for being a deserter. She knew that the minute you opened your big mouth and told her you used to be a soldier like that fellow who sent you there. Only a low-class person mocks his fellow beings, and Miss Plumblossom is not a low-class person."

Tora sneered. "Because she once slept with some fat bastard

with a title? So have half the sluts in the Willow Quarter. Besides, the woman probably lies. Look at her! Who'd want to sleep with that? She's as big as a bear and as bald as an egg. A man would be afraid she'd smother him if she got on top for the rain and the clouds."

Akitada had raised both hands to his head, which pounded viciously, and covered his ears.

"You filthy-mouthed bastard!" Genba shouted, purple with fury. He rose with clenched fists.

Tora shot up and bared his teeth in a snarl. "You call me that again and you're a dead man."

"Enough!" roared Akitada, stepping between them. He winced at an excruciating stab of pain, closed his eyes, and waited until the throbbing abated. When he opened them, he saw Tora and Genba staring at him openmouthed. He said more quietly, "Sit down, both of you!" and gingerly returned to his cushion.

They obeyed, and after regarding them bleakly, he said, "Tora, if your manners are as bad in public as they were here today, you are useless to me. Worse than useless, for your behavior reflects on me."

Tora blanched.

"And you, Genba, seem to have allowed a casual acquaintance with a female of dubious background to get in the way of an investigation."

Genba flushed and hung his head.

"Since neither of you can be trusted any longer, you will henceforth confine yourselves to duties around the house."

"Sir!" they both protested.

"Please, sir. I promised to meet the little acrobat tonight," Tora added.

It was the last straw. "Get out!" Akitada ground out between clenched teeth, fixing Tora with such a look that he flinched back. "Get out of my sight! All you're good for is chasing women. Go clean the stable. Perhaps that will remind you of your place in this household."

They trooped out with hanging heads, and Akitada sagged on his cushion, staring at his clenched hands. He slowly opened them and watched his fingers tremble. His heart pounded, and every heartbeat throbbed in his skull. He had lost control. The fact that he had passed a miserable day was no excuse.

Reaching for some paperwork, long postponed, he tried to distract himself with figures and accounts, but he could not shed his sense of failure.

Tora's disparagement of actors resembled his own disdain for merchants and their kin. Tora's attitude had severed the bond of friendship between himself and Genba, as he, Akitada, had destroyed the affection his younger sister had for him. The silent, pale young woman who had submitted to his commands today no longer looked at him with trust and fondness. He had seen resignation and fear in her eyes.

The hours passed. Seimei crept in with the evening rice and replenished the coals in the brazier. But neither warmth nor food cheered Akitada. He pushed his tray aside untouched, unrolled his bedding, and tried to forget the onerous and painful responsibilities of being a husband and family head.

FIFTEEN

The Empty Storehouse

Akitada woke up feeling exhausted and depressed. Nothing in his household seemed to be going right. They had barely returned from the long assignment up north when the very foundations of his life started crumbling. First Yoshiko got entangled with a commoner who was in jail on a murder charge. Then she rebelled against her brother's authority and caused Tamako to take her side, the first rift in Akitada's marriage. And now the quarrel between Genba and Tora further destroyed the peace and harmony he had hoped to feel after years of struggle and hardship.

Akitada knew he had been too harsh with Tora and Genba. How could he expect them to be all business on their first night out in the capital? So what if after years of near abstinence, Genba had been attracted to a woman who, from all accounts, combined feminine wiles with an interest in competitive sports? Such a thing was natural and human. And Tora had pursued every available light-skirt in town because that was *his* nature. The quarrel had been provoked by the actor Danjuro, not Tora. A man like Tora could not tolerate insults; his respectability had been too hard-won. No, the fault for all this trouble lay with himself, with his cursed temper. Instead of dealing calmly with the strain produced by recent events, he had flared up and become judgmental and punitive.

With a sigh, Akitada got up, folded his bedding, put it away, and started dressing. He felt old and tired. Apparently neither age nor experience had corrected his character flaws.

He thought about the Nagaoka case, where he had made no progress whatsoever because of all the family distractions. The wretched prisoner remained in custody and at the mercy of the brutal guards and their bamboo whips. The man had not fit the image Akitada had formed of him, that of an upstart commoner who seduces unprotected daughters of the aristocracy in hopes of bettering himself, and so he had made a poor job of questioning him. The truth of it was that Akitada could not even dislike this Kojiro who had caused all the trouble in his home. The man had behaved with unexpected dignity and courage. And Nagaoka had proved to be a man of culture, well-read and knowledgeable. This did not, of course, clear him of suspicion in his wife's murder.

Akitada paced, considering the case against Nagaoka. Nagaoka took an interest in the theater, and actors stayed at the temple on the night of the murder. Nagaoka could have hired one of them to kill his wife when he discovered her infidelity. Tora, for all his prejudices, had been quite right about actors. An acting job, particularly with a traveling troupe, was often a cover for all sorts of criminals on the run from the authorities. What better place to find a killer for hire?

It had been foolish to dismiss Genba and Tora before they had had time for a full report, and even more foolish to prevent Tora from getting information from the girl acrobat.

Still feeling languid and vaguely ill, though the headache was much better, Akitada thought some tea might help. It was early and Seimei was probably still asleep. Making his way to the kitchen, where the sleepy-eyed maid Kumoi was just starting the water for the morning rice gruel, he made himself a pot of tea and took it back to his room.

Sipping on the veranda outside his study, he looked at his garden. It was barely dawn, but the clouds seemed to be clearing. In the pine, some sparrows rustled, chirping softly. The fish were sluggish. He must get them some food.

Seimei appeared suddenly. He glanced at the teacup in Akitada's hand and apologized for having overslept, adding, "Genba is outside, sir. He begs for a moment of your time."

"Good! Ask him to come!"

Genba came to him hesitantly, head still hanging low. He stood for a moment, awkwardly clenching and unclenching his big fists, then said hoarsely, "We are very sorry, sir."

"Sit down, Genba." Akitada made his tone friendly. "I have been too harsh and forgot that neither you nor Tora have had any leisure since our return. You have both served faithfully during the long years of hardship up north and on the strenuous journey back. Then you got back and had to deal with ruined stables and a funeral. I should have been more appreciative. Instead I lost my temper. Please forgive me, and take the rest of the day and the night off. Tomorrow we will discuss your new assignments."

Genba's face broke into a wide grin. "Whew!" he cried fervently. "Thank you, sir. But you were quite right. We shouldn't have quarreled. Well, I came to tell you, we've made up. Tora's been worried because you wouldn't let him go see the little acrobat. He told her to meet him in the Willow Quarter, which is not a good place to send a nice young girl on her own."

"I am sure she came to no harm." Akitada wondered why Tora should be concerned about the reputation of a girl who had agreed so readily to sleep with him on first acquaintance. "You said very little yesterday. Do you have anything to add to Tora's report?"

Genba scratched his head. His once-shaven pate was once again covered with a thick brush of hair not yet long enough to twist on top. Genba attempted to make it lie down flat by wetting it periodically and plastering it as close to his skull as he could. But as it dried, stubborn sections of hair popped up again. Having disturbed the careful arrangement, he quickly patted it back down. Watching him, Akitada noticed for the first time that Genba was turning gray. He had never asked his age but guessed that Genba must be well into his forties.

"About Tora's worries, sir. Miss Plumblossom, the lady who runs the training hall, is very concerned about some villain who's been going around slashing prostitutes. Her maid's one of the bastard's victims. She must've been good-looking until she lost her nose and part of her upper lip. Her whole face is a mess, what with all the knife scars. Being disfigured like that, she couldn't work anymore and was starving. She was going through the refuse behind the training hall when Miss Plumblossom found her."

Akitada frowned. There seemed to be many stories of disfigurement recently, but the matter hardly concerned him. "It is horrible, of course, but prostitution provokes abnormal behavior in some men," he said carelessly. "Has she identified her attacker to the police?"

Genba shook his head. "Prostitutes don't complain to the authorities. And she may not have got a good look at him. Probably met him on a dark street and went home with him. Miss Plumblossom says some people found her half dead in an abandoned temple. They thought she'd been attacked by demons."

This sounded familiar, but Akitada could not immediately place it and put it from his mind. "A terrible tale," he said, "but I don't see that it helps us with the actors. We know they spent the night at the temple. Did they talk about the murder?"

"No. And that's a bit queer. Tora says nobody would talk to him after Danjuro warned them off. By the way, the maid was spying on Tora and his girl and he grabbed her. She bit his hand and ran off screeching that she'd been attacked."

"Not surprising under the circumstances," Akitada said dryly.

"There's some trouble between the actors and Danjuro. Seems Uemon recently turned over the running of the troupe to Danjuro, who's come into some money."

"Hmm." Akitada slowly shook his head. "I don't see that any of this gets us closer to the Nagaoka case. Well, perhaps Tora will have better luck with his girl tonight. If he turns up nothing, either, we will have to start interviewing the monks."

Having made his peace with Tora and Genba, Akitada decided to speak to his wife.

Tamako was up, peering into a large round silver mirror. The shutters of the room were still closed, but daylight seeped in. Only a single candle was burning next to her, and in the golden light and the soft rosy glow from the glowing coals in the brazier, she looked ethereal. She was still in her undergown of white silk, which alternately clung and floated as she moved, revealing and concealing the soft curves of her body. Akitada felt a strong surge of desire, and an even stronger need to hold and touch her.

She barely looked up. "Forgive me, Akitada. I am hurrying to get dressed. It was a long day yesterday, and I overslept. Do you mind terribly if I go on with my makeup?"

Crushed, he turned to go. "No," he mumbled, "of course not. I just came to . . . talk."

She caught up with him before he reached the door. "Wait." Peering up at him, she cried, "What is wrong? Are you ill?"

"No. Just tired. And worried about Yoshiko."

"You look terrible. Yoshiko will get over it. Fortunately, both Toshikage and Akiko agreed with me and we convinced her to obey you in this matter. Come sit down." She led him to the bedding, which still lay spread out, and made him loosen the upper part of his robe. He submitted meekly, marveling at how he had misjudged her. She had been on his side all along.

Kneeling behind him, Tamako massaged and stroked his neck and shoulders with her strong, gentle hands until he felt his muscles ease and allowed himself to relax, closing his eyes and sighing with pleasure.

He did not know how it came about, but at some point he caught one of her hands and kissed it gratefully. She paused for a moment, then moved around in front of him to slip his robe off his shoulders. Her fingers touched his skin like the wings of butterflies, or like the mouths of the fishes in the pool last night, moving over his chest, down to his waist, and back again. His breath caught in his throat. He looked at her, hoping she would read the naked hunger in his eyes.

Tamako extinguished the candle, and helped him out of his clothes.

——+——

Later, when he was back at his desk, warm and happy, Seimei brought fresh tea along with the morning rice. Akitada thought the old man looked pale and drawn. The tray seemed almost too heavy for him. Eating the thick rice gruel, he watched Seimei pour a cup of the tea with a hand that shook so badly that he spilled a few drops. Akitada lowered his bowl. "Are you feeling quite well, Seimei?"

"Yes. Fine, sir. Fine. Sorry about this." Seimei dabbed at the drops of tea with the sleeve of his dark cotton robe. Then, instead of leaving quietly, he remained, his eyes downcast.

"Is anything else wrong?"

"Nothing wrong—precisely—sir. Only . . ."

"Only what?"

"I wondered if all is well with Miss Yoshiko, sir? Her ladyship mentioned to me that the policeman had brought some very disturbing news. I couldn't help worrying."

"Heavens. I thought you knew." Akitada tried to remember: had Seimei somehow missed being told? He realized that this was the first time he had not discussed family matters or a case with the old man. He set down his bowl. "I am sorry, Seimei. I should have kept you informed, but so much has happened lately that I forgot. Please take a seat, for this will take a while."

Seimei obeyed, his eyes suddenly moist. Akitada told him of

Yoshiko's relationship with Kojiro, her trips to the prison, and Kobe's assumption that Akitada had used her to get to the prisoner. Then he explained the agreement he had reached with Kobe and the present status of the case. When he was done, Seimei nodded and dabbed his eyes.

"Why, what is the matter now?" Akitada asked.

Seimei smiled a little. "Nothing now, my lord. I'm overcome with gratitude. I was afraid that I had lost your confidence." He made Akitada a deep bow. "I shall do my utmost to be always worthy of it."

"You are and will be." Akitada's conscience smote him. In his pique he had slighted the old man and hurt his feelings. "It was just an oversight, Seimei. Stop worrying so much. Er, how is Yori doing? Are you still teaching him his brushstrokes?"

Seimei sat up a little straighter. His smile widened. "The young master is improving. It is said that one is never too young or too old to learn the way of the brush. He is not always patient as you were at his age, but he has a steadier hand, I think."

Akitada chuckled, relieved to hear the old Seimei quoting his wise sayings again. "I am sure," he said, "that you have reminded him that even the poorest archer will hit the target with enough practice."

"Ah, yes. I did mention that, and also the one about a drop of water piercing a rock if repeated often enough. He did not care for that one too much. But the day he complained of his fingers being too cold to hold the brush, I explained that a turning waterwheel does not have time to get frozen. He worked quite industriously after that." Seimei chuckled.

With a lighter heart, Akitada reached for his gruel. On second thought, he carried it out into the garden and fed grains of rice to the fish. They rose eagerly to the surface, twisting and splashing for the bits of food. Their excitement pleased him and he laughed.

"You remind me, my old friend, that I have neglected other duties," he said, turning to Seimei, pleased to see the quick flush of joy the familiar form of address brought to the old man's cheek. "I'm afraid that I have also not been much of a father lately."

Seimei smiled. "Impossible, sir. A parent's love for his son is greater than the son's for his father."

"Well, I hope Yori does not think too badly of me." Akitada looked at the sky. It was still slightly overcast, but here and there a patch of blue showed and the sun shone fitfully. Two squirrels chattered in the pine and then chased each other up and down the trunk. The air smelled fresh and clean. "What do you say, shall we have a game of football in the courtyard? Tora and Genba can use some exercise, I expect, and you can keep score for us."

Seimei clapped his hands. "Excellent, sir. The young master will be happy. A man may be known for his sportsmanship as much as his erudition."

Akitada found Yori with his mother. The boy greeted the suggestion with whoops of joy, crying *"kemari, kemari,"* while he looked for the leather ball. Father and son sat down together on the veranda steps to put on their leather boots and then ran out into the courtyard. Yori's excited shouts brought Tora and Genba from the stables. Their playing field, ten feet square, was quickly marked out in the gravel. Four potted trees marked the corners, and the players, booted and their trousers tied up, arranged themselves between them.

The object was to kick the ball from player to player without letting it touch the ground. Yori, not yet four years old, was already amazingly adept at the game, and the others lost points rapidly. Akitada called for time out to remove his heavy outer robe, and noticed Tamako and Yoshiko on the veranda. Tamako was smiling, but his sister still looked pale and dispirited.

Akitada's performance gradually improved. It had been a

long time since he had played the game. Once he had been very good at it. He took great care to make it easy for his young son, but Yori had the energy of ten and threw his whole small body into each effort. Tora and Genba, unaccustomed to this pastime of the "good people," caused Yori to burst into gales of laughter at their clumsy efforts.

When they finally broke off, the adults were breathless and perspiring, while Yori, declared the winner, raced about the courtyard, shouting, "I won! I won!" as Seimei and the ladies applauded. In a sudden glow of happiness, Akitada caught up his son and swung him high into the air. Yori shrieked with delight and flung his small arms about his father's neck. Akitada had not felt so well, so whole, in many months, and, hugging the child to him, he made a courtly bow toward the veranda.

Back in his office, his newly found optimism still with him, he called for his outdoor clothes. "I am going to pay another call on Nagaoka," he told Seimei, who helped him dress. "There must be any number of things the man has not told. I did not pry into his relations with his wife last time, but her personality is the most intriguing mystery in her death. It now seems to me he avoided the subject."

Seimei pursed his lips. "In autumn there is no need for a fan. From what you said, Mr. Nagaoka was too old for his wife. He may feel great relief."

Seimei was a terrible misogynist, but Akitada considered the possibility that Nagaoka might have tired of an immature and expensive wife. He said dubiously, "From all accounts, she was very beautiful and he loved her."

Seimei shook his head. "An angel outside often hides a demon inside." He recalled himself quickly. "Of course, there are exceptions to this rule."

Akitada, on his way out, chuckled.

— ◆ —

A short walk brought him to the tree-lined street where Nagaoka lived. Once again he was struck by the quiet gentility of the wealthier merchants' lifestyle. The trees were completely bare now, and it was possible to see many roofs beyond Nagaoka's wall. A well-to-do antiquarian might easily live as luxuriously as a member of the imperial family, forever changing the displays in his house from goods stored away for sale or trade.

Nagaoka's gate stood wide open, a fact which puzzled Akitada, considering his train of thought. Who was guarding the valuable contents of the residence? Last time he had seen only a single disgruntled servant; this time even that slovenly individual was absent.

He strolled in. The courtyard had not been swept in days and reminded him of his first visit. He called out, but no one answered. Taking this as an invitation to look around, he walked past the entrance of the main house and into the rear courtyards and gardens. Everywhere he went, he saw the same neglect. Furthermore, back here, away from visitors' eyes, the buildings were in poor repair and the gardens as overgrown as his own. Paint peeled off the lacquered eaves and railings. A stair step had warped out of place. Shutters hung crookedly. There had been times when the Sugawara property had looked something like this because they had been too poor to fix the damage of time. But would a wealthy man allow his home to become run-down like this?

And the place was deserted. Where were the servants to look after things? Could Nagaoka have taken flight because he was afraid he would be implicated in the murder?

Akitada passed quickly through a small garden, its fishpond choked with leaves and empty of koi, and entered the service courtyard. In its center stood a large storehouse. Unlike the residence, it was built of stone and plaster and had a tile roof. Such storehouses stood in all the compounds of wealthier families for safekeeping of valuables and heirlooms from the many fires which plagued the wooden buildings of the capital. Nagaoka's treasure-house stood open like his gate.

Akitada stepped on the large slab of rock at the door and peered in. The shelves which stretched along the windowless walls inside were bare except for a few small bags of what looked like rice or beans, a small pile of turnips, and some chestnuts. An earthenware pitcher and a sake barrel sat next to a large basket. Stepping inside, Akitada looked into the basket. It contained charcoal. He raised the pitcher and smelled its mouth: cheap oil. The sake barrel was empty, the dregs in the bottom as clouded and sour-smelling as the most inferior brew. Against the back wall stood some metal-bound wooden chests, their locks unfastened. He looked inside. They were empty except for remnants of packing material. Where were all of Nagaoka's antiques?

Akitada reemerged and stood for a few moments in the courtyard, digesting the discovery and wondering about its significance. His first fear, that there had been some strong-armed robbery, possibly resulting in the death of the owner and his servants, was proved wrong by the fact that the storehouse had been put to use as a sort of pantry after its costlier contents had been removed. The types of foods stored were hardly what one expected to content the palate of a wealthy merchant, but someone seemed to have been living here since the treasures had disappeared.

Thoughtfully Akitada retraced his steps to the front of the house and pounded on the door.

"Stop that racket," a voice shouted from the street. "I'm coming. Can't a man have even a moment's peace in this forsaken place?" The figure of the servant rounded the open gateway. He was walking in a leisurely fashion, perhaps a little unsteadily, and carried a slightly steaming bundle which looked like a hot meal from some eatery. His appearance had deteriorated further since last time. He had not bothered to tie up his hair or shaved in days, and his robe was filthy.

When he saw Akitada, he stopped, narrowed his eyes, and peered blearily at him. "Oh, it's you again," he finally said rudely. "What do you want this time? He's not been home for days, and I have work to do."

"Mind your manners," Akitada snapped. "Where is your master?"

The man scowled. "Who knows? Took his money and ran, is my guess. Either that or he's jumped off a bridge and is explaining his sins to the judge of the underworld. Leaving me behind with nothing to eat or drink, not to mention without my pay."

Akitada regarded the man suspiciously. His appearance and behavior showed that he did not expect his master to return very soon. He said brusquely, "It is cold out here. You may take me to your master's room and answer some questions."

The servant bristled. "I don't see why. Him not being here, I'm not allowed into the house."

"What is in that parcel?" Akitada asked, narrowing his eyes.

"Just some food. A man's got to eat."

"And where did you get the money for it? You said you had not been paid."

The servant's bluster faltered. "I had some saved up," he muttered sullenly.

Akitada glared. "You are a liar! I think you stole the money from your master. I shall inform the police." Stepping down into the courtyard, he approached the man threateningly. "In fact, I don't believe your master has left. Why should he do so, with his wife recently dead and his brother in jail and about to go on trial? Perhaps you murdered him. What have you done with him? Come on, you lout! Speak up!"

The servant, turning pale, backed away so suddenly that he dropped his parcel. An unappetizing mess of glutinous morsels spilled onto the gravel. Its smell and the man's strong odor of sour wine and unwashed skin turned Akitada's stomach.

"I told the truth," the man wailed. "He went off last week,

looking terrible, all white like a ghost. He never said a word. Just walked past me out the door. And he never came back. Maybe he *is* dead someplace, but I didn't lay a hand on him."

Akitada looked at him long and hard. "We shall see. Open the door to the house!"

The door was unlocked, as had been the gate, the storehouse, and the chests.

"Why are you not guarding this house better?" Akitada growled as he followed the fellow down the dark hallway to the room where he had last spoken with Nagaoka.

"What for? There's nothing left to steal."

And there was not. Akitada looked around the dim room, and went to throw the wooden shutters open. There were no picture scrolls on the walls, the shelves were empty, even the heavy carved desk was gone. Only the thick floor mats remained and the two cushions they had sat on during his last visit. "What happened to your master's goods and furniture?" he asked, looking about him in surprise.

"He sold 'em."

"Everything? All his antiques? His stock as well as his own possessions?"

The servant nodded. "Every stick of it."

"Why would he do a thing like that?"

"Business hasn't been exactly flourishing for a long time, and her ladyship had to have fine clothes, maids, and baubles, not to mention what he paid for her to start with. The master just kept selling off stuff to pay for it all." The man's tone became increasingly resentful. "He paid that snooty maidservant of hers and the lazy cook better'n me. The maid took off the minute she heard of the murder. And the cook went when she saw that the master hardly had money left for a decent funeral. They knew the good life was over. Guess who got stuck with all the work and no pay? Call me the biggest fool, for hanging around!"

"I told you once to watch your tongue!" Akitada snapped. "I

won't do it again. You have eaten your master's rice and owe him respect and loyalty."

"More like millet and beans of late," grumbled the man.

"When did your master begin to liquidate his property?"

The servant stared at him. "Liquid what? He didn't drink. Not like that brother of his!"

"I meant, when did he begin selling off everything?"

The man chewed on his lower lip. "He started selling the last of the antiques right after it happened. The buyers went away grinning. I guess word got around, for after that more and more people came, and then he sold all his wife's things. Good riddance, I thought! We had a bit of fish with our rice after that, and the wine barrel was filled with better stuff."

Akitada recalled Nagaoka handling the *bugaku* mask during his last visit. He had been planning to sell it below its value. In retrospect, he should have wondered then what would cause a shrewd antiquarian to sell a rare object at a loss. "Go on!" he told the servant. "When were the other things sold, his personal things?"

"After the visit of his wife's father, I suppose. He lost his spirit. I guess it finally sank in that she was gone. And when that police officer came again to tell my master to stop visiting his brother in jail, that was the final straw. The very next day, people came and carried away the rest of the furniture, and when they were done, my master sat right there, on his cushion, looking around the empty room like a dying man. The next morning he left."

"How long has he been gone?"

The servant pondered. Using his fingers to count off the days, he said, "Seven days, maybe."

Seven days! What could have happened to Nagaoka? Had Kobe threatened him and sent him into a panic? Nagaoka had not seemed the kind of man who would leave a servant to look after a house without money for food.

The servant suggested, "Maybe he really killed himself."

Akitada rejected that explanation. Having systematically sold all his things and taken whatever money he received for them, he was surely not planning to commit suicide. Unless . . . Perhaps he had left his affairs in the hands of another before ending his life.

"Does he have any family or friends whom he might visit?"

"Only his brother in jail."

The other possibility was, of course, that Nagaoka, afraid of a murder charge, had made his escape, leaving his brother to his fate. Akitada did not want to believe this.

"When your master left here, was he carrying anything? A box, or bundle of clothes? Was he dressed for a long journey? Boots for riding? A warm robe?"

"He carried a bag, the kind you'd strap to a saddle. And boots on his feet and his best quilted robe." The servant squeezed his eyes shut, trying to remember. "I think I saw the handle of a short sword in his sash, too." Opening his eyes in wonder, he cried, "So the old b—— he went off on a trip after all! How about that?"

"Where would he have gone? Does he have property in the country?"

"Just his brother's place. At Fushimi. He'd hardly be going to see his father-in-law." He guffawed.

Akitada raised his brows. "And why not?"

"They had a quarrel right after the funeral. You never heard such shouting! The master all but threw him out, and the old man left shaking his fist at him."

"Really?" Akitada was intrigued. "Where does his father-in-law live?"

"He's got a farm someplace near the brother's. Gives himself airs like a gentleman but wears a patched robe and straw boots."

"Hmm." The servant seemed to have run out of useful information, and Akitada turned to leave. "Very well. I shall check your story. If you have lied to me, I'll have you arrested. Meanwhile, you had better straighten up the place in case your master returns."

Greatly relieved, the servant promised to get started immediately, but Akitada had a strong premonition that Nagaoka would not return to this empty shell of a house.

SIXTEEN

Yin and Yang

"It's too late now," grumbled Tora, when he and Genba returned to the stable from the game of football and Genba suggested he go to see Gold. "No telling what she'll think of me for standing her up. She hated the idea of going to the pleasure quarter to meet me."

"Well, why don't you go and explain? Buy her something pretty and apologize."

Tora brightened a little. He never lacked confidence when it came to women. "You going, too?" he asked tentatively. Their peace was still recent, and bad feelings might linger.

Genba shook his head. "No. I think I'll exercise the horses." He slapped the rump of Akitada's gray, who snorted playfully and danced about on his rope.

Tora hesitated. "I'm sorry for what I said about, you know, the lady."

"I know." Genba busied himself with one of the saddles.

"She was really good with the bamboo staves. No fear at all."

"I know."

"D'you suppose she wrestles, too?"

"I wouldn't be surprised."

"I didn't like getting beaten by a female. Would you wrestle with her?"

Genba placed the saddle on the back of the gray and pulled the leather straps tight. Then he leaned on it to look at Tora. "After what she did to you? No." He grinned slowly.

Tora returned the grin. "Well, remember what you told me. Don't be discouraged. There are lots of ways to get close to a woman. Tell her you're afraid of hurting a delicate creature in a real bout. Then show her other uses for holds and clinches."

Genba smiled a little sadly. "She doesn't like me. She likes you."

"That's because you haven't sweet-talked her. Tell her how pretty she is, and how bright her eyes are, and how sweet her voice sounds."

Genba made a face. "She's an intelligent woman, not a silly young girl. We talk about important things."

"That's where you make your mistake. Women like it when you talk about their beauty and make soulful eyes at them. It's their nature. A woman who doesn't like pretty speeches is as rare as a square egg. You want me to stay and teach you some good lines?"

"No, thanks. I'll do my own courting. Go on and find your girl."

Relieved that all seemed to be well between him and Genba, Tora walked into the city in a more cheerful mood. The sun was already high; it was time for the midday rice. Gold would hardly be at the training hall except at night, and then only on their practice nights. He remembered that she stayed at the Golden Phoenix Inn, but his first stop was the Willow Quarter, on the off chance that she might still be waiting.

In broad daylight the quarter looked shabby and deserted. A few elderly maids swept doorways and porters delivered supplies to the restaurants and wineshops. The house he was looking for was in a backstreet and quite small, squeezed between two more substantial neighbors. It had a tiny entrance courtyard behind a wicker gate. A morning glory vine grew here in summer, but now the wooden posts were bare. Tora opened the gate and quickly walked the few stepping-stones to the door. A small bell with a wooden clapper hung there and he rang it vigorously. When there was no immediate answer, he pushed the door open and stepped into the small, dirt-floored entry, shouting, "Ho! Mitsuko?"

"Yes? Who's there?" came a soft voice from the back.

"Tora. Can I come in?"

"Tora?" The voice was filled with sudden pleasure. "Yes. I'll be right there."

Tora grinned and took off his boots. After a moment, a middle-aged woman, very small like her house, and dressed in a plain blue cotton robe, came hurrying down the dim corridor. She moved with the peculiar half-sliding, half-swaying gait of the trained woman of pleasure and had, in fact, once been a famous courtesan. She was still beautiful in all but her face, which was severely disfigured by smallpox.

"It *is* you, Tora, my fierce animal!" she cried. "At last, after all this time. It's been six years almost, hasn't it? Come in, come in. Let me look at you."

Tora stepped up onto the wooden floor of the hallway. It was highly polished and, like everything else in the small house, very plain and very clean. He looked down at her from his height. "You look well, little flower," he said, and bowed. "It gives me great pleasure to find you as charming as ever."

She laughed at his formality, brushing at her hair, which she wore gathered into a heavy bun. It was still glossy and the sound of her laughter was pleasant, like that of very small smooth pebbles being poured into a ceramic bowl. It rippled melodiously, and used to make men feel quite weak with pleasure. "You're such a handsome liar," she said, reaching up and pulling Tora's nose. "I have some decent wine. Shall we share a cup while you tell me your adventures and help a poor lonely old woman pass an afternoon?"

"Never an old woman, but"—he looked at her anxiously—"have you been lonely, Mitsuko?"

She patted his arm. "No more than usual. Since you have rid me of that horrible man, I can go anywhere and my friends can visit me again."

The "horrible man" was a hunchbacked fishmonger who had attempted to force Mitsuko to become his personal property by paying a debt for her and then claiming that she had sold herself to him. Like many women of her class, Mitsuko was unable to read the documents she signed with her mark. Tora had made certain that the fishmonger not only relinquished the documents, but never approached her again.

"I was hoping the bastard had died." Tora seated himself in a tiny reception room hardly large enough to hold two people. Mitsuko produced the wine and cups with the conscious grace of the professional companion and served him with slender, beautiful hands. "Welcome home, my tiger," she said with a smile.

Tora raised his cup to her and drank. The wine was good, but he drank sparingly, knowing she had little money. Putting his cup down, he asked, "Did a young woman come here last night, asking for me?"

Mitsuko raised her brows. "You have made new friends before visiting your old ones?"

"I'm sorry, Mitsuko. I met her on an assignment for my master. I haven't had time off until today."

"Ah. I forgive you. No. Nobody came. Perhaps you are not as irresistible as you think?"

Tora was disappointed. "I guess not, though I would've bet she liked me. Maybe you know her? She's an actress. Her professional name's Gold. She and her twin Silver work for a guy called Uemon."

Mitsuko thought. "No. I've seen Uemon's shows. They're very good. Is she pretty?"

"Pretty, yes. Not beautiful like you."

She smiled a little sadly. "You are always kind, Tora. Sometimes I need to hear that. After the smallpox, people stopped looking at me. Just the one glance, you know, and then they turn their eyes elsewhere as they talk to me."

Tora looked at her. "Not all of them. I like looking at you. Your eyes are as large and handsome as ever and you still smile like a goddess. It's just the skin that's a bit marred. Nothing to get upset about. I've seen much worse, and not so long ago."

She laughed bitterly and reached up to touch a pitted, discolored cheek. "Not worse. None of the other women lost their looks like I have."

"You had more to lose. Most people die from smallpox."

"I usually wish I had."

Tora never knew how to respond when she said things like that. "The girl I saw looked really horrible. Some man carved her a new face. Took off the nose and part of her upper lip. Then he cut a couple of extra mouths on her face."

Mitsuko's eyes widened. "So she's still alive. We thought she drowned herself. She worked here in the quarter for a while. Seemed a better-class girl, but couldn't find good customers." Mitsuko earned a very meager income arranging appointments between men and certain women of the quarter. Some of her own former clients had taken pity on her and sent a little business her way. "She was very pretty and promising, I heard, and I was going to talk to her when she disappeared."

"What happened?"

"Some of the common people blame it on demons, but it must have been a client. Lately there have been rumors of someone . . . strange." She sighed, looking down at her hands.

"You mean one of her customers did that to her?"

"Sometimes men can only enjoy the rain and clouds if they hurt the woman."

Tora was appalled. "That's disgusting! Why would a girl let a man do such things to her?"

"I don't suppose she expected it."

"The bastard's got to be stopped before he does it again. Did she tell anyone who he was?"

"I don't think so. You'll have to ask her yourself. I wish someone could find out. The girls are worried."

"Hmm." Tora stared at her. He had often regretted that his master seemed to do most of the investigating himself—as if he did not trust Tora to have enough sense for the trickier bits. The recent reprimand still rankled. What if he could solve a case all by himself? Perhaps this slasher was his chance to prove himself. "Suppose I caught the bastard?" he asked Mitsuko.

She looked at him with a smile. "You might. Nobody else seems to bother. The police have better things to do than protect poor women."

"Well, then, wish me luck!" He hurriedly finished his wine and rose.

"But you just got here."

"And I'll be back, sweetheart." Mitsuko shook her head and looked at him quizzically. He was not sure whether she was hurt or amused by his short visit, but he put his arm around her and gave her a squeeze before heading out the door.

In his new role as hunter of criminals, Tora was no longer hampered by the fact that Gold might not want him to pursue her too openly. A madman who preyed on the women of the pleasure quarter was loose. What if she had run into that animal on the way to meet him? Tora asked the way to the Golden Phoenix.

It was near the river and Miss Plumblossom's training hall, a backstreet business offering cheap accommodations to poor travelers and those who needed a place to sleep for a few weeks. When Tora ducked under the torn and faded curtain separating the inn's interior from the narrow street outside, he found himself face-to-face with two small boys. They sat on the wooden platform, their feet dangling, engaged in a game of dice.

The smaller of the two snapped, "Yes? What do you want?"

in an irascible tone and a gravelly voice which seemed to have broken prematurely.

Tora peered at him, adjusting his eyes to the dimness after the outdoors. The little one could not be more than five or six. He had tiny hands and feet. But that voice! "Your mother needs to teach you manners, boy," he growled. "Where is she? Who's in charge here?" He looked at the older boy, who merely grinned foolishly. Probably an idiot, Tora thought. What were these children doing, gambling for money? The pile of coppers in front of the little one was impressive.

The small boy hopped up. He used his arms to do this, much like a little monkey. When he was standing, his head seemed too large for his compact short body. Tora thought him the ugliest child he had ever seen. Ratlike eyes peered over a bulbous nose, and large protruding ears looked like handles stuck onto a melon; besides, he was glowering up at Tora with a thoroughly malevolent expression. "Look who's talking about manners!" he croaked. "What mangy cat dragged you in by that moth-eaten mustache?"

The insult to Tora's trim and dapper facial ornament was too much. He took a large step forward. "Let me save your parents the trouble and blister your sorry behind, you little lout!" He seized the boy by the scruff of his jacket, intending to put him over his knee, but a closer look stopped him. The "child" had gray hair and the wrinkled face of an elderly man. Shocked, Tora let him drop back on the platform.

"Ouch!" The little old man fell on his behind, then bounced up and retaliated with a well-placed kick to Tora's groin.

Tora doubled over. "Why, you little bastard," he said when he came up for breath.

The dwarf hopped around like an excited bird and laughed with an unpleasant cackle. "I have other tricks, if you want to try me, big bastard," he crowed.

Tora saw the humor in the situation and chuckled. "Sorry,

uncle," he said. "It was dark after the street outside. I meant no harm."

The ugly little man narrowed his eyes, then nodded. "All right," he said grudgingly. "I'm the manager. What do you want?"

"One of Uemon's girls. The one called Gold. I was told she stayed here."

The dwarf and the grinning boy looked at each other. When the small man turned to Tora, his expression was grim. "Gone!" he said.

"Gone? All of them? So suddenly? Where?"

"How should I know? The handsome one paid and they all walked out. I don't ask people for their travel plans."

Tora looked from one to the other. There was a certain wariness in their eyes, as if they were waiting to see how he would take this information. He sighed and pulled out his meager string of coppers, weighing it in his hand. "How much?" he asked the dwarf.

The beady eyes guessed at the number of coins in Tora's hand. "Twenty," the dwarf ventured.

It was all Tora had for his midday meal. He counted out twenty coppers and stacked them on the platform. "I need to know when they left, where they went, and if the girl was with them," he said without removing his hand from the stack.

The dwarf's eyes lit up. "Sometime yesterday, don't know, and yes."

Tora did not take his hand off the money. "What about your young friend there? Does he know anything?"

The boy was still grinning. Shaking his head violently, he made a snorting sound which might have been suppressed laughter or an idiot's speech defect. After a moment, Tora released the money. The dwarf scooped it up so quickly that his fingers touched Tora's hand as it withdrew.

Well, at least the girl was fine. Tora nodded to the gamblers and stepped back out into the street. It was well past noon, and his stomach grumbled. He looked unhappily about him. His master would want him to find the actors. Maybe they left for an engagement in the country, but with the end of the year approaching they had to be rehearsing. Probably they had just changed accommodations. Tora did not relish the thought of trudging up and down streets to check every inn or rooming house. He decided to stop by Miss Plumblossom's. Surely she would know what their plans were. Besides, he needed to talk to that maid if he was going to find the slasher.

As he walked, he thought of a third reason. His hungry imagination conjured up the memory of Miss Plumblossom eating. A woman with such an appetite might offer a leftover morsel to a starving man.

Miss Plumblossom was indeed just finishing her meal. Seated on her thronelike chair, she eyed the tray held by the scarred maid regretfully and dabbed her lips. "Take the rest away, my dear. That was quite delicious, but Mr. Oishi is waiting for his wrestling lesson and too much food makes me sluggish."

The doorkeeper being absent, Tora had slipped in unnoticed. Mr. Oishi, a very large, blubbery figure already stripped to his loincloth, was waiting anxiously for his lesson, and the maid walked away with the tray.

Seeing his meal disappearing, Tora shouted, "Wait!" Six astonished eyes turned toward him. Then disaster struck. The maid shrieked and dropped the food. Tora cursed, rushed up, and was met by Miss Plumblossom's heel placed squarely and violently in his groin, which was still sore from the kick by the dwarf. Miss Plumblossom packed quite a different force from the tiny old man. Tora shrieked and fell backward, writhing with pain. Almost instantly a crushing weight landed on his body, choking off his second scream. He mercifully lost consciousness.

Akitada was in Kobe's office reporting Nagaoka's disappearance when a sergeant walked in to announce that the "slasher" had been captured.

Kobe rose excitedly. "Well, I hope it's good news this time!" he cried. "We've tried to catch that monster for months now."

Akitada was not pleased by the interruption but asked politely, "A dangerous criminal?"

"So far he's only preyed on prostitutes and loose women in the quarter of the untouchables, but you never know. Six dead that we know of." He turned to the sergeant, who stood waiting. "How did you catch him? In the act, I hope?"

The sergeant looked embarrassed. "Er, sort of," he mumbled. "Actually . . ."

"What? Speak up, man! It could mean special recognition for one of our guys."

"Er," stammered the sergeant, "it wasn't one of our men that caught him, sir. It was a female."

Kobe stared. "A female? You mean one of the whores fought back? Good for her!"

"Not really, sir. It was Miss Plumblossom."

"The idiot attacked Miss Plumblossom?"

Akitada chuckled. Kobe looked at him suspiciously. "You know her?"

"Only from what my men told me. If it is the same woman, she is a character, a former acrobat who runs a training hall."

Kobe nodded glumly. "The same. Not the easiest person in the world to deal with. She's forever complaining about us. Well, I suppose I had better face the dragon. Do you want to come?"

Akitada hesitated. "Can we discuss the Nagaoka case on the way?"

"Nothing to discuss, but if you must."

Akitada bit his lip. "In that case, I will come. If Kojiro does not know where his brother has gone, there may be trouble."

"The man's not accountable to his brother. Besides, I warned him away."

They walked out of the administrative hall of the prison and crossed the courtyard, where a contingent of constables was practicing with weighted steel chains and *jitte*, iron prongs designed to deflect swords.

"Nagaoka has been gone too long," Akitada urged. "And he carried money."

Kobe considered it. "I suppose Nagaoka could be behind the murder. If so, he has by now disappeared into the mountains."

"Will you let me help you find him?"

Kobe stopped and looked at Akitada. "Where would you go? What do you know?"

"Nothing I have not told you. But there are obvious places to ask questions. The servant said he was dressed for a journey. Boots, quilted robe, a bag, and possibly a short sword."

"Let me think about it."

They resumed their rapid pace and were approaching the eastern market. In spite of the cold weather, crowds of shoppers were coming and going, casting curious or nervous glances at the red-coated police constables who were preceding the two officials.

"A sword, eh?" Kobe pondered. "He didn't strike me as the type."

"If he carried all the money he got from selling his possessions, he would take a weapon. The roads are not safe."

"No. But where would you look?"

"His brother's farm is an hour's ride from the capital. So is the home of his late wife."

"Hmm. I don't see the point of going there." Kobe turned to his sergeant to discuss the case of the slasher and ignored Akitada until they arrived at Miss Plumblossom's establishment.

Inside, Akitada looked around curiously. The place reminded him of another training hall, in faraway Kazusa province, though this one was far larger and better equipped. But the memory brought sadness and he put it from his mind. The proprietress awaited them seated in a chair on the dais at the end of the hall, in the company of a very fat young man and a young woman who hid behind a fan.

Since chairs were by no means common—in fact, not even the emperor used such a piece of furniture—Akitada stared in surprise. If it had not been for the elaborate coils of shiny black hair trimmed with red ribbons and the chalk-white face with heavy "moth" eyebrows painted somewhere high above the kohl-rimmed eyes, he would have taken Miss Plumblossom for a fat abbot of a Buddhist monastery.

"Well, if it isn't the superintendent himself!" fluted the lady in the chair. "How very gratifying!"

"How do you do, Miss Plumblossom," said Kobe, stiff-faced. "Now, where is this man you suspect of being the slasher?"

The painted eyebrows rose another inch. "Tsk. Tsk. Superintendent. Is that mannerly? Surely there is no need to be so abrupt, seeing that I have saved the police months, maybe years of trouble, by catching the monster."

"Madam," snapped Kobe, "I have little time to waste. Let me see the fellow now. We have absolutely no proof that you have the right man."

"Ah! But I have. Identified by his victim, Superintendent. When he was about to attack her again."

Kobe glanced at the young woman with the averted face. "If I recall, last time I spoke with her, your maid said she could not describe her attacker. She said it was too dark and she passed out. How, then, can she be sure now?"

"She knew him, all right. The monster grabbed her again. The other night, right outside my establishment. Out in the alley. Meant to kill her this time, no doubt, to keep her from identifying him. We would have caught him then, but it was dark and he got away."

Kobe muttered something that sounded like a curse. Miss Plumblossom's eyebrows climbed again and she pursed her red lips disapprovingly.

"If he got away," Kobe said with forced patience, "how is it that you have him now?"

"Hah! The fool made another attempt in broad daylight, thinking he hadn't been recognized. Walked right in here, bold as brass. Poor Yukiyo happened to be with me." Miss Plumblossom put a pudgy hand on the head of the young woman, who seemed to shrink into herself. "Yukiyo's eyes almost popped out, she dropped the dishes and screamed so loud the tiles rattled on the roof. That's when the animal rushed forward to wring her neck, but I kicked him in the jewels. Appropriate, don't you think?"

Kobe grimaced. "Ouch!"

"Well, of course that brought him to his knees. Then Mr. Oishi here, who was waiting for his wrestling lesson, jumped on top of him, and flattened him out proper. We tied him up and threw him in the back room. I doubt he'll give you any trouble, but you'll have to carry him back."

"All right, let's have a look at him!" Kobe's impatience carried him in the direction of the door behind the dais, but Miss Plumblossom stopped him.

"A moment, Superintendent!" she cried, rising majestically from her chair.

He paused, and she preceded him to the door. Willy-nilly the superintendent of the capital police and a highly entertained Akitada followed a mere female, famed acrobat though she was. The constables and Mr. Oishi pressed after them.

Because Miss Plumblossom's bulk and the broad shoulders of Kobe blocked Akitada's view of the captured criminal, his first inkling that something was amiss was Kobe's indrawn breath and the words, "But that's . . ." before he stepped aside for Akitada to see the bound man on the floor. The shock of recognition propelled Akitada forward. Pushing both Kobe and Miss Plumblossom rudely aside, he fell down on his knees beside Tora.

Tora was conscious, his face white and glistening with perspiration. "Thank heaven, sir," he whispered. "Take me home."

Akitada touched Tora's face and found it ice-cold. He used a sleeve to dab gently at the beads of sweat. "Yes, of course." He looked up at Kobe. "I want him untied. Tora was working for me. I trust you remember him?" When Kobe nodded, he went on, "The women have made a terrible mistake. Tora may be badly injured and needs a doctor immediately—if there is a decent one available in this neighborhood. And then perhaps an oxcart to take him home. I will pay the costs." He turned back to Tora and, tugging at the knots in the rope which tied his hands, asked, "How badly are you hurt, do you think?"

"Don't know. My ribs. Can't breathe well." Tora paused, took a careful breath, and added, "That fiend of a woman kicked me in the groin. The second kick today." He closed his eyes. A tear escaped and slowly trickled down the side of his face. Akitada, sick with worry, tossed aside the rope and dabbed Tora's face again.

Kobe finished untying Tora's feet and then confronted a very nervous Miss Plumblossom. "Well, it looks like you put your foot in it properly this time, madam," he growled. "What do you have to say for yourself?"

Miss Plumblossom stammered, "B-but he *was* attacking Yukiyo right in front of us. We saw him. Didn't we, Mr. Oishi?"

"Well," said Mr. Oishi, with a voice surprisingly high for a man of his bulk, "he was certainly walking fast. When you kicked him, I naturally assumed he meant you harm. Else why would you do such a thing?"

"Quite right." Miss Plumblossom nodded. "I was provoked into a defensive action. The law permits me to protect myself and members of my family. I know my rights, because I had a learned man read my license to me."

"Get the doctor!" Akitada was on his feet, glaring at her, furious at the delay. "He is in pain and may have suffered permanent damage. We can unravel the tale later."

Miss Plumblossom flushed and offered timidly, "I have some knowledge of treating injuries. I'll take a look at him."

"No!" Tora gasped, wild-eyed. "Keep the fiend away from me! Get Seimei!"

Akitada laid a soothing hand on Tora's wrist. "Seimei is too far away. You need some help now, and then we'll take you home." Turning back to Miss Plumblossom, he demanded, "Who is the best doctor hereabouts? Quick, woman, before I lose my temper completely and lay charges for your arrest! You are clearly a menace who should never have been licensed in the first place."

Miss Plumblossom shrank back before his flashing eyes. "The Temple of the Twelve Divine Generals is just around the corner. One of the monks there practices healing. But he's getting old—"

Akitada told one of the constables, "Get the man!" The constable looked at Kobe, who nodded.

"Tell him to bring ice!" cried Miss Plumblossom after him, adding for Akitada's benefit, "To bring down the swelling of the jewels."

Tora groaned and turned his face away. Akitada knelt back down by his side. "My poor fellow. I am so sorry. I suppose you were looking for that girl. Gold, was it?"

Tora nodded.

"I should not have spoken to you the way I did yesterday. Please accept my apologies."

Tora nodded again, then reached for Akitada's hand and squeezed it.

"What's this about a girl?" asked Kobe, startled by Akitada's humble apology to a servant.

"I asked Tora to find a group of actors who may have witnessed the murder in the temple. One of the young women promised to meet him last night in the pleasure quarter. I would not let him go, so he came today, no doubt worried about her safety."

Miss Plumblossom gave a little gasp. "Gold! I might have known!" Raising her voice, she called, "Yukiyo! Come here this instant!"

The maid crept in. Her face was averted, but Akitada saw enough of it to be appalled.

"Come here, girl," commanded Miss Plumblossom. "Look at this young man well! Are you certain that *he* cut your face?"

The maid trembled and wept, but she shook her head mutely.

"He didn't?" roared Miss Plumblossom. "Then how could you say so?"

"I . . . I . . . he grabbed my arm outside . . . in the alley. He frightened me." The maid's speech was marred by her missing upper lip, but they understood her.

"But, stupid girl, that is not the same as taking a knife to your face. Look at what you made me do to him! Was grabbing your arm in the alley worth that? The man may never enjoy a woman again!" Tora went rigid and clutched at Akitada's hand. Miss Plumblossom, in full spate, continued, "He may never have a wife or beget children! A eunuch the rest of his life! And all because you made us think he was the slasher!"

The maid burst into hacking sobs.

Akitada said grimly, "Enough! It has happened. Let us try to make sure your predictions don't come true. Now get out of here."

Miss Plumblossom left meekly, taking the sobbing maid with her. Kobe slammed the door after them, then crouched down next to Akitada.

"You poor fellow," he said to Tora. "Women can be devils, but don't believe what she said. The doctor will fix you up like new."

Tora compressed his lips, stared at the ceiling, and said nothing. An old monk, bent almost double and wearing a threadbare black cotton robe liberally stained across the chest and sleeves, eventually made his appearance and examined the patient with many head-shakings and mumblings. To Akitada's irritation, his leisurely examination began with Tora's face, eyes, and tongue, and moved on to the feeling of his pulse and his abdomen, before it focused on his injuries. After considerable manipulation with his gnarled fingers—during which Tora went absolutely rigid until Akitada snapped, "enough!"—he pursed wrinkled lips and announced, "The cold and wet appearance of the skin, along with the extreme paleness, suggests that the life force has withdrawn and that the patient is therefore in a state of negativity. This indicates that the male force of *yang* has been weakened and overpowered by the female *yin* force, thereby creating a severely abnormal imbalance."

Tora's eyes grew round with horror. "She unmanned me!" he groaned. "I knew it. Just make an end of me right now. I can't bear life as a eunuch."

Kobe was shaking his head in pity, but Akitada glared at the monk. "Stop talking nonsense," he snapped. "Surely you can do something to bring down the swelling and reduce the pain. What about that ice?"

The monk rummaged in his bundle and brought out a stoneware jar and an ointment box, muttering, "The human body is transient, weak, and impotent." He applied the thick black ointment. "It is untrustworthy, impure, and full of filthiness." He took up the jar dubiously. Jerking his shaven head toward the door, he said, "*She* always orders ice for injuries that swell. I won't say she's wrong, since swellings attract heat, but in a case of severe negativity it's a very dangerous thing to do. I don't advise it. Leeches would be my choice. They'll bring the swelling down without chilling the flesh further."

With Tora's fingers gripping his painfully, Akitada said, "Put on the ice! In her business the woman should know what works best."

The monk grunted. "The love of women leads to delusion. Don't have any leeches anyway," and transferred the ice to a square of cotton, which he tied and placed on the injured groin. Tora sighed and relaxed a little.

Next the old monk fingered the purple bruises on Tora's chest. "No broken ribs," he pronounced, "but some of the vital organs may have been displaced or injured. The patient's coldness and the sweating suggest a rupture may have occurred, but it is too soon to tell."

"What if there is a rupture?" asked Akitada, visions of Tora's slow and agonizing death from internal injuries passing through his mind.

But the monk knotted up his bundle and rose, saying piously, "We must all prepare to leave this world of nothingness."

A miserable silence settled over the room after the monk had left. Then Tora said tentatively, "The ice helps."

"Good," cried Kobe. "You see! All will be well."

"What about your breathing?" asked Akitada.

"The same." Tora looked up at him. "I'm not afraid to die."

"You are not going to die," cried Akitada, and jumped up. "Where is that oxcart? You are going home, where Seimei will make you well."

The door opened. Miss Plumblossom said, "There's a messenger outside for you, Superintendent."

Kobe left the room, and Miss Plumblossom inched in. She had been weeping, for black smudges ringed her eyes like a badger's. "I'm very sorry, Tora," she told the patient. "I'll try to make it up to you. Whatever I have, it's yours."

Tora waved a languid hand. "Forget it!"

"No, no," she insisted, wringing her hands, when Kobe put in his head again.

"The oxcart is ready. But I have to leave. Looks like they found Nagaoka. Dead. His skull bashed in."

284

SEVENTEEN

Switched Boots

Since Kobe had rushed off without giving particulars about Nagaoka's death, Akitada merely saw Tora settled under Seimei's care before he went looking for the superintendent. Unfortunately, at his headquarters nobody knew or wanted to tell him where he had gone. He met with the same results at the prison, but here Akitada fretted and complained, and finally demanded to see Kojiro. The officer in charge relented and took him to the cell.

Kojiro rose as soon as Akitada entered. He looked much better than the last time they had met. Apparently there had been no further beatings, and he had been allowed to wash and shave. When he recognized his visitor, he bowed, his eyes intent. "Is there news, my lord? Have they found Nobuko's murderer?"

Evidently Kobe had not bothered to inform the man of his brother's death. Akitada steeled himself for the ordeal. "There is news, but it does not concern your sister-in-law." He searched for the right words. "I was hoping," he finally confessed, "that the superintendent had told you. He received an unsubstantiated report that your brother has met with a mishap."

Instant anxiety appeared in the other man's eyes. "Mishap? What kind of mishap? Is he wounded? Ill?"

"I have no details, nor do I know where he was found."

" 'He was found'? Then it must be serious." Kojiro clenched his manacled fists and glared at the locked cell door. Frustrated, he started pacing back and forth. The chain on his legs clinked and limited his path to no more than three steps either way. Like a caged beast, he had learned when to turn. "He may even be dead," he muttered, then stopped. "Is he dead?"

Akitada spread his hands helplessly. "There is a chance that the man they found is not your brother after all," he evaded awkwardly.

"But they found a dead man and think he's my brother?"

Akitada nodded.

Kojiro sat down abruptly and put his head in his hands. After a moment he said dully, "Thank you for telling me. This way I shall be prepared when Kobe finally bothers to inform me."

"This is bad news, and I am very sorry to be the one to bring it." Akitada crouched down near him. "A number of strange things have been happening. Perhaps they have something to do with the death of your sister-in-law, and if the man they found is indeed your brother and he was murdered also, the same killer may be responsible. The best thing you can do now is to help me find justice for both. Can you explain why your brother might sell all his goods, everything except the house? And why he would then disappear without telling anyone where he was going or why?"

Kojiro raised his head from his hands and looked at him bleakly. "Perhaps, but I doubt it has anything to do with Nobuko's death. My brother's business affairs have not been going well for a few years now. I offered money on a number of occasions, but he always refused it. Too much pride. His reputation was excellent, and his creditors did not press him for payment as a rule, but perhaps this time their patience ran out. Paying his debts is a matter of conscience with him. He would do so even if it meant selling everything. My brother had much honor." Tears welled up in his eyes, but he controlled himself immediately. "Could he have been killed because he carried the money on him?"

"Possibly. His servant said he left with a saddlebag, and was dressed for a journey. He may have rented a horse. Did he have any creditors outside the capital?"

"Yes. He sometimes bought art objects from temples and from country manors. I'm afraid he kept business details to himself, perhaps because he did not want me to help him out."

"The last time I was here, I asked you to think about your sister-in-law."

Kojiro rubbed his face as if to remind himself of his own problems. "I don't know what you have heard, so I had better tell you what I saw and thought of her." He told about his encounters with Nobuko, from their first meeting to the calamitous trip to the temple. He described her beauty and said he had distrusted her for marrying his middle-aged brother, but had accepted her when he saw his brother's happiness and pride in his young wife's talents.

"She could play the zither like a professional and knew wonderful songs. Sometimes she even danced for us. My brother was completely enchanted, and in time so was I. I was stunned, appalled, when she approached me one day to suggest we become lovers because my brother was . . . inadequate and she wanted a child. Torn between disgust and pity, I stopped my visits to my brother's house. But he sent for me and I went back reluctantly. To my relief, my sister-in-law was cold and distant. I assumed she was embarrassed about the incident."

"Could she have been angry with you for rejecting her advances?"

Kojiro nodded. "She may have been. At the time I said some things to her that I regret now, but I meant to shock her into having more sense."

"Do you think she could have found another lover?"

He shook his head. "I have wondered, but don't see how. My brother never entertained, and the only men who came to his house were clients who never met his wife."

"What about her life before her marriage? Were there any men in it?"

Kojiro shook his head helplessly. "I know only what she or my brother told me about her family life. Her father is a retired scholar. He moved to Kohata after his wife's death. Nobuko was raised in the country, but she received a good education from her father. From what she said, I gathered that her life must have been entertaining. They had celebrations on all the festival days, sometimes with singers and musicians, and her father encouraged her to ride and took her with him on hunting trips. I always thought that she must be dreadfully bored in my brother's house."

Akitada pulled his earlobe and pondered. "Surely your brother showed her the famous sites of the capital? Or took her to the palace for horse races, and to temples for the festival dances and play performances?"

"No. My brother used to take an interest in theater in his younger years, but lately he considered public entertainments unsuitable for a man in his position and he would never have taken his wife. I thought she had settled for children and a quiet family life." He flushed a little.

"There were some actors staying at the temple where she died. Uemon's Players, they called themselves. It may not mean anything, but I knew of your brother's interest and now you tell me your sister-in-law also may have met such performers."

Kojiro looked blank. "I did not see them and know nothing of this."

In the hallway outside the cell, steps and voices approached, followed by the grating of a key in the door. It opened and Kobe stepped in. Kojiro rose, his mouth set and his face expressionless.

Kobe nodded to him and turned to Akitada. "They told me you were here. Does Kojiro know?"

"I only told him what I knew. Was the report correct?"

"Yes, I'm afraid so. Sorry, Kojiro. Your brother was found bludgeoned to death near the southern highway. You have my sympathy."

The prisoner looked down at his shackled hands. They were clenched so tightly that the knuckles showed white against the sun-darkened skin. "Thank you, Superintendent," he said tonelessly. "I can only hope it was not my arrest and imprisonment which caused my poor brother to undertake this tragic journey." He grimaced, then looked up at Kobe. "I don't suppose you would let me out to find the bastards who killed him?"

"You know I cannot do that. There is still a murder charge against you."

Akitada said, "All the evidence we have points away from Kojiro and to someone else. Now that Nagaoka himself has been killed—and Kojiro certainly could not have done that—is it not likely that the two murders are connected?"

"Why? From all accounts, the man carried money, which has disappeared. He must have been set on by bandits."

Akitada sighed and rose. It was all too likely. "How is it that you are back so early?" he asked.

"I met my sergeant at the city gate. He was bringing back the body. I suppose you would like to see it for yourself?"

"Yes." Akitada turned to Kojiro. "I promise to do my best to find who is responsible for this. I liked your brother, you know. His knowledge of the antique trade was admirable, and he had great affection for you."

Kojiro struggled to his feet. "I know. Thank you," he said with a bow.

◀━┼━▶

Akitada and Kobe crossed the prison courtyard to the same small building which had held the corpse of Nagaoka's wife only a month earlier.

Nagaoka lay in much the same spot. He, too, had suffered dreadful wounds to the head, but his thin, sharp features were untouched and looked strangely noble in death. He wore the clothes the servant had described, but there was something odd about the way the body lay, and Akitada stared for a moment before he realized what bothered him.

"Are his legs broken?"

Kobe looked, then bent to manipulate one of them. "No."

Behind them the door opened, admitting Dr. Masayoshi, the coroner.

"A new case?" He came forward and stared at Akitada. "You again? Do you make a habit of visiting the dead?"

"And a good day to you, Doctor." Akitada made him a tiny bow, which the coroner returned in the same deliberately rude manner. Akitada pointed. "What is wrong with this man's feet?"

Masayoshi looked at the corpse, briefly felt one of the legs, then grinned. "Your little joke, my lord? Forgive me, but it was rather puerile even for you."

Akitada stared, then flushed at the insult. Controlling his fury with an effort, he walked to the body and jerked off one of the boots. Nothing at all was wrong with Nagaoka's leg. His boots had been put on the wrong feet. Akitada's eyes flew to Masayoshi's face and caught the moment the coroner realized that it had not been a joke after all, but a mistake. Masayoshi's eyebrows rose mockingly.

Akitada was tempted to wipe the sneer off the man's face, but he clenched his fists and turned his back abruptly on the grinning coroner. He told Kobe, "Did your men do this?"

But they had not, and it changed everything. Even Kobe could not see bandits taking off their victim's boots and then replacing them.

Kobe scratched his head. He removed the other boot and looked at Nagaoka's feet. They wore clean white socks.

"Strange!" he muttered. "I thought they might have tortured him. Maybe they tried on his boots and they didn't fit."

"Nonsense! They would not have bothered to put them back."

Masayoshi had knelt to examine the head wound, probing it gently with his fingers. He was pursing his lips. Moving forward, he lifted the dead man's eyelids and then smelled his mouth. He got to his feet with a satisfied grunt. "Even stranger than the boots," he said, "is the fact that this man died from poison."

"Poison!" yelled Kobe. "How poison? Even an idiot can see he's been clubbed to death. Why poison him, too? Are you mad?"

Grinning, Masayoshi folded his arms across his small paunch and rocked back and forth on his heels. "Not at all." He chuckled. "I must say, you present me with the most interesting cases, Superintendent," he said appreciatively. "But actually you got it backward. He was poisoned first and clubbed afterward. You notice that there is very little blood in the wound. Dead men don't bleed, you see."

Silence greeted his explanation.

Much as he detested Masayoshi's manner, Akitada did not question his professional expertise. In fact, he should have seen the lack of blood himself. He asked brusquely, "Can you tell when he died? And how much later the head wounds were inflicted?"

Masayoshi became businesslike. He returned to the body, flexing its limbs and joints down to the fingers and toes, then pulled apart the clothing to study Nagaoka's torso and poke his thin belly. Finally he pinched the skin in a few places. Straightening up, he said, "Hard to tell. Depends on whether he was left lying around outside or inside near a fire. He's been frozen, of course, so he was outside at least part of the time and probably all of it. My guess would be several days. The head injury happened shortly after death, probably while the body was still slightly warm. There are some residual traces of bleeding in the wounds."

"Several days! That's not much help for the time of murder," exploded Kobe. "What about the poison? How soon before he died did he take it?"

"Ah. That is even more difficult. Some poisons work quickly and some are quite slow. And we do not know how much he consumed. He may have lasted a few heartbeats, or taken a whole day and night to die, or even several days. I cannot be certain what he took until I dissect him and make certain tests. These, as you will hardly wish to spare any of your prisoners, will involve rats, whose tolerance for poison is different from that of humans. Still, we'll know if it was quick, and may be able to guess at what it was. Though I have an idea about that."

"Which is?" demanded Kobe.

"No, Superintendent! You must wait. I don't enjoy making a fool of myself and avoid it at all costs." His eyes slid to Akitada, and he smirked.

Akitada bit his lip. "Well," he challenged Kobe, "either way, it eliminates highway robbery as a motive. Poisoning a man requires thought and selection. It is not random. Are you ready to admit that you made a mistake about Kojiro?"

"Certainly not. This does not clear him of the other charges."

"Your people should not have moved the body. The killer may have left clues to his identity. Footprints, for example."

"I know." Kobe cursed. "It looked like a robbery. The money was gone, along with his horse. He was lying by the road. And my sergeant was so pleased with himself for identifying the missing Nagaoka that he decided to bring him back here for us to see. I'll have his balls for this and fry them in oil. How's Tora, by the way?"

Akitada suppressed a chuckle. "Seimei thinks he will do well." Suddenly and perversely he felt a great deal better about the Nagaoka case. "Shall we go take a look at the scene while your capable coroner does his job?" he suggested, with a smile and bow toward Masayoshi, who looked at him in blank astonishment.

Kobe cursed again. "I suppose we'd better. Before it gets dark."

—◆—

Dusk fell early, before they were well out of the city. It was bitterly cold. A sharp northerly wind pushed them onward and brought heavy dark clouds on their train. Kobe muttered something about the failing light, but Akitada would not turn back. The smell of snow was in the air, and he was afraid all tracks would disappear if they waited for the next day.

So they rushed on at a gallop, on horses requisitioned for government business, followed by the cowed sergeant and six mounted constables.

It was difficult to talk over the sound of the horses' hooves and the gusts of wind, and for a while they simply covered ground. Soon the horses were steaming; flecks of foam from their muzzles flew back past the riders.

To the right and left of the raised highway, fallow rice fields and withered plantings of soybeans stretched into the murky distance. A few small farms huddled under dark groves of trees, like birds gone undercover from the freezing cold.

It began to snow when they were about halfway. The low dark clouds had steadily caught up with them, moving faster and lower, and when the first flakes materialized in the cold air, they stung their cold faces like pins and dusted their clothes and the horses' manes.

The sergeant pulled up beside Akitada, perhaps to avoid catching more of Kobe's wrath. He was eager to make up for his mistake and scanned the distance anxiously. "See that line of pine trees up ahead?" he shouted, pointing at a shadowy bank of darkness in the general murk. "That's a canal. It crosses the road. About a mile after that is the turnoff."

Minutes later they passed over the small bridge and turned down a narrower track.

"Where does this road lead, Sergeant?" Akitada asked.

"To a village called Fushimi."

The name was familiar. "Isn't that where Kojiro's farm is?"

"Yes, sir. Though it's a pretty large place, actually."

Well, Nagaoka had said that his brother's hard work had made his farm prosper. Akitada had a strong desire to see for himself. Since it was not far from where Nagaoka had been found, he thought Kobe might accept the need for a visit.

Eventually the narrow road cut through a forest of pines and leafless trees, and the sergeant called out to slow down. They came to a place where the ground was churned up by the hooves of horses and boots of men, and stopped. The sergeant pointed. "He was right over there! Against that rock!"

The sergeant, Kobe, and Akitada dismounted. Akitada cast a hopeless glance around. Those who had found the dead man, and those who had come later to get him, surely had destroyed any tracks left by his killers.

But when they reached the rock, the sergeant pointed out hoof marks in the soft ground. "They brought him on a horse," he said. "We came on foot and carried him back to the highway."

" 'They'?" Akitada crouched to stare at the indentations. His heart started beating rapidly. "A single horse! Perhaps his own? And whoever brought him took it away again. Could a single person manage? One man ... or woman?"

The sergeant glanced back at the waiting constables on the road. "His companions may have stayed on the road."

"Not likely under the circumstances, Sergeant," snapped Kobe. "He was poisoned. I hardly think the murderer would bring along an escort while disposing of the body."

The sergeant flushed. "The body was sort of flung down," he said to Akitada, "not laid flat or sat up or anything. I suppose a strong woman, if she had a dead man draped over the saddle of a horse, could pull him off. A man, definitely. Getting him on is a bigger problem."

They all crouched, studying the prints, but there were too many to make sense of. Akitada gave up first and followed the hoofprints away from the rock. The tracks slanted toward the road more or less along the same line on which they had arrived, and rejoined the tightly packed dirt track about fifty feet from the rock. The horse's hooves had left clear marks in the moist earth of the grassy verge. To Akitada's eye, the impressions looked the same both coming and going. "Come here, Sergeant," he called. "Have a look at this. All the hoofprints are the same depth. Yet we know that, coming, the horse carried the body. That means the person who brought the body must have led the horse to the rock, and then ridden back to the road. Do you agree?"

The sergeant nodded eagerly. "You are right, sir. Let's look for his footprints here."

Akitada turned to Kobe, who had come up. "There was only one horse," he said. "And only a single individual leading it. This individual lives within walking distance from here."

Kobe glanced down the road where it disappeared among the trees in a haze of blowing snow. He scowled. "How far is the brother's place?" he snapped at the sergeant.

The man flinched. "A couple of miles, sir. I can't make out any footprints, except in this place here."

In the growing darkness, they gathered and peered at a shallow impression. "Maybe a boot, not big, but not a woman's, either," guessed Kobe. Nobody could improve on this, and after another look around they gave up. The light was failing rapidly, and the snow fell more thickly.

"Let's go to Kojiro's farm," said Akitada, swinging back in the saddle. "The weather is worsening and we will probably have to seek shelter anyway."

Kobe scowled at the sky, but he nodded with a grunt, and the small cavalcade set out again.

They reached their destination just before it became necessary to light their lanterns. To Akitada's amazement, Kojiro's property was a manor house in a compound of buildings which was larger than his own in the capital. The entire compound was walled and had an imposing roofed gate.

"Are you sure we have the right place?" Akitada asked the sergeant. "This looks like some nobleman's estate."

The sergeant assured him that there was no mistake and applied the wooden clapper to the bell.

Kobe joined Akitada. "What do you make of this?" he asked, clearly thunderstruck. "The man acts like the merest peasant. If he has this much wealth, why didn't he make an outcry? Where are all his wealthy friends? Or the poor officials who would gladly put in a good word for him for a small present?"

Akitada was completely out of his depth. "Perhaps he just does not have any connections and friends. Or maybe he does not believe in bribes."

Kobe was snorting his derision when the gate opened on oiled hinges.

A boy of ten or eleven stood there, holding up a lantern and looking at them. Behind him an elderly man in a simple cotton robe came hobbling up, leaning on a stick. The wide courtyard was neat in the light of torches fixed to the walls of the manor house before them.

"You are welcome," the old one said, a little out of breath. "I suppose you need lodging for the night?"

Akitada glanced up at the sky, which was nearly black and filled with swirling, dancing snowflakes. "Yes, thank you for your hospitality. The weather caught us unprepared. We are from the capital, investigating a murder which happened nearby.

This is Police Superintendent Kobe with his men, and I am Sugawara Akitada."

It was doubtful if the old man took in Akitada's name, but when he heard Kobe introduced, his expression changed, and his eyes became fixed on the superintendent. "Are you the one that's put my master in jail?" he asked, suddenly belligerent.

Akitada glanced nervously at Kobe to see how he would react to the sudden defiance of the old man.

Kobe scowled, being used to abject bows from mere peasants, then glanced around the compound again and cleared his throat. "In a manner of speaking," he said. "I am in charge of the prisons in the capital. Who are you?"

Completely unimpressed, the man stood a little straighter. "I'm Kinzo. Senior retainer in charge of the manor while my master is away, jailed, though he is as pure and innocent as Saint Zoga." He glared back at Kobe.

Kobe cast a glance at the sky. "I don't blame you for your feelings," he said peaceably, "but your master cannot be released until the evidence against him is either disproven or we find another suspect. That is why we are here now."

The old servant's fierce expression softened marginally. "You'd better come in," he said grudgingly, and turned to lead the way.

They rode in, and the boy closed and latched the gate behind them. Kobe and Akitada dismounted at the house, where the boy took their horses. The others followed him to the stables.

Not unexpectedly, the house was dark and empty. Kinzo lit a lantern in the entry while they removed their boots. Then they followed him down dark corridors into a spacious room with a fire pit in its center. Heavy shutters to the outside were closed against the night and the weather. The room contained little beyond necessities: a few mats and cushions, several candlesticks with candles, and a large wooden chest of the type used by traveling merchants. It was reinforced with decorative metal corners, hinges, and locks on its drawers and had metal hafts at both ends to push carrying poles through. The only item in the room which was not utilitarian was a large and very fine scroll painting of a waterfall in a mountain landscape.

"Your master must be prosperous," said Akitada, looking around.

"He has been blessed by Daikoku, god of farmers, but suffers the injustice and cruelty of the emperor Chu."

"A well-read peasant," whispered Kobe to Akitada, as Kinzo removed the wooden lid from the fire pit and lit the neat pile of charcoal at its bottom. Then he arranged cushions around it and invited them to sit.

"You may spend the night," he said to Kobe. "Like the sainted Kobo Daishi, my master would not turn his worst enemy out on a night like this. Maybe you are trying to help him, but you've taken your time about it. Four times I've traveled to the capital and asked to see him, and four times your constables have turned me away. May Amida grant my master the unshakable spirit of Fudo. Last time, one of the constables said that not even my master's wife was admitted any longer. I ask you, what wife may that be? My master does not have a wife."

Akitada and Kobe looked at each other. Akitada said, "The constable made a mistake. The visitor happened to be my sister. She met your master once, and when she heard of his troubles, she took him some food."

Now he had the old man's full attention. "Ah! Forgive me, your honor. I didn't catch the name."

"Sugawara. I am a government official, and I, too, have taken an interest in your master's case and am here to help."

Kinzo suddenly smiled and bowed deeply. "An illustrious name! You walk in the footsteps of your noble ancestor who defied tyranny. You are indeed welcome. May the Buddha reward you for your help and may he reward your noble sister's kindness. It is good to work on the side of the just. My master would never have killed his brother's wife. He loves his brother more than his life. I told him so only a week ago."

"Told whom?" snapped Kobe, coming to attention.

"Why, Master Nagaoka, of course. Your guards would not let me see my master, remember. Master Nagaoka stopped by to check on things and bring me news. I told him what the constable at the prison had said about a wife, and Master Nagaoka said it wasn't true. I don't suppose he knew about your sister, sir. He said the superintendent had warned him away, too, and that we must hope for a miracle to happen, for there was nothing that could be done anymore." Kinzo shot an accusing glance at Kobe, who was staring at him fixedly.

"You say Nagaoka was here a week ago?" the superintendent asked. "When did he leave?"

"Why, the very next day. He had business elsewhere."

"And how did he look when he left?" Kobe asked, giving Akitada a meaningful nod.

The old man had sharp eyes. He frowned suspiciously, but said, "As you'd expect. Like Kume after he saw the washerwoman's legs."

Kobe looked blank. "Who is Kume? What washerwoman?"

"It's another story. Kume was a fairy," Akitada explained. "The story has it that he lost his supernatural powers because he lusted after a mortal woman."

The old man nodded. "A woman ruined Kume. A woman ruined Nagaoka. Her and that father of hers."

"What is he talking about?" Kobe asked. "All I want to know is if Nagaoka was sick when he left here."

"There was nothing wrong with his health," snapped the old man. "If you're afraid to spend the night here, you can ride home in the storm."

Akitada said quickly, "No, no. You misunderstood. Nagaoka was found dead not two miles from here. He may have died the day he left here. The superintendent and I are trying to find out what happened to him. Do you know where he was going?"

Kinzo's jaw dropped. "Master Nagaoka's dead?" He shook his head in disbelief. "Oh, his karma was very bad! And now my poor master will be even more wretched than Fujiwara Moroie when his beloved died."

"Come on, man," snapped Kobe, "where was Nagaoka headed when he left here?"

Kinzo's eyes widened. "Hah," he cried. "That woman got him! I knew it. They say the spirit stays in its home for forty-nine days. Hers must have gone to Kohata. That's where Master Nagaoka was going. Just over the hill to Kohata. And that evil demon was lying in wait for him." He shook his head at the pity of it.

EIGHTEEN

Two Professors

Kinzo treated them well that evening. There was a hot bath for them, a substantial meal of hot rice and vegetables, with steamed fish fresh from a nearby river, and bedding for a restful night.

Akitada had rarely slept better. Outside, the snow fell silently and it was a cold night, but the large pile of charcoal in the fire pit continued to glow, making the room very comfortable.

When they rose the next morning, Kinzo reappeared, followed by the youth who had opened the gate and now brought a tray with steaming bowls of rice gruel.

"It stopped snowing," announced Kinzo. "On horseback you shouldn't have any trouble crossing the mountain to Kohata."

It turned out to be a hard ride after all, but the weather had cleared and there was even some sun. The snow was so bright, it was almost blue in the shadows, and the trunks and branches of the trees stood out sharply like black brushstrokes against white paper.

They saw the village of Kohata when they made their way down the other side of the mountain. It consisted of a few straggling farmhouses, a post house, and a somewhat larger complex of buildings on the outskirts of the small town. The latter turned out to be the farm belonging to Nagaoka's father-in-law, known locally as "the professor."

It was certainly not as prosperous as Kojiro's place, and had seen better days. The fence gaped in places, but the gate still had two panels, and the dwelling looked a comfortable size. Smoke rose in a thin spiral from a derelict outbuilding, no doubt the kitchen, and someone had swept a makeshift path to the entrance of the house.

No one was about, so the sergeant went to knock on the door. There was no answer.

After a few more attempts to rouse someone, Akitada and Kobe dismounted and walked around to the back. A leaning wooden gate led into what must once have been a small garden; now the overgrown plants were towering shapes under the snow. A single set of footprints skirted the corner of the house, and these they followed to a small pavilion at the back of the garden.

Its doors stood wide open, and inside huddled a figure. It was covered from head to toe with layers of old quilts and covers, and was bent over a desk spread with papers. Only one hand protruded, laboriously writing a few characters before raising stiff fingers to blow on them.

The occupant did not hear their muffled steps in the snow outside until they stepped onto the small veranda. Then he started and turned, the covers slipping to reveal an elderly man with bright black eyes and a dripping nose.

Kobe said, "Sorry to interrupt, but nobody answered our knocks. Would you be Professor Yasaburo?"

The elderly man sniffed and dashed the moisture from the tip of his nose with a stained sleeve. "No, I'm not, I'm glad to say." He spoke in the nasal voice of someone with a bad cold. "Yasaburo is a disgusting tightwad, a damnable slave driver, a vulgar boor, an inferior poet, a vile cook, a contemptible conversationalist, a wretched scholar, a shocking father, an execrable calligrapher, and he serves inferior wine. No, thank the heavens, I'm not Yasaburo."

"Your name, then?" demanded Kobe.

The elderly man wiped his nose again and sniffed. "Cursed

cold," he muttered. "I don't remember an introduction. Your turn first."

Kobe snapped, "I'm Kobe. Superintendent of police."

"Ridiculous." The man chuckled. "What would a police superintendent from the capital be doing out here? Try again."

Kobe bristled. "Don't waste my time!"

Without rising, the little man managed to sketch an obeisance. "Harada. Formerly professor of mathematics at the Imperial University. Presently a lowly drudge."

"I am investigating a crime. Are you familiar with the name Nagaoka?"

The little man stared at him. "Nagaoka's in trouble? You surprise me. He was just here."

"When?"

Harada sniffed and turned the leaf of his account book, running a finger blue with cold down a line of entries. "That's the day," he mumbled. "Yes, I make it the second day of this month."

"Ah!" Kobe was hitting his stride. "We're getting somewhere. By the way, what in hell are you doing out here?"

"In hell or not, I'm working. True, at the moment I'm in hell: cold sober, suffering from a bad cold, and keeping the tightwad slave driver's accounts in an unheated garden pavilion while a policeman's shouting at me."

Akitada suppressed a smile. Kobe was certainly not getting much respect in the country. He asked the irreverent Harada, "Where is your master?"

"My master?" Harada drew himself up and attempted to look at Akitada over his nose. The effect was spoiled by another droplet forming at its end. He dashed it away with the much-abused sleeve and said haughtily, "If you—a total stranger to me, by the way—are referring to Yasaburo, you have not been listening. That man is nobody's master. He's incompetent at everything, a total failure. I work for him, but I am certainly his master in most things. A fine distinction, young man. Remember it!"

Akitada smiled. "Forgive me, Master Harada. My name is Sugawara. I take an interest in the case of one of Superintendent Kobe's prisoners, Nagaoka's brother."

"Hah! The unfortunate Kojiro." Harada eyed him, then said, "Hell opens its jaws in many nooks and corners. Beware of the demons among the living."

"What do you mean?" asked Akitada sharply.

But Harada had turned away, shaking his head. "Nothing, nothing. You'd better wait for Yasaburo. He's out with his little bow and arrow, wreaking death and destruction among the crows." He huddled back into his quilt and rubbed more ink.

Kobe angrily opened his mouth to show Harada who gave the orders, when there was the sound of shouting from somewhere beyond the house. They turned.

Another strange-looking creature was approaching rapidly through the snow-covered garden, this one tall and thin and with a gray-streaked beard and bristling eyebrows. He was dressed in an old-fashioned fur-trimmed hunting cloak, fur cap, and long, snow-caked fur boots. Except for the fact that he was carrying a bow and had several arrows sticking up from a quiver behind his left shoulder, he might have been an emaciated old bear walking on his hind legs.

"Who in the name of the forty-eight devils are you and what do you want here?" the creature shouted shrilly, shaking his bow, as soon as he saw them. "Get away from him! He's working. That's what I pay him for, not to chat with every fool who's lost his way."

"Are you Yasaburo?" roared Kobe, his patience gone.

The furry man—well into his sixties, to judge by the beard—stopped to glare at them. "I asked first," he snapped.

Kobe's face darkened. He had clearly had it with insubordinate civilians. "Police," he snapped. "We have some questions. In the house."

Yasaburo's glance flicked over them. "I am retired," he grumbled. "If you want an expert, go to the young fellows at the university."

Kobe jumped down into the snow. "I said, in the house. If you don't move now, I'll have my constables tie you to a horse and trot you back to the capital."

Wordlessly Yasaburo turned and marched toward the house. A string of birds tied to his belt flopped and swung like the tail of some large upright beast. Akitada thought he heard a soft cackling behind his back, but when he turned, Harada was bent over his account books making entries.

The main house was an old manor with a steep roof, sturdily built of massive timbers, but blackened by age and generations of smoky fires. In the dirt-floored entry, Yasaburo flung the string of birds into a corner and sat down to remove his snow-caked boots on a stone step leading up to the wooden flooring of a dark corridor. "Cursed birds!" he grunted. "Nothing worse than crows for making a racket." He issued no invitations to his guests to join him.

Neither Akitada nor Kobe commented, but simply removed their own boots and followed Yasaburo. He shuffled ahead and brought them to a large room with a central fire pit, much like Kojiro's, except that this room contained along the back wall a wide wooden dais, raised about two feet above the rest of the flooring. On this dais rested many strange objects, indistinctly seen in the general gloom until Yasaburo struck a flint to a couple of oil lamps.

They stared in surprise at a large hide-covered drum decorated with wood carvings of orange flames and a black and white yin-yang symbol, several smaller shoulder and hip drums, folding stools, a zither, and a couple of lutes. Suspended from nails in the wall hung several flutes, both the long, transverse kind and the short ones.

"I see you have musical performances out here in the country," Akitada said.

Yasaburo grunted. "Not anymore. Used to when the girls lived here. Nothing to do now but sit around and wait to die." He kicked a few dusty, faded pillows their way, and stirred the coals in the fire pit. Tossing some dried wood and pinecones onto these, he started a fire, which shot several feet up toward the soot-blackened rafters. Smoke filled the room.

Kobe and Akitada sat on the cushions at a safe distance from the pit.

Their host barely waited for the flames to die back before suspending a blackened iron kettle from the chain above the pit and filling it with wine from an earthenware pitcher. Then he pulled off his fur cloak and cap, tossed both on top of a huge clothing trunk in a corner, and sat down with his visitors.

"Well, what d'you want to know?" he demanded. His manner was belligerent, but Akitada thought he sounded uneasy.

"I'm Kobe. Superintendent of police in the capital," Kobe told him. "You have had a recent visit from your brother-in-law, Nagaoka?"

Yasaburo did not quite suppress a start. "What about it?"

"Why did he come here?"

Yasaburo shifted on his cushion, then said, "A condolence visit."

"Involving money, I gather," Akitada put in.

Yasaburo glanced at him from under his bristling brows. Instead of answering, he got up and ladled wine into three cups, passing two to Kobe and Akitada. "You don't look like police," he said to Akitada. "Who are you?"

"I am Sugawara Akitada and represent the interests of Nagaoka's brother." The warm wine was sour and cloudy. Either the man was desperately poor or the miser Harada had called him.

Yasaburo glowered. "The bastard who killed my girl? You have no business in my house. Get out!"

Kobe said, "He stays. And you talk. Now!"

"What do you want from me?" Yasaburo's voice took on a whine. "I have lost my child, my beloved daughter, beautiful and talented beyond compare, and you come and torment me with stupid questions. So what if Nagaoka showed up a week ago? He took his time. It's only right he should apologize for what his brother did to my little girl. And he did not stay. Arrived one morning and left again. Had business elsewhere, he said."

"What sort of business where?"

"How should I know. Probably tracking down some rare object, hoping to cheat semiliterate monks so he could sell it in the capital for a fortune. That's all he was good for, money. That's why I let my little girl marry him. So she would have some of the better things in life. Hah!" He made a choking sound, shook his head, and covered his eyes with one hand.

Akitada thought the show of emotion unconvincing. This Yasaburo was full of contradictions, playing many roles simultaneously. One moment he was the rustic hermit, then an eccentric academic, then again the grieving father or the worldly cynic. He was intensely curious about this man, but thought it better to let Kobe do the questioning, particularly since he was no longer a welcome visitor.

"Speaking of Nagaoka's wealth," continued Kobe, "how much blood money did he pay you?"

There was a startled pause; then Yasaburo growled, "Not enough!"

Kobe turned to Akitada. "Well, that explains what happened to the money. Not highway robbery, then."

Yasaburo's head came up. "He might have carried more. How do you know he was not killed for his money?"

"Did I mention he was killed?"

Yasaburo said angrily, "What else would a superintendent of police be doing here? Well, he deserved it. He is responsible for my daughter's murder by that depraved brother of his. And how much do you think her life was worth to him? A mere eighteen bars of silver, that's all! I told him what I thought of him, my wealthy son-in-law. He tried to excuse himself. Said business had been bad. Even had the nerve to claim Nobuko's tastes had been expensive. Hah! The miser kept her locked up in his house day and night like a slave." He paused, drank deeply from his cup, and slammed it down. "And then the cold fish sent her off with his randy brother. For all I know, he told the bastard to get her with child. When my poor girl fought the fellow off, he killed her. No, no, Superintendent, eighteen bars of silver is not enough for such an outrage!"

A brief silence followed that shrill outpouring of venom. Then Akitada said, "That is a scandalous accusation. And a cowardly one. It takes little courage to heap abuse on the head of the dead."

"Spare me that drivel." Yasaburo glared at Akitada, then asked Kobe, "Well, have you got what you came for?"

Kobe said, "Not quite. We have reason to believe that Nagaoka died here and was taken later to the place where he was found."

Yasaburo stumbled to his feet. "What? When? He left here the way he arrived. Alive. On his horse. My boy can tell you. You're not going to pin this on me."

"Sit down! Let's talk about his visit."

Suddenly both strength and fight seemed to go out of the old man. He muttered, "I know nothing about Nagaoka's death. He left here alive. Must have run into robbers on the way."

"No. Tell me about the blood money."

"Eighteen bars. He owed me more. We agreed on thirty-five bars when I went to see him in the capital. He gave me five bars then and promised me the rest later. But he brought only eighteen."

Akitada interjected, "Why would he pay you? He did not believe in his brother's guilt."

Yasaburo sneered. "What difference what he believed? The

police said he was guilty. The moment I heard about it, I went for my money. And Nagaoka did not refuse. Just asked for time."

"Hmm," said Kobe, scratching his short beard. "Let me get this story straight. You made certain demands on Nagaoka, he gave you a down payment, and was bringing the rest here in person?"

"That's what I said."

"But he did not bring enough, and so you got angry, eh? Very angry, I would say."

Yasaburo bit his lip. "I was not pleased and let him know it. He left right away."

"What about refreshments? After a long, cold journey?" Kobe raised his cup. "Some of your hot wine? After all, the man was related to you by marriage."

Was there a nervous flicker in Yasaburo's eyes? He definitely hesitated before answering. "A cup of wine, that was all."

"Ah!" Kobe nodded and smiled. "Do you keep poison? For the birds, perhaps?"

Yasaburo paled. He was clearly frightened now. "He was alive. I swear he was!"

Kobe clapped his hands. A thin boy with bulging eyes and open mouth appeared so instantly that he must have been eavesdropping. "Where are the other servants?" Kobe barked.

"There's only me and Mr. Harada." The boy was lost in amazed contemplation of his master, who sat wringing his hands and moaning into his beard.

"Do you remember a visitor a week ago?" asked Kobe. "Middle-aged. Thin. Came on a horse?"

"A horse?" The boy was still staring at Yasaburo, who had turned beseeching eyes on him.

"His name is Nagaoka. The antique dealer who married your master's daughter."

"Oh, him."

"Pay attention!"

The boy reluctantly took his eyes off Yasaburo. "He came in the morning. On a horse. I took the horse. Then he came for his horse." The boy frowned. "He was scared, maybe. Like there were demons after him."

Yasaburo gave another moan and hid his face in his hands. "The boy's a half-wit," he mumbled. "Tell them that he rode away!" he cried.

Kobe glared at him and snapped, "Stay out of this!" Then he asked the boy, "Did he look ill? You know, like he needed to vomit or relieve himself?"

The boy fell into a fit of giggles.

Kobe looked disgusted. "We had better call Harada!"

"Can't. He's gone," the boy volunteered.

"Gone? What do you mean?"

"He took the master's horse."

Yasaburo cried, "The dissembling cheat has stolen my horse and run. No doubt with my money. Quick, after him!"

Kobe snapped, "Fetch my sergeant!"

The sergeant was sent in pursuit of the flighty Harada, and Kobe began pacing, muttering under his breath. The boy stood staring at Yasaburo and picking his nose. Akitada got up to wander about the room.

"You!" Kobe snapped suddenly at the boy. "Look at me! Who was here the day Nagaoka visited?"

The boy said, "*She* was here. With him. *He* gives me coppers."

Yasaburo cried, "I told you the boy is slow. He is confused and remembers an earlier visit by my daughter and her husband."

Akitada paused in his examination of the musical instruments to cast a surprised glance at Yasaburo. So the man had another daughter. Come to think of it, he had referred to daughters earlier. There was no reason why he should not, but neither Nagaoka nor his brother had mentioned this.

Kobe asked the boy, "Did they come the same day as Mr. Nagaoka?"

The boy thought. "It was before. He gave me five coppers."

"A boat without oars," Kobe muttered under his breath. He tried again, "Your master's daughter and her husband, did they meet Mr. Nagaoka? Talk to him?"

But he had run out of luck. The boy shook his head. "Maybe they did, maybe they didn't."

"What about Mr. Nagaoka's horse? Did he leave his horse behind?"

The boy grinned. "I was tending his horse."

With a sigh, Kobe let him go. Yasaburo started up again about Harada's duplicity. Kobe snapped, "Shut up! You're in enough trouble," and started pacing and muttering again.

After a while, Yasaburo tried again. "I confess I'm as surprised as you at Harada's flight, Superintendent," he said. "It must mean he is involved in this murder. Frankly, I never did like the man. With all his crazy talk, I always thought he was half-mad, but I never dreamed he would kill anyone. He knew about the eighteen bars of silver. No doubt he thought Nagaoka carried more. Harada drinks like a fish, and nobody knows what he does in the capital. Maybe he gambles." Yasaburo glanced nervously at the dais, where Akitada was still looking at the instruments.

"I am curious, Professor Yasaburo," Akitada asked him, "what made you employ a man as untrustworthy as Harada?"

Yasaburo fidgeted. "Oh. He was a colleague. Lost his university position because of his drinking after his family died. Smallpox. But he was good with numbers. His fingers play tunes on that abacus of his, and his bookkeeping is immaculate. He got no wine from me while he was working, but once a month I let him off for a few days in the capital." Seeing disbelief in their faces, he added grudgingly, "And he worked cheap."

Akitada drifted on. In a niche hung a calligraphy scroll above a vase filled with dead branches. Both the scroll and the ledge for the vase were covered with thick dust, but a large trunk next to it looked clean. Idly Akitada opened it. It was filled with brilliant robes and gowns. On top lay a carved mask of some magic creature. He opened his mouth to ask if Yasaburo's daughters had taken part in theatrical performances, but thought better of it.

It was becoming obvious that Harada had made good his escape. Kobe stopped in front of Yasaburo. "We will take you back to the capital for further questioning. You may pack some clothes and enough money to purchase food from the prison guards."

"Why?" wailed Yasaburo. "I've done nothing. You cannot do this!"

While Kobe had Yasaburo readied for the return journey, Akitada made a quick tour of the house.

At one time, the dwelling and an adjoining smaller building must have accommodated comfortably a family and several servants, but now Yasaburo seemed to be living in one room, for the other rooms were not only shuttered and empty, but thick layers of dust lay on everything. Managing with only Harada and the boy, Yasaburo would not expect much in terms of service. However, in the other wing, one room was the exception to the general state of dereliction. Here a few grass mats covered the floorboards and trunks held clean bedding. Several braziers and oil lamps stood around and the room had been cleaned recently. No doubt this was where Nagaoka's other daughter stayed with her husband on their visits.

He walked back to the courtyard. The sergeant and his men were getting off their horses with glum faces. No Harada. Since the man knew the area better than the constables, he could have hidden anywhere and nobody the wiser. Harada was the biggest puzzle of all.

Kobe came out with Yasaburo and two constables. Yasaburo's hands were tied behind his back. Kobe said, "One of the horses

312

in the stable bears the marks of a post station in the capital, and my men found poison. Arsenic. He says it's for the birds, but I charged him. Dr. Masayoshi will be able to tell what Nagaoka took. Ready? It's a long ride back."

They rode ahead of the others. Akitada felt vaguely uneasy. He asked Kobe what he thought about the visit of the other daughter and her husband.

"That half-wit of a boy! I doubt they are involved, but we'll get the truth out of Yasaburo." After that they fell silent, each caught up in his own thoughts.

Akitada found the recent revelations confusing rather than enlightening. Until now they had not been aware that the dead woman had had a married sister. And the costumes in Yasaburo's trunk were even more intriguing. Yasaburo had claimed his interest had ended when his daughters had moved away, but as dusty as the rest of the room had been, Yasaburo seemed to have cared lovingly for the reminders of a happier past. Most troubling were the ubiquitous ties to the acting profession. Everyone connected with the case so far had some interest in or involvement with actors.

The snowy landscape was mostly empty. Few people took to the road this time of year, and those were walking, mainly local peasants or itinerant monks. But when they topped the final rise, they saw a lone horseman ahead of them.

The rider, covered in some large colorful garment, slouched and drooped, leaning alarmingly first to one side, then to the other, and was alternately kicking the beast into bursts of speed and reining it in again.

"Heavens," cried Kobe, "that's Harada, isn't it?" and kicked his own horse into a gallop.

It was. When Harada heard the pursuit, he glanced over his shoulder and whipped up his mount. The animal reared and took off madly across a barren, snow-covered field, with Harada clinging on for dear life, the strange robe fluttering behind like a huge pair of multicolored wings. At first they gained only slightly on him. Then, abruptly, his horse became airborne, and Harada flew off.

When they reached him, he was sitting on the edge of a frozen irrigation ditch, shaking his fist after the escaping horse. He was surrounded by the colorful folds of a quilt, one of those which had covered his shivering body in the unheated pavilion. He seemed to have fashioned it into a cloak by cutting a hole in it for his head.

Kobe swung himself out of the saddle and said happily, "Not a bad haul. Two prisoners on a single murder charge. Trouble is, I don't have chains or rope to tie him up with. Do you?"

Akitada shook his head and dismounted. "It's just as well," he said. "I have a feeling this man is a witness rather than an accomplice. Let's go easy with him."

Harada made no effort to get up. Instead he greeted them with the words, "I hate horses and they hate me. It's a measure of the misery to which I have been reduced since I entered the service of that man that I should choose his horse to escape it."

Kobe looked baffled. "Better than facing a murder charge, surely."

"Is it murder, then?" Harada shook his head. "It wasn't me."

"Then why did you steal the horse and run away?" Kobe growled.

"From the purest of motives, Superintendent, I assure you. Even Confucius would approve. A man should not add to his employer's troubles if he can avoid it."

Akitada asked, "Are you hurt?"

Harada felt various parts of his body and shook his head. "Good thing I brought the quilt against the cold. It cushioned the impact." He eyed his surroundings. A little distance from them one of the many little groves of trees hid a small farmhouse. "I suppose I must impose on the good farmer's hospitality tonight."

"Nonsense. You're under arrest," snapped Kobe. "Who do you think you're dealing with? A couple of yokels? This is a murder case."

Harada heaved a shuddering sigh. "I knew it wouldn't work, but it was worth a try. I'm not getting on a horse, though."

Kobe raised his brows. "You want to walk?"

"Perhaps a palanquin?"

Kobe roared with laughter. "You think you're the emperor himself, do you? You either ride or walk. And seeing that we are in a hurry to get your master locked up, you may have to run."

"You've arrested Yasaburo for the murder of his son-in-law?" Harada finally made a move to disentangle himself from the quilt and get to his feet.

"I did. What do you know about it?"

"Not much. I was drunk at the time."

"I thought you were supposed to have no wine except on your visits to the capital," said Akitada.

"Yes, yes. Part of the contract. A roof over my head and a bit of food, plus a monthly binge. Except that day. He sent me a pitcher of wine—very superior stuff, by the way, which is astonishing in itself—with the message that I was to take it for my cold. I did. All of it before the sun went down. And forgot my cold and slept. When I woke up it was the middle of the next day, I was feeling a lot worse, and Nagaoka was gone."

Kobe said, "What about Yasaburo's daughter and husband?"

"Them? A more disreputable pair you'll never meet. I stay out of their way when they show up. They cavort about, dressed up like lions with masks and long manes of hair, the daughter in man's pants, lifting her legs up in the air, screeching like a demon possessed. And the old man is beating a drum and shouting encouragement. And he complains about my drinking! I ask you, would you let your daughter act that way?"

Kobe looked baffled by the question. "Let's go," he said gruffly. "We can't spend the rest of the afternoon chatting in a field."

Since Kobe climbed back on his horse and seemed to expect the shivering Harada to trot behind, Akitada said, "You can ride with me. If you sit in front, I'll hold you and make sure you don't fall again."

Harada thought about it and nodded. The ascent was accomplished with difficulty, observed by a smirking Kobe, but eventually they were on their way to the highway, where the others awaited them.

Yasaburo greeted Harada with abuse and demands for his horse. He was ignored.

Slowed down by Harada, Akitada fell in behind the cortege. Harada gradually relaxed, and talked a little about his life. The loss of his family had shaken him to the point that he cared for little but periodic wine-induced bouts of forgetfulness.

"How long have you worked for Yasaburo?" Akitada asked.

"Almost a year."

"Then you don't know much about the performances they used to give?"

"Not much. I watched once, then stayed away when they played the fools."

"So you did not take your meals with the family?"

Harada looked back at him over his shoulder. "What, me? Never. I would not have accepted had they asked. I stay in the garden pavilion and sleep in the stable."

Akitada had suspected as much from close contact with Harada's quilt.

By the time they reached the capital, Harada had unburdened himself about his work: Yasaburo rented out plots to poor farmers in exchange for rice, which he traded for silver or invested in more land purchases. Harada's function had been to collect rents, and to keep the books in such a way that the annual tax collector's visit might pass with minimal losses. He glossed over illegalities, but his tone implied them. He had disapproved, but, unattractive as working for Yasaburo was, he had

316

little choice in the matter. Besides, he pointed out, it left him time to read and write, and to make periodic trips to the capital.

He shivered a little and sighed. "I suppose I could have saved myself that terrifying ride out of loyalty to a man I have no respect for."

Long before they reached the eastern jail, Harada began to sag more heavily against Akitada, and when they arrived, he had fallen into a fitful sleep.

"We'll put him in one of the cells," said Kobe when he saw them trudging into the prison courtyard, Harada slumped forward across the horse's neck and Akitada grimacing as he tried to keep him from falling off.

"He feels feverish," Akitada said. "I think he is too ill to stay here. It is not just that Harada should now die in prison because of Yasaburo's misdeeds. If you agree, I will take him home, where Seimei can look after him. Besides, I have a feeling he knows something about the murders without being aware of it."

NINETEEN

The Temple of Boundless Mercy

Saburo opened the gate and helped Akitada with the semiconscious Harada. When they had him standing on wobbly legs, Harada mumbled, "Sorry, must've had a drop too much. Head hurts," and pitched forward. Akitada caught him and picked him up bodily. Harada weighed little, even with his assorted blankets.

"Get Seimei and send him to my room," Akitada told Saburo, and carried Harada into the house.

In his study, he laid him down. Harada opened his eyes and blinked at him. "What ... where ... ?"

"Don't worry! My secretary is quite good with herbal remedies, and so is my wife. They will have you feeling better in no time."

"Tha's very good of you," mumbled Harada. He looked at Akitada uneasily. "Er, who are you? I seem to have forgotten."

"Sugawara. You are in my house. I brought you here because you seem a bit feverish."

"Hmm," said Harada, and fell into a dry coughing fit which left him shaking and gasping.

The door opened and Seimei came in.

"Another patient for you," said Akitada. "This is Professor Harada. He was manager for Nagaoka's father-in-law, Yasaburo, who was arrested for Nagaoka's murder. Our guest is a witness in the case. I brought him here because he is too sick to go anyplace else."

Seimei was immediately all interest and attention. He knelt, greeting Harada with a bow, before peering at his face intently. Harada peered back. Seimei bowed again and touched Harada's forehead. "A fever is burning your life force and you must be put to bed immediately, sir," he informed the sick man. Then he turned to Akitada. "Shall I put Professor Harada in Miss Akiko's room?"

"Yes. And see what you can do for him." Harada had closed his eyes and was either asleep or unconscious. Akitada took Seimei aside and gave him a sketchy outline of Harada's misfortunes, adding, "He has suffered more misery than one man deserves."

Seimei shook his head with pity, but remarked, "As to what he deserves, sir, we do not know what he may have been guilty of in his previous life." Seimei was a strong believer in karma as the ultimate leveler of human lives, punishing transgressions and rewarding virtues in subsequent lives.

"How is Tora?" Akitada asked.

Seimei smiled. "Much improved, though he won't say so in front of the ladies."

"The ladies?"

"Oh, yes. He has visitors every day."

Akitada scooped the sick man up again, and carried him to another wing of the house where his sister Akiko's room had stood empty since her marriage to Toshikage. There, Seimei spread bedding from a trunk. Together they divested Harada of an odd assortment of patched blankets and robes and tucked him under the quilts.

The small room Tora shared with Genba was crammed full of people. Tora, covered by a quilt and leaning on an armrest, reclined on a mat in its center. Next to him sat Miss Plumblossom, enthroned on an upturned water barrel on which someone had placed one of the silk cushions from Akitada's room. Apparently she refused to sit on the floor like everyone else.

Slightly behind her was her maid, her scarred face hidden behind a fan, and on Tora's other side knelt a very pretty young girl with sparkling eyes. Genba's bulk filled the rest of the room. All of them looked up at Akitada's entrance, smiled, and bowed.

"Well!" Akitada looked around. "I hope I see you all well. Especially you, Tora."

"Pretty well, pretty well," Tora said with an expression of patient suffering. "The company helps, but the nights are bad, and I can't seem to move without much pain." The pretty girl by his side took his hand and stroked it, murmuring, "My poor tiger."

The rascal, thought Akitada, and sat down. He kept a straight face and told Miss Plumblossom, "I am happy to see that you have made your peace." Sitting down had put him at a distinct disadvantage, because the formidable Miss Plumblossom now towered over him.

She was untroubled by the impropriety. "The four of us have come to an understanding," she informed Akitada, and smiled with fashionably blackened teeth. "Yukiyo, the foolish girl, will make up for falsely accusing poor Tora by helping him find the slasher. Between us we'll get the bastard, if it's the last thing we do." She nodded emphatically and her red hair ribbons bounced.

Akitada looked at Tora, who looked back uneasily. "It's what I'd planned to do all along, sir," he pleaded. "In fact, that's one reason I went to Miss Plumblossom's. I've finally got a case of my own to solve."

Akitada opened his mouth to point out some small problems—such as the fact that Tora needed rest, or that, once he was well, he had certain duties to perform, or that the slasher had so far escaped the superior manpower of the police as well as the watchful eyes of people. Something about Tora's face made him keep his thoughts to himself. "Excellent!" he said heartily. "I wish you the greatest success. Given your experience and special talents and Yukiyo's description of the man, you will triumph where Superintendent Kobe has failed."

Tora flushed with pleasure, but Miss Plumblossom said, "The silly girl says she couldn't see in the dark. All she's sure of is that he was smallish and thinnish but very strong. Humph!"

"After such a vicious attack, it is a wonder she recalls anything. Perhaps in time she will remember more."

The maid mumbled something.

"Oh, yes. She says she smelled him," interpreted Miss Plumblossom with a toss of her head. "As if we could go around smelling people."

"What sort of smell was it?" Akitada asked, interested in spite of himself.

Tora moved impatiently. "Never mind, sir. We'll get it all sorted out. How was your trip? Catch any murderers?"

"Superintendent Kobe has arrested Nagaoka's father-in-law, and I brought home a guest, a Professor Harada. He used to work for Yasaburo. He is pretty sick, but may be able to give us some information. Seimei is tending to him now." Akitada looked curiously at the pretty girl. "Is this young woman by any chance a member of Uemon's Players?"

"Yes, Gold's an acrobat. She's fantastic." Tora smiled proudly at the girl, who returned the adoring look.

"In that case, Gold," said Akitada, "you may be able to answer a question. You stayed at the temple where the woman was murdered, didn't you? On the fifth day of last month?"

"Yes, sir. Tora's already asked me about that. I saw nothing, and neither did any of the others, sir."

Akitada hid his disappointment. "You did not leave your room after dark?"

"No. We had performed that afternoon and I was tired. Besides, it was raining."

"You slept alone?"

"No. My sister and Ohisa shared the room. They came to bed later, but my sister also saw nothing."

"And Ohisa?"

"Ohisa took off before either of us awoke."

"Took off?"

Gold made a face. "Ohisa used to be Danjuro's girl. Danjuro is our lead actor, and all the women are wild about him." Tora glowered and she added with a smile, "Except me. I can't stand the arrogant bastard. Anyway, he dumped Ohisa and she left in a snit, just like that. We would've been short a dancer if Danjuro's new girlfriend hadn't stepped in."

"And none of the others saw anything suspicious?"

She shook her head. "They would've told me. We talked about the murder all the way back to the capital."

Akitada thanked her and turned to Genba. "I trust everything was quiet in my absence?"

Genba nodded. "But there was an odd little man here a little earlier. He asked for you. Something about a screen he's supposed to paint for your lady, so I took him to her. I hope that was all right?"

"Heavens, Noami!" Akitada jumped up. "He is a very unpleasant person. I had better see him before he upsets my wife."

He met Tamako in the corridor outside her quarters. She had heard of his arrival and was coming to look for him.

"I am glad you are back safely." She bowed in her restrained and formal manner, but her eyes searched Akitada's face.

"I looked in on Tora first and found him surrounded by admiring females, plotting how to catch the slasher." Seeing her incomprehension, he explained, "A man who has been mutilating and killing young women in the city."

Her eyes grew round. "How very horrible," she breathed. "I had no idea such things were happening. Is it safe to go out?"

"Safe enough, provided you go in the daytime, take a maid with you, and don't venture into unsavory parts of town. By the way, I brought you another patient." He explained briefly about Harada.

She nodded, then took his arm. "Come! I have someone waiting to talk to you. The painter of the pretty scroll has called. I
left him giving a drawing lesson to your son."

An irrational fear seized Akitada. "You left him with Yori?"

But the scene which met his eyes was harmless enough. The
defrocked monk, dressed in a decent gray robe, his short hair
brushed back, knelt next to Akitada's son. Both held ink brushes
and were bent over a large sheet of paper.

The boy looked up and a broad smile lit his face. Jumping to
his feet, he ran to his father and wrapped his arms around his
thighs. "I'm painting," he cried. "I painted cats. Come see!"

Akitada nodded to Noami, who bowed with unexpected
politeness.

"I called, sir," he said in his grating voice, "to see if you
wished me to proceed with the screen for your lady. Since you
were not here, it was my great fortune to meet the beautiful lady
herself and your charming son."

The compliments were courteous, but Akitada did not want
this man near his family. "It was good of you to come," he said
brusquely, "but we have not really had time to consider the
matter."

Yori tugged at his sleeve.

"I was perhaps a little unreasonable about the price," Noami
suggested.

Still easily shamed by money problems, Akitada felt the color
rise to his face. "No, no. I have been too busy to consider and
will let you know when we make up our minds." He hoped
Noami would get the idea that the visit was over.

But the painter lingered. "Young Yori has something to show
you," he reminded Akitada.

Reluctantly Akitada allowed his son to draw him over to
Noami's side. The sheet of paper was covered with pictures of
cats. Some were admirably true to life, their catlike postures
sketched with consummate skill: a cat jumping for a mouse, a

cat staring down into a fishbowl, a cat toying with a beetle, a cat hissing, and a cat eating a bird. The others were childish copies by Yori, painstakingly executed, the black-on-white scheme enlivened by vivid touches of red.

"Your son has a lively sense of color," Noami commented, his eyes watching Akitada's face.

The red touches looked like blood, were meant to be blood. Yori had got the idea from the just-killed bird and applied a thick layer of red grease paint from his mother's cosmetics to the bird and to the face of the cat. Pleased with the effect, he had then given all the other cats red muzzles. He pointed, quite unnecessarily. "Blood! Cats eat birds and mice and they get blood on them."

Tamako came to take a look and clasped her hand to her mouth.

Noami chuckled, a dry coughlike sound. "A boy after my own heart," he said, and put a hand on Yori's shoulder. "So young and already so observant. What a man you will be some-day!"

Tamako jerked up the child. "It is time for his nap," she cried, and ran from the room, Yori protesting loudly.

Akitada looked at the painter with hatred in his heart. Controlling himself with difficulty, he said coldly, "We won't keep you any longer. And there is no need to return. I will send for you if we decide on the screen."

Noami nodded. "I am told you saw the hell screen at the temple?"

"Yes. It is greatly admired."

The painter cocked his head. "But not by you?"

Akitada said stiffly, "I do not hold with the Buddhist theory of hell."

"Ah! I, on the other hand, have problems with the Western Paradise." Noami stepped closer and fixed Akitada with his deep-set, burning eyes. "What pleasure can be so great that it matches pain? We all suffer the agonies of hell, but none has tasted the joys of paradise." With that he turned and walked out.

—◆—

When Tora felt well enough to begin his investigation two days later, he dressed in the worst clothes he could find: baggy pants, liberally stained and torn in places; a ragged cotton shirt; a quilted jacket with unmatched patches, tied about the waist with a hemp rope; and old straw sandals. He untied his long hair, rubbed it with some greasy lamp oil, and wrapped a rag around his head. Finally, putting a scowl on his unshaven face, he left.

He was headed for the western city, where poor people, criminals, and outcasts lived in tenements, abandoned ruins, or squatters' shacks in open fields. There was the heart of the underworld of the city, the refuge of gangs and notorious criminals, of vagrants, beggars, cripples, and the insane.

The day was overcast and cold. Tora walked at a comfortable pace to avoid undue strain to his recent injuries and thought about Yukiyo. She had tried her best to describe her ordeal. In a shamefaced whisper, she had spoken of her wounds, the horrible disfigurement of her face, the deep slashes across her breasts and abdomen. The monster had taken pleasure in the cutting, it seemed, but was not bent on killing her, or he would have stabbed or disemboweled her. Appalled by the viciousness of it, Tora had wondered if she encountered a demon instead of a man. His small size, his superhuman strength and cruelty, and his acrid stench all pointed to it. But Yukiyo had shaken her head stubbornly. He had been a man. As for the smell, it been more like hot lacquer or lamp oil, maybe.

Some sort of craftsman, thought Tora as he walked. It was not a useful clue. There were too many of them in the city. Tora planned to retrace Yukiyo's steps that night, beginning with the place where she had met the slasher, at a cheap brothel. She had been soliciting there without any luck, but as she was walking away a hooded figure had reached out from an alley and drawn her into the shadows. In a hoarse whisper, the man had offered to pay her thirty coppers to go home with him. Thirty coppers was wealth; it would pay for food for weeks, and she had agreed eagerly.

They had walked a long way, through a warren of back alleys in the far western city wards. Once she had glimpsed the roof ornament of a pagoda, and not long after that they had come to a grove of bamboo and entered an empty unlit house. There, in the darkness, he had given her a cup of wine. After that she remembered nothing until she woke in another alley in horrible pain, looking up into the horrified eyes of people who found her half-naked and bleeding.

Tora found the brothel easily. It was a rickety wooden building with the impressive name Crane Terrace. A cheap wineshop occupied the street level and a few rooms above served prostitutes and their customers. The entrance was remarkable only for the stained and torn door curtain with a misshapen bird painted on it. Tora noted the narrow passage along the side of the building. Here, among the remnants of broken sake casks and vegetable peelings, the slasher had lurked that dark night, catching his victim by the simple expedient of grabbing her arm as she passed by. Tora shook his head. Even a half-starved whore should have had the good sense to run.

He ducked under the curtain into the semidarkness of the wineshop. A thick, fetid vapor of food smells and smoke almost took his breath away.

He stood on a dirt floor. On his right, a set of steep stairs led above. Straight ahead a fire pit was putting out the smoke and the indescribable smells from a large cauldron stirred by a shaggy-haired hag. On his left, a one-eyed brute sat next to a keg. Three ragged creatures eyed the newcomer blearily. The innkeeper growled, "Wine's a copper, take it or leave it. For another copper, you can eat."

Tora suppressed his revulsion. "Wine," he said gruffly, joining the three guests.

"Show me the money first!"

Tora dug out a copper coin. The man snatched it from his hand, held it up to his eye, and nodded. Dropping the coin down the front of his shirt, he dipped out a measure of dark, cloudy liquid from the keg. It was easily the worst wine Tora had ever tasted and almost choked him. "I'm looking for a girl," he said when he found his voice.

"I don't provide whores," snapped the host. "You get your own around here." One of the customers snickered.

"She's my sister," said Tora, improvising. "Our mother's dying and she's asking for her, so I came to the capital to look for her. I was told she works this part of town."

The one-eyed man said gruffly, "She must be hard up. Sorry about your troubles. What does she look like?"

This could not be answered easily, so Tora said vaguely, "About this high, kinda small bones, pretty hair. Ordinary, you know."

"It's not fat Mitsu," volunteered one of the guests.

"And Kazuko's a good lay, but bald as an egg," added another.

The one-eyed man turned to the old hag stirring the cauldron. "What do you think, Mother?"

She wiped the sweat from her face with her sleeve. "Maybe she's the sickly little thing. Only came a few times. Seems like her name was Yukiyo."

Tora asked eagerly, "Any idea who she went with?"

The old woman said, "Nobody. She came in, but there were no takers. She looked so sick I gave her some soup on account and she left."

Tora dug out another copper. "Here. We may be poor, but we pay our debts."

This gesture worked wonders. They all fell to a serious discussion of every man or woman Yukiyo might have talked to, but the men who visited the brothel were mostly transients, nameless laborers, vendors, porters, beggars, or monks.

"Monks?" Tora asked. "Looking for women?"

His naïveté caused general hilarity. "Some of 'em are worse than ordinary men," cackled the old woman, "and, come to think, there was one who kept looking at the girl. Getting up his courage, I guess. But he never talked to her that I could see."

"Is there a monastery around here?" Tora asked, thinking of the pagoda.

There was not. It was a dead end. Tora thanked them and left.

He walked northward, passing through alleys and poor streets, and began to suspect that the slasher had avoided landmarks which his victim might recall. He had zigzagged through quarters, always skirting their main gates. No wonder Yukiyo could not give a clear account of their route.

He wished he could have talked to her some more, but after his master had returned, Yukiyo had refused to visit again. Miss Plumblossom had snorted. "I don't know what's come over the girl. When we were leaving, she grabbed my arm and started rushing for the gate. And now she won't come back!"

But her unexplained fright was not the only thing troubling Tora. Apparently all the slasher did was cut her. Yukiyo was certain that she had not been raped. Lust, even perverted and sadistic lust, Tora could understand, but this was something else entirely.

The quarter he was entering now was more depressing than the previous one. People lived here, if you could call it that, but there were far too many loitering men. No work meant high crime or slow starvation. And that reminded Tora of another troubling fact. The slasher had offered Yukiyo thirty coppers to go home with him. That was a lot of money for an employed laborer, let alone an outcast or mendicant monk.

He raised his eyes to scan the rooftops once again for the spire of a pagoda, when he was suddenly jostled, and a string of curses rang in his ears. Before he could blink, he was flung violently against a house wall, and punches rained on his head and chest. Tora raised his arms to protect his face and waited for his chance. But the onslaught ended as abruptly as it had begun. His assailant spat disgustedly and turned to walk off.

Hot fury washed over Tora. He raised himself from his half-prone position and rushed after his assailant. Grabbing his elbow, he spun him about, cried, "That's for hitting a man for no reason, bastard," and landed a fist squarely on the other's chin. He stepped back instantly. The other man, young and poorly dressed, wore a bloody bandage over part of his face.

He raised his arm to protect himself, but Tora said, "Never mind! I wasn't done with you for the thrashing you gave me, but I'll put it on your account, seeing that someone else has already done the job. I don't like an uneven fight."

The other man growled, "Don't let that stop you. I can beat you any day, turd."

He was slightly taller and much wider in the shoulders than Tora, but the fight had gone out of him.

"Why did you hit me?"

Slowly the other man lowered his arm. "You pushed me, bastard. Nobody does that to me."

"I didn't see you. I was looking for a pagoda."

The eye not covered by the bloody bandage narrowed, looking Tora up and down. "You're a stranger here?"

There was no sense in inventing new lies. Tora told the story of his dying mother and lost sister again, adding some heart-rending detail which brought tears to his own eyes.

The ruffian rubbed his bristly chin, reddened from Tora's fist. "Sorry, buddy," he said hoarsely. "Looks like you're worse off than me. Didn't mean to lay into you, but I've had a bad day with some rough fellows. My head's sore as hell itself and when you bumped into me I was seeing stars."

"Oh, in that case," said Tora, "allow me to make up for it with a cup of wine. My name's Tora, by the way."

"Junshi." The other man grinned, revealing a large recent gap in his front teeth. "Thanks. I won't say no. There's a place around the corner sells some decent muck."

The place was worse than the Crane Terrace, being smaller, dirtier, and smellier, but the wine was slightly better.

"Now, about your sister," said Junshi awkwardly. "She may be dead, you know. I work for the warden and I can tell you, street girls have a hard life in this quarter."

"I know, but I've got to keep looking till I know one way or another."

Junshi sighed. "Most men here can't pay more than a copper or two for a woman, and there's a lot of rough stuff. My boss could tell you how many dead girls they fish out of the canals or find among the garbage in the alleys."

"By heaven! The warden!" Tora slapped his forehead with his hand. "Why didn't I think of that? Where's his office?"

Junshi snorted. "A warden with an office? In this quarter? If there ever was one, it's long gone. The position is what you might call 'by popular acclaim.' My boss runs things here and he's usually somewhere around the temple in the daytime."

Tora sat up. "What temple? Does it have a pagoda? And monks?"

Junshi laughed. "They call it the Temple of Boundless Mercy—which is a laugh, seeing that mercy's the last thing you expect to find there—but yes, it's got a pagoda. The monks left long ago. There's only the one hall and the pagoda left. People think demons roam about at night there. That makes it a fine meeting place for thugs. Either way, it's unhealthy after dark." He touched his bandage and grimaced.

Tora shuddered. However, he merely needed to find the

house where the slasher had taken Yukiyo, and it was still broad daylight. "Can you introduce me to your boss?"

Junshi guffawed. "Not today. He'll send me back after the bastards tonight. I'll show you the way to the temple, but you'll have to find him yourself. And don't mention you've seen me."

Tora paid for their wine, and they walked northwestward through slums and open fields with squatters' shacks. People glanced at them and crossed the street. Junshi filled Tora in on the dangers of the quarter. "Bodies in the street almost every day," he said in a matter-of-fact tone. "If it wasn't for the boss, it'd be worse. The police don't come here. They don't like to deal with outcasts. The boss doesn't care what a man is or has, so long as he doesn't hurt people."

"He sounds good to me," said Tora. "Any bamboo groves near the temple?"

"No groves. The fox shrine has some pines around it." They emerged into the square in front of the ruined temple. Junshi stiffened and grabbed Tora's arm, saying, "There's the boss now. Good luck!" and was gone before Tora could thank him.

A bearded giant stood in front of the remnants of the temple gate, his arms folded across a barrel-like chest. A group of young boys surrounded him. Tora crossed the square slowly. The semilegal standing of this individual did nothing to reassure him. He looked more like a robber chief than a representative of the law in his sector.

The giant was laughing with the boys, but his eyes found Tora immediately and sharpened. He detached himself from the youngsters and strolled up. "Good day to you," he said. His voice rumbled from the depth of his chest like a rock slide.

Tora returned the greeting with a grin. "I am told you're the warden," he said. "Could you tell me where I might find a bamboo grove around here?"

The warden's eyes narrowed suspiciously. "What's your purpose for asking?" he demanded.

Tora bristled. "Look, I'm a stranger here, asking for directions. What's with the third degree?"

"I like to know what strangers are up to in my district," snapped the big man. "You either tell me what you want here, or you leave."

Tora considered his options and said in an ingratiating tone, "Well, it's a bit embarrassing. But here goes. I'm looking for my sister, who's disappeared. She's been working as a whore. Now our mother's on her deathbed and wants to see her. Someone told me she worked around here and might have gone off with a monk. To a bamboo grove."

The eyes narrowed even further, moving speculatively from Tora's trim mustache to his hands. "Who told you that?"

"Er, the landlord of a tavern."

The boss sneered and opened his mouth, but was suddenly distracted by the sounds of a fight inside the temple grounds. He snapped, "No monks in my district and no bamboo groves, either. You'd better go look in another part of town." He strode off to investigate.

Tora wondered for a moment about the man's reaction. Everyone else had swallowed the tale of the dying mother. He looked down at himself. His clothes looked no worse than the warden's rags. Maybe the guy had a hangover or a toothache.

Shaking his head, he also went into the temple grounds, where a pitiful sort of market seemed to be in progress. The fight had attracted scant attention. Human scarecrows sat about on the muddy ground with items spread out for sale which looked like the garbage tossed out by the servants of the better houses, and probably was. Tora strolled about and tried to strike up conversations, but after a glance at him people turned uncommunicative. He was an outsider and his rags made him unwelcome here, for clearly he had no money for purchases, but might be there to steal from them.

It was already long past midday, and so far Tora was no closer to his objective than before. Glancing up at the old pagoda, he got an idea. If he climbed up there, he could look over the rooftops for miles. A bamboo grove within a few blocks of the pagoda should be easy to find.

Luck was with him—the entrance to the tower had not been boarded up. Inside, however, his heart fell. The steep stairs were missing steps, and a pile of rotten timbers had fallen from the upper floors. Tora peered up. The floor above him was missing so many planks that he could see through it to the one beyond. But he decided to risk it. At least there was enough daylight so he could see where he was putting his feet.

The climb was tedious because each step and each board must be tested before he dared put weight on it, and when he reached the top floor, he was sweating in spite of the cold. Slowly he made his way around all four sides, looking out over the quarter. There were only a few spots of green among the wintry huddle of dull brown roofs. All but one of these were the dark green of pines, but one was paler, the jade green color of bamboo. It was smaller than a grove or woods, but larger than the yards of houses thereabouts, and it lay only two blocks to the southeast of the temple.

Elated, Tora started downward, but in his hurry he took a misstep, lost his footing, and, twisting wildly, plunged through space.

When he regained consciousness, he was in darkness but knew immediately where he was. His back rested across a beam, his hips and legs, slightly higher than the rest of his body, were supported by more solid flooring, but his head hung over empty space. He was conscious of pain everywhere, but the worst of it in his head. After cautiously checking to see if he could move his limbs without falling again, he shifted just enough on his beam to support his head. After resting for a few moments, he tried to sit up, but a wave of dizziness hit him and he grasped desperately around him to keep from tipping over the edge. After a moment the nausea passed and his eyes adjusted to the darkness. He could make out vague shapes of flooring and part of the stairs. Carefully, inch by inch, he moved toward them, testing each plank before heaving his bruised and aching body onto it.

After a short rest, he felt his head and found his hair wet with blood and a large, painful swelling behind his right ear. Otherwise he seemed whole, though very sore in places. He looked up. If memory served, he had fallen from the fourth level to the second. The beam had caught his shoulders and kept him from landing headfirst on the stone floor of the entrance level. He must have been unconscious for hours if it was nighttime. He listened. All was silent outside the pagoda. The market was over, and people had left without discovering his fall. Or, more likely, they had ignored it.

He got to his hands and knees and crept backward down the stairs. In the almost complete darkness he had to trust his sense of touch not to step through a hole and fall the rest of the way. When he finally reached solid ground and stood up, the world spun dizzily for a moment. He staggered toward the lighter rectangle of the doorway and looked out.

The night was moonless, and the courtyard lay deserted. In the darkness, the shapes of trees, buildings, and walls loomed strangely, and he suddenly remembered the reputation of the temple. Sweat broke out on his body and his hair bristled unpleasantly. Everybody knew deserted temples were dwelling places for demons and hungry ghosts. With a shudder he shrank back into the doorway. But a strange rasping sound, followed by a skittering noise, came from under the stairs, and with a mighty leap Tora plunged down the stone steps and into the open.

Almost immediately a loud wail rose from somewhere near the monstrous black shape of the old temple hall. Tora froze. Several dark figures detached themselves from the hall and moved toward him, gliding low across the ground and wailing loudly. With a hoarse cry, Tora ran for the gate.

When he had put some distance between himself and the haunted temple, he stopped to orientate himself. He wished himself elsewhere with all his heart, but having come this far he would find that bamboo grove.

After a false turn and falling once over some garbage in an alley, setting off a dog's barking, he found a wall over which a thick tangle of bamboo branches drooped their rustling leaves, sere and shredded by the winter winds but still dense enough to hide the house behind the closed gate. The wall was too high to climb and the gate looked sturdy. Tora tried to make out the inscription over the gate, but the characters were in Chinese. Inside, a sleepy crow gave a hoarse croak.

At that moment, the gate creaked open. Tora shrank into the shadow of the wall. A small hooded figure emerged, relocked the gate, and walked slowly up the street.

Tora was after him in an instant. "Stop!" he cried, grabbing the other man's shoulder. "Let's have a look at you."

The hood slipped back, and he caught a brief glimpse of a round, ugly face under bristly gray hair. Then the man seized his arm with both hands, twisted, and jerked. Pulled off balance, Tora released his hold and tried to recover. Too late. With another mighty shove in the back, he went sprawling, and when he scrambled to his feet, the hooded man had disappeared.

Cursing, Tora ran this way and that before giving up and returning to the gate. He decided to see how large the area was. A narrow path followed the wall toward the back. He had only taken a few steps along this track when it happened. A moment before the excruciating blow struck the back of his head, he had a dim impression of running steps. Then he pitched forward and passed out.

TWENTY

A Hell of Ice

Yori disappeared the day of Tora's adventures.

Because Harada's condition had worsened, everyone in the Sugawara household was preoccupied with his care, and the boy was left to amuse himself. Yori's absence was not noticed until the hour of the midday rice. At first it caused only mild concern, because Yori had wandered off before. But when time passed without his return and it grew colder outside, a search was organized, first of the house, gardens, and stable, then of the immediate neighborhood.

By midafternoon both Tamako and Akitada were pacing the floor. Unable to wait any longer, Akitada threw on an extra robe, put on his warm boots, and rushed out into the street. He knocked on every gate and personally questioned every resident of the surrounding streets, every passerby, every vendor, every beggar, and every passing servant, asking if they had seen the child. Nobody had.

Toward dusk, Akitada, now frantic with fear, picked up the first news at one of the mansions in the next quarter. A house-boy had passed the Sugawara mansion on an errand during the morning and noticed a small man with short bushy gray hair hovering by the open gate. The man had been gesturing to some-one inside.

Then Saburo came rushing up with more news. In the next block, a cook's children were playing in the alley when a hooded monk passed them, leading a small boy by the hand. They had stared because the boy had worn a very pretty red silk robe. It had to be Yori. And the hooded monk?

Akitada was seized with a sudden, gut-wrenching, irrational fear, but he told Saburo calmly, "I believe I know where he is. Tell your mistress that I have gone to bring him back and not to worry."

Noami! It must have been Noami. The bushy hair, barely grown out; the children thinking of a monk, because Noami, dressed in monk's robes, had probably covered his head against the cold. It did not explain why he had taken Akitada's son.

Akitada set out for the painter's home at a loping run, telling himself that there was a perfectly reasonable explanation for what had happened.

What was more likely than that Yori, bored and left out of his elders' activities, had spied Noami passing the house? The boy, remembering the interrupted painting lesson, would have begged the artist for another one, and Noami, unwelcome in Akitada's house, would have offered to teach Yori at his home.

The distance between Akitada's house and Noami's Bamboo Hermitage was nearly two miles, and Akitada kept to the most direct route. Rushing along, he attracted stares and soon began to perspire in spite of the freezing cold.

He was no longer accustomed to exercise and soon tired, but he kept up his pace until he reached the artist's place. It was getting dark, and the narrow street was as deserted as it had been the last time. When he pounded on the gate, the dry leaves of the bamboo rustled mysteriously and he half expected to hear the raucous cry of the crow again. Instead there was the sound of someone shuffling through the fallen leaves inside. A wooden bar was pulled back and the gate swung slowly open.

Noami stood before him. A slow smile stretched the wide mouth, his large yellow teeth making him look more than ever like a grinning monkey.

Like the monkey that ate the plum, Akitada thought, and snapped, "Do you have my son here?"

"But certainly, my lord." Noami bowed and threw the gate wide. "The youngster has enjoyed himself enormously. Please come in."

Relief washed over Akitada and left him wordless. He followed Noami down the path to his studio. At the entrance they both removed their boots. Akitada said peevishly, "May I ask why you brought him here?"

"To paint." Noami raised his brows in surprise. "I came by to see if he might like a lesson. The boy told me that you and your lady were busy, but that he might visit my studio. I was about to bring him back."

It sounded plausible. Yori was very likely to have said such a thing if he wished to go. Still, Noami's high-handed invitation had put them all to immense trouble and worry. Akitada said brusquely, "We did not know and have been searching for him since he left."

"Oh, dear," said the painter blandly. "I am so sorry. It is amazing what youngsters can get up to. Please come in."

Yori sat on the floor, surrounded by pieces of paper and small containers of paints. Noami had removed his quilted red robe and given him a short cotton shirt which covered his full trousers and jacket. It was liberally stained with paint. Yori turned a smiling face to his father.

"Look at my paintings," he cried.

The studio looked much like the last time, except that all the sliding doors were closed against the winter chill. Noami had lit a lamp near some cushions. A large brazier warmed the room.

"May I offer refreshments?" Noami asked.

"Please do not bother," Akitada said quickly. He disliked the man intensely, but felt it would be boorish to express his feelings, when the painter had done no more than entertain Yori for an afternoon. "We must return immediately. His mother is anxious."

"Yes, of course. I forgot. But let me get something to clean him up a little. Please do have some wine. You look chilled. Surely on such a cold night...?"

Akitada saw a wine flask on the brazier. His fingers and ears felt nearly frozen, and the sweat was like ice against his skin. "Very well." He seated himself. Noami poured and offered the wine with a bow, then hurried away.

Akitada warmed his frozen hands by holding them over the brazier. Yori was dipping his fingers into some yellow paint and making hand prints on the paper.

"Stop that!" his father snapped. "Why did you run away without permission?"

Yori turned round eyes to his father. "But I asked permission. You were reading some papers and nodded your head."

Akitada did not remember. Seimei had been busy with the sick Harada, and Akitada had worked over the accounts himself. An unpleasant draft passed through the studio, chilling him to the bone but doing little to disperse the strong smell of paints and pigments which hung about the studio. He sipped a little of the spiced wine and found it strange but not unpleasant. Papers lay scattered about the floor, Yori's handiwork. He remembered the last painting lesson and became angry again. "Wipe your hands and come here."

Yori obeyed, using Noami's shirt for the purpose. Picking up some of the papers, he brought them to his father. "Look!"

The boy had tried to draw people this time, strange creatures with large heads, open mouths, huge eyes, and missing hands or feet. Childish distortions because he had found them too difficult to draw? Akitada took another sip, letting the wine warm and settle his stomach, and rose to look at the other sheets. As he did so, he came across a drawing by Noami. This, too, was of a human being, a small boy, whose eyes were wide with fear and his mouth open in a scream. Akitada dropped the paper in sudden revulsion. This drawing also had only stumps where the

339

hands and feet should have been. How dare the man show such things to a child!

Then two memories coalesced in Akitada's mind: the bleeding wounds of the tortured souls on the hell screen and the maimed son of the poor woman in the market nearby. At first his mind refused a connection too horrible to contemplate, but he sifted through the rest of the papers with frantic haste, turning up two more sketches of children with missing limbs. Remembering the rolls of drawings Noami had so angrily prevented him from seeing, Akitada took up the lamp, found the pile in the corner of the studio, and unrolled sketch after sketch, letting each fall from his trembling hands. Most were of women and children, though there were two frail old men. All of them poor weak creatures, and all of them horribly wounded or burned. Several sketches showed Yukiyo, her face slashed and her naked body bleeding from the breasts and abdomen. Akitada's stomach turned, and the sour taste of wine rose to his mouth.

He thought too late of what might happen if Noami returned and found him so. Yori! He must get the boy away.

Akitada swayed, suddenly dizzy. With shaking hands he rolled up the papers and pushed them back in their corner. Then he staggered back to Yori. He was barely in time.

Noami came in, carrying a bowl of water and some towels. For a moment, Akitada could not focus. The room swam before his eyes.

Noami busied himself wiping paint off Yori's face and hands.

"Papa saw my pictures." Yori's voice sounded a long way off, but quite cheerful. "I shall come back to paint the puppies soon."

Noami put down the dirty towels and took off the stained shirt. "I shall look forward to it, young master," he said in his grating voice. Yori ran to Akitada. Catching the child in his arms, Akitada stared at the painter. He must act naturally, or Noami would prevent their leaving.

"Are you quite well, my lord?" asked Noami. "You look very pale."

"No, I'm . . . I'm fine. His coat? We must g . . . g . . ." Yori was already struggling into his red coat.

"We must go home," Akitada managed to say quite clearly. He felt strangely light-headed. Making an attempt to get to his feet, he found that his legs would not support him.

"Perhaps another cup of wine before your long walk back?" asked Noami, pressing the cup into his hand.

Anything to get to his feet. He must leave. He must take Yori. Akitada drank and staggered up. "Come, Yori," he said, and bent to take his son's hand. But he miscalculated, overbalanced, and fell to his hands and knees.

"Oh, dear, oh, dear," said Noami. "Sit down and rest, my lord. Shall I get you some water?"

Akitada nodded. "Some water. Yes."

The light was very poor, but the man seemed to be grinning as he left. For a moment, Akitada stared after him nervously. It seemed darker in the room. Then he realized that he had left the lamp in the corner with Noami's drawings. The painter knew he had seen them. Almost at the same moment, another thought worked its way through the haze of his mind: the wine he had just drunk must have been drugged to make him so dizzy and weak.

Akitada made a superhuman effort. "Yori," he mumbled, "you must run home *now!*"

Yori nodded. "We'll run home, Papa. I'm hungry."

"No. You must go home alone. Can you . . ." Akitada's tongue would not obey. "Alone. Now! Can you . . . run alone?" He had meant to ask if the child could find the way. Silly question. "Get Genba . . . tell Genba . . ." No time! He raised his voice. "Run, Yori! Now! *Run!*"

The boy stood irresolute, staring at him wide-eyed. Outside, there were the returning steps of Noami.

341

"Please, Yori," Akitada begged. "Please, hurry! And don't look back!" He gave the child a little push toward the entrance.

His urgency must have registered, for Yori nodded and ran. In a moment, he was gone. Akitada staggered to his feet again, grabbing for a pillar to stay upright. He must prevent Noami from going after Yori. Pushing himself away from the pillar, he stumbled toward the rear of the studio and slid open the doors to the garden.

"What are you doing?" cried the painter.

Akitada staggered forward and fell headlong down some steps. The pain to his knees and the cold air cleared his head a little. Noami, a vague presence in Akitada's confused state, attempted to lift him to his feet. Akitada mumbled, "Yori . . ."

"Where's the boy? Did he run out?"

Akitada clutched the shoulders of the small man and nodded. "Li'l rascal was looking for the . . . dogs," he slurred.

"Let's get you back in first," said Noami. "Then I'll go find the boy!"

He half supported, half dragged Akitada back into the studio and let him drop onto the cushion.

Waves of nausea washed over Akitada; the room spun and receded crazily; someone pressed a cup to his lips. He tried to shake his head, opened his mouth to say no, but the liquid poured between his teeth; he gagged and swallowed.

Before him hovered the broad, grinning face of Noami. "There, now," he rasped. "That should put you to sleep." His laughter sounded like a cracked bell. "I was right about you. I knew you'd come yourself and alone, my lord. Men like you are too arrogant to think common folk would dare lay a finger on them."

Akitada lurched forward, his hands reaching for the man's throat, but Noami pushed him back and laughed. The sound reverberated in Akitada's ears as he lay helplessly on the floor and watched the painter's disembodied head recede and fade on waves of mocking laughter.

Then he was alone.

As long as the walls kept whirling and the floor bucking like a wild horse, he despaired of making his escape, but something forced him to try. He got to his knees.

Concentrate! Move! Get away from here! If necessary, on all fours, or crawling like a snake, pulling himself along by his fingernails across the wooden floor, board by board. To the entrance and beyond. Yori must be well clear by now.

On that thought, Akitada passed out.

❈

When he regained consciousness, he was first aware of bitter cold. There were sounds of rustling and more faintly of someone moaning. It was very dark, and he could not see where the sounds came from. He was freezing. There was also pain, great pain in his wrists and shoulders. His arms were stretched above his head. He tried to move, and the moaning turned into an agonized groan. His groan. His wrists were tied and attached to something above him. Most of the weight of his body depended from his wrists, because he was sagging. He straightened, and the pain eased a little.

He tried to shout, but something was stuffed in his mouth, a rag with the nauseating taste and smell of paints. He gagged and felt the bile rising in his throat. No! He must not vomit or he would suffocate. Closing his eyes, he concentrated on subduing his nausea. Finally the urge subsided.

His wrists were held together by a rope tied so tightly that he could not feel his hands. His feet were also tied at the ankles, but not so tightly. He could feel sharp gravel biting into the soles of his feet. But when he tried to move his legs, his shoulders, arms, and wrists were in agony. If only he could get some slack in the rope from which he was suspended. He attempted to pull on it, but another excruciating pain ran from his shoulders across his entire torso, and he desisted instantly. To ease the pain, he raised himself to his toes.

He balanced like this for a while, afraid to move until the waves of pain subsided a little. As he waited, it dawned on him that he was strung up in Noami's garden and that he was alone.

The darkness was not impenetrable. A patch of starlit sky showed between the fronds of rustling bamboo and bare branches. He must be tied up to a tree. It was incredibly cold, and he realized that he was naked except for his loincloth.

The madman had stripped him of his clothes, tied him up to the tree, and left him to freeze in agony. It was a great deal of trouble to go to, in order to eliminate a witness. Why not kill him outright? What did Noami have in mind?

The memory of those sketches of bleeding bodies returned vividly. Perhaps he was about to be carved up while the monster busily sketched away. He, Akitada, would become a character on the hell screen. He had a sudden freakish image of lines of people passing by to stare at his writhing body. Would his friends or acquaintances recognize him? He giggled at the thought of their faces, and then felt warm moisture running down his cheeks.

Oh, no! Dear heaven, no! He must not give the man the satisfaction of seeing him cry. Searching for something to distract his mind, he decided to concentrate on a scheme for freeing himself, impossible as that seemed.

For a while now his contracted leg muscles had protested against supporting his weight on the balls of his feet. They began to cramp in earnest, his ankles wobbled, and he dropped forward. The sudden jerk was agonizing to his already injured shoulder joints. He closed his eyes and slowed his breathing: Inhale! Exhale! Inhale! Exhale! Over and over again, until he became inured to the pain in his shoulders and the cramping in his legs.

His head cleared a little, but breathing was difficult. In his present position, he could not catch deep breaths. The thought of not getting enough air panicked him. Noami had left him here to suffocate slowly.

Back on his toes again and with a little slack to work with, he began to test the rope. If only he had some sensation in his fingers! He might be able to feel a knot, find out how he was attached to the tree limb. He could not raise his head enough to see what was directly above him.

He tried twisting. At the cost of another wave of pain to his shoulders and wrists, he managed it. A wasted effort. It was too dark to make out details, and his hands were in the way. Straightening his body with another painful effort, he slowly transferred his weight to his feet again, rested, and thought.

Had Yori made good his escape? Had he found his way home? Probably not. He was only three years old and two miles from home, in a strange neighborhood. He remembered Takenori's warning with a shudder. How long would a small child in expensive silk robes last among people who attacked grown men? His heart contracted with fear and grief. Poor child! Poor boy! Sent out by his own father to face more horrors.

Still, it was marginally better than to have let him fall into Noami's clutches. Any one of the cutthroats roaming the street of the western capital at night would take more pity on a child than that monster.

Besides, there was a chance, a very small chance, that Yori would find help. Even if he did not reach home, he might find someone who would listen to his story and come to investigate. But Akitada thought about how long he had been unconscious, and knew that help would have come by now if the boy had found a friend. Besides, Yori had not been aware of the danger his father was in. And who would listen to the babblings of a lost child in the middle of the night? If only Yori was safe, it was enough. Somewhere inside, because he would freeze to death in this cold. Akitada had begun to shake so badly that the rope vibrated and he could see the bare twigs above him trembling among the icy stars. Strangely, death by freezing was less upsetting than the pain he was in and the thought of his torturer's return.

He found himself gasping for breath again and shifted his weight for a few minutes' relief. He could no longer control his shaking. The thought that he would soon be past caring about escape was almost welcome.

But either the instinct to survive or some perverse pride intervened, and he began to tug at the rope to test its strength. It bit cruelly into his wrists and sent shock waves of hot pain along his arms and into his shoulders, but he persisted. Hemp rope was stretchable. If he got enough slack to ease his arms and shoulders, he might also have enough purchase to loosen the knot around his wrists. He pulled and jerked and twisted. Then he rested and began again. Now and then he stopped to check his progress. Then he started the whole process over again—pull, twist, rest—until he lost all sense of time. He could feel the warm blood running into his hands and dripping down his arms and back. Strangely, it did not hurt as much as before, and the moment came when he could bend his elbows a little and move his head.

At that moment, Noami returned. Akitada saw the light of his lantern first. It gleamed eerily through the dense stalks of bamboo. Then the painter appeared. In addition to the lantern, he carried a large basket, which he dropped before Akitada's feet to raise the lantern.

"Ah, you're awake," he said, his eyes glowing like live coals in the flickering light. "Tsk, tsk. Look at what you have been doing to your wrists! Does it hurt very much?" He jerked sharply at the bonds, while his eyes watched Akitada's face intently. "Cold enough for you? Yes, I expect it is. Not cold enough for a freezing hell, though. But I can always paint in the snow and ice later." He set down the lantern and began to remove painting supplies from the basket and set them out neatly before Akitada.

The basket he turned upside down to seat himself on. Some time was taken up by adjusting both basket and lantern so all of Akitada's strung-up body was well lit, and Noami could see it from the proper angle. When he was satisfied, he began to rub ink and water.

All of these activities the painter accompanied by a steady flow of chatter. "I don't like to disappoint a man of your stature," he said, as he let his eyes travel over Akitada's body. "Both figuratively and literally. Those are very nice muscles. I am strong for my size, but I hate to think what trouble you would have been without the sleeping draught."

Akitada managed only a faint growl from behind the stinking rag in his mouth.

Noami laughed. "I would enjoy a conversation, but it's not advisable. I live like a hermit here, and I doubt anyone would pay attention to your screaming, but then you never know. By the way, your son seems to have disappeared. I was sorry to lose him. A child is always much more effective in conveying horror than a grown man, though a nobleman of your stature should make a rather neat point. On the other hand, Yori was such a charmingly pampered child. A child of a noble house. All my previous subjects have been the spawn of untouchables."

Without his efforts to stretch the rope, Akitada was beginning to shake again. His relief at Yori's escape from this maniac was tempered by the knowledge that, even if he managed to loosen the rope enough to free himself, he would by then be in no condition to defend himself, let alone walk away. Dear heaven, what did Noami have in mind?

"I expect you are afraid," the painter said, sketching rapidly with his brush while casting sharp glances at Akitada. "Yes, I can see it in your eyes."

Akitada attempted a glare and another grunt of protest.

"No? I don't believe you. Your situation is quite hopeless, you know. You cannot get away from me, and soon even your sturdy

347

constitution will succumb to the frigid temperatures." He glanced about him. "Regrettable that the snow did not last. But what I need for my last panel, for my hell of ice, is the suffering produced by freezing to death. You, my lord, will be immortal-ized."

Akitada did not think that he would freeze to death very readily. Perhaps the man would be satisfied with some sketches and untie him when he was done. If Noami was the slasher, and there was little doubt he was, he had never actually killed any of his victims, though some had died from their wounds. Some remnant of his Buddhist training probably caused him to shy away from actual murder.

Noami paused to stare at Akitada. "You asked for this, you know," he said. "If you had not started snooping at the temple, we might never have met. But you could not leave it alone. You had to come here, claiming to be a customer! Hah! I'm not such a fool that I could not tell you wanted to inspect my studio for evidence. Then I caught you back at the temple, asking more questions. I suppose the abbot asked you to investigate? I thought he looked at me strangely after he saw the first panels of the screen. Imagine my shock when I came to your house and saw a girl there that I'd used as a model for the hell of knives. I heard you calling me a slasher, a common criminal! That was when I was sure that you were about to call in the police, and I could not let you do that. Not before my screen was com-pleted."

Akitada's foolish hope that Noami might be satisfied with a few sketches collapsed. Noami would not let him go. There was nothing left now but the feeble hope that Yori somehow would make people understand where his father was.

"Hmm," said Noami, looking at his sketch critically and nodding. "This will have to do. More extreme suffering will have to wait till later." He held up the sketch for Akitada to see.

Akitada did not recognize himself in the pitiful, twisted

creature suspended from a bare branch. Was his face really so contorted? He attempted to straighten up.

Noami grinned. "My compliments on your self-control, by the way. Your position must be quite painful by now." He rose and came to check Akitada's bonds again. "Tsk, tsk. You've been pulling on the rope. All you accomplished was to tighten the knots on your wrists. Your hands are already blue and quite swollen. I doubt if you have any feeling left in them. You should be safe enough." He suddenly cocked his head and listened, then turned abruptly and padded off into the garden.

Akitada immediately returned to jerking on the rope. He discovered that he could manage ten sharp pulls before the pain on his wrists and arms became too great and he had to rest. At least he had some leverage by now. Sweat was running down his face despite the cold. He thought at first it was blood, that somehow the cold had thinned his skin until the slightest exertion cracked it wide open. Relieved that it was not, he began his routine again. There was a little more slack than before. Blood started trickling from his wrists again, but he did not care and gave more and harder pulls on the rope. By now his whole torso was a mass of fiery pain, and he was almost certain he had dislocated both of his shoulders, but he finally had some hope that he might have enough purchase to loosen his bonds or break the rope.

He had hardly thought this when the painter reappeared, muttering to himself. He was carrying two heavy pails and some rags. The pails he set down next to Akitada and, dropping the rags into the first pail, he began to wash Akitada's body down.

Although he was thoroughly chilled already, the shock of the icy water was so great that Akitada groaned and flinched back violently. He could not fathom the purpose of this bath. If Noami wanted to get rid of the blood, he had no need to wet his head, chest, and abdomen.

When Akitada was completely wet, Noami moved the second pail next to Akitada's feet, then bent to lift them into the pail.

Having his legs knocked out from under him pushed Akitada forward, his whole weight suddenly suspended again from his raw wrists and damaged shoulders. He screamed in agony, a muffled groan because of the gag, and closed his eyes against the excruciating pain which ran down his arms to the rest of his body like hot lightning. When his feet touched ground again and took the weight from his arms, the relief was so enormous that he did not realize right away that Noami had inserted his bound feet into a pail of freezing water halfway up his shins. He shrank into himself, then flinched violently as Noami draped the icy cloths about his bare body, covering him from his head to his hips.

When the wet cloth slapped against his nose and cheeks, robbing him of sight and air simultaneously, his terror was so great that he reared up, and the back of his head somehow struck Noami. He heard a sharp cry, and then felt a vicious blow to his head, which made him sag abruptly. He almost wished for unconsciousness at that moment, but Noami had been careful. He still needed him, needed him conscious and in agony.

Akitada could not see, but when Noami had struck him he had loosened the wet cloth on his face enough that he could breathe. He heard Noami muttering as he moved about.

"There," he said suddenly quite close to Akitada's ear as he adjusted one of the wet rags, "that should freeze nicely to your skin in the next hour. Not quite as natural as chaining you in a frozen pond, but I expect to see much the same expressions of pain and fear. It is very difficult to arouse certain emotions through art, but people will see my hell screen and be terrified. Nothing moves one's heart like utmost terror and pain in the faces of other creatures. Terror has many faces, you know. Its variety would surprise you. I am quite curious how you will look when I return. If the effect is as fine as I hope, you will occupy the foreground, a lesson to all sinners. Through my art, the terror of one person, you, becomes the terror of all who see you, and terror is the only emotion which moves men's hearts from sin. Thus a small sacrifice produces a great good. Now do you under . . . ?"

The rest was drowned out by the gush of icy water from the other pail. It hit Akitada squarely across head and shoulders and soaked his whole body.

Without another word, Noami left.

The cold was unbelievable and produced a totally new kind of pain, perversely almost akin to burning. Not in all those years in the snow country had Akitada felt such deadly cold. He tried to think back to the stories of people who had barely escaped freezing to death. They had become sleepy and felt nothing after a while. So Noami would be disappointed after all. Akitada thought that he was beginning to lose sensation in most parts of his body already. Then the memory of amputated limbs came to him. Those who had not died in the frozen north had lost hands and feet, ears and noses to the cold. Ice was as effective as a sharp knife.

Movement and physical exertion had warmed him earlier, and he tried to move again, to pull against the rope, but his muscles were stiffening, cramping, refusing his commands. For the first time he considered seriously the fact that he was about to die. To die slowly, forgotten in this overgrown bamboo grove, while a demented artist sketched his final moments. To die without a single act of courage or affirmation. The thought of being mocked in death, and again mocked after death by the thousands who would pass by Noami's masterpiece, revolted his very soul.

He began his struggle again, straining, his teeth grinding against the rags in his mouth, his own groans filling his ears till they drowned out the rustling of the bamboo and the distant sound of temple bells marking the hours. He gained enough purchase that his arms and shoulders could move a little and he celebrated that moment with a brief period of rest during which

351

he attempted to move his fingers and wrists. Without them he could not work the knot loose. But his exertions were in vain. He had no idea if his fingers were capable of movement, and his wrists hurt too badly. But the physical effort had counteracted the freezing water against his skin, and one of the rags had actually come loose and fallen.

He considered his situation. Once or twice during some of his more violent efforts of pulling against the rope, he had brushed the bark of the tree trunk behind him. Perhaps he could get close enough to rub the rope against it.

Belatedly he remembered the bucket he stood in. He had lost contact with his feet when he stopped feeling them. With a convulsive kick forward, and a resulting new tear to his shoulder muscles, he overturned the bucket. He barely felt the ground under his feet, but the bucket touched his ankle. If he could get his feet on top . . .

It took another vicious pull on his arms and shoulders to raise his legs. He missed, sliding off the wooden surface of the bucket with the soles of his feet. Clamping his teeth into the gag, he tried again, clung precariously for a moment; then somehow the bucket must have rolled slightly and settled into the mud under him. He stood on it, supported totally by his feet, but swaying weakly, perilously, on its curved surface.

The resulting slack had brought his tied wrists close enough to see that the rope was knotted too tightly to undo, even if he could have moved his hands, which no longer resembled human hands at all. He blocked the thought of losing both hands from his mind.

Instead he concentrated on severing the rope some other way. If the trunk of the tree was immediately behind him, he could lean backward against it. If not, he would tumble off the bucket again. He tried not to think of the pain which would follow, and reached back. And touched the tree. He leaned back cautiously, feeling the sharp bark against his back, letting it support some of his weight. But there was very little slack in the rope now and pushing his bound wrists up and down against the bark of the tree required him to stretch upward from his shoulders and against the pull of the rope. Each movement sent new arrows of pain through his shoulders and caused him to teeter on the bucket beneath his feet.

He persisted. The bucket settled more deeply into the mud, and at some point of the continuous push and pull he dislodged the cloth covering his face and sucked in a deep breath of clean air and gazed at the stars. The relief brought tears he could not stop.

The rubbing motion became automatic, the pain a fact of existence, proof he was alive. He was hardly conscious of the moment when the sharp bark of the tree bit into his skin.

And then the rope parted and he fell.

He fell hard, totally unprepared for freedom, and lay there for a time, too stunned to form any plan for further action. Above him rose the massive trunk of the tree, splitting into black branches and twigs against the midnight blue, star-spangled sky.

After a while, he rolled on his side and brought his arms down, cradling them against his chest. Lowering his arms in itself was exquisitely painful, and even after that agony dulled, there was more pain, though the worst spasms were different from the earlier ones. He rested some more and tried to move his fingers again. Evidently the rope, once severed, had parted completely, because his wrists, black with blood, were free. He tried to warm his hands against his belly and could feel them moving. Thank heaven.

He next thought of getting rid of the gag. He tried raising his hands to his face, but was unable to make his fingers take hold of the fabric and instead rubbed the side and back of his head against the ground. A protruding tree root shifted the cloth strip enough that he could force the gag from his mouth with his tongue.

He vomited, but felt better afterward, and struggled into a sitting position. The strip which had held the gag in place still encircled his head, covering one of his eyes. He pushed it up and off and looked around. The tree stood in the middle of dense bamboo. The sky above had paled and the stars were becoming faint. Almost dawn. How much time had passed? Noami had said he would return in an hour. Akitada could call for help now, but that might simply bring his tormentor back, and how was he to deal with him in his present condition? His ankles were still hobbled together; he could not untie the knot, because his hands were useless. Besides, his knees shook so badly when he tried to stand that he fell down again.

He must crawl, hide somewhere in the garden, give himself time to recover more strength, perhaps untie his legs.

He crawled, slithered, rolled, more like a snake or worm than a two- or four-legged creature, deeper and deeper into the bamboo thicket, until he reached the boundary wall and could go no farther. Here he sat up, leaning his back against the wall, and rested.

All was still blessedly silent. After a while he began to work on his hands again. The icy skin felt like something alien against his chest and cheek, and he put his fingers in his mouth to warm them. Then, taking them out, he watched his fingers move in the dim light, one by one, reluctantly and eerily, since he could not feel the movement. One finger at a time, they all moved, pale white like the underbelly of a dead fish against the dark, oozing flesh of his wrists. He exercised them again and again, warming them briefly in his mouth in between.

Finally came the moment when he felt a faint itching in one of his thumbs. It spread and changed to an unpleasant tingling, but he was so encouraged that he increased his hand exercises, adding slow stretches of his arms and shoulders.

He was just starting to explore the rope around his ankles when he heard a distant shout.

Noami! He had found his prisoner gone.

Akitada sagged hopelessly as the sounds of thrashing and breaking bamboo began. Too soon. He could not get up yet. Not even walk a few steps, let alone run. The sounds of frantic searching, loud in the still predawn air, were coming closer. He had left a trail for Noami to follow.

Pointless though it seemed, Akitada bent to work the knot, his half-raw fingers protesting until blood trickled from under his fingernails. The knot was wet, partially frozen, and sharp bits of ice were cutting his skin. It was no use. Looking around, he saw a chunk of stone the size of an infant's head. Scooting over, he tried to pick it up. But his fingers would not grasp, nor would his arm muscles support, even such a slight weight in their present condition. He staggered to his feet, bent, and scooped it up by placing both his hands underneath and lifting with his back. Then, cradling the stone against his bare belly, he shuffled the few feet back to the wall and propped himself upright against it to wait for Noami.

TWENTY-ONE

The Mended Flute

When Tora regained consciousness, he thought at first that he had fallen the rest of the way down the ruined pagoda. But the rustling of leaves eventually penetrated the thick fog of pain in his head, and he rolled onto his back to stare up at the night sky. Fronds of bamboo dipped over a garden wall and soughed dryly at the slightest breath of air. He sat up and immediately reached for his head. The stars above were dancing wildly, and the wall undulated like a snake. He had to blink hard several times before the world settled down to its usual solidity.

At that point memory returned. The bamboo grove. The slasher. And someone had jumped him from behind. He felt for the string of coppers in his sash and found it. At least the bastard had not got the rest of his money. That amounted to a miracle. Then Tora recalled the short hooded figure who had twisted from his grip at the gate.

He felt his head again. The crusty lump he had sustained in his earlier fall had spawned a twin. The whole back of his skull was swollen and tender. A short man had struck this blow, and that convinced him that his attacker had been the hooded fellow—the slasher himself?

It seemed wise to move in case he returned to finish the job.

Tora staggered to his feet, waited a moment for his stomach to settle, then groped along the wall toward the rear of the property. The place was large and the wall high and well maintained but appeared to have no other gates.

The blind backs of storage sheds, belonging to the next street and surrounded by broken fencing, weeds, and shrubbery, adjoined in the rear. Feeling dizzy, Tora sat down to think over his options.

If his attacker had been the slasher himself, it was strange that he had left him unconscious next to his hideout. Why not make sure his victim would not raise an outcry? Maybe he had gone back for his knife. Tora shuddered. On the other hand, leaving a murdered man lying about would cause some awkward questions even in this part of town.

Tora started feeling better, but the sharp night air penetrated his thick clothing. He got to his feet and became aware of a faint moving glow above the dark mass of bamboo behind the wall. Someone was walking around inside with a lantern. He listened and thought he heard a faint voice. So the bastard was not alone!

Tora continued along the wall until he reached the street again, verifying his suspicion that there was no back gate. What now? He could go home and tend to his wounds. After all, it was the middle of the night. Besides, he had probably alerted his quarry. Tomorrow, by daylight, he could return with Genba, knock on the gate, and force his way in. The little creep might be strong for his size, but he was no match for the combined skills of Tora and Genba.

It was the wisest choice, but something held Tora—a strange and perverse urge to get over the wall and into the slasher's lair as soon as possible.

Shivering with cold and light-headedness and in spite of a monstrous headache and assorted other pains, Tora retraced his steps to the back of the property and took a closer look at the ramshackle storehouses.

He found a section of broken but sturdy fencing, just long enough to prop against the wall for a ladder. He listened. Everything was quiet, and he decided that whoever was inside had gone to bed.

Tora climbed up, straddled the wall, and looked down on the other side. A far jump, but it could not be helped. Thick stalks of bamboo grew close to the wall and he leaned out to take hold of one to break his fall and jumped. The bamboo bent and made an infernal noise, creaking and rustling as if a huge bear were rampaging about, but Tora landed quite softly. After the bamboo had snapped back with more hideous racket, he waited for a few moments, but all remained quiet.

Carefully he made his way through the grove, pausing from time to time to make sure that the rustling sounds around him were no more than the night breeze in the leaves or some small animal. In the darkness it took him a long time to get close enough to the house to see its size and layout. It was larger than he had expected and in good repair. But the garden had been allowed to grow into a tangled wilderness, the bamboo covering everything except a small area surrounding a large leafless tree some distance away.

The house was plunged in silence and darkness. Tora considered going inside, but without knowing precisely where the slasher was, this was impracticable. At a loss, Tora glanced around the garden again. A distant crackling sound attracted his attention. Whatever was moving through the bamboo sounded larger than a rat or cat. He decided to explore.

The sounds came from the direction of the tree. He followed a narrow well-trodden path through the bamboo thicket to the clearing and stopped. Pale in the murky darkness, rolls of paper lay scattered about. A large upturned basket rested among them, and a long rope dangled from a branch of the tree. There was nobody about.

Tora approached cautiously. A container of brushes and a large inkstone and water container stood near the basket. Beside the tree, a water bucket lay on its side among some rags. Whoever had worked here was messy, Tora decided. He kicked one of the papers and it unrolled.

There were drawings on it. In the gloom it was hard to see, but they seemed to be pictures of a nearly naked man tied to a tree. Tora eyed the tree and the rope. Then he picked up the picture, and another, and a third. Swallowing sudden nausea, he went to take a closer look at the rope and rags.

The rags had been wet and were beginning to stiffen in the freezing temperature. The rope, also wet, looked frayed. Some shorter pieces of rope on the ground showed dark stains. Picking up one of these, Tora raised it to his nose. Blood! He had found the slasher, and he had been torturing some other poor bastard even as Tora closed in on him. Tora wondered if the monster had dragged away a corpse to bury it. Perhaps that was when he had heard something. He glanced around the perimeter of the clearing.

He was lucky, for at that moment he caught sight of someone rushing down the path toward him. In this light, it seemed an apparition, moving silently, its face distorted like a goblin's and a long knife in its right hand.

Shaking off a superstitious panic, Tora dropped the piece of rope and sidestepped the slashing ball of fury, tripping him as he passed. The creature was, thank heaven, real enough, and he flung himself on top of the thrashing figure. This time, he took no chances. He remembered the strength of this small, agile creature. Catching the flailing knife arm, he twisted it back so violently that the man's shoulder dislocated with a snap. With a shrill scream, the slasher stopped moving.

Tora threw the knife deep into the bamboo, made sure his captive had fainted, and got the rope pieces to tie him up securely.

Meanwhile, the night had become less murky. His surroundings began to take shape with sharp outlines. It must be close to dawn. In the faint light, Tora saw that the rope ends he was using were frayed and torn, not cut. Whoever had been tied to that tree had managed to free himself. Breaking the heavy rope must have taken extraordinary patience and strength.

Tora rose to his feet. The clearing lay empty and silent. He called out, "Hey! It's safe! You can come out now."

No response. Somewhere a bird chirped sleepily. It occurred to Tora that whoever had escaped the slasher's torture would hardly emerge from his hiding place at the invitation.

Making a methodical circuit of the clearing, he saw where dried weeds and fallen leaves had been disturbed by something large rolling or dragging through the bamboo. For a moment, Tora feared that the slasher had managed to kill his victim after all and had dragged the corpse away. But then he found the partial print of a bare foot. The monster's victim had been too weak to walk and had crawled away, pushing and clawing forward with toes and hands. Cursing under his breath, Tora followed the track as quickly as he could, prepared at any moment to stumble over the dead or unconscious body of a mutilated person.

Preoccupied with the ground, he did not see the wall or the pale figure leaning against it. One moment his eyes were fixed on the earth, the next there was a flash of movement, and he felt a blinding pain on the back of his skull. Sagging to his knees, he plunged into darkness.

--+--

Tora was the last person Akitada had expected to see emerging from the bamboo thicket. Thinking only of Noami, he put the last shred of his remaining strength into raising and bringing down the rock at the precise moment when the leaves parted. It seemed an eternity passed, and when the moment finally came, Akitada's arms acted independently. He could do no more than slow the violent descent of the rock at the last moment. Too weak to control the downward stroke, he watched in horror as

Tora crumpled before him. Letting the stone drop from his life-less hands, he began to shake again. He had killed his friend who had come to his rescue.

He fell to his knees beside Tora. "I'm sorry. I'm sorry," he sobbed, hot tears stinging his cheeks as he rocked back and forth. He stroked Tora's head and his swollen hands were cov-ered with warm blood. With an inarticulate cry, he collapsed across Tora's broad back.

"Sir? Sir? Is that you, sir?"

When the words penetrated the fog of weakness and misery, Akitada struggled up. "Are you alive, Tora?" he asked feebly. "I thought you were Noami, come back to finish me off."

Tora sat up, too, holding his head. He chuckled weakly. "And I thought you were the slasher's accomplice. That's the third knock my head caught tonight."

The sky above had turned a silvery gray, and birds chirped all around them.

"I'm sorry," Akitada said again. He was still shaking, and his teeth chattered uncontrollably, but he looked at Tora with joy. "I'm so glad you came. Yori got home, then?"

"Yori?" Tora lowered his hands and stared at his master. "Holy heaven!" he exclaimed. "What did that bastard do to you?"

Akitada smiled bitterly through chattering teeth. "An experi-ment in artistic realism. The effect of freezing on the human body. For the hell screen," he said with some difficulty, and struggled to his feet. "Never mind that. What about Yori?"

Tora stood up. "I don't know about Yori. I haven't been home since yesterday morning."

Akitada suddenly felt faint. "Dear heaven! Then the child is still lost. Come. We must find Yori." He grasped Tora's shoulder for support. "Before Noami catches us."

"If he's an ugly little runt with spiky hair, I've caught him." Tora slipped off his ragged coat and shirt. These he wrapped around his master and then put his arm about him to support him. "Your hands, sir," he muttered. "They look terrible." Akitada hid them inside Tora's quilted jacket.

Together they staggered back to the clearing. Noami was conscious and moaning. He glared balefully when he saw them. "Untie me this instant!" he shrieked. "You've broken my shoulder. I may never be able to paint again!"

"Good!" remarked Akitada, sinking weakly on the upturned basket. "Make sure, Tora, that he cannot escape before the police get here."

Tora glanced at the rope dangling from the tree, grinned, and jerked Noami to his feet. The painter screamed. Tora carried him to the tree, attached the rope to his bound wrists, and pulled it taut. The painter screamed again and fainted. His weight caused him to flop forward.

"I wrenched his shoulder out of the socket earlier," Tora explained with great satisfaction. "When he comes to, he won't try to move if he can help it."

Akitada grimaced. "Let him down enough so his feet support his weight," he said.

Tora obliged, but the unconscious man still drooped forward. Akitada got up from his basket. "Here, set him on this and then let's go." As Tora adjusted the unconscious Noami, Akitada flexed his arms and legs experimentally to get some circulation and warmth back into his muscles. But he was too weak and in too much pain and would have fallen if Tora had not caught him in his arms.

Subsequent events were a haze in Akitada's mind. When they emerged from Noami's gate, they encountered the giant warden and Genba. Reassured by them that Yori was home safe, Akitada felt his knees buckle under him. He was placed on a litter and whisked home.

His trials, however, were far from over. Fussed over by a white-faced Tamako, he was stripped and immersed in lukewarm water by Genba and Seimei, an experience which turned out to be excruciatingly painful to his nearly frozen flesh. Later Seimei treated his lacerated wrists by applying ointments and herbal packs, which he changed every few hours. Akitada's hands began to swell and burn. The skin cracked in places and oozed blood.

In spite of this, the satisfaction of knowing Yori was safe was enough in itself, and after drinking a sleeping draught, Akitada asked no questions and slept.

But the exposure during the freezing night had undermined his strong constitution, and his sleep turned into a virulent fever filled with hallucinatory images from the hell screen.

He tossed between nightmare and waking for six days and nights. Finally, on the seventh day, exactly a week after his escape, he woke up clearheaded and hungry. His eyes fell on his sister. Yoshiko sat by his bedside, quietly sewing some child's garment, no doubt Yori's. Memory returned abruptly, and he was filled with an immense gratitude that both he and his son were alive, that he might see him grow up after all, play games with him, and laugh at his childish antics together with Tamako.

He longed for Tamako, but perhaps she had gone to rest. He had given them all too much trouble. Yoshiko looked drawn and tired, quite as pale and worn as she had been when he had first seen her on his return from the north. He lay comfortably warm in his silken bedding—how different from that hellish night in Noami's garden—and wondered if he had done the right thing, forbidding his sister her last chance for happiness. It struck him now that he owed his own happy family to her, for it was Yoshiko who had brought him Tamako.

If only that fellow Kojiro could be cleared of the murder charge. He was innocent, and a much better—and wealthier—man than Akitada had expected. Well, he must see what he could do for him as soon as he was up and about again. He cleared his throat.

Yoshiko's head shot up. "Akitada?" She looked at him anxiously. "You are awake?"

Silly question. Akitada meant to say yes, but managed only a croak.

"Don't try to talk," she cried, and put her sewing by to reach for a teapot on the brazier at her side. She poured a cup and supported his head as he drank.

He was very thirsty and emptied the cup.

"More?"

He nodded and she gave him another cup.

"Thank you," he managed to say after that. "Where is Tamako?"

"Playing with Yori in his room. Shall I fetch them?"

He felt a little hurt that Tamako had left him, but shook his head. "Later."

"How are you feeling, Elder Brother?"

He managed a lopsided grin. "Hungry. How's Tora's head?"

She got up. "Fine. You know Tora. He recovers quickly. He and Genba have been spending most of their time with Miss Plumblossom and the young actress. If you think you will be all right by yourself for a few minutes, I will go heat some rice gruel in the kitchen."

Akitada nodded and she left. Just as well, for he did not relish the idea of having her company for a trip to the privy. Testing his limbs, he found them pain-free but strangely languid. He pushed the covers back and saw the white silk bandages about his wrists. His hands were no longer swollen, but stiff and covered with scabs. Getting to his feet was easier than he thought, but he had to catch hold of a screen when he took his first step. Fortunately, his head cleared and he negotiated the hallway and gallery to the privy without incident.

Feeling better when he emerged, he decided to find his wife and son.

They were, as Yoshiko had said, in the boy's room, kneeling over some papers and busy with brush and ink.

This brought back memories of Noami's lessons and momentarily nauseated him. He grabbed hold of the open doorway. Tamako looked up.

"Akitada!" She was on her feet and, flinging her silk skirts aside, rushed to him to put her arms around his waist.

"A fine greeting for your husband, madam," he teased. "Have you been taking lessons in the Willow Quarter?"

She immediately dropped her arms and flushed scarlet. Bowing primly, she said, "Forgive my immodesty, please. I thought you were going to fall and . . . and . . ."

Akitada reached out and pulled her into his arms, burying his face in her soft, sweet-smelling hair. "You may take me into your arms anytime, my wife," he murmured.

"I have missed you," she whispered.

Feeling her pliant body press against his, he took a ragged breath and reached for her sash.

Yoshiko appeared in the corridor, carrying a small footed tray with a steaming bowl on it. "Oh," she cried, "so here you are. You should not have tried to get up so soon after having been in a fever for a whole week."

Akitada released his wife reluctantly. "A week?" he asked, flabbergasted.

The women nodded and half pushed, half drew him into the room to sit on a pillow. Wrapping him into Yori's quilts, they made him eat his gruel. He smiled at Yori between sips, wondering why the boy was so quiet. He tried to talk to him, to ask questions about what had happened, but the women would not permit it until he had emptied the bowl.

The boy sat wide-eyed, watching his father finish. Then he held up a sheet of paper. It bore the wobbly and smudged character for "A Thousand Years."

A New Year's wish. Of course, it was almost that time. Akitada nodded and smiled. "A remarkably fine sign, and very appropriate."

"Do you really like it, Father?" Yori whispered, perhaps out of respect for his father's condition. "It's Chinese for having a long life and good fortune in the coming year. Mother showed me how to write it."

Tamako read and wrote Chinese because her father, a professor at the Imperial University, had taught her as if she had been a son.

Putting the empty bowl aside, Akitada asked, "Do you remember the night at the painter's house?"

Yori nodded. "You sent me home, but I got lost. I asked a man to show me the way. I said, 'Take me to the Sugawara mansion!' He was quite rude and laughed at me, so I stomped on his foot and told him I would have him beaten if he did not obey instantly. He grabbed me by the arm and shook me, saying he would wring my neck like a chicken, but a huge giant appeared and snatched me away. The giant was bigger than Genba, but very dirty. He took me to his hut and gave me soup. He did not laugh when I told him to take me home, but he was not terribly polite and he did not obey me. I went to sleep then."

"You were very brave!" Akitada complimented him.

Yori nodded. "I was."

So the warden had saved the boy. Good man! He would have to do something for him. If only Yori had told the warden where Akitada was. He could have been rescued before Noami strung him up in the garden. But that was ungrateful. He looked at the women. "How did you find out what happened?"

Tamako said, "The warden brought Yori home. When we asked about you, he remembered that Yori had said something about his father. We woke up the child and he told us about the painter's house. After that it was easy. The warden and Genba went to find you. They got there just as Tora carried you out in his arms."

Akitada corrected her. "I was walking. But I must thank the warden in person for returning Yori. He appears to be a very decent fellow and an excellent influence in a bad section of the capital. Besides, I have some questions about Noami's activities. By the way, what happened to the man?"

The two women looked at each other. Tamako said diffidently, "Superintendent Kobe called daily to inquire about your condition. He mentioned that the painter hanged himself."

"What? In prison? They must have been unusually careless."

Tamako avoided his eyes. "Not in prison. They found him hanged in his garden."

Akitada stared at her. "In his garden? But we left him alive."

"Oh. The superintendent thought it strange. He wants to ask you about it."

How was this possible? Akitada thought back to his last sight of Noami. Tora had fastened Noami's wrists to the rope from the tree branch and then shoved the basket under him to prop him up. How could Noami have hanged himself? Even if he had gained consciousness and, like Akitada, climbed on the basket, he could not have tied the rope around his neck with that dislocated shoulder. He shook his head in bafflement.

When Kobe came to see him, Akitada had had a bath and been shaved by Seimei. He had spoken with Genba, Tora, and the recovered Harada, had eaten a light meal of fish soup, and was resting comfortably in his study.

The superintendent approached warily, his face anxious. Akitada greeted him affably. "Good afternoon, my friend. I am grateful for your concern during my illness."

"Oh," said Kobe, sitting down with a sigh of relief, "you do look much better now. Yesterday I was afraid you would not make it."

Akitada chuckled and poured two cups of wine. "My wife says that Noami hanged himself?"

Kobe gave Akitada a sharp look. "It is true that we found

him hanging by the neck from a rope tied to a tree branch." He paused, then added, "His hands and feet were tied, and one of his shoulders was dislocated."

"Then someone killed him. Tora fought with the man and dislocated his shoulder, but we left him alive, tied to the rope by his wrists. It is impossible that he could have hanged himself!"

Kobe said nothing.

Akitada stared at him. In disbelief he asked, "Do you think we hanged him?"

"It does not matter. He deserved it." Kobe emptied his cup of wine. "I had my men dig up the garden. They uncovered four skeletons. Two were children, one an old man, and one a woman."

Akitada shook his head. What was it that Noami had said about the children's visits? "It's getting rid of them that's hard." The disposal of the dead and the barely alive must have taxed even his strength. Akitada looked the superintendent in the eyes. "Kobe, I swear to you, we did not hang Noami. I was in no shape to stand, let alone string up a man, and Tora was with me the whole time. We left the man unconscious but alive. Noami got a more humane treatment than he accorded me."

Kobe's eyes went to Akitada's bandaged wrists. He nodded. "We found the sketches. Tora says you freed yourself."

"It was either that or die. He doused me with cold water and left me to freeze because he wanted me in sufficient agony for his cursed hell screen. After that . . . well, by then he knew that I knew."

Kobe clenched his big fists. "He was a demon! I am glad he is dead. But I wish he had suffered like those poor creatures. Someone cheated us of the pleasure of lawful torture."

Akitada frowned. "I don't understand what happened. Perhaps someone took private vengeance before you got there. How long before—" He broke off. It occurred to him suddenly that it must have been the warden who had taken justice into his own hands. It certainly fit his character of running his quarter by his own set of laws.

"Well, we won't pursue it." Kobe regarded him worriedly. "You still look tired. I won't stay long. Noami is dead, and good riddance, but there is another matter which troubles me more. Yasaburo was found poisoned in his cell."

Akitada sat up. "What?"

"He had had a visitor, an old priest, just before he fell into convulsions. Nobody knew the monk, but he seemed harmless enough and Yasaburo greeted him as an old friend. Since it was a religious visit, the guard left them alone together. Yasaburo was all right when his visitor left, but shortly afterward he started vomiting and screaming with pain. He died before the guard could question him."

"Well, did anyone look for that priest?"

Kobe bristled. "Of course. What do you take us for? We scoured all the temples around and questioned anyone who was in the street at the time the priest came and went. Nothing. The man disappeared into thin air as soon as he left the prison grounds."

"Have you asked Harada?"

"Harada was still pretty sick, but he said that he never knew Yasaburo to associate with priests. In fact, he says his employer despised Buddhists."

"Yet he knew him. Strange." Akitada caught a momentary glimpse of a pattern, but it was all still too vague to share. He asked, "What about Nagaoka's brother? How long are you going to hold him? You must know now that someone else is responsible for the deaths in the Nagaoka family."

Kobe nodded glumly. "I had him released this morning. He will remain in the capital until the case is cleared up."

Akitada thought of Yoshiko. For the past month, he had struggled with the problem of Yoshiko and Kojiro, or rather with himself. While Kojiro was in jail, Akitada had concentrated on the murder cases and pushed the decision about his sister's future aside. Now the inevitable moment had come when he would have to weigh centuries of his family's tradition against Yoshiko's happiness.

He glanced out into the wintry garden. Had Seimei remembered to feed the fish? How pointless his resentment toward the old man seemed now. Tradition-bound, Seimei had chosen loyalty to Akitada's father over love for his son. Where lay one's duty?

Kobe moved restlessly. "I must go," he said. "When you are better ..." He hesitated. Akitada looked at him questioningly. Such diffidence was out of character for Kobe. "When you feel more yourself," Kobe blurted, "I would be very glad to have your help with the unsolved cases."

The humble plea marked an extraordinary reversal of their previous roles, and Akitada was profoundly moved. He said quickly, "Of course. I look forward to it."

Kobe nodded and left.

A quite ridiculous sense of happiness filled Akitada all of a sudden. He was alive. Yori was safe. They were all together again. He looked around the room. It had once been his father's and a hated room, but now it was his, truly his, and he was pleased with it. Filled with his books and papers, it was the heart of his home and a refuge against the demons lurking outside. The uncertainties of life were offset by such islands of peace among one's family.

His eye fell on an unfamiliar oblong brocade-wrapped package on his desk. Curious, he took it up, untied the silk cord, and unrolled the fabric. It contained his broken flute, now miraculously restored. He turned it slowly in his hands, looking for the seam between the broken halves. He could not find it. Bemused, he raised the flute to his lips and blew. The sound was pure and clear, hanging in the air for a moment like a silken ribbon before he let it dissolve into a shower of trills as joyous as the song of a nightingale outside his veranda door.

He played remembered tunes, "Mist and Rain over a Mountain Lake" and "Bells on a Snowy Night," surprised that he recalled them, immersed in the music, totally happy for a time. When he finally lowered the instrument, a soft sound of applause came from the door to the corridor. It had been pushed ajar a little, and in the opening appeared the smiling face of Yoshiko.

"Oh, that was lovely, Elder Brother," she cried. "The flute maker promised it would play as well as ever. Do you like it?"

"Please come in, Little Sister." Akitada smiled. "It sounds better than before, I think. A miracle. Was it you who had it mended?"

She blushed and bowed. "It gave me great pleasure."

Yoshiko was no longer the laughing young girl Akitada remembered. She was a grown woman, Tamako's age almost, though she looked older, more worn, quietly composed instead of bubbling with energy as she used to be. He was partially to blame for that. What her mother had started by denying Yoshiko a life of her own, he had finished by extorting a cruel promise. He had taken her last hope of happiness with the man she loved.

"Yoshiko," he said humbly, "I find I must beg your pardon. I have given you much pain when I had meant to make you happy. And in spite of this, you have gone to have my flute mended. It was too kind and I don't deserve it."

She gave a little gasp. "Oh, no, Akitada. The flute was nothing. And . . . you meant well," she said softly.

"Do you truly love Kojiro?"

"Yes," she said without qualification, her voice matter-of-fact.

"He has been released."

A slight flush rose to her cheeks. "I am glad. Poor man, he has suffered so much. I hope his future will be blessed."

"And you? Do you still wish to be a part of his future?"

For a moment the color receded from her face and he

thought she would faint. But the blush returned as abruptly. She looked at him in wonder. "Akitada," she breathed, "have you changed your mind? For me nothing has changed. I shall always love him. He may only be a farmer and a merchant's brother, but I am a part of him. But what about you, and the family? If you allow this marriage, must we part forever?"

"No. I was wrong to forbid the marriage and I was wrong about Kojiro's character. He is a much better man than most people of rank. However, that does not mean that things will be easy for you. You must be prepared for rejection by people of our rank, perhaps even by your own sister."

She smiled. "As long as you and Tamako will not disown me, I shall manage quite well. And Akiko will come around in the end because Toshikage is a kind man."

Akitada nodded, remembering that he had once also doubted this brother-in-law. "In three weeks' time the forty-nine days of mourning for your mother will be up. I see no reason why you cannot have a quiet wedding in the spring. If you like the idea, I shall speak to Kojiro about a marriage contract. I mean to give you the same dower as Akiko."

His sister covered her face with both hands and began to weep.

"Yoshiko!" Akitada struggled up in dismay. "What is it? What have I said?" He went to kneel beside her.

She buried her face against his chest. "Nothing, everything," she sobbed, half crying and half laughing. "Oh, Akitada. Thank you so much. Oh, and Kojiro will thank you also. We are both forever in your debt."

"Well," said Akitada, dabbing his own eyes and patting her shoulder. "In that case, I had better get busy clearing up three murders, and you will have to use your needle on your own gowns instead of Yori's. It is high time we got out of these dark clothes."

TWENTY-TWO

The Dance of the Demon

On the next to the last day of the year, Akitada was well enough to leave the house. The weather was gray, but the bitter cold had finally broken. Akitada wore elaborate court dress—his new robe, made by Yoshiko from the silk he had bought so many weeks ago—because he was on his way to court to present his official report.

Years ago this would have been a highly stressful affair for him. Even men older and higher in rank than Akitada quaked at the prospect of making their bow to the chancellor and assorted ministers and imperial advisers. But Akitada had just been given back his life. That sort of experience put the present ordeal and even his six years in the frozen north into a new perspective.

He therefore arrived calmly smiling at the officious young nobleman who had pitied his frayed costume on his last visit. The young man flushed with embarrassment and bowed Akitada obsequiously into the presence of the great men. Oblivious to their sharp-eyed scrutiny, Akitada extended New Year's wishes with goodwill and more smiles to the three ministers and the haughty and bored chancellor. Then he presented his official report. He spoke easily and concisely on matters of national security, handing over sheaves of neatly written documents, answered their questions, and stated his recommendations for the region with strong arguments and to such good effect that even the chancellor sat up and listened. What should have been a stiff and formal affair suddenly became a lively exchange of views, and the eminent men consulted Akitada's opinion with flattering interest and respect.

He left the palace smiling and whistling under his breath, the recipient of several invitations to seasonal parties. Strange, when one stopped caring so much about impressing the great, they became entirely human and quite likable.

After changing from the stiff silk gown with its long train into a more comfortable robe, Akitada set out again for the Nagaoka house.

This time the gate was answered by the old man who had entertained them at Fushimi, the one who loved old stories. Akitada racked his brain for a name. Kinzo! That was it.

"Well, Kinzo," Akitada said, "I hope you remember me."

"Sugawara," snapped the old man. "I'm not senile yet. Lord Sugawara, I suppose I should say, though your ancestor held a much higher rank. Well, my master got out of jail without your help. Never mind! We can't all be brilliant."

Akitada chuckled. Lest he become arrogant after the flattering reception by the chancellor and ministers, here was Kinzo to remind him that greatness was a matter of opinion. He patted the old man's shoulder. "True, but I am as happy as you that your master is finally free."

Kinzo grunted as he slammed the gate shut behind them. "Maybe if he had chanted sutras in jail like Shuncho, the holy Fugen would've come to release him."

"In that case, perhaps the god could have solved the murder of his sister-in-law. And prevented the killings of Nagaoka and Yasaburo."

Kinzo pushed out his lower lip and considered. "It reminds me of the story of the Somedono Empress," he said. "She was possessed by a demon who was her lover." He shook his head. "The demon did terrible things and many people died for it."

Akitada looked at him sharply. It was a strange parallel. But perhaps the old man was getting senile. He asked, "How is your master?"

"He's the invisible man. Demon spit will make you invisible, you know."

More demons. Akitada sighed inwardly. "I hope to bring him good news."

Kinzo nodded. "Lord Kinsue comes to see the hermit," he muttered, and climbed the steps to the house.

Akitada followed, frowning. Lord Kinsue? Another reference to demons? He only recalled one tale in which that lord had sought out a priest to be cured of a fever. Did this apply to himself? He was quite well again, and surely Kinzo could not know of his recent illness.

Kinzo's allusion was partially explained when he saw Kojiro. The man was sitting listlessly in his brother's study, staring at a blank wall where once his brother's paintings had hung.

Kinzo said, by way of introduction, "Here's company. And just in time before you forget you have speech." He gave them both an admonitory look and said, "Remember Fujiwara Moroie!"

Akitada again searched his memory for the allusion and failed. Kojiro turned red and came to his feet. "How are you, my lord?" Then, scanning Akitada's face, he asked, "What happened? Have you been ill?"

Kinzo snorted and left.

"Yes, but I am recovered," said Akitada, "and take the first opportunity to see you and congratulate you on your release. What did Kinzo mean just now?"

Kojiro flushed again. "It was nothing. He believes old tales hold meaning for our lives." He invited Akitada to sit and looked around helplessly. "Some wine? I don't . . ." He raised his voice. "Kinzo!" There was no response and he sighed. "Forgive me. I'm afraid I get no visitors, so we are unprepared."

"It is my fault for coming unannounced. Besides, I had better not have any wine. Seimei, my secretary, says it brings on a fever, and I have had enough of that."

Kojiro visibly pulled himself together. He said formally, "I owe you my gratitude. You took the trouble to make my imprisonment easier. May I take this opportunity to wish you better health and fortune in the New Year?"

"Thank you. I return the wishes." Akitada smiled. "Most sincerely, believe me. In fact, that is the reason I came. Tomorrow is the last day of the year. It is customary to discharge one's debts."

Kojiro looked puzzled. "What debts?" He gestured toward the account books. "There is nothing in my brother's papers to suggest you did business with him."

"My debt is to you. Weeks ago I made a promise to clear you of the murder charge. I have failed to do so. You were released from prison only because there have been two more murders, one of them your brother's. I am afraid I cannot bring your brother to life again, but by tomorrow night, before year's end, I shall try to pay that debt. I hope to solve not only the murder of your sister-in-law but also identify the killer of your brother and his father-in-law."

Kojiro stared at Akitada, then burst into a bitter laugh. "Don't blame yourself on my account, my lord. I no longer care much about what happened."

"I understand how you feel." Akitada hesitated. "Did you ever meet Nobuko's sister?"

"What?" Kojiro shook his head. "No. Yugao died soon after Nobuko came here. I doubt my brother met her more than once. Look, I wish you would leave it alone, my lord. I doubt I shall be arrested again, and as for the rest, I don't care. My brother's wife was a demon who deserved to die, and her father was not much better. As for my brother, well, he was a very unhappy man at the end."

"Nevertheless, you shall be cleared and your brother's murderer shall be punished. Justice demands it."

Kojiro grimaced. He looked thinner and older than Akitada remembered, more like his brother now than the ruddy, muscular young man he had seen in the mountains, or even the bloodied and defiant prisoner. As with Yoshiko, some life force seemed to have gone out of him. "There is another debt I owe you," Akitada said more diffidently. "It concerns my sister Yoshiko. I was very wrong to force my sister to break her word to you. I ask your forgiveness for my insensitive behavior."

Kojiro said nothing for a long time. He sat so still he seemed hardly to breathe, but his face was closed and his back stiff. He looked like a man who was fighting a fierce struggle with conflicting emotions. Finally he said harshly, "Have you apologized to your sister, my lord?"

Akitada flinched. "I have spoken to Yoshiko. She was . . . very happy. In fact, she thought you would be glad also."

"That you have relented and are willing to accept a connection with a mere commoner?"

This was not going well. Akitada felt the blood rise to his face. He was angry with himself and with this stiff-necked farmer. Surely the man could see that Akitada had taken an enormous and unprecedented step, one which would lay him, and the rest of his family, open to calumny and censure from his associates and friends. For Yoshiko's sake he controlled himself.

"I had hoped that we might become friends," he said mildly. Thinking of Toshikage, he added, "Brothers, even. I never had a brother and have discovered great pleasure in the relationship with my other sister's husband."

Kojiro wilted. "Please forgive me," he said softly. "I have misjudged you again. I had no right to reject your generous offer of friendship and . . ." He moved uncomfortably. "You say Yoshiko is still . . . that Yoshiko still wishes . . . ?"

"Oh, yes. But perhaps you are of a different mind now, after all that has happened?"

Kojiro said fervently, "No. Never! There will never be

another woman for me as long as I live. I have always known that, almost from the first. It has not changed in all the years and it will not change in the future."

A little embarrassed by such raw emotion, Akitada looked down at his hands and smiled. "I have gone over my accounts and find that I shall be able to give Yoshiko the same dower as her sister." He mentioned figures—silver, rice fields, bolts of silk—and then asked, "Is this satisfactory to you?"

Kojiro had listened in amazement. "My lord," he gasped, "there is no need. You are exceedingly generous, but I assure you, I am quite well-to-do. My property in the country is large. I can support Yoshiko in the style she was born to in spite of my station in life."

"Well, then it's settled and you must call me Akitada," said Akitada with a nod. "Yoshiko shall have what I promised and you shall also make provisions for her and her children. We can work out the details later. Yoshiko has had a hard life in the past. But I am determined that shall change." He rose, smiling.

Kojiro stumbled to his feet. "I—don't know what to say," he stammered. "Can I see her?"

"Of course. Come tonight and join us for a family meal. I shall ask my brother-in-law. Yoshiko's sister is due to give birth and will be unable to come." This was fortunate under the circumstances. Akiko would need time to adjust to Yoshiko's marriage to a commoner. At the gate he stopped. "And I trust you will join us for an outing tomorrow night. It is the day of the spirit festival, and there will be music and dances in the Spring Garden. I am told a fine group of actors and acrobats will perform the demon chase."

Kojiro looked too overwhelmed to protest. He bowed and nodded with a smile. He bowed and smiled again when Akitada made his farewells. And when Akitada glanced back over his shoulder some distance from Nagaoka's house, Kojiro still stood in the open gate, smiling and raising his arm to wave. It was then that Akitada remembered the story of Fujiwara Moroie, who had lost his true love by wasting time.

※

The last day of the year dawned with a clear sky. In the Sug-awara house, preparations for the New Year's festivities were in full swing. Tora and Genba were climbing all over the gate and roof of the house, fixing pine branches to the rafters and string-ing sacred ropes of rice straw. In the kitchen, foodstuffs piled up and the cook directed hired helpers in the preparations for the New Year's banquet Akitada planned to give for friends and col-leagues. Tamako, her silk gown covered with a cotton jacket, stuffed New Year's rice cakes with sweet bean paste, and handed them to her little maid to shape into perfect, auspicious moon shapes.

Akitada still took it easy, but on this morning he set out early to make seasonal calls and deliver invitations. Some of these were for the banquet, but the others were for this very night, the last night of the old year, when evil spirits were exorcised and driven from the capital.

Akitada's party would attend the celebration sponsored by the crown prince for the officials and clerks who worked in the government complex. Many of these were commoners and would bring their families. Akitada's party included not only his family and retainers, but also Superintendent Kobe and Miss Plumblossom.

Two hours before sunset, the women and Yori climbed into the ox-drawn carriage which they shared with hampers of food and pitchers of wine, and everyone set out for the Spring Gar-den.

A sizable crowd had gathered around the lake pavilion for the event. Viewing stands awaited the noble families and ropes sepa-rated the rest of the crowd from an open area and the tent and raised stage reserved for the performers. Akitada led his family and guests to one of the stands, and saw the women and Yori settled behind the bamboo screening which protected them from the curious eyes of the crowd. When Miss Plumblossom protested that she would not be able to wave to her friends, Tamako persuaded her that she was needed to explain the acrobatics.

Akitada joined Kojiro, Toshikage, and Kobe in the front seats, while Seimei, Harada, Genba, Tora, and Saburo sat behind them. Hired servants scrambled back and forth with wine and refreshments.

Toshikage had accepted Kojiro easily. His happiness almost matched that of the bridegroom. His son Tadamine had been recalled from military duty in the east and was back in the capital to take up his post in the Palace Guard.

Kobe alone was irritable. He had tried to refuse, claiming police business, and Akitada had been forced to resort to hints of important disclosures before he relented. As it was, he fidgeted impatiently as old friends and colleagues stopped by to wish Akitada well.

When the music started, the crowd around their viewing stand thinned.

Customarily the first dances were formal and traditional, performed by young men or boys of the nobility. They wore gorgeous robes with long stiff trains and danced the ancient court rites with solemn perfection.

Kobe glared at them. "Very pretty," he grumbled, "if you have nothing else to do with your life. Give me a wrestling match any day. At least that might teach me something about dealing with criminals. What are we waiting for?"

Akitada was becoming uneasy about his plan, but said, "Patience! You will find out soon enough." He was taking a chance, but it was his only chance. He cast a glance at Kojiro and wished it had been possible to warn him, but everything depended on a spontaneous reaction.

When the acrobats came on, the tone of the entertainment changed abruptly to noisy good humor. The twins Gold and Silver were particular favorites, and Tora roared his approval of Gold's somersaults so vociferously that Seimei clapped a hand over his mouth. In the sudden lull, Miss Plumblossom's voice came from the screened enclosure. "Higher! Higher! Another flip, girls! Show them your bottoms! Bravo! I knew you could do it!"

Seimei looked outraged and plucked his master's sleeve, but Akitada laughed. He was watching the area below the stage where Uemon's Players were gathering for their turn.

Someone had chosen the farce *Priest Fukko Begs for Robes,* a piece which delighted both gentry and commoners because it made fun of a certain type of greedy Buddhist priest. Silence fell when Uemon himself, a thin, venerable-looking man in an elegant black silk robe, climbed the stage to recite the part of the much-provoked benefactor. Danjuro was to play the title role of the gluttonous monk.

After a brief interlude of music, a fat monk staggered onto the stage and began his antics. Danjuro's performance was impressive. He looked, spoke, and acted exactly like the fat, middle-aged cleric: lazy, sniveling, pompous, and self-indulgent. The crowd roared its approval.

Given his dislike for all things Buddhist, Akitada enjoyed the farce, but he found it hard to laugh. Behind the mask of comedy was an odious truth.

Beside him, Kobe moved restlessly again. "Look at him," he whispered into Akitada's ear. "He makes it seem so easy. Do you suppose the fellow who poisoned Yasaburo could've masqueraded as a Buddhist priest?"

Akitada compressed his lips, his eyes on the actor. "Why not? I would not be surprised if he looked exactly like Fukko."

Kobe stared from him to the stage and frowned. "You're right. If that's why you brought me here, you could have told me instead."

"There is more."

The farce closed and Uemon announced the dance of the celestial fairies. This was what Akitada had been waiting for. His heart started pounding. It was getting late, and he had not counted on the early darkness and their distance from the stage.

With some relief he saw that attendants were lighting lanterns on the eaves of the main pavilion and the viewing stands. Around the stage, more colored paper lanterns swung from ropes and from tall bamboo poles. The fading daylight was the color of pale wisteria and, combined with the colored lights, it made a fairyland of the scene. From behind the screen, Akitada could hear the women exclaim with delight.

The musicians struck up again, a dainty, otherworldly piece in which the flutes predominated over the drums. Then the dancers climbed to the stage one by one, eight women in all. They wore tall gilded crowns with softly tinkling bells and pendants on their heads and were dressed in diaphanous silk robes, each in a different shade from azure blue through rose, golden yellow, copper, leaf green, plum purple, and cherry red to the palest violet, and they moved with slow grace to the music of the flutes. Their faces and hands were covered thickly with white paint, charcoal outlined their eyes, and their mouths were tiny crimson bows. The masklike makeup made them all look the same, beautiful but remote. This illusion was heightened because they performed all movements and turns in unison, seeming to float above the wooden boards of the stage.

"Beautiful," breathed Toshikage beside Akitada.

Akitada did not answer. He was beginning to despair. It was impossible to tell the women apart. The tallest was the lead dancer, and her gestures seemed to him a little more abrupt, her movements more designed to attract the eyes of the crowd. Yes, he thought, that's the one. She is not quite in step with the others and a show-off besides. He glanced at Kojiro, who smiled back cheerfully. Akitada clenched his hands.

The dancers bowed to great applause and then, led by the tall fairy, descended from the stage to parade past the viewing stands, pausing now and then to perform movements of the dance. Akitada's heart started pounding again. He had forgotten about this custom, which distinguished professionals from noble amateurs. The actors had a living to make, and looked for sponsors and protectors among the crowd. It gave him another chance, but might also precipitate an ugly incident. He sat in an agony of apprehension as the young women approached the Sugawara stand. Half-hopeful, half-fearful, he awaited the confrontation.

The lead dancer started a new routine. Akitada's eyes went from her to Kojiro. Kojiro had been watching with polite interest, but suddenly his face changed, he stiffened, looked momentarily confused, and opened his mouth to say something. At that moment the short dance ended, and Tora jumped up to shout his compliments down to Gold, one of the eight fairies. The lead dancer gave him an angry glance, tossed her head so that the bells of her headdress jingled loudly, and pranced off, followed by the others. Akitada sagged with relief.

A pale Kojiro passed a shaking hand over his face as he stared after the disappearing dancers. Touching his arm, Akitada asked softly, "What is it? You look as if you had seen a ghost."

"A ghost?" Kojiro laughed shakily. "Yes. Or a devil!" He gave a shudder. "It's the night for it. I thought that first dancer . . . I could have sworn . . . heaven help me, but I thought I was looking at Nobuko. That woman will haunt me the rest of my life."

Akitada exhaled with relief. It had worked. "Relax," he said, giving Kojiro's arm a squeeze. "It was no ghost. Yes. That was your brother's wife. I hoped you would recognize her earlier. Thank the heavens she did not see you and make a run for it." He turned to Kobe. "You heard? That lead dancer is Nagaoka's wife, alive and well. The murdered woman was someone else, possibly one of the actresses who left the company about that time. You may recall I questioned her identity."

Kobe gaped at him. "Is this some sort of joke? Nagaoka himself identified the body."

"Nagaoka was overwrought and identified the expensive gown he had just given to his wife."

"But then . . ." Kobe's mind was working furiously. He muttered conjectures to himself. "One of the actresses? Then the actors are involved . . . but why would the Nagaoka woman . . . did *she* kill the other woman? Why? No, it makes no sense." He glared at Akitada. "Was this your surprise?"

"Yes. The actor Danjuro was her accessory. The motive, or motives, were greed and a passion for theater. They extorted blood money from Nagaoka and then killed him. Yasaburo was poisoned by Danjuro, who was wearing the costume of the priest, to protect himself and Nobuko. Do you want to make the arrests now or wait until after the crowd has left?"

Kobe's startled expression changed to one of anger. "You planned this to show off your brilliant detective work and made me look an idiot," he charged. "Even if you are right, and I don't for a moment believe your far-fetched tale, how do you expect me to conduct an investigation and arrest here and without constables?"

"Come, there are only two of them. And we have Tora and Genba. Besides, Kojiro and Toshikage will lend a hand. It should not be too difficult to capture two individuals, and one of them a woman." Kobe looked irresolute, and Akitada urged, "We could at least confront them with Kojiro and see what happens."

Kobe bit his lip and glanced around. It was completely dark by now. The attendants were taking down the colored lanterns and replacing them with torches. "Very well," he said, rising to his feet. "Let's go see what that dancer has to say."

As they made their way behind the viewing stands to the actors' tent behind the stage, the booming sounds of the big drum announced the demon chase. The other drums followed, the beat against the taut leather a rising crescendo like approaching thunder. Then the higher notes of the shoulder drums, tapped out with the drummers' fingers, followed, and unearthly squeals produced by flutes and human voices tore through the throbbing noise until the night air vibrated with the din.

They caught a glimpse of the stage, filled with shrieking, jumping creatures in fearful masks and costumes. Kobe stopped when the drumming paused abruptly and the flutists broke into high wailing trills. A large figure burst into the middle of the hopping goblins. This creature wore a brilliant orange silk costume with embroidered apron and train and fiery red trousers. A huge, snarling black mask with rolling eyes and large white fangs rested on its broad shoulders, and long tufts of red hair shot out of its head like flames, which licked its back and shoulders. The king of demons had begun his dance. The monster jumped and twisted, facing this way and that as if scanning the crowd for victims, its talons slashing wildly about.

The audience screamed.

"The king of the demons," said Akitada. "I expect Danjuro will soon appear as the demon-slaying general and engage him in fierce combat. Perfect timing to confront Mrs. Nagaoka and force a confession out of her."

Nobody paid attention to the six men as they skirted the stands and ducked under the rope by the actors' tent. There was no one about. Most of the actors were on the stage, jumping about and screeching. The red-maned demon king faced off against a figure in gilded helmet and armor. The battle had begun.

Akitada and Kobe slipped into the tent, while Kojiro waited outside with Toshikage. Tora and Genba left to intercept Danjuro when he returned from his performance.

Inside the tent the noise of the drums and shrieks receded, but they walked into the middle of a noisy confrontation.

"I'll teach you manners," the little acrobat called Gold shouted, advancing with balled fists toward the tall lead dancer.

Nagaoka's widow was without her headdress but still wore the pasty makeup, while Gold had stripped down to a pair of full trousers. Both looked murderous.

"How dare you hit our master?" Gold demanded, waving her fist in the other woman's face. "What kind of filth are you? Uemon's like a father to us."

The beautiful Nobuko retreated a step. "You're fired," she shrieked. "You and your sister can pack up and leave. And take the old man with you. You're nothing without Danjuro and my money, do you hear?"

Gold slapped her hard, just as Kobe roared, "Quiet! In the name of the emperor!"

They all jumped and turned to look at them. Old Uemon still sat on a stool, pale, the imprint of a hand stark against his skin. Gold dropped her arm; her adversary stood frozen, a hand raised to her cheek.

"I am Kobe, superintendent of police," snapped Kobe, glaring around at the cowering women in various stages of undress, "and this is a murder investigation."

Old Uemon groaned and buried his face in his hands.

"You there," snapped Kobe, pointing at the tall dancer. "Step over here!"

Mrs. Nagaoka approached slowly. "What's all this about?" she asked. "I know nothing about any murders. I just joined these people. Whatever it is they've done, it has nothing to do with me."

Kobe snorted. "That's what you think!" He reached back to lift the tent flap. Kojiro, followed by Toshikage, ducked in and faced the woman. Kojiro nodded.

"*You!*" She stared at Kojiro, her eyes suddenly wide with fear.

Kojiro made her a mocking bow. "Surprised to see me, sister-in-law?"

She drew herself up. "You are mistaken, Kojiro. I may look like Nobuko, but I'm her sister Yugao. And you killed her! How

386

is it that you're allowed to run around free? Where is the justice in this country, when a man can murder a woman and soon after consort with the superintendent of police?" She glared at Kobe, who looked dumbfounded.

Akitada said, "It won't work, Mrs. Nagaoka. Your sister died years ago. Your father tried to confuse us the same way when we asked him questions about your husband's murder. He did it to protect you. Even in prison he suffered flogging without revealing your murderous plot. But you sent your lover Danjuro, disguised in his Fukko costume, to kill your own father so he would not reveal your identity."

She paled slightly but raised her chin. "I don't know what you're talking about. My *husband* and I know nothing about any murders. We are actors. My father gave out the story that I had died because he was ashamed of me for running away with Danjuro."

Kobe frowned and looked at Akitada.

Akitada shook his head. "No. Your sister has been dead for years. You only joined Uemon's Players a few weeks ago at the Eastern Mountain Temple. You took the place of the girl Ohisa after you and Danjuro killed her. As for running away, you ran away from your husband Nagaoka, not your father. And after the murder, you sent your father to collect blood money from him."

A shocked muttering passed among the other women. Gold cried, "So that's what happened to poor Ohisa!" She glared at Nobuko. "May you both rot in the worst hell for what you did. I remember how Danjuro came to us that morning, bringing you along, claiming Ohisa had left to go home, but that you were a dancer who happened to be on a pilgrimage—some pilgrimage, you she-devil—and that you'd fill in until he could find another professional. It was all lies, wasn't it? What did you two do to Ohisa?"

There was a moment's silence.

Then Akitada said softly, "Yes, Mrs. Nagaoka. What did you two do to Ohisa?"

She had no time to answer. The tent fabric parted and, in a flurry of orange and red silk, the demon king shot in. He slid to a halt, painted eyes goggling and red mane flaring wildly about the snarling features. Nobody said anything. With a grunt, he turned and ducked out again.

Mrs. Nagaoka cried out and made a move to go after him. Akitada cursed under his breath, caught her by the arm, and tossed her back to Kobe. Shrieking, she twisted, biting, scratching, and clawing like a wild animal, as Kobe and Kojiro struggled with her. Gold ended the tussle by planting her balled fist squarely in the other woman's face and breaking her nose. Gushing blood, the tall dancer crumpled to the floor.

Kojiro looked aghast and bent to stem the bleeding.

"Leave her," snapped Kobe harshly. "Go see what's happened to her lover!" Snatching a sash from among the discarded costumes, he tied the unconscious woman's hands behind her back. Toshikage knelt, following his example with her feet.

Akitada, aware only of having made a crucial mistake, waited just long enough to see the woman secured, then rushed out of the tent after Kojiro.

All hell seemed to have broken loose. Drums, flutes, screeches, and screams created a cacophony of noise. Lanterns and torches flickered and bobbed about as dark figures of demons and guests rushed pell-mell this way and that. Amid the shrieks, laughter mingled with curses and shouts. The demon chase had turned into a crowd-participation affair. Kojiro stood hesitant, turning his head this way and that. He was about to plunge into the melee when Akitada grabbed his arm.

"Listen," he shouted over the din, "I was wrong. Danjuro is not the general; he's the demon king. The demon king, do you hear? Stay away from him and tell the others!"

Kojiro stared at him blankly. In the flickering light his eyes gleamed strangely. "What?" He pointed at the milling crowd. "There's no time for that! They've all gone mad. Yoshiko and the ladies are not safe." He rushed off.

"Wait!" Akitada shouted after him, but it was too late. Kojiro had been swallowed up by the darkness and the crowd.

Akitada followed more slowly, dodging running figures of demons and guests, his eyes scanning the bobbing heads for the red-maned mask of the demon king. At one point, he rushed after a masked figure in orange, tackled it, and brought it down, only to discover he had caught one of the minor goblins who had become entangled in a red streamer. Immediately three or four spectators threw themselves upon them, wielding paper whips and rice straw brooms with abandon. Dizzy from the struggle and the wine-filled breath of the celebrants, Akitada staggered up. He plunged back into the swirling, shrieking crowd, but conditions deteriorated when someone began to extinguish lanterns, and the crowds helped themselves to torches in their mad pursuit of demons. The light diminished to isolated flames, and the screams now held real terror and pain.

Akitada gave up and cursed his carelessness. He had failed. Danjuro would hardly stay in his costume and more than likely had already fled the park.

Behind the actors' tent, he found the discarded mask of the demon king. He also found Tora and Genba, who stood holding a torch and staring dismally at a weeping man in gilded armor who sat on the ground between them, clutching his groin. An elaborate gilded helmet and a broken wooden sword lay beside him.

Tora saw Akitada first. "Wrong man," he said. "Poor bastard."

"What happened?"

"We thought he was that snooty bastard Danjuro and had some fun with him."

Genba bent down to the weeping man and patted his shoulder. "We're sorry," he said. "We thought you were someone else."

The man sniffled. "You bastards!"

Akitada asked, "Is he hurt badly?"

"He'll be all right," said Tora. "We didn't hit him near as hard as Miss Plumblossom kicked me."

"Well, it was my fault," said Akitada, fishing a gold coin from his sash and pressing it into the sobbing man's hand. "I told you to look for the general, but Danjuro played the demon king. And by now he knows what's up and got away in the confusion."

Tora cursed.

Genba helped the unfortunate general to his feet. The actor held the coin to his eyes, then made Akitada a deep bow before scooping up his helmet and limping away.

Genba asked, "What about the woman?"

"Kobe has her safe."

A new burst of screams drew their attention to the viewing stands. Someone had managed to set one of them on fire, and red flames shot up from the wooden, fabric-covered construction.

Appalled, Akitada cried, "Come on!" and rushed off.

But already panic had seized the crowd. People were running everywhere, and acrid smoke drifted on the night air. The noble families were departing in terror, their ox-drawn carriages adding to the confusion. Everywhere drivers where shouting and whipping their oxen or other drivers. The crown prince and his court had withdrawn to the gallery of the lake pavilion, whence they were fearfully gazing at the fire among the stands.

Their own frantic progress was impeded by the stream of people leaving the grounds. Flames cast a lurid light on the milling scene, smoke obscured other areas, actors in demon costumes dodged in and out of the crowd. The demon chase had become real.

They came to a halt when three carriages suddenly collided. The ensuing hysterics of the elegant ladies inside and of the plunging oxen outside stopped all traffic and blocked the way to the Sugawara stand. Directing Tora and Genba to lend a hand, Akitada climbed the tall wheel of one of the carriages to peer over its roof. He caught a glimpse of Seimei outside the screened enclosure. The old man was walking anxiously back and forth, scanning the crowd. Thank heaven all seemed well. Jumping back down, Akitada lent a hand to the drivers. After a few minutes of concentrated effort, the carriages finally pulled apart and moved off. Akitada turned toward their viewing stand.

But Seimei was gone and instead Kojiro was there, backing away from a figure in red and orange silk. As Akitada looked, the demon king lunged forward and pushed the much smaller Kojiro so violently into the screened enclosure of the stand that it toppled inward.

Shouting for Tora and Genba, Akitada tried to push through the milling crowd, but another carriage blocked his way. The huge wheel almost ran over Akitada's foot, and when he jumped out of the way, he fell over someone behind him. Scrambling up and forward again, he saw that his stand had collapsed and its occupants were in full view of the crowd. Danjuro jumped about among fallen benches, flinging the elderly Seimei aside and making for the cluster of women in the corner. Akitada vaulted over some debris in the road and shouted. He saw Danjuro dodging a bench which came flying through the air. The bench was followed by Miss Plumblossom's large bulk in a flutter of black silk skirts and red ribbons. She collided violently with the fiery demon king, bringing both of them down with a crash that Akitada could hear over the noise of the fleeing crowd.

Pushing people out of his way, dodging the hooves of oxen, and squeezing between two carriages barely in time before one of the large wheels almost caught him again, Akitada managed finally to reach his family. To his relief, Tamako and Yoshiko huddled together on a bench, their arms around each other and Yori. Kojiro stood over them, his face flushed and an ugly bruise marring one cheek.

They all looked at a pile of overturned seats where Miss Plumblossom sat among the broken boards and splintered bench legs. She had lost her wig, and her bald scalp shone in the torchlight. Her gown was ripped down the front, and a broad streak of mud decorated her ruddy face. But she looked triumphant.

"Miss Plumblossom," gasped Akitada, sliding to a halt, "are you hurt?"

Groping for her wig with its red ribbons, she grinned. "Not a bit, sir. Look, I caught me the head goblin himself. If that isn't good luck, I don't know what is."

Seimei staggered over, rubbing his shoulder and holding his head. "Thank heaven you've returned, sir. This madman attacked Mr. Kojiro and then ran into the ladies' enclosure. But fleeing from the tiger's den, he ran into the dragon. If it hadn't been for Miss Plumblossom, I don't know what we should have done."

Akitada stepped closer. On the ground, pinned between Miss Plumblossom's massive haunches, lay a figure dressed in orange and red silk. Danjuro was on his back, his eyes closed and his face contorted with pain. Miss Plumblossom chuckled and stuck her wig on his head. The actor jerked away and started bucking and moaning. His struggle had perversely sexual overtones. Dressed in his orange finery, with the wig on his head, and straddled by a bald Miss Plumblossom, he resembled the female partner of a lecherous priest.

The resemblance had not escaped Miss Plumblossom. She giggled and bounced. "Come on, lover," she cooed. "Get it up. I've got you right where I want you. If you were a bit more of a man, I think I'd take you home with me."

392

Seimei gasped.

Danjuro stopped struggling and moaned again. Akitada shot a glance at his wife and sister and said sternly, "Miss Plumblossom, get up! There are ladies watching."

Miss Plumblossom made no move to obey. "Time they learned the way to please a man, if they haven't by now. I don't mind giving them pointers while Goblin here is twitching between my thighs, but the poor creature's rod is a limp noodle. I wonder what all those girls have been seeing in him."

Seimei gave a choking cry and clutched at Akitada's arm. He looked so profoundly shocked that Akitada thought he was about to faint.

TWENTY-THREE

The Twofold Truth

The night between the old year and the new was long. Akitada did not return to his home and bed until just before dawn, to the cheerful noise from the Imperial Palace, where the members of the Imperial Guard were twanging their bows and officials were ringing bells to mark the new beginning.

After the capture of Danjuro in the Spring Garden, Akitada sent his family home and arranged to have Miss Plumblossom escorted by Tora and Genba. The tumult of the demon chase died down gradually, as Kobe and Akitada accompanied the prisoners to jail.

Kobe insisted on interrogating Danjuro and Nobuko immediately and separately. He commandeered the prison director's office and sent the sleepy constables and guards rushing about, carrying messages and summons to clerks, physicians, and the women's prison matron. Danjuro was dragged in first. Someone had decided that he was not injured badly enough to rate a litter. Danjuro did not agree and refused to cooperate. The two burly guards had to grip him under the arms and drag him in between them. They expressed their frustration by handling him as roughly as they could, and Danjuro cursed and screamed.

"Put him down!" shouted Kobe over the din. "Why is he screaming like that?"

They dropped him like a load of firewood. One guard grinned. "Broken rib, sir."

"Oh." Kobe eyed the whimpering prisoner on the floor. "Well, he's calmed down," he said carelessly. "The doctor can take a look at him later. But you shouldn't have roughed him up before I had a chance to talk to him."

"We didn't," protested the men. "That rib was already broken."

Kobe turned to Akitada. "Did you have trouble with the bastard?"

"No. But Miss Plumblossom did."

Kobe's eyes widened. "Not that woman again? She's better than any of my men. I may have to give her a job." He chuckled. "That would stop her from criticizing the police. I could make her a warden of her quarter, maybe?"

"I should think she would like that very much," Akitada said with a laugh.

Danjuro cursed again. One of the guards unhooked his two-pronged metal *jitte* from his belt and gave him a sharp prod with it.

"Sit up, you!" Kobe snapped.

"I can't. She broke my back," whined Danjuro. "She finished me. I'll never act again. I want compensation."

"You what?" Kobe guffawed. "Don't worry! You'll be compensated. And if you don't sit up, I'll make certain you cannot lie down for weeks."

Danjuro bestirred himself weakly and with many moans and cries. His face was wet with sweat and tears when he finally faced them.

Kobe burst into another shout of laughter. "Behold the fierce demon king! You look more like an old woman without your mask. What a crybaby! How can someone like you play famous heroes and gods? You're an insult to men everywhere."

Danjuro shot him a malevolent glance and sniffled. "I'm an actor," he said with an attempt at dignity, "not a crude soldier or constable. Besides, I've been viciously attacked and injured. Imagine finding yourself pushed into an enclosure where some man starts hitting you! I was defending myself as best I could when that female monster joined in and tried to kill me. You'd do better to arrest that pair than to torture me. Tomorrow I shall lay charges before a judge against my attackers and all of you. Now I demand to be treated by a physician." He snapped his mouth shut and glared.

The guard jabbed Danjuro again with his *jitte* while his partner reached for his whip, but Kobe shook his head. "It is late, and I am tired," he said, "so we'll dispense with your amusing pretense of innocence. You are charged with murdering three people, specifically the actress Ohisa, the antiquarian Nagaoka, and the retired professor Yasaburo."

"Ridiculous," said Danjuro, feeling his ribs.

"Not at all. The actress Ohisa was a member of your troupe and one of your women. You strangled her during a stay at the Eastern Mountain Temple because you had tired of her, and had a new lover. Her murder may have been instigated by your new lover, Nagaoka's wife. We know she helped you contrive an elaborate plot in which Ohisa's body would be disguised as hers so that the murder could be pinned on Nagaoka's brother."

"Lies," cried Danjuro. "Ohisa left to go home to her parents."

"That will be easy enough to disprove," Kobe said coldly. "Your next murder, that of your paramour's husband, happened at Kohata in the home of her father. After extracting a fortune in blood money from him, you poisoned him and dumped him by the side of the highway, hoping we would blame it on robbers."

Danjuro looked at the ceiling. "I know nothing of the man. Total stranger!"

"Then there is murder number three, also by poison. I suppose you found it worked very well the last time, or you had a supply left over. In any case, you entered the eastern jail disguised as a Buddhist monk and asked to see Yasaburo. When you were admitted to his cell, you passed him the poison in a gift of food and departed."

"What a fantastic tale!" scoffed Danjuro. "Just because I'm an actor and you've seen me play a priest, you accuse me of murder. Why would I do such a thing?"

"Because you were afraid that Yasaburo would identify his daughter and because he knew or suspected that you killed Nagaoka. Believe me, Danjuro, your game is up. You can save yourself some pain by confessing now."

"You can't scare me. I'm innocent," Danjuro blustered.

"Don't forget," said Kobe, smiling ferociously, "we have your lover in custody. She will talk soon enough once the guards take the bamboo whips to her pretty backside. And she'll blame it all on you."

Danjuro sagged. Like a cornered animal's, his eyes moved frantically this way and that. "Then she'll be lying," he muttered.

He was taken away to the doctor, and Nobuko was brought in. She was in tears, but had washed the makeup off her face and managed to rearrange her hair and fairy princess gown. She knelt without urging and bowed deeply to Kobe and Akitada.

"This insignificant person is the actress Yugao, daughter of Yasaburo Seijiro and wife of the actor Danjuro. I humbly ask your honors' explanation of the charges brought against me."

Kobe regarded her bowed figure with contempt. "You can stop acting now, Mrs. Nagaoka. We know who you are and what you and your current husband have done. It is in your interest to confess quickly and completely to your involvement in the triple murder of the girl Ohisa, your husband Nagaoka, and your father Yasaburo."

Her eyes widened. She opened her mouth, then raised a hand to it and bit her knuckles. "Oh," she wailed, "that you should think I could lay a hand on my own father for whom I grieve day and night. I have not always been a dutiful daughter to him and the guilt weighs heavily on me. May the gods of heaven and earth forgive me!"

Akitada thought it a fine performance, though perhaps just a little overdone. That last phrase especially sounded quaint, like some ancient Shinto prayer.

"Guards!" shouted Kobe. Two uniformed constables entered and stood to attention. "Bamboo whips!" Kobe ordered.

The prisoner dropped her pose, her beautiful face suddenly a mask of fear. "No, please not that," she cried. "Ask me anything! I shall answer."

Kobe dismissed the constables and glowered at the prisoner. "Did you join Uemon's troupe on the sixth day of the Frost Month on the occasion of a pilgrimage to the Eastern Mountain Temple?"

"Yes. I had always aspired to be an actress, and our father encouraged us to participate in private performances. Theater was his passion. When I heard some actresses in the temple's visitors' quarters talking about one of their troupe having deserted them, I acted on impulse and offered to take her place. It was to be for only one performance, but I fell in love with Danjuro and stayed."

Regardless of what she called herself, this woman was not only beautiful and self-possessed but very clever. The story hung together. Both her father and Harada had spoken of performances with visiting actors, and Nagaoka and Kojiro had mentioned her talents in singing and dancing. A lonely middle-aged bachelor like Nagaoka would have been enchanted by her. Even now her manner was consciously flirtatious, the lips full and moist, every movement of her body provocative. Such a woman would hardly settle for the quiet devotion of a reserved, older husband, but would try to seduce the stolid Kojiro. Danjuro, a dashing ladies' man and part-time hero onstage, would have been irresistible to her. Akitada leaned toward Kobe and whispered.

Kobe nodded. He asked the woman, "Did Uemon's Players ever perform at your father's house while you lived there?"

The question made her pause. "I . . . I can't remember. They may have. It was such a long time ago."

Kobe leaned forward. "We have a witness who says you met Danjuro there and later had an affair with him."

She flushed. Kobe smiled triumphantly. Then she lowered her eyes. "Yes. It's quite true. I was ashamed to admit it. It is the reason my father and I quarreled. He was terribly angry when he found out. I wanted to leave with Danjuro, but he forbade it."

Kobe and Akitada looked at each other. What was this? A confession wrapped into the old story of the maiden seduced and ruined by the villain?

Kobe muttered to Akitada, "That old man may have dug his own grave when he raised his daughter to associate with such riffraff."

Akitada murmured back, "In this case, I suspect the woman corrupted the man."

Kobe snorted and turned back to the prisoner. "We are not getting anywhere," he snapped. "You lied earlier, claiming to be your sister Yugao. Are you now admitting the truth? That you are Nobuko, widow of the late Nagaoka?"

"The truth? Oh, no. The truth is that poor Nobuko was murdered. I'm Yugao. You must believe me. We look . . . looked as much alike as twins."

Kobe frowned. "Do you claim that you and your sister spent the same night at the Eastern Mountain Temple? How could you not meet?"

She sighed. "It rained. Neither of us left her room, or I might have saved her life that night."

She was good, thought Akitada. He cleared his throat. "This is pointless, Mrs. Nagaoka. Your brother-in-law told us that your sister Yugao died shortly after your marriage, certainly long before the night at the temple. There has been only one of you for years."

She tossed her head. "You take the word of the drunken sot who murdered my poor sister?" Raising her chin, she glared at

Kobe. "I ask you again, why is it that that murderer runs free, while I am accused of his crime?"

Kobe growled, "Do you want me to send for the whips again? You know very well that your sister's death can be proven easily."

She smiled sadly. "*My* death, you mean. I'm afraid you'll not prove it. You see, my father was so angry when I ran away that he announced my death. He even went so far as to have an empty coffin cremated and a marker erected with all due ceremony. Father enjoyed making fun of the Buddhists that way."

Akitada felt the first stab of unease. This sounded remarkably like Yasaburo. His unease changed into dismay when he realized how difficult it would be to prove the woman wrong. Who had seen both women together? Their father Yasaburo and Nobuko's husband, both dead. The retarded servant? Harada, a recluse?

Kobe gave a disgusted grunt. "So! You persist in your tale! Very well. We shall prove your identity in court. You would do well to remember that the punishment for lying to a judge is one hundred lashes. Some have been known to die from it."

She paled, but managed a smile. "Then I'm safe," she said.

"Take her away!" Kobe snapped to the guards.

She walked out gracefully, her hips swaying lightly. One of the guards watched her and swallowed visibly. Kobe cursed.

Akitada shared Kobe's frustration. If this was indeed Yugao, where was Nobuko? Dead? And what of the missing Ohisa? Worse! If this was not Nobuko, then the whole case against her and Danjuro fell apart and Kojiro would once again stand accused of Nobuko's murder. But Akitada was certain that they had been right. He thought furiously.

Kobe looked despondent. He muttered, "Bitch! They did it, all right! That actor gave himself away. He's the weak link, and we'll beat it out of him. You'd think the woman would fall apart first, but she is the real demon. I was hoping to tie the case up before the New Year."

Akitada nodded. He felt responsible. If he had checked the background of the people involved more carefully, this would not have happened. Yasaburo's confusing references to daughters should have warned him. It had never been quite clear if he referred to Nobuko or both sisters. Kojiro had cleared up the discrepancy, but his information should have been checked, particularly since he had never met Nobuko's sister. Harada had been vague also, probably because he never spent time with Yasaburo's family and saw the girls only from a distance. It explained also why he had not recognized Nobuko in her makeup and costume.

Kobe growled, "Curse that man for producing two such daughters! What now?"

Akitada rose with a sigh. "We will go out and ask more questions." He was still sore and tired easily, but he owed Kobe another effort and had made a promise to Kojiro. "I shall talk to Miss Plumblossom and the other actors again. Perhaps you could send someone to Kohata?"

Kobe nodded glumly. "I'll go myself. A fine New Year's Day, plodding through the mud for hours to talk to drunken farmers and locals. Not to mention that half-wit."

The night air was thick with the scent of pine torches and greenery as Akitada walked south toward the river. A faintly lit haze of smoke hovered over the dark rooftops and towering pines. People were still celebrating with muffled cries and laughter, and here and there groups of drunken revelers staggered home. Some of them would tumble into the frozen canals and sober up quickly. Some perhaps would not have the strength to save themselves and would die an icy death.

Akitada shivered and walked faster, hoping to find Miss Plumblossom and the others still awake. He was encouraged by the sounds of lute and zither coming from the houses in the pleasure quarter, and by the many people crowding the streets.

Lights shone from behind the high paper-covered windows of the training hall, and he heard laughter. The old doorkeeper let him in, pointing toward the end of the hall. Apparently all the oil lamps and lanterns had been gathered around Miss Plumblossom's dais. She held court on her chair, her maid on the dais beside her and a group of actors and acrobats clustered around. Tora and Genba sat on the floor at her feet.

They had been celebrating. Cups and pitchers of wine and trays of food littered the floor, and their faces were flushed. Tora and Genba jumped up guiltily when they saw Akitada.

"We were invited for a nightcap," Genba said.

Tora asked, "Is something wrong, sir?"

"No, but we have run into a problem. Mrs. Nagaoka claims to be her sister."

Something clattered and there was a gasp. Surprised, they looked at the maid, who had dropped her fan and raised a hand to her mouth, staring at Akitada with wide, horrified eyes.

"Yukiyo," said her mistress severely, "you've been acting very peculiar ever since we got back. What is the matter with you?"

The maid snatched up her fan and hid her face again. "Nothing, nothing."

"Nonsense, girl! You know something. I recall you asking a lot of questions about Danjuro and his wife. Out with it!"

The maid cried out and struggled to her feet, but Miss Plumblossom's pudgy hand clamped around her arm. "Sit, girl! I'll not have you cause more trouble after all I've done for you. You've made enough of a mess already. Look what you did to poor Tora! Is that any way to pay me back, you ungrateful girl? I took you off the streets when you were starving and gave you a home. I've been a mother to you."

Yukiyo collapsed like a straw doll and wrapped her arms

around Miss Plumblossom's knees. "I'm sorry," she sobbed. "By the gods of heaven and earth, I would do anything for you."

Akitada tensed. That strange phrase about the ancient gods again! The upper-class speech belied the maid's present status. And that peculiar gesture. She, too, had raised her knuckles to her mouth. His heart pounding, he asked, "Who are you really?"

Miss Plumblossom frowned. "Yukiyo? Is there something you haven't told me?"

Yukiyo mumbled something unintelligible.

"What?" she asked. "You gave your word about what?"

Akitada stepped closer. "Are you Yugao?"

More whispers. Miss Plumblossom's painted eyebrows rose.

Akitada urged, "Miss Plumblossom, if she is Yugao and protecting her sister Nobuko, she must testify. She is our only hope in bringing the murderers of three people to justice."

Miss Plumblossom reached down and touched the sobbing woman's head. "He is right, child," she said.

"Answer my question!" Akitada cried impatiently. "If you are Yugao, your sister plotted the murders of your own father and her husband. If we cannot prove her identity, the killers will go free and the dead will have no peace."

Yukiyo clutched Miss Plumblossom tightly and wailed. Miss Plumblossom looked old and sad, her rounded cheeks and double chin sagging. "Poor child," she murmured, patting the weeping girl's back, "poor child. Don't grieve! You'll always have a home with me, no matter what happens. You shall be the daughter I never had. Now sit up proper and wipe your face. You're among friends and you've nothing to be ashamed of. You've done your filial duty. Which is more than I can say for that evil creature."

They all held their breath. Yukiyo laid down her fan, and raised her disfigured face to Akitada. Struggling to speak through torn lips, she said tonelessly, "Yes, you found out the truth. I'm Yugao. I don't know how you guessed. My own sister did not recognize me."

Akitada smiled encouragingly. "You have a grace of gesture and an old-fashioned manner of speaking in common. Both of you called on the 'gods of heaven and earth,' for example, when most people would invoke the Buddha."

"Our father did not want us to refer to Buddhist gods. When Nobuko first came here with Uemon's people, I was so happy to see her. I thought we might live together, but she didn't want me—and she was married to Danjuro. Danjuro . . . well, I was in love with Danjuro once, and the way I look now, I didn't want him to know who I was. I begged Nobuko to keep my secret, and she agreed if I would keep hers. I thought then it was because she had run away from her husband. We swore by our mother's soul." She stopped, hid her face in her sleeve, and wailed again. Miss Plumblossom put an arm around her.

Akitada released his breath slowly and sat down. So there had been more than one mystery. How had the temple scroll put it? A Twofold Truth. The case was solved, but at what human cost! He said gently, "I understand, Yugao. It is a difficult thing to testify against your own sister even under normal circumstances, but you must do so in this case. You see, quite apart from your duty to your dead father, there are the living to be considered. Nagaoka's brother Kojiro is a good man who was cruelly set up for the murder of the girl Ohisa. He would never be cleared of this suspicion except for your honesty. Think of it as a gift you make to the victims, dead and alive, a debt you pay to make good your sister's crimes."

Clutching Miss Plumblossom's hand, Yugao-Yukiyo nodded her head.

Akitada looked at the graceful way she sat, her pretty shape, slender neck, and glossy hair all in stark contrast to the ruined face. "Will you tell us your story?"

She nodded again.

"My father always invited actors to perform for him at the farm, and when we got older it pleased him if we dressed up and acted small parts with them. We thought it fun, and the actors liked us because we were both pretty." She flushed. "I was pretty then. Danjuro preferred my beauty to my sister's. He asked me, not my sister, to be his wife and to go away with him. Father was furious when I told him. He ordered Danjuro and the others to leave. I cried for days. Then Danjuro wrote to me, and I ran away to be with him." She shivered and pulled her robe more closely about her. "Only it wasn't what I had expected. Danjuro didn't marry me, and after a while he had other women. I was upset and acted poorly, and one day Uemon fired me. Danjuro told me to go home. But I couldn't because my father had declared me dead. So I roamed the city, looking for work, and found there was only prostitution. After that nothing much mattered except the next meal. Until I met the slasher."

A dismal silence fell. "Well," Miss Plumblossom finally said firmly, "I think your father treated you abominably for a little mistake, and then that bastard Danjuro did you wrong. Men! And your own sister, instead of opening her arms to you with love, tells you to leave her alone. Your whole family has a lot to answer for."

Akitada looked on helplessly. Hell had little to compare with the sufferings of the living. In the face of such misery—the loss of her family, her lover, her beauty, and the hope for future happiness—he felt humbled.

Tora, characteristically unsentimental, looked at the practical side of the situation. "You know," he pointed out, "your sister can't inherit your father's place, and that leaves only you. You'll have the farm, and if you're the girl I think you are, you'll make a go of it."

The thought surprised Yugao. She stared at him. "Kohata mine? Do you really think so? But who will believe me? How can they tell I'm Yugao when my own mother would not recognize me?"

Tora looked at his master in consternation.

"I think," said Akitada, "considering your great service to the capital in identifying Noami as the slasher, and your testimony in the present case, the authorities will help you prove your identity by the details you remember of your home and past. I see no great difficulties in your claiming your inheritance."

Yugao rose. Looking down at Miss Plumblossom, she reached for her hand. "Will you come with me?"

"Of course," said the other woman gruffly, getting up. "You're a brave girl. Let's go and get it over with."

Yugao suddenly smiled. It was startling, a horrible grimace, but it touched their hearts and they all smiled back at her. Miss Plumblossom nodded and dabbed her eyes.

When they arrived, Kobe stared in surprise at the ill-assorted group of men and women who crowded into the prison director's office.

"What's this?" he demanded of Akitada. "I'm dead tired and have a hard day ahead of me. As you well know."

"You don't have to go to Kohata. I brought Kohata to you." Akitada pulled Yugao forward.

Kobe flinched when he saw her face. "Miss Plumblossom's maid? The one who identified the painter?"

"Yes," the maid said, her voice trembling a little. "But I am also Yugao, Yasaburo's younger daughter. I have come to identify my sister Nobuko so she can atone for what she has done."

Kobe stared at her. Slowly a broad grin replaced his scowl. He shouted for a guard and ordered both prisoners brought back.

Danjuro tottered in first. A doctor had tended to his broken rib, but he looked ill and hopeless. Nobuko entered with her head held high. She saw her sister immediately and looked away. Except for small beads of perspiration on her face and a slight trembling of her hands, she gave no sign of recognition. Glancing at the others, she sneered, "I see you've brought this has-been of an acrobat and a parcel of untalented actors to speak against me. It won't do you any good."

Yugao stepped forward. "It's no use, Nobuko," she said. "I told them. Our father was not always kind, but you should not have let Danjuro kill him. It was a terrible crime against the mandate of heaven."

The beauty raised her chin. "Who is this deformed freak? Are you scouring the gutters to trump up your charges, Superintendent?"

Akitada said, "Your sister has proven her identity. Do not waste time on pointless denials."

Danjuro had been staring at the scarred sister. "Yugao? You're Yugao?" He took a step toward her. Kobe signaled the guard to release him. Danjuro's eyes roamed over Yugao's face and figure. She stood still, flushing painfully, but bearing it. Moving behind her, he lifted her heavy hair.

Nobuko cried out, "Danjuro, don't touch her! She's dirty scum!"

Too late. Everyone in the room had seen the small birthmark at the nape of Yugao's neck. Danjuro dropped Yugao's hair and looked at Nobuko. "It's no use. It's Yugao, all right. It's all over."

For a moment, Nobuko stood staring at him stonily. Then she spat at him. "I take pleasure in the knowledge that you will die, coward." She turned to Kobe. "Well, you have what you wanted. I wish to go to my cell now."

Kobe was complacent. "Very well." He nodded to the officer of the guard. "We shall begin the interrogation tomorrow. I expect she'll confess but, just in case, have the green bamboo whips ready." The guards marched both prisoners out.

Akitada was sickened by Kobe's order. Green bamboo was thin and pliant and could shred a prisoner's skin. "I suppose we had all better go home," he muttered. "I cannot say I shall remember this day with any pleasure."

Yugao was weeping softly. Miss Plumblossom put an arm around her, and they turned to go.

Kobe was about to say something when there was a muffled

noise outside. He looked toward the door. They all heard it now: a high, thin screaming and male shouts. Running steps approached, the door was flung open, and a breathless constable appeared. The screams were horribly clear now.

The man cried, "Sir, the prisoner tried to escape—"

A second figure appeared behind him. One of Nobuko's guards, his pale face rigid. He raised his right hand, which held the two-pronged *jitte*. Both his arm and the *jitte* were covered in gore. Outside, the screaming stopped.

Kobe asked, "What happened?"

The guard choked on his words. "When we got to the court-yard, she ran. We gave chase. Someone cornered her, but she slipped past them. She didn't see me. I stepped in her way and ... and just raised the *jitte* ... so ... to stop her." The man turned faintly green and gulped. "She ran into it ... with her face, sir." He gulped again. "It went into her eye and mouth, sir. All the way. She's dying." He turned his head to listen to the silence outside. "Dead," he amended.

Epilogue

Superintendent Kobe did not, after all, spend the holiday riding all over the countryside in the chilly winter air. Instead he was invited to the Sugawara house, where an enormous dinner was laid on, with mountains of moon cakes, fish stews and game soups, pickled eggs, rice cakes filled with vegetables, rice gruel with red beans, salted chestnuts, sliced sea bream, boiled taro, marinated radish, and any number of other delicacies.

There was much more to celebrate than even Akitada had anticipated. When he woke on New Year's morning to the excited shouts of Yori and a large pitcher of spiced New Year's wine, Seimei made an unexpected appearance. He never intruded when Akitada spent the night in his wife's room. On this occasion, he entered only after being invited, his eyes strangely bright and with an air of suppressed excitement. He blushed and averted his eyes from the pile of bedding where Yori was tumbling about with his parents.

"Sir," he murmured, "my apologies to both of you, but I just found that a document was delivered from the palace. A messenger must have brought it while we were out last night, and that fool of a boy forgot to mention it." He bowed and scuttled out of the room quickly.

Akitada had a reasonably clear conscience for once and proceeded to his study after calmly completing his toilet. Seimei and Harada were there, kneeling on either side of his desk as if in prayer to the imperial missive. The document, a tightly rolled tube of thick paper, tied with purple silk ribbons, rested on a black-lacquer tray in the center of his desk. He recognized what it was at once and stopped. Many years ago he had seen something like it. It had been addressed to another man and occupied the place of honor on his ancestral altar. It was official notice of rank promotion, traditionally handed with due ceremony to the recipient by his superior shortly before the official posting on the public board outside the palace gate on New Year's Day. The fact that he had just returned and was between assignments apparently had made this normal procedure impossible.

His heart suddenly pounding, he bowed toward the imperial letter, then approached his desk reverently and took it up with both hands.

After his last assignment as provisional governor of the northern province of Echigo, he had hoped at most for a confirmation of the honorary rank he had held along with the temporary title. But this promised more.

He unrolled the scroll with trembling fingers and skimmed over the formal greeting, looking for the news. There it was: Junior Sixth Rank, Upper Grade!

This was not merely a confirmation of the honorary Junior Sixth, Lower Grade, but a whole step beyond that. He finally held administrative rank. Not only did this provide considerable protection against his enemies in the administration, but it promised another challenging assignment.

Akitada let the document fall back on the desk—whence Seimei took it tenderly—and walked out into his garden. It was still chilly, but the sun was rising, its first rays gilding the rocks and warming his shoulders through the silk gown. In the pond, golden shapes moved about the muddy bottom, no longer winter-sluggish. When Akitada's shadow fell across the water, one—a large, spotted carp—rose to the surface to greet him.

Akitada regarded it sadly. His satisfaction was tempered by

guilt. What would Tamako say if he was dispatched again to some distant province? They had just returned, and she had expressed her deep happiness about being home only a short while ago as they drank to each other's health on the New Year. Was it fair to his family to drag them away again to some uncertain or dangerous place? Was it fair to himself to leave them behind?

He stood in his garden and turned slowly to look about him. He would miss his home, the fish in his pond, the twisted cherry in the corner of the garden. The sharp pang of anticipated loss reminded him that only a short time had passed since he had taken possession of this, his patrimony. Much had happened, much had changed, he himself most of all. The woman he had thought his mother was gone forever, but he had somehow regained his father, a shadowy but benevolent presence.

What was it the old abbot of the Eastern Mountain Temple had said to him? *That which seems real in the world of men is but a dream and a deception.* There was certainly truth in that. He had discovered that his mother was not his real mother and that she had deceived him all his life about his father's love. And the words applied as well to the murder cases he had finally solved. The corpse at the temple had not been Mrs. Nagaoka but the girl Ohisa. And on that deception had hung a series of others. Kojiro was not as he had seemed, and neither were Yasaburo and Yugao. And the slasher Noami had seemed a mere talented painter, one who was thought his neighbors' benefactor.

The old abbot himself had seemed senile, irrational, and his words mere gibberish, but Akitada was no longer sure of that, either. Had Genshin not made certain that Akitada would be shown Noami's hell screen? What was it Genshin had said after the line about deception? *The reverse is also true.* So as truth is deception, deception may be truth. The hell screen, of course.

The painted suffering was real. Each picture showed a human being, tortured and wounded by a man who had become a monster in the service of his art.

Akitada shivered. What chance had brought him to the Eastern Mountain Temple on that night? What tasks lay still ahead? And in the general scheme of things, was not everything arranged for a purpose?

Deeply moved, he turned toward the eastern mountains and bowed to the rising sun.

Historical Note

In the eleventh century, Heian Kyo (Kyoto) was the capital of Japan and its largest city. Patterned after the capital of China, it was laid out in a rectangle of two and a half by three and a half miles, with an even grid of avenues and streets which ran due north and south and east and west. Its population was about two hundred thousand. The Imperial Palace, a separate walled and gated city encompassing the emperor's residence and the ministries and bureaus of the government, occupied the northernmost center. From it the broad, willow-lined Suzaku Avenue led south, bisecting Heian Kyo into a western and eastern half and ending at the famous gate called Rashomon. The city was said to have been quite beautiful, with its broad avenues, parks, canals, rivers, palaces, and temples. (For details on the city and its buildings during the Heian period, see R. A. B. Ponsonby-Fane, *Kyoto: The Old Capital of Japan.*)

Law enforcement in eleventh-century Japan followed the Chinese pattern to some extent, in that each of more than sixty-eight city quarters had its own warden who was responsible for keeping peace. The government offices and the palace were protected by divisions of the Imperial Guard. In addition, a separate police force, the *kebiishi*, investigated crimes and made arrests and judges pronounced sentence. The most serious crimes, as defined by the Taiho code (A.D. 701) were (1) rebellion against the emperor, (2) damage to the Imperial Palace or royal tombs,

(3) treason, (4) murder of one's kin, (5) murder of one's wife or of more than three members of a family, (6) theft or damage of imperial or religious property, (7) unfilial acts toward parents or senior relatives, and (8) murder of a superior or teacher. There were two prisons in the capital, but imperial pardons were common and sweeping. Convictions required confession by the accused, but these could be encouraged by the interrogating officers. The death penalty was rare because the Buddhist faith opposed the taking of life, but exile under severe and often fatal conditions was often substituted.

The two state *religions*, Shinto and Buddhism, coexisted peacefully, sometimes in the same temple complex and during the same religious festival. Shinto, the native faith, is tied to Japanese gods and agricultural observances. Buddhism, which entered Japan from China via Korea, exerted enormous influence over the aristocracy and the government through numerous monasteries. Most emperors and many powerful nobles ended their careers by taking the tonsure. The Buddhist hell inflicts on sinners a variety of physical sufferings: in addition to the fiery torment associated with the Christian hell, it offers slashing with swords and knives, freezing, starvation, and other unpleasant fates. Paintings of such scenes were common in Buddhist monasteries in China and Japan. The story of the demented artist of the hell screen in the present novel was inspired by Akutagawa's short story "The Hell Screen," in which a painter immolates his own daughter in order to achieve verisimilitude.

Japanese customs in connection with *death* partook of both faiths. Taboos prohibiting contact with the dead were based on Shinto beliefs, while funeral ceremonies (cremations) were in the hands of Buddhist monks. It was thought that the spirit of the deceased resided for forty-nine days in its home and that angry spirits could haunt the living.

As far as eleventh-century *popular entertainment* (later known as the "floating world") is concerned, historical evidence is skimpy. Prostitution was certainly known, but as far as we know Kyoto's two famous pleasure quarters did not exist until two centuries later. However, in the centuries before the shoguns, there was no prohibition against female entertainers who earned a living by dancing, singing, and playing instruments. The great age of Noh and Kabuki theater came later, but the precursors were the bards who recited famous tales, the sacred dances of *bugaku* which mimed stories, short farces called *kyogen*, and acrobatics. All of these are well attested to before and during the eleventh century.

Finally, the plot of the Nagaoka case is based on case 64A of the twelfth-century Chinese collection of criminal cases *T'ang-yin-pi-shi* (translated by Robert Van Gulik), a text which was imported to Japan during the Ming dynasty.